THE MYSTERY OF THREE QUARTERS

Also by Sophie Hannah

Little Face
Hurting Distance
The Point of Rescue
The Other Half Lives
A Room Swept White
Lasting Damage
Kind of Cruel
The Carrier
The Orphan Choir
The Telling Error
Pictures Or It Didn't Happen
A Game for All the Family
The Narrow Bed
Did You See Melody?

Hercule Poirot mysteries

The Monogram Murders
Closed Casket

Agatha Christie®

The Mystery of
Three Quarters

THE NEW HERCULE POIROT MYSTERY

SOPHIE HANNAH

HarperCollins*Publishers*

HarperCollins*Publishers*
1 London Bridge Street
London SE1 9GF
www.harpercollins.co.uk

Published by HarperCollins*Publishers* 2018
1

A catalogue record for this book
is available from the British Library

ISBN 978-0-00-826445-1 HB
ISBN 978-0-00-826446-8 TPB

Set in Sabon by Palimpsest Book Production Ltd,
Falkirk, Stirlingshire.

Printed and bound in Great Britain by
CPI Group (UK) Ltd, Croydon CR0 4YY

MIX
Paper from
responsible sources
FSC
www.fsc.org **FSC™ C007454**

For Faith Tilleray,
who has gone above and beyond,
and taught me so much

Acknowledgements

I am hugely grateful to the following people:

James Prichard, Mathew Prichard and everybody at Agatha Christie Limited; David Brawn, Kate Elton and everyone at HarperCollins UK; my agent Peter Straus and his team at Rogers, Coleridge & White; my wonderful publishers William Morrow in New York, and all my Poirot publishers all over the world who have helped to distribute the books far and wide; Chris Gribble, who read and enthused at a crucial early stage; Emily Winslow who made editorial suggestions that were meticulous and invaluable, as always; Jamie Bernthal-Hooker, who did a million helpful things, from proof-reading to researching to title brainstorming; Faith Tilleray, who designed me a stunning new website and then became my marketing guru; my family—Dan, Phoebe, Guy . . . and Brewster in particular on this occasion, for reasons that will be clear to anyone who reads the book!

Thank you to competition winners Melanie Vout and

Ian Mason, who supplied the names Peter Vout and Hubert Thrubwell respectively. They are both wonderful names! A massive thank you, also, to all the readers who have loved *The Monogram Murders* and *Closed Casket*, and my other books, and have written/tweeted/messaged me to tell me so—your enthusiasm makes it all feel so worthwhile.

Contents

THE FIRST QUARTER

1. Poirot is Accused   3
2. Intolerable Provocation   12
3. The Third Person   20
4. The Odd One Out?   30
5. A Letter with a Hole in it   48
6. Rowland Rope   55
7. An Old Enemy   65
8. Poirot Issues Some Instructions   74
9. Four Alibis   79

THE SECOND QUARTER

10. Some Important Questions   99
11. Emerald Green   108
12. Many Ruined Alibis   116
13. The Hooks   128
14. At Combingham Hall   136
15. The Scene of the Possible Crime   147
16. The Opportunity Man   155
17. Poirot's Trick   168

18. Mrs Dockerill's Discovery   184
19. Four More Letters   192

THE THIRD QUARTER

20. The Letters Arrive   203
21. The Day of the Typewriters   213
22. The Solitary Yellow Square of Cake   216
23. Meaning Harm   222
24. Ancient Enmities   236
25. Poirot Returns to Combingham Hall   244
26. The Typewriter Experiment   261
27. The Bracelet and the Fan   266
28. An Unconvincing Confession   274
29. An Unexpected Eel   279
30. The Mystery of Three Quarters   284

THE FOURTH QUARTER

31. A Note for Mr Porrott   301
32. Where is Kingsbury?   309
33. The Marks on the Towel   317
34. Rebecca Grace   328
35. Family Loyalty   339
36. The True Culprit   353
37. The Will   366
38. Rowland Without a Rope   376
39. A New Typewriter   381

THE FIRST QUARTER

CHAPTER 1

Poirot is Accused

Hercule Poirot smiled to himself as his driver brought the motorcar to a stop with satisfying symmetry. As a lover of neatness and order, Poirot appreciated such perfect alignment with the entrance doors of Whitehaven Mansions where he lived. One could draw a straight line from the middle of the vehicle to the exact point where the doors met.

The luncheon from which he was returning had been *très bon divertissement*: the most excellent of food and company. He alighted, bestowed a warm thank-you upon his driver, and was about to go inside when he had a peculiar feeling that (this was how he put it to himself) something behind him was in need of his attention.

He expected, on turning, to observe nothing out of the ordinary. It was a mild day for February, but perhaps a light breeze had put a tremor in the air around him.

Poirot soon saw that the disturbance had not been caused by the weather, though the well-turned-out woman approaching at a great pace did, in spite of her fashionable pale blue coat and hat, resemble a force of nature. 'She is the whirlwind most fierce,' Poirot murmured to himself.

He disliked the hat. He had seen women in town wearing similar ones: minimal, without ornament, fitted close to the scalp like bathing caps made of cloth. A hat ought to have a brim or some manner of embellishment, thought Poirot. At least, it should do something more than cover the head. No doubt he would soon get used to these modern hats— and then, once he had, the fashion would change as it always did.

The blue-clad woman's lips twitched and curled, though no sound came from her. It was as if she was rehearsing what she would say when she finally reached Poirot's side. There was no doubt that he was her target. She looked determined to do something unpleasant to him as soon as she was close enough. He took a step back as she marched towards him in what he could only think of as a stampede—one consisting of nothing and nobody but herself.

Her hair was dark brown and lustrous. When she came to an abrupt halt directly in front of him, Poirot saw that she was not as young as she had looked from a distance. No, this woman was more than fifty years old. She was perhaps sixty. A lady in her middle age, expert at concealing the lines on her face. Her eyes were a striking blue, neither light nor dark.

'You are Hercule Poirot, are you not?' she said in the loudest of whispers. Poirot noted that she wished to convey anger but without being overheard, though there was nobody nearby.

'*Oui*, madame. I am he.'

'How *dare* you? How *dare* you send me such a letter?'

'Madame, pardon me, but I do not believe we know one another.'

'Don't act the part of the innocent with *me*! I am Sylvia Rule. As you know perfectly well.'

'Now I know, because you have told me. A moment ago, I did not know. You referred to a letter—'

'Will you force me to repeat your slander of me in a public place? Very well, then, I shall. I received a letter this morning—a most disgusting and objectionable letter, signed by *you*.' She stabbed the air with a forefinger that would have poked Poirot in the chest had he not hopped to one side to avoid it.

'*Non*, madame—' he tried to protest, but his attempt at denial was swiftly demolished.

'In this travesty of a letter, you accused me of murder. *Murder*! Me! Sylvia Rule! You claimed that you could prove my guilt, and you advised me to go at once to the police and confess to my crime. How *dare* you? You cannot prove anything against me, for the simple reason that I am innocent. I have not killed anybody. I am the least violently inclined person I have ever met. And I have never heard of a Barnabas Pandy!'

'A Barnabas—'

'It is monstrous that you accuse *me*, of all people! Simply monstrous. I shall not stand for it. I have a good mind to go to my solicitor about this, except I don't want him to know I have been so defamed. Perhaps I shall go to the police. The slur I have suffered! The insult! A woman of my standing in the world!'

Sylvia Rule went on in this manner for some time. There was a lot of hiss and fizz in her agitated whispering. She made Poirot think of the loud, turbulent waterfalls he had encountered on his travels: impressive to watch, but mainly alarming on account of their relentlessness. The flow never stopped.

As soon as he could make himself heard, he said, 'Madame, please accept my assurance that I have written no such letter. If you have received one, it was not sent by me. I too have never heard of Barnabas Pandy. That is the name of the man you are accused of murdering, by whoever wrote the letter?'

'*You* wrote it, and do not provoke me further by pretending you didn't. Eustace put you up to it, didn't he? You both know that I have killed nobody, that I am as blameless as it is possible for a person to be! You and Eustace have hatched a plan together to send me out of my wits! This is exactly the sort of thing he would do, and no doubt he will claim later that it was all a joke.'

'I know of no Eustace, madame.' Poirot continued to make his best effort, though it was plain that nothing he said made the slightest bit of difference to Sylvia Rule.

'He thinks he's so clever—quite the cleverest man in England!—with that disgusting smirk that never leaves his appalling face. How much did he pay you? I know it must have been his idea. And you did his dirty work. You, the famed Hercule Poirot, who are trusted by our loyal and hardworking police. You are a fraud! How *could* you? Slandering a woman of my good character! Eustace would do anything to defeat me. Anything! Whatever he has told you about me, it's a lie!'

If she had been willing to listen, Poirot might have told her that he would be unlikely to cooperate with any man who considered himself to be the cleverest man in England for as long as he, Hercule Poirot, resided in London.

'Please show me this letter you received, madame.'

'Do you think I *kept* it? It made me ill to hold it in my hand! I tore it into a dozen pieces and tossed it on the fire. I should like to toss Eustace on a fire! What a pity such actions are against the law. All I can say is that whoever made that particular law must never have met Eustace. If you *ever* traduce me in this way again, I shall go straight to Scotland Yard—not to confess to anything, for I am entirely innocent, but to accuse *you*, M. Poirot!'

Before Poirot could formulate a suitable response, Sylvia Rule had turned and marched away.

He did not call her back. He stood for a few seconds, shaking his head slowly. As he mounted the steps to his building, he muttered to himself, 'If she is the least violently inclined person, then I do not wish to meet the most.'

Inside his spacious and well-appointed flat, his valet awaited him. George's rather wooden smile turned to an expression of consternation when he saw Poirot's face.

'Are you quite well, sir?'

'*Non.* I am perplexed, Georges. Tell me, as one who knows much about the upper echelons of English society . . . do you know a Sylvia Rule?'

'By reputation only, sir. She is the widow of the late Clarence Rule. Extremely well connected. I believe she sits on the boards of various charities.'

'What about Barnabas Pandy?'

George shook his head. 'That name is not familiar to me. London society is my area of special knowledge, sir. If Mr Pandy lives elsewhere—'

'I do not know where he lives. I do not know *if* he lives, or if he was, perhaps, murdered. *Vraiment,* I could not know less about Barnabas Pandy than I do presently—that would be an impossibility! But do not try, Georges, to tell this to Sylvia Rule, who imagines that I know all about him! She believes I wrote a letter accusing her of his murder, a letter I now deny having written. I did not write the letter. I have sent no communication of any kind to Mrs Sylvia Rule.'

Poirot removed his hat and coat with less care than he usually took, and handed both to George. 'It is not a pleasant thing, to be accused of something one has not done. One ought to be able to brush the untruths aside, but somehow they take hold of the mind and cause a spectral form of guilt—like a ghost in the head, or in the conscience! Someone is certain that you have done this terrible thing, and so you start to feel as if you have, even though you know you have not. I begin to understand, Georges, why people confess to crimes of which they are innocent.'

George looked doubtful, as he frequently did. English discretion, Poirot had observed, had an outward appearance that suggested doubt. Many of the politest English men and women he had met over the years looked as if they had been ordered to disbelieve everything that was said to them.

'Would you like a drink, sir? A *sirop de menthe*, if I might be permitted to make a suggestion?'

'*Oui*. That is an excellent idea.'

'I should also mention, sir, that you have a visitor waiting to see you. Am I to bring your drink immediately, and ask him to wait a little longer?'

'A visitor?'

'Yes, sir.'

'What is his name? Is it Eustace?'

'No, sir. It's a Mr John McCrodden.'

'Ah! That is a relief. No Eustace. I can cherish the hope that the nightmare of Madame Rule and her Eustace has departed and will not return to Hercule Poirot! Did Monsieur McCrodden state the nature of his business?'

'No, sir. Though I should warn you, he seemed . . . displeased.'

Poirot allowed a small sigh to escape his lips. After his more than satisfactory luncheon, the afternoon was taking a disappointing turn. Still, John McCrodden was unlikely to be as vexatious as Sylvia Rule.

'I shall postpone the pleasure of *sirop de menthe* and see Monsieur McCrodden first,' Poirot told George. 'His name is familiar.'

'You might be thinking of the solicitor Rowland McCrodden, sir?'

'*Mais oui, bien sûr.* Rowland Rope, that dear friend of the hangman—though you are too polite, Georges, to call him by the *soubriquet* that suits him so well. The gallows, they are not allowed by Rowland Rope to have a moment's rest.'

'He has been instrumental in bringing several criminals to justice, sir,' agreed George, with his customary tact.

'Perhaps John McCrodden is a relation,' said Poirot. 'Allow me to settle myself and then you may bring him in.'

As it transpired, George was prevented from bringing in John McCrodden by McCrodden's determination to stride into the room without help or introduction. He overtook the valet and positioned himself in the middle of the carpet where he stopped as if frozen in the manner of one sent to play the part of a statue.

'Please, monsieur, you may sit down,' Poirot said with a smile.

'No, thank you,' said McCrodden. His tone was one of contemptuous detachment.

He was forty years old or thereabouts, Poirot guessed. He had the kind of handsome face that one rarely encountered apart from in works of art. His features might have been chiselled by a master craftsman. Poirot found it difficult to reconcile the face with the clothes, which were shabby and showed patches of dirt. Was he in the habit of sleeping on park benches? Did he have recourse to the usual domestic amenities? Poirot wondered if McCrodden had sought to cancel out the advantages that nature had bestowed upon him—the large green eyes and the golden hair—by making himself look as repellent as possible.

McCrodden glared down at Poirot. 'I received your letter,' he said. 'It arrived this morning.'

'I'm afraid I must contradict you, monsieur. I have sent you no letter.'

There was a long, uneasy silence. Poirot did not wish to leap to any hasty conclusions, but he feared he knew the direction the conversation was about to take. But it could not be! *How* could it be? Only in his dreams had he encountered this sensation before: the doom-laden knowledge that one is trapped in a predicament that makes no sense and will never make sense, no matter what one does.

'What did it say, this letter that you received?' he asked.

'You ought to know, since you wrote it,' said John McCrodden. 'You accused me of murdering a man named Barnabas Pandy.'

CHAPTER 2

Intolerable Provocation

'I must say, I was rather disappointed,' McCrodden went on. 'The famous Hercule Poirot, allowing himself to be used for such frivolities.'

Poirot waited a few moments before answering. Was it his particular choice of words that had proved so ineffective in persuading Sylvia Rule to listen to him? Then, for John McCrodden, he would make an effort to be clearer and more persuasive. 'Monsieur, *s'il vous plait*. I believe that somebody sent you a letter and that, in it, you were accused of murder. The murder of Barnabas Pandy. This part of your story I do not dispute. But—'

'You are in no position to dispute it,' said McCrodden.

'Monsieur, please believe me when I tell you that *I was not the writer of the letter you received*. To Hercule Poirot, there is nothing frivolous about murder. I would—'

'Oh, there won't have been any murder,' McCrodden interrupted again with a bitter laugh. 'Or, if there has, the police will already have caught the person responsible. This is one of my father's childish games.' He frowned, as if something disturbing had occurred to him. 'Unless the old gargoyle is more sadistic than I thought and would actually risk my neck in a real and unsolved case of murder. I suppose it's possible. With his ruthless determination . . .' McCrodden broke off, then muttered, 'Yes. It *is* possible. I should have thought of that.'

'Your father is the solicitor Rowland McCrodden?' asked Poirot.

'You know he is.' John McCrodden had already declared himself disappointed, and that was how he sounded—as if Poirot was sinking lower in his estimation with each word he spoke.

'I know your father by reputation only. I have not personally made his acquaintance, nor have I ever spoken to him.'

'You have to maintain the pretence, of course,' said John McCrodden. 'I'm sure he's paid you a handsome sum to keep his name out of it.' He looked around the room he was standing in, seeming to notice it for the first time. Then he nodded as if confirming something to himself, and said, 'The rich who need money least—like you, like my father—will stop at nothing to get their hands on more of it. That's why I've never trusted it. I was right not to. Money is corrosive to character once you're accustomed to it, and you, M. Poirot, are the living proof.'

Poirot could not recall when someone had last said something so unpleasant to him, so unfair or so personally wounding. He said quietly, 'I have spent my life working for the greater good and the protection of the innocent and—yes!—the wrongly accused. That group includes you, monsieur. Also, today, it includes Hercule Poirot. I too am wrongly accused. I am as innocent of writing and sending the letter you received as you are of murder. I too know no Barnabas Pandy. Not a dead Barnabas Pandy and not an alive Barnabas Pandy do I know! But here—ah! Here is where the similarities between us end, for when you insist you are innocent, I listen. I think, "This man might be telling the truth." Whereas when I—'

'Spare me the fancy words,' McCrodden cut in again. 'If you imagine I'm likely to trust dazzling rhetoric any more than I trust money, reputation or any of the other things my father holds in high regard, you're grievously mistaken. Now, since Rowland Rope will doubtless require you to relay to him my response to his sordid little scheme, please tell him this: I'm not playing. I have never heard of a Barnabas Pandy, I have killed nobody, therefore I have nothing to fear. I have enough confidence in the law of the land to trust that I won't hang for a crime I didn't commit.'

'Do you believe your father wants that to happen?'

'I don't know. It's possible. I have always thought that if Father ever runs out of guilty people to send to the gallows, he'll turn his attentions to the innocent and pretend they're guilty—both in court and in his own mind. Anything to feed his lust for the blood of his fellow human beings.'

'That is a remarkable accusation, monsieur, and not the first one you have made since you arrived.' McCrodden's brisk, business-as-usual way of speaking chilled Poirot. It lent an air of objectivity to his words, as if he was merely conveying the plain and uncontroversial facts.

The Rowland Rope about whom Poirot had heard so much over the years was not the man his son was describing. He was a strong advocate of death as a punishment for the guilty—a little too strong for Poirot's taste, for there were circumstances that called for discretion—but Poirot suspected McCrodden Senior would be as horrified as he himself would be at the prospect of an innocent man or woman being sent to the gallows. And if the man in question was his own son . . .

'Monsieur, I have not, in all my years, met a father who sought to have his son condemned to death for a murder he did not commit.'

'Ah, but you have,' John McCrodden responded swiftly. 'Despite your protests to the contrary, I know you must have met my father, or at least you have conversed with him, and the two of you have conspired to accuse me. Well, you can tell Dear Father that I no longer hate him. Now that I see how low he is willing to stoop, I pity him. He's no better than a murderer. Neither are you, M. Poirot. The same is true of anyone in favour of choking wrongdoers at the end of a rope, the way our brutal system does.'

'Is that your opinion, monsieur?'

'All my life I've been a source of embarrassment and frustration to Father: refusing to bow down, to do what he wants, think what he thinks, work in *his* chosen profession. He wants me to take up the law. He's never forgiven me for not wanting to be him.'

'May I ask what is your profession?'

'Profession?' McCrodden sneered. 'I work for a living. Nothing fancy. Nothing grand that involves playing with other people's lives. I've worked in a mine, on farms, in factories. I've made trinkets for ladies and sold them. I'm good at selling. At the moment I've got a market stall. It keeps a roof over my head, but none of that's good enough for my father. And, being Rowland McCrodden, he won't admit defeat. Never.'

'What do you mean?'

'I hoped he had given up on me. Now I see that he never will. He knows a man accused of murder will need to defend himself. It's rather clever of him, actually. He's trying to provoke me, and harbouring all sorts of fantasies, I imagine, of me insisting on defending myself against the charge of murder at the Old Bailey. To do that, I would have to take an interest in the law, wouldn't I?'

It was evident that Rowland McCrodden was to John McCrodden what Eustace was to Sylvia Rule.

'You can tell him from me that his plan has failed. I will never be the person my father wants me to be. And I would rather he didn't attempt to communicate with me again— directly, or using you or any of his other toadies as a conduit.'

Poirot rose from his chair. 'Please wait here for a few moments,' he said. He left the room, taking care to leave the door wide open.

When Poirot returned to the room, he was accompanied by his valet. He smiled at John McCrodden and said, 'You have already met Georges. You will, I hope, have heard me explain to him that I would like him to join us for a short while. I raised my voice so that you would hear everything I said to him.'

'Yes, I heard,' said McCrodden in a bored voice.

'If I had said anything else to Georges, you would have heard it too. I did not. Therefore, what he is about to tell you will, I hope, convince you that I am not your enemy. Please, Georges—speak!'

George looked astonished. He was not accustomed to receiving such vague instructions. 'About what, sir?'

Poirot turned to John McCrodden. 'You see? He does not know. I have not prepared him for this. Georges, when I returned from luncheon today, I told you about something that had just happened to me, did I not?'

'You did, sir.'

'Please repeat the story that I told you.'

'Very well, sir. You were accosted by a lady who introduced herself as Mrs Sylvia Rule. Mrs Rule mistakenly believed that you had written a letter to her in which you had accused her of murder.'

'*Merci*, Georges. Tell me, who was the supposed victim of this murder?'

'A Mr Barnabas Pandy, sir.'

'And what else did I tell you?'

'That you were not acquainted with a man of that name, sir. If there is such a gentleman, you do not know if he is alive or dead, or if he has been murdered. When you tried to explain this to Mrs Rule, she refused to listen.'

Poirot turned to John McCrodden in triumph. 'Monsieur, perhaps your father wishes also for Sylvia Rule to defend herself at the Old Bailey? Or are you finally willing to concede that you have misjudged and most unfairly maligned Hercule Poirot? It might interest to you to know that Madame Rule also accused me of conspiring with one of her enemies to cause her distress—a man named Eustace.'

'I still say my father is behind it all,' John McCrodden said after a short interval. He sounded markedly less certain than he had before. 'He enjoys nothing more than the challenge of an elaborate puzzle. I'm supposed to work out why Mrs Rule received the same letter I did.'

'When one has a driving preoccupation—yours with your father, or Sylvia Rule's obsession with her Eustace—it colours the way one sees the world,' said Poirot with a sigh. 'I don't suppose you have brought the letter with you?'

'No. I tore it up and sent the pieces to my father with a note telling him what I think of him, and now I'm telling you, M. Poirot. I won't stand for it. Even the great Hercule Poirot cannot accuse innocent people of murder and expect to get away with it.'

It was a considerable relief when John McCrodden finally removed himself from the room. Poirot stood by the window in order to watch his visitor's departure from the building.

'Are you ready for your *sirop de menthe* now, sir?' George asked.

'*Mon ami*, I am ready for all the *sirop de menthe* in the world.' Seeing that he might have caused confusion, he clarified. 'One glass please, Georges. Only one.'

Poirot returned to his chair in a state of agitation. What hope was there for justice or peace to prevail in the world when three people who might have made common cause—three wrongly accused people: Sylvia Rule, John McCrodden and Hercule Poirot—could not sit together and have a calm, rational discussion that might have helped them all to understand what had happened? Instead there had been anger, an almost fanatical refusal to entertain a point of view other than one's own, and the ceaseless hurling of insults. Not from Hercule Poirot, however; he had behaved impeccably in the face of intolerable provocation.

When George brought him his *sirop*, he said, 'Tell me—is there anybody else waiting to see me?'

'No, sir.'

'Nobody has telephoned to request an appointment?'

'No, sir. Are you expecting someone?'

'*Oui*. I am expecting an angry stranger, or perhaps several.'

'I'm not sure what you mean, sir.'

Just then the telephone started to ring. Poirot nodded permitted himself a small smile. When there was no other pleasure to be taken from a situation, one might as well enjoy being correct, he thought. 'There he is, Georges—or there *she* is. The third person. Third of who knows how many? Three, four, five? It could be any number.'

'Number of what, sir?'

'People who have received a letter accusing them of the murder of Barnabas Pandy—signed, fraudulently, in the name of Hercule Poirot!'

CHAPTER 3

The Third Person

At three o'clock the next day, Poirot was visited at Whitehaven Mansions by a Miss Annabel Treadway. As he waited for George to show her in, he found himself looking forward to the encounter. For those of a different temperament, it might have been tedious to field the same accusation time after time from a succession of strangers united in their determination not to listen to a word that was said to them; not so for Hercule Poirot. This third time, he resolved, he would succeed in making his point. He would convince Miss Annabel Treadway that he was telling the truth. Perhaps then progress might be made and some more interesting questions asked.

The puzzle of why most people, even intelligent people, were so illogical and pig-headed was one to which Poirot had devoted quite enough consideration while lying awake the previous night; he was eager to turn his attention to Barnabas Pandy himself. Of course, that was assuming that Barnabas Pandy had a self. It was possible that he did not exist, had never existed, and was no more than a figment of the letter-writer's imagination.

The door opened and George ushered in a thin woman of average height, with fair hair and dark eyes and clothes. Poirot was alarmed by his reaction to the sight of her. He felt as if he ought to bow his head and say, 'My condolences, mademoiselle.' Having no reason to believe that she had suffered a loss, he restrained himself. A letter accusing her of murder might provoke anger or fear, but it could hardly be considered a tragedy; it would not, Poirot thought, make a person sad.

As surely as John McCrodden had filled Poirot's room with cold contempt, Annabel Treadway had brought sorrow in with her. 'The aching heart,' Poirot thought. He felt it as keenly as if it were his own.

'Thank you, Georges,' he said. 'Please, sit down, mademoiselle.'

She hurried to the nearest chair and sat in a manner that cannot have been comfortable for her. Poirot observed that her most striking facial feature was a deep vertical groove that started between her eyebrows: a pronounced crease that seemed to divide her forehead into two neat halves. Poirot resolved not to look at it again, lest she should notice.

'Thank you for allowing me to come here today,' she said quietly. 'I expected you to refuse.' She looked at Poirot five or six times as she spoke, turning away quickly on each occasion as if she didn't want him to catch her in the act of observing him.

'From where have you come, mademoiselle?'

'Oh, you won't have heard of it. Nobody has. It's in the country.'

'Why did you expect me to refuse to see you?'

'Most people would go to any lengths to prevent someone they believed to be a murderer from entering their home,' she said. 'M. Poirot, what I came here to tell you is . . . Well, you might not believe me, but I am innocent. I could not murder another living soul. Never! You cannot know . . .' She broke off with a ragged gasp.

'Please continue,' said Poirot gently. 'What is it that I cannot know?'

'I have never caused pain or injury to anybody, and nor could I. I have *saved* lives!'

'Mademoiselle—'

Annabel Treadway had produced a handkerchief from her pocket and was dabbing at her eyes. 'Please forgive me if I sounded boastful. I did not mean to exaggerate my own goodness or my achievements, but it is true that I have saved a life. Many years ago.'

'A life? You said "lives".'

'I only meant that if I had the opportunity to do so again, I should save every life that I could save, even if I had to place myself in danger to do so.' Her voice trembled.

'Is that because you are especially heroic or because you think other people matter more than you do?' Poirot asked her.

'I . . . I'm not sure what you mean. We must all put

others before ourselves. I don't pretend to be more selfless than most, and I'm far from brave. I'm a terrible coward, in fact. Coming here to talk to you took all my courage. My sister Lenore—she's the brave one. I'm sure you are brave, M. Poirot. Wouldn't you save every life that you could, every single one?'

Poirot frowned. It was a peculiar question. The conversation so far had been unusual—even for what Poirot was calling in his mind 'the new age of Barnabas Pandy'.

'I have heard of your work and I admire you greatly,' said Annabel Treadway. 'That is why your letter pained me so. M. Poirot, you are quite wrong in your suspicions. You say you have proof against me, but I don't see how that is possible. I have committed no crime.'

'And I have sent you no letter,' Poirot told her. 'I did not accuse you—I *do* not accuse you—of the murder of Barnabas Pandy.'

Annabel Treadway blinked at Poirot in astonishment. 'But . . . I don't understand.'

'The letter you received was not written by the true Hercule Poirot. I too am innocent! An impersonator has sent these accusations, each one with my name signed at the bottom.'

'Each . . . each one? Do you mean—?'

'*Oui.* You are the third person in two days to say this very thing to me: that I have written to you and accused you of murdering a Barnabas Pandy. Yesterday it was Madame Sylvia Rule and Monsieur John McCrodden. Today it is you.' Poirot watched her closely to see if the names of her fellow accusees had any noticeable effect. There was none that he could see.

'So you didn't . . .' Her mouth moved for a while after she stopped speaking. Eventually she said, 'So you don't think I'm a killer?'

'That is correct. At the present moment, I have no reason to believe you have murdered anybody. Now, if you were the only person to come to me as you have and talk about this letter of accusation, I might wonder . . .' Deciding against sharing any more of his thoughts, Poirot smiled and said, 'It is a cruel joke that this trickster, whomever he is, has played upon us both, mademoiselle. The names Sylvia Rule and John McCrodden are not known to you?'

'I have never heard of either of them,' said Annabel Treadway. 'And jokes are supposed to be funny. This is not funny. It's appalling. Who would do it? I'm not important, but to do such a thing to a person of your reputation is shocking, M. Poirot.'

'To me you are extremely important,' he told her. 'You alone, of the three people to receive this letter, have listened. You alone believe Hercule Poirot when he says that he wrote and sent no such accusation. You do not make me feel I must be going mad, as the other two did. For that I am profoundly grateful.'

An oppressive air of sorrow still lingered in the room. If Poirot could only bring a smile to Annabel Treadway's face . . . Ah, but that was a dangerous way to think. Allow a person to affect your emotions and your judgement suffered, always. Reminding himself that Miss Treadway might, despite seeming forlorn, nevertheless have murdered a man named Barnabas Pandy, Poirot continued with less effusiveness: 'Madame Rule and Monsieur McCrodden, they did not believe Poirot. They did not listen.'

'They surely didn't accuse you of lying?'

'Unfortunately, they did.'

'But you're Hercule Poirot!'

'An undeniable truth,' Poirot agreed. 'May I ask, have you brought the letter with you?'

'No. I destroyed it at once, I'm afraid. I . . . I couldn't bear for it to exist.'

'*Dommage*. I should have liked to see it. *Eh bien*, mademoiselle, let us take the next step in our investigation. Who should want to make mischief in this particular way—for you, for me, and for Madame Rule and Monsieur McCrodden? Four people who do not know this Barnabas Pandy, if he exists at all, which, for all we know—'

'Oh!' Annabel Treadway gasped.

'What is the matter?' Poirot asked her. 'Tell me. Do not be afraid.'

She looked terrified. 'It's not true,' she whispered.

'What is not true?'

'He does exist.'

'Monsieur Pandy? Barnabas Pandy?'

'Yes. Well, he *did* exist. He's dead, you see. Not murdered, though. He fell asleep and . . . I thought . . . it was not my intention to deceive you, M. Poirot. I should have made it clear straight away . . . I simply thought . . .' Her eyes moved quickly from one part of the room to another. There was, Poirot sensed, great chaos in her mind at that moment.

'You have not deceived me,' he assured her. 'Madame Rule and Monsieur McCrodden were adamant that they knew no one by the name of Barnabas Pandy, and neither do I. I made the assumption that the same must be true of you. Now, please tell me all that you know about Monsieur Pandy. He is dead, you say?'

'Yes. He died in December of last year. Three months ago.'

'And you say it was not murder—which means you know how he died?'

'Of course I do. I was there. We lived together in the same house.'

'You . . . you lived together?' This Poirot had not been expecting.

'Yes, since I was seven years old,' she said. 'Barnabas Pandy was my grandfather.'

'He was more like a parent to me than a grandparent,' Annabel Treadway told Poirot, once he had succeeded in convincing her that he was not angry with her for misleading him. 'My mother and father died when I was seven, and Grandy—that's what I called him—took us in, Lenore and me. Lenore has also been like a parent to me, in a way. I don't know what I'd do without her. Grandy was terribly old. It's sad when they leave us, of course, but old people do die, don't they? Naturally, when it's their time.'

The contrast between her matter-of-fact tone and the air

of sadness that seemed to cling to her led Poirot to conclude that, whatever was making her unhappy, it was not her grandfather's death.

Then her manner changed. There was a flash of something in her eyes as she said fiercely, 'People mind so much less when old people die, which is dreadfully unfair! "He had a good innings," they say, as if that makes it tolerable, whereas when a child dies everyone knows it's the worst kind of tragedy. I believe every death is a tragedy! Don't *you* think it's unfair, M. Poirot?'

The word 'tragedy' seemed to echo in the air. If Poirot had been ordered to pick one word to describe the essence of the woman before him, he would have chosen that one. It was almost a relief to hear it spoken aloud.

When he didn't immediately answer her question, Annabel Treadway blushed and said, 'When I spoke of old people dying and nobody caring as much as . . . well, I didn't mean . . . I was talking about really *very* old people. Grandy was ninety-four, which I'm sure is *much* older than . . . I hope I have caused no offence.'

Thus, reflected Poirot, did some reassurances cause greater alarm than the original remark upon which they sought to improve. Somewhat dishonestly, he told Annabel Treadway that he was not offended. 'How did you destroy the letter?' he asked her.

She looked down at her knees.

'You would prefer not to tell me?'

'Being accused of murder—not by you, but definitely by somebody—makes one a little nervous of revealing anything.'

'I understand. All the same, I should like to know how you disposed of it.'

She frowned. '*Alors!*' thought Poirot to himself as the crease between her eyebrows deepened. That was one mystery solved at least. Frowning was a habit of hers and had been for many years. The groove in her forehead was the proof.

'You'll think me silly and superstitious if I tell you,' she said, raising her handkerchief to just below her nose. She was not crying, but perhaps expected to be soon. 'I took a pen and scored thick black lines through every word, so that nothing of what was written remained visible. I did it to your name too, M. Poirot. Every single word! Then I tore it up and burned the pieces.'

'Three distinct methods of obliteration.' Poirot smiled. 'I am impressed. Madame Rule and Monsieur McCrodden, they were less thorough than you, mademoiselle. There is something else I should like to ask you. I sense you are unhappy, and perhaps afraid?'

'I have nothing to be afraid of,' she said quickly. 'I've told you, I'm innocent. Oh, if only it were Lenore or Ivy accusing me, I would know how to convince them. I would simply say, "I swear on Hoppy's life," and they would know I was telling the truth. They already know, of course, that I did not kill Grandy.'

'Who is Hoppy?' asked Poirot.

'Hopscotch. My dog. He's the most darling creature. I would never swear on his life and then lie. You would love him, M. Poirot. It's impossible not to love him.' For the first time since arriving, Annabel Treadway smiled, and the thick layer of sadness in the room's atmosphere lifted a little. 'I must get back to him. You'll think me foolish, but I miss him dreadfully. And I'm not afraid—truly. If the person who sent the letter wasn't willing to put his name to it, then it's not a serious accusation, is it? It's a silly trick, that's all it is, and I'm very glad to be able to see you and straighten it out. Now, I must go.'

'Please, mademoiselle, do not leave yet. I would like to ask you more questions.'

'But I must get back to Hoppy,' Annabel Treadway insisted, rising to her feet. 'He needs . . . and none of them can . . . When I'm not there, he . . . I'm so sorry. I hope whoever sent those letters causes you no further trouble. Thank you for seeing me. Good day, M. Poirot.'

'Good day, mademoiselle,' Poirot said to a room that was suddenly empty apart from himself and a lingering feeling of desolation.

CHAPTER 4

The Odd One Out?

The next morning felt peculiar to Hercule Poirot. By ten o'clock, no stranger had telephoned. Nobody had appeared at Whitehaven Mansions to accuse him of accusing them of the murder of Barnabas Pandy. He waited in until forty minutes after eleven (one never knew when a faulty alarm clock might cause an accusee to oversleep), then set off across town to Pleasant's Coffee House.

Unofficially in charge at Pleasant's was a young waitress by the name of Euphemia Spring. Everyone called her Fee for short. Poirot liked her enormously. She said the most unexpected things. Her flyaway hair defied gravity by refusing to lie flat against her head, though there was nothing floaty or flighty about her mind, which was always sharply in focus. She made the finest coffee in London, then did all she could to discourage customers from drinking it. Tea, she was fond of proclaiming, was a far superior beverage and beneficial to health, whereas coffee apparently led to sleepless nights and ruination of every sort.

Poirot continued to drink Fee's excellent coffee in spite of her warnings and entreaties, and had noticed that on many subjects (other than the aforementioned) she had much wisdom to impart. One of her areas of expertise was Poirot's friend and occasional helper Inspector Edward Catchpool—which was why he was here.

The coffee house was starting to fill with people. Moisture dripped down the insides of the windows. Fee was serving a gentleman on the other side of the room when Poirot walked in, but she waved at him with her left hand: an eloquent gesture that told him precisely where to sit and wait for her.

Poirot sat. He straightened the cutlery on the table in front of him as he always did, and tried not to look at the teapot collection that filled the high shelves on the walls. He found the sight of them unbearable: all angled differently and apparently at random. There was no logic to it. To be someone who cared about teapots, enough to collect so many, and yet not to see the need to point all the spouts in the same direction . . . Poirot had long suspected Fee of creating a deliberately haphazard arrangement solely to cause him distress. He had once, when the teapots were lined up in a more conventional fashion, remarked that one was positioned incorrectly. Each time he had come to Pleasant's since that day, there had been no pattern at all. Fee Spring did not respond well to criticism.

She appeared by his side and slammed a plate down between his knife and fork. There was a slice of cake on it, one Poirot had not ordered. 'I'll be needing your help,' she said, before he could ask her about Catchpool, 'but you'll have to eat up first.'

It was her famous Church Window Cake, so called because each slice comprised two yellow and two pink squares that were supposed to resemble the stained glass of a church window. Poirot found the name bothersome. Church windows were coloured, yes, but they were also transparent and made of glass. One might as well call it 'Chess Board Cake'—that was what it brought to Poirot's mind when he saw it: a chess board, albeit too small and in the wrong colours.

'I telephoned to Scotland Yard this morning,' he told Fee. 'They say that Catchpool is at the seaside on holiday, with his mother. This did not sound to me likely.'

'Eat,' said Fee.

'*Oui, mais*—'

'But you want to know where Edward is. Why? Has something happened?' She had started, in recent months, to refer to Catchpool as 'Edward', though never when he was present, Poirot noticed.

'Do you know where he is?' Poirot asked her.

'Might do.' Fee grinned. 'I'll gladly tell all's I know, once you've said you'll help me. Now, eat.'

Poirot sighed. 'How will it help you if I eat a slice of your cake?'

Fee sat down beside him and rested both her elbows on the table. 'It's not my cake,' she whispered, as if talking about something shameful. 'Looks the same, tastes the same, but it isn't *mine*. That's the problem.'

'I do not understand.'

'Were you ever served by a girl here, name of Philippa—all bones, teeth like a horse?'

'*Non*. She does not sound familiar.'

'She wasn't here long. I caught her pilfering food and had to have words. Not that she didn't need feeding up, but I wasn't having her taking food from plates of those who'd paid fair and square. I told her she was welcome to leftovers, but that weren't good enough for her. Didn't like being spoken to like a thief—thieves never do—and so she never came back after. Well, now she's at the new coffee house, Kemble's, near the wine merchants' place on Oxford Street. They can keep her and good luck to 'em—but then customers start telling me she's making *my* cake. I didn't believe 'em at first. How could she know the recipe? Passed down from my great-granny, it were, to my granny, then my ma, then to me. I'd cut out my own tongue before I'd tell it to anyone outside the family, and I haven't, to no one—certainly not to *her*. I've not written it down. Only way she could know's if she's secretly watched me making it . . . and when I thought carefully, I thought, yes, she might've. She'd have only needed to do it once if she'd paid attention, and I can't swear she didn't. All that time, the two of us together in a tiny kitchen . . .'

Fee pointed an accusatory finger, as if the kitchen of Pleasant's were to blame. 'Easy enough to look like she's busy with somethin' else. And she was a proper little sneak-about. Anyhow, I had to go and try it, didn't I? And I think they're right, those who've told me she's making my cake.

I think they're dead right!' Her eyes blazed with indignation.

'What would you like me to do, mademoiselle?'

'Haven't I said? Haven't I been saying? Eat that and tell me if I'm right or wrong. That's hers, not mine. I shoved it in a coat pocket when she wasn't looking. She never even knew I was in her coffee house, that's how careful I was. I went in disguise—wore a proper costume!'

Poirot did not wish to eat a slice of cake that had been in anybody's pocket. 'I have not sampled your Church Window Cake for many months,' he told Fee. 'My memory of it is not strong enough to judge. Besides, one does not remember taste accurately—it is impossible.'

'D'you think I don't know that?' said Fee impatiently. 'I'll give you a slice of mine next, won't I? I'll get it right now.' She stood up. 'Have a little bite of one, then the other. Then do it again, a little bite from each. Tell me if they couldn't all come from the same slice.'

'If I do this, you will tell me where is Catchpool?'

'No.'

'No?'

'I said I'd tell you where Edward is if you'll help me.'

'And I have agreed to taste—'

'The tasting's not the helping,' Fee said firmly. 'That'll come after.'

Hercule Poirot rarely allowed himself to be bent to the will of others, but to resist Fee Spring was a fool's enterprise. He waited until she returned with another slice of Church Window Cake that looked identical to the first and then, obediently, sampled both. To be certain, he tasted three pieces from each one.

Fee watched him closely. Finally she could control herself no longer and demanded, 'Well? Is it the same or not?'

'I can taste no difference,' Poirot told her. 'None at all. But, mademoiselle, I am afraid that there is no statute that prevents one person from making the same cake as another, if she has observed with her own eyes—'

'Oh, I'm not after using the law against her. All's I want to know is if she thinks she's stolen from me or not.'

'I see,' said Poirot. 'You are interested not in the legal offence but in the moral one.'

'I want you to go to her coffee house, order her cake, and then ask her about it. Ask where she got the recipe.'

'What if she says, "It is the one used by Fee Spring of Pleasant's"?'

'Then I'll go see her myself, and tell her what she doesn't know: that the Spring family recipe's not to be used by anyone else. If it's an honest mistake, that's how I'll treat it.'

'And what will you do if she answers more evasively?' Poirot asked. 'Or if she says boldly that she got the recipe for her cake from somewhere else, and you do not believe her?'

Fee smiled and narrowed her eyes. 'Oh, I'll soon have her regretting it,' she said, then quickly added, 'Not in a way as'd make you wish you hadn't helped me, mind.'

'I am glad to hear that, mademoiselle. If you will allow Poirot to offer you a piece of wise advice: the pursuit of revenge is rarely a good idea.'

'Neither's sitting around twiddling your thumbs when folks have made off with what's rightfully yours,' said Fee decisively. 'What I want from you's the help I've asked for, not advice I didn't asked for.'

'*Je comprends*,' said Poirot.

'Good.'

'Please. Where is Catchpool?'

Fee grinned. 'At the seaside with his ma, just like Scotland Yard said.'

Poirot's face assumed a stern look. 'I see that I have been tricked,' he said.

'Hardly! You didn't believe it when they told you. Now I'm telling you it's true, so's you know. That's where he is. Great Yarmouth, out east.'

'As I said before . . . this does not sound likely.'

'He didn't want to go but he had to, to get the old girl to leave him be. She'd found another perfect wife for him.'

'Ah!' Poirot was familiar with Catchpool's mother's ambition to see her son settled with a nice young lady.

'And this one had so much going in her favour—a right looker, Edward said she was, and from a respectable family. Kind, too, and cultivated. He found it harder than usual to say no.'

'To his mother? Or did the *jolie femme* make to him the proposal of marriage?'

Fee laughed. 'No—it was his ma's notion and that was all. It knocked the stuffing out of the old girl when he said he wasn't interested. She must've thought, "If he won't be persuaded, even for this one . . ." Edward decided he had to do something to lift her spirits, and she loves Great Yarmouth, so that's where they are.'

'It is February,' said Poirot crossly. 'To go to an English seaside resort in February is to invite misery, is it not?' What a dismal time Catchpool must be having, he thought. He ought to return to London at once so that Poirot could discuss with him the matter of Barnabas Pandy.

'Excuse me, M. Poirot? M. Hercule Poirot?' A tentative voice interrupted his thoughts. He turned to find a smartly attired man beaming at him as if suffused with the greatest joy.

'Hercule Poirot, *c'est moi*,' he confirmed.

The man extended his hand. 'How delightful to meet you,' he said. 'Your reputation is formidable. It's hard to judge what one ought to say to such a great man. I'm Dockerill—Hugo Dockerill.'

Fee eyed the new arrival suspiciously. 'I'll leave you to it, then,' she said. 'Don't forget you've promised to help me,' she warned Poirot before leaving the table. He assured her that he would not forget, then invited the smiling man to sit.

Hugo Dockerill was almost completely bald, though not yet fifty, Poirot guessed.

'I'm terribly sorry to accost you in this manner,' Dockerill said, sounding jolly and not at all regretful. 'Your valet told me I might find you here. He encouraged me to make an appointment for later this afternoon, but I'm awfully anxious to clear up the misunderstanding. So I told him I'd rather seek you out sooner, and when I explained to him what it was all about, he seemed to think that you might want to see *me* rather urgently—so here I am!' He guffawed loudly, as if he'd told a hilarious anecdote.

'Misunderstanding?' Poirot said. He was starting to wonder if perhaps a fourth letter . . . but no, how could that be? Would any person, even the most enthusiastic and optimistic, beam with delight in such circumstances?

'Yes. I received your letter two days ago, and . . . well, I'm sure the fault is entirely mine and I'd hate you to think I'm levelling any sort of criticism at you—I'm absolutely not,' Hugo Dockerill chattered on. 'In fact, I'm a keen admirer of your work, from what I've heard of it, but . . . well, I must have unwittingly done something that's given you the wrong idea. For that, I apologize. I do sometimes get into a bit of a muddle. You'd only need to ask my wife Jane—she'd tell you. I planned to track you down at once, after I got your letter, but I misplaced it almost immediately—'

'Monsieur,' said Poirot sternly. 'To which letter are you referring?'

'The one about . . . well, about old Barnabas Pandy,' said Hugo Dockerill, beaming with renewed vitality now that the crucial name had been uttered. 'I wouldn't normally dare to suggest that the amazing Hercule Poirot might be wrong about something, but on this occasion . . . I'm afraid it wasn't me. I thought that . . . well, if you could tell me what has led you to believe it was, maybe between us we could get this funny mess ironed out. As I say, I'm sure the misunderstanding is entirely my fault.'

'You say it was not you, monsieur. What was not you?'

'The person who murdered Barnabas Pandy,' said Hugo Dockerill.

Having declared himself innocent of murder, Hugo Dockerill picked up an unused fork from the place setting opposite Poirot and helped himself to a chunk of Fee Spring's Church Window Cake. Or perhaps it was Philippa the pilferer's slice; Poirot could no longer remember which was which.

'You don't mind, do you?' Dockerill said. 'Shame for it to go to waste. Don't tell my wife! She's always complaining I've got the table manners of a guttersnipe. But we boys are a bit more robust when it comes to filling our bellies, eh?'

Poirot, aghast that anyone would find a half-eaten slice of cake tempting, made a tactfully non-specific noise. He permitted himself to reflect, briefly, upon similarity and difference. When many people do or say precisely the same thing, the effect is the opposite of what one might expect. Now two women and two men had come forward to communicate the same message: that they had received a letter signed in the name of Hercule Poirot and accusing them of the murder of Barnabas Pandy. Instead of pondering the similarities between these four encounters, Poirot found himself intrigued by the differences. He was now firmly of the view that if you wanted to see clearly how one person's character diverged from that of another, the most efficient method was to place both in identical situations.

Sylvia Rule was egotistical and full of proud rage. Like

John McCrodden, she was in the grip of a powerful obsession with a particular person. Both believed Poirot must have done the bidding of that person in writing the letters, be it Rowland 'Rope' McCrodden or the mysterious Eustace. John McCrodden's anger, Poirot thought, was equal to Sylvia Rule's but different: less explosive, more enduring. He would not forget, whereas she might if a new and more pressing drama occurred.

Of the four, Annabel Treadway was the hardest to fathom. She had not been angry at all, but she was withholding something. And afflicted, somehow.

Hugo Dockerill was the first and only letter-recipient to remain cheerful in the face of his predicament, and certainly the first to demonstrate a belief that all the world's problems could be solved if only decent people sat down at a table together and set things straight. If he objected to being accused of murder, he concealed it well. He was still doing his best to split his face across the middle with a radiant smile, and muttering, between mouthfuls of Church Window Cake, about how sorry he was if anything he'd done had created the impression that he might be a killer.

'Do not keep apologizing,' Poirot told him. 'You spoke of "old Barnabas Pandy" a moment ago. Why did you refer to him in that way?'

'Well, he was on his way to being a hundred years old when he died, wasn't he?'

'So you knew Monsieur Pandy?'

'I had never met him, but I knew about him, of course— because of Timothy.'

'Who is Timothy?' asked Poirot. 'I should explain, monsieur, that the letter you received did not come from me. I knew nothing of a Barnabas Pandy until I was visited by three people who were all sent the same letter. And now a fourth: you. These letters were signed "Hercule Poirot" by a deceiver. A fraud! They did not come from me. I have accused nobody of the murder of Monsieur Pandy—who, I believe, died of natural causes.'

'Golly!' Hugo Dockerill's broad smile dipped a little as his eyes filled with confusion. 'What a rum do. Silly prank, was it?'

'Who is Timothy?' Poirot asked again.

'Timothy Lavington—he's old Pandy's great-grandson. I'm his housemaster at school. Turville. Pandy himself was a pupil there, as was Timothy's father—both Old Turvillians. As am I. Only difference is, I never left the place!' Dockerill chortled.

'I see. So you are acquainted with Timothy Lavington's family?'

'Yes. But, as I say, I never met old Pandy.'

'When did Barnabas Pandy die?'

'I couldn't tell you the exact date. It was late last year, I think. November or December.' This matched what Annabel Treadway had said.

'In your capacity as housemaster, you were told, I assume, that the great-grandfather of one of your charges was deceased?'

'Yes, I was. We were all a bit glum about it. Still, the old boy lived to a ripe old age. We should all be so lucky!'

The joyous smile was back in place. 'And if one has to go, I suppose there are worse ways than drowning.'

'Drowning?'

'Yes. Poor old Pandy fell asleep in his bath and sank down under the water. Drowned. Horrible accident. There was never any talk of it being anything else.'

Annabel Treadway had spoken of her grandfather falling asleep. Poirot had assumed this meant he had died naturally in the night. She had said nothing about a bath or drowning. Had she deliberately withheld that part of the story?

'This was what you believed until you received a letter signed in the name of Hercule Poirot—that Monsieur Pandy drowned in his bathtub, accidentally?'

'It's what everybody believes,' said Hugo Dockerill. 'There was an inquest that returned a verdict of accidental death. I remember hearing Jane, my wife, commiserating with young Timothy. I suppose the inquest must have got it wrong, what?'

'Do you have the letter with you?' Poirot asked him.

'No, I'm sorry, I don't. As I said, I mislaid it. I lost it twice, in fact. I found it the first time—that's how I had your address—but then it went astray again. I looked for the blasted thing before I set off for London, but couldn't lay my hands on it. I do hope one of our boys hasn't got his grubby mitts on it. I should hate for anybody to think I stand accused of murder—especially when, as it turns out, you have accused me of no such thing!'

'Do you and your wife have children?'

'Not yet. We're hoping to. Oh—I'm speaking as a

housemaster when I say "our boys". We've got seventy-five of the little blighters! My wife is a saint to put up with them, I always say, and *she* always says that they're no trouble at all, and if she's a saint then it's for putting up with *me*.' A predictable guffaw followed.

'Perhaps you could ask your wife to help you search the house?' said Poirot. 'So far, not one person has brought me their letter. It would be very helpful if I could see at least one.'

'Of course. I should have thought of that. Jane'll find it, I have no doubt. She's tremendous! She has a talent for finding things, though she denies it. She says to me, "You'd find all the same things I find, Hugo, if you'd only open your eyes and engage your brain." She's marvellous!'

'Do you know a woman by the name of Annabel Treadway, monsieur?'

Hugo's smile widened. 'Annabel! Of course. She's Timothy's aunt, and old Pandy's—what would it be? Let me think. Timothy's mother Lenore is Pandy's grand-daughter, so . . . yes, Annabel was his . . . erm . . . She's Lenore's sister, so . . . she was also Pandy's grand-daughter.'

Poirot suspected that Hugo Dockerill was one of the stupidest people he had ever met.

'Lenore is usually accompanied by both Annabel and her daughter Ivy—Timothy's sister—when she comes to Turville, so I've got to know Annabel rather well over the years. I'm afraid, M. Poirot, that *therein lies a tale*, as they say. I proposed to Annabel some years ago. Marriage, you know.

Quite head over heels, I was. Oh—I wasn't married to my wife at the time,' Dockerill clarified.

'I am glad to hear, monsieur, that you did not make a bigamous proposal.'

'What? Golly, no. I was a bachelor then. It was peculiar, actually. To this day I can't make sense of it. Annabel seemed thrilled when I asked her, and then, almost immediately, she burst into tears and refused me. Women are nothing if not changeable, as every man knows—apart from Jane. She's tremendously reliable. But still . . . saying no seemed to upset Annabel dreadfully—so much so, I suggested to her that changing her "no" to a "yes" might make her feel more chipper.'

'What was her reaction?'

'A firm "no", I'm afraid. Ah, well, these things have a way of working out for the best, don't they? Jane's so wonderful with our boys. Annabel assured me when she rejected me that she would have been *hopeless* with them. I don't know why she thought that, devoted to Timothy and Ivy as she is. And she truly is—like a second mother to them. I've wondered more than once if she was secretly afraid of having her own children—in case it weakened her motherly bond with her niece and nephew. Or maybe it was the sheer number of boys in my house that discouraged her. They are rather like a herd of beasts sometimes, and Annabel's a quiet creature. But then, as I say, she dotes on young Timothy, who's hardly the easiest of boys. He's given us a spot of trouble over the years.'

'What kind of trouble?' asked Poirot.

'Oh, nothing serious. I'm sure he'll shake out all right. Like a lot of Turville boys, he can be rather self-congratulatory when no such congratulations are in order. Sometimes carries on as if school rules don't apply to him. As if he's above them. Jane blames it on . . .' Hugo Dockerill broke off. 'Whoops!' he laughed. 'Mustn't be indiscreet.'

'Nothing you tell me will go any further,' Poirot assured him.

'I was only going to say that as far as his mother is concerned, nothing is ever Timothy's fault. Once when I felt I absolutely had to punish him for insubordination—Jane *insisted*—I got punished myself by Lenore Lavington. She didn't speak to me for nearly six months. Not one word!'

'Do you know a John McCrodden?' Poirot asked.

'No, I'm afraid not. Should I?'

'What about Sylvia Rule?'

'Yes, I know Sylvia.' Hugo beamed, happy to be able to answer in the affirmative.

Poirot was surprised. He had been wrong again. There was nothing he found more disconcerting. He had assumed that there were two pairs of two, he mused, like the two yellow squares and two pink squares in a slice of Church Window Cake: Sylvia Rule and John McCrodden, who did not know Barnabas Pandy and had never heard his name; and the other pair, the pair who had known Pandy or at least known of him, Annabel Treadway and Hugo Dockerill.

Incorrectly, Poirot had assumed these pairs would remain neatly separate, as distinct as the yellow squares and the pink squares of the cake. Now, however, things were messy: Hugo Dockerill knew Sylvia Rule.

'How do you know her?'

'Her son Freddie is a pupil at Turville. He's in the same year as Timothy Lavington.'

'How old are these two boys?'

'Twelve, I think. Both in the Second Form, at any rate, and both in my house. Very different boys. Goodness me, they couldn't be more different! Timothy's a popular, gregarious young fellow, always surrounded by a crowd of admirers. Poor Freddie is a loner. He doesn't seem to have any friends. Spends a lot of time helping Jane, in fact. She's tremendous. "No boy here will be lonely if I've got anything to do with it," she often says. Means it, too!'

Had Sylvia Rule lied about not knowing Pandy? Poirot wondered. Would a person necessarily know the name of their son's school acquaintance's great-grandfather, particularly when the surnames were different? Timothy's last name was Lavington, not Pandy.

'So Madame Rule has a son who is in the same house at school as the great-grandson of Barnabas Pandy,' Poirot muttered, more to himself than to Hugo Dockerill.

'Golly. Does she?'

'That is what we have established, monsieur.' Perhaps it was only family relationships that Hugo Dockerill struggled with. That and knowing where things were—things like important letters.

Dockerill's smile dimmed as he struggled to make sense of Poirot's announcement. 'A son who . . . the great-grandson of . . . Of course! Yes, she does. She does indeed!'

This meant, thought Poirot, that it was not so simple as two pink squares and two yellow; it was not a case of pairs. Three recipients of the letter could be linked to Barnabas Pandy most definitively, and one could not—at least, not *yet*.

Two questions interested Poirot: had Barnabas Pandy been murdered? And was John McCrodden the odd one out? Or was he also connected to the deceased Pandy in a manner that was not yet clear?

CHAPTER 5

A Letter with a Hole in it

I am producing this account of what Poirot later decided to call 'The Mystery of Three Quarters' on a typewriter that has a faulty letter 'e'. I don't know if anyone will publish it, but if you are reading a printed version, all of the 'e's will be flawless. It is nevertheless significant that in the original typescript there is (or should I say for the benefit of future readers, was?) a small white gap in the middle of the horizontal bar of each letter 'e'—an extraordinarily tiny hole in the black ink.

Why is this important? To answer that question immediately would be to rush ahead of my own narrative. Let me explain.

My name is Edward Catchpool and I'm an inspector with Scotland Yard. I'm also the person telling this story—not only now, but from the beginning, though I have been helped by several people to fill in those parts of the drama for which I was absent. I am especially grateful to the sharp eyes and the loquaciousness of Hercule Poirot, who, when it comes to detail, misses nothing. Thanks to him, I do not feel that I, in any meaningful sense, missed the events I have so far recounted, all of which occurred before I returned from Great Yarmouth.

The less said about my infuriatingly tedious stay at the seaside, the better. The only relevant point is that I was compelled to return to London sooner than planned (you can imagine my relief) by the arrival of two telegrams. One was from Hercule Poirot, who said he urgently needed my help, and could I come back at once? The other, impossible to ignore, was from my superintendent at Scotland Yard, Nathaniel Bewes. This second telegram, though not from Poirot, was about him. Apparently he was 'making life difficult', and Bewes wanted me to stop him.

I was touched by the Super's quite unjustifiable confidence in my ability to alter the behaviour of my Belgian friend, and so, once back in Bewes's office, I sat quietly and nodded sympathetically as he gave vent to his dismay. The essence of what was at stake seemed clear enough. Poirot believed the son of Rowland 'Rope' McCrodden to be guilty of murder, and had said so, and claimed to be able to prove it. The Super didn't like this one bit because Rowland Rope was a chum of his, and he wanted me to persuade Poirot to think otherwise.

Instead of paying attention to the Super's loud and varied expressions of disgust, I was busy rehearsing my answer. Should I say, 'There's no point in my talking to Poirot about this—if he's sure he's right then he won't listen to me'? No, that would make me sound both truculent and defeatist.

And, since Poirot wanted to talk to me as a matter of urgency, presumably about this very same business, I decided to promise the Super that I would do my best to make him see sense. Then, from Poirot, I would find out why he believed Rowland Rope's son was a murderer when apparently no one else did, and convey his thoughts back to the Super. All of this seemed manageable. I saw no need to upset the apple cart at work by pointing out that 'He's my friend's son' is neither proof of innocence nor a viable defence.

Nathaniel Bewes is a mild, even-tempered and fair-minded man—apart from in the immediate aftermath of something that has especially upset him. In those rare moments he is incapable of realizing that he is greatly distressed and that his emotional state might have skewed his perspective. Because his judgement is so often sound, he assumes it will always be, and is therefore liable to make the most absurd pronouncements—things which, in his usual calm frame of mind, he would be the first to call idiotic. Once restored to sanity after one of his episodes, he never refers to the period during which he emitted a series of ridiculous statements and directives, and, as far as I know, no one else ever refers to them either. I certainly don't. Though it sounds fanciful, I am not convinced that the normal Super is aware of the existence of his deranged counterpart who occasionally understudies for him.

I nodded judiciously as the understudy ranted and growled, striding up and down his small office, pushing his spectacles back up to the bridge of his nose as they slid down with disconcerting frequency.

'Rowly's son, a murderer? Preposterous! He's the son of Rowland McCrodden! If you were the son of a man like that, Catchpool, would you take up murder as a way of passing the time? Of course you wouldn't! Only a fool would! Besides, the death of Barnabas Pandy was an accident—I've availed myself of the official record of his passing and it's all there in black and white, plain as day: *accident!* The man drowned in his bath. Ninety-four, he was. I mean, I ask you—*ninety-four!* How much longer was he likely to live? Would you risk your neck to murder a ninety-four-year-old man, Catchpool? It beggars belief. No one would. Why would they?'

'Well—'

'There could be no reason,' Bewes concluded. 'Now, I don't know what your Belgian chum thinks he's up to, but you'd better make it clear to him in no uncertain terms that he is to write to Rowly McCrodden at once and convey his most profuse apologies.' Bewes had clearly forgotten that he too was on friendly terms with Poirot.

There were, of course, many reasons why someone might murder a nonagenarian: if he had threatened to expose their shameful secret to the world the very next day, for instance. And Bewes—the real Bewes, not his unbalanced *doppelgänger*—knew as well as I did that some murders are initially mistaken for accidents. To grow up as the son of a man famous for helping to dispatch miscreants to the gallows could, arguably, warp a person's psyche to the point where he might decide to kill.

I knew there was no point saying any of this to the Super

today, though in a different mood he would have made the same good points himself. I decided to risk only a minor challenge. 'Didn't you say Poirot sent this letter of accusation to Rowland Rope's son, not to Rowland Rope himself?'

'Well, what if he did?' Bewes rounded on me angrily. 'What difference does that make?'

'How old is John McCrodden?'

'How old? What the devil are you talking about? Does his age matter?'

'Is he a man or a young boy?' I continued patiently.

'Have you taken leave of your senses, Catchpool? John McCrodden is a grown man.'

'Then wouldn't it make more sense for me to ask Poirot to apologize to *John* McCrodden, not his father? Assuming he's mistaken and John McCrodden is innocent. I mean, if John is not a minor—'

'He used to be a miner, but not any more,' said Bewes. 'He worked in a mine somewhere up in the north-east.'

'Ah,' I said, knowing that my boss's ability to understand context would return sooner if I said as little as possible.

'But that, Catchpool, is beside the point. Poor Rowly's the one we need to worry about. John is blaming him for the whole mess. Poirot must write to Rowly immediately and grovel for all he's worth. This is a monstrous accusation—an outrageous slur! Please see to it that this happens, Catchpool.'

'I'll do my best, sir.'

'Good.'

'Can you tell me any more about the particulars of the

case, sir? I don't suppose Rowland Rope mentioned *why* Poirot has got hold of this idea that—'

'How the devil should I know why, Catchpool? Man must have lost his grip on his faculties—that's the only explanation I can think of. You can read the letter for yourself, if you like!'

'Do you have it?'

'John tore it into pieces, which he sent to Rowly with a note of accusation of his own. Rowly taped the pieces together and passed the letter on to me. I don't know why John thinks Rowly's behind it. Rowly plays a straight bat. Always has. His son, of all people, should know that. If Rowly had something to say to John, he'd say it himself.'

'I'd like to see the letter if I may, sir.'

Bewes walked over to his desk, opened one of the drawers and grimaced as he pulled out the offending item. He handed it to me. 'It's the purest nonsense!' he said, in case I was unsure of his opinion of the matter. 'Malicious rubbish!'

'But Poirot is never malicious,' I nearly said; I stopped myself just in time.

I read the letter. It was brief: only one paragraph. Nevertheless, given what it sought to communicate, it could have been half the length. In a muddled and artless way, it accused John McCrodden of the murder of Barnabas Pandy and claimed that there was proof to vindicate the accusation. If McCrodden did not immediately confess to this murder, then this proof would be turned over to the police.

My gaze settled upon the signature at the bottom of the

letter. In a sloping hand was written the name '*Hercule Poirot*'.

It would have been useful if I could have recalled my friend's signature, but I could not, despite having seen it once or twice. Perhaps whoever had sent the letter had meticulously copied Poirot's handwriting. What they had not done was manage to sound at all like the man they hoped to impersonate, nor to write the sort of letter he might have written.

If Poirot believed that John McCrodden had murdered this Barnabas Pandy fellow and successfully passed his death off as an accident, he would have visited McCrodden accompanied by the police. He wouldn't have sent this letter and allowed McCrodden the chance to escape or to take his own life before Hercule Poirot had looked him in the eye and explained to him the chain of errors that had led to his unmasking. And the nasty, insinuating tone . . . No, it was impossible. There was no doubt in my mind.

I had not had time to work out what effect my revelation would have upon the Super, but I felt I must tell him at once: 'Sir, the situation seems not to be exactly what I . . . or what you . . . That is to say, I'm not sure that an apology from Poirot . . .' I was making a hash of it.

'What are you trying to say, Catchpool?'

'The letter is a fake, sir,' I said. 'I don't know who wrote it, but I can tell you for certain that it was not Hercule Poirot.'

CHAPTER 6

Rowland Rope

The Super's instructions were clear: I was to find Poirot at once and ask him to accompany me to the offices of Rowland Rope's firm of solicitors, Donaldson & McCrodden. Once there, we were to explain that the letter sent to John McCrodden had not been written by Poirot, and to apologize fulsomely for the distress caused by neither one of us.

Having already wasted too many days in Great Yarmouth, I had urgent work to catch up with and was displeased to have this task assigned to me. Surely a telephone call from Bewes to Rowland Rope would have sufficed? The two were great friends, after all. But no, the Super had insisted that McCrodden Senior was a more than usually cautious man who would require an assurance from Poirot that he had not written the offending letter. Bewes wanted me to be present so that I could report back to him that the matter had been satisfactorily dealt with.

'This should all be straightened out within an hour or

two,' I thought to myself as I set off for Whitehaven Mansions. Alas, Poirot was not at home. His valet told me he was likely to be *en route* to Scotland Yard. He was apparently as keen to locate me as I was to find him.

I made my way back to Scotland Yard and discovered that Poirot had been there, asking for me, and even waited a short while, but was now gone. There was no sign of Superintendent Bewes either, so I could not ask him how I ought to proceed. I tried Pleasant's Coffee House, but Poirot was not there either. In the end, exasperated, I decided to visit Rowland McCrodden's offices alone. I reasoned that he would prefer to know as soon as possible that his son did not stand accused of murder by Hercule Poirot; the word of a Scotland Yard inspector ought to be enough even for Rowland Rope.

Donaldson & McCrodden Solicitors occupied the top two floors of a tall stucco-fronted terrace on Henrietta Street, next to the Covent Garden Hotel. I was greeted by a smiling young woman with a pink face and dark brown hair cut into a short and severely geometrical style. She wore a white blouse and checked skirt that brought to mind a picnic blanket.

She introduced herself as Miss Mason before asking me a series of questions that prevented me from stating the nature of my business as easily as I might have if I had simply been asked 'How may I help you?' Instead, an absurd amount of time was wasted by her 'And if I might enquire as to your name, sir?', 'And if I might ask to whom you wish to speak, sir?', 'And might I enquire as to whether you have an appointment, sir?', 'And are you able to divulge the purpose of your visit?' Her method of enquiry ensured that I was only able to utter two words at a time, and all the while she stared with undisguised prurience at the envelope in my hand, which was the letter sent by somebody to John McCrodden, accusing him of murder.

By the time Miss Mason led me along a narrow corridor lined on both sides with leather-bound books about the law, I was tempted to run in the opposite direction rather than follow her anywhere. I noticed—no one could fail to—that she did not so much walk as forward-bounce, on two of the tiniest feet I have ever observed.

We reached a black-painted door with the name 'Rowland McCrodden' painted on it in white. Miss Mason knocked and a deep voice said, 'Come!' We entered, and were met by a man with curly grey hair, a vast expanse of forehead that seemed to occupy an unreasonable amount of his face, and small beady black eyes that were closer to his chin than eyes should be.

Since McCrodden had agreed to see me, I was expecting to be able to commence our conversation at once, but I had not accounted for Miss Mason's capability to hinder progress. There ensued a frustrating attempt to persuade McCrodden to allow her to enter my name in his appointments diary. 'What would be the point of that?' asked McCrodden with obvious impatience. He had a thin, reedy voice that brought to mind a woodwind instrument. 'Inspector Catchpool is already here.'

'But, sir, the rule is that no one can be admitted without an appointment.'

'Inspector Catchpool has already been admitted, Miss Mason. There he is—*you* admitted him!'

'Sir, if you're meeting Inspector Catchpool, shouldn't I make an appointment for, well, *now*, and record it in—?'

'No,' Rowland McCrodden cut her off mid-question. 'Thank you, Miss Mason, that will be all. Please be seated, Inspector—' He broke off, blinked several times, then said, 'What is it, Miss Mason?'

'I was only going to ask, sir, if Inspector Catchpool might wish to partake of some tea. Or coffee. Or perhaps a glass of water? Or if, indeed, *you* might wish to—'

'Not for me,' said McCrodden. 'Inspector?'

I could not immediately produce an answer. A cup of tea was exactly what I wanted, but it would necessitate the return of Miss Mason.

'Why don't you have a little think, Inspector Catchpool, and I'll come back in a few moments and—'

'I'm sure the inspector can make up his mind,' said McCrodden briskly.

'Nothing for me, thank you,' I said with a smile.

Finally, mercifully, Miss Mason withdrew. I was determined to waste no more time, so I pulled the letter out of the envelope, laid it on McCrodden's desk and told him that there was no question of it having come from Hercule Poirot. McCrodden asked how I could be sure of this, and I explained that both the tone and the message left me in no doubt.

'So, if Poirot did not write the letter, who did?' asked McCrodden.

'I'm afraid I don't know.'

'Does Poirot know?'

'I have not yet had the chance to speak to him.'

'And why did they pretend to be Hercule Poirot?'

'I don't know.'

'Then your general bearing, if I may say so, is erroneous.'

'I'm not sure I understand what you mean,' I confessed.

'You said you were here to clear something up, and your manner suggests that you now believe it to be cleared up: Hercule Poirot has not accused my son of murder, therefore I have nothing to worry about. Is that your opinion?'

'Well . . .' I cast about for the correct answer. 'I can see that it's an upsetting thing to happen, but if the accusation was some sort of prank, then I wouldn't concern myself unduly, if I were you.'

'I disagree. I am, if anything, more disturbed now.' McCrodden stood up and walked over to the window. He looked down at the street below for a moment before moving two steps to the right and staring at the wall. 'When I thought it was Poirot, I was confident of a proper resolution. He would eventually admit his error, I thought. I have heard that he is proud, but also honourable and, most importantly of all, amenable to reason. He treats character as if it were a concrete fact, I'm told. Is this true?'

'He certainly believes knowledge of character is essential to the solving of crime,' I said. 'Without knowing the motive, you can't solve anything, and without understanding character, motive is unknowable. I have also heard him say that no man can act in a way that is contrary to his own nature.'

'Then I would have been able to convince him that John could never commit a murder—to do so would be at odds with his principles. The idea is laughable. Now, however, I learn that Hercule Poirot is not the one I need to convince, for he did not write the letter. Furthermore, I am able to draw the inescapable conclusion that the letter's true author is a liar and a fraudster. That sort of person might stop at nothing in his quest to destroy my son.'

McCrodden returned quickly to his chair as if the wall at which he had been staring had silently instructed him to do so. 'I must know who wrote and sent the letter,' he said. 'It is imperative, if I'm to ensure John's safety. I should like to engage the services of Hercule Poirot. Do you think he would agree to investigate for me?'

'He might, but . . . it's not at all certain that the letter-writer believes what he claims to believe. What if it's no more than a horribly misjudged joke? This might be the end of it. If your son receives no further communications—'

'You are naïve in the extreme if you think that,' said McCrodden. He picked up the letter and threw it at me. It landed on the floor at my feet. 'When someone sends something like that, they mean you harm. You ignore them at your peril.'

'My superintendent tells me the death of Barnabas Pandy was an accident,' I said. 'He drowned while taking a bath.'

'That is the story, yes. Officially, there is no suspicion that the death was a murder.'

'You sound as if you think it could have been,' I said.

'Once the possibility is raised, one has a duty to consider it,' said McCrodden.

'But the likelihood is that Pandy was not murdered, and you say your son could never commit a murder, so . . .'

'I see,' said McCrodden. 'You think I am guilty of wilful paternal blindness? No, it's not that. No one knows John better than I do. He has many faults, but he would not kill.'

He had misunderstood me; I had simply wanted to say that since no one was looking for a murderer in connection with Pandy's death, and since he knew his son was innocent, McCrodden really had nothing to worry about.

'You will have heard that I am a strong advocate of the death penalty. "Rowland Rope", they call me. I do not care for the name, and no one would dare say it in my presence. Now, if they were to call me "Rowland Just and Civilized Society For the Protection of the Innocent". . . Unfortunately, that does not trip so easily off the tongue. I'm sure you agree, Inspector, that we must all be accountable for our actions. I don't need to tell you about Plato's Ring of Gyges. I discussed it with John many times. I did everything I could to instil proper values in him, but I failed. He is so passionately against the taking of human life that he doesn't support the death penalty even for the most depraved monsters. He contends that I am as much a murderer as the bloodthirsty reprobate who slits a throat in an alleyway for the sake of a few shillings. Murder is murder, he says. So you see, he would never allow himself to kill another person. It would make him look ludicrous in his own eyes, which would be intolerable to him.'

I nodded, though I was not convinced. My experience as a police inspector has taught me that many people are able to regard themselves with inordinate fondness, no matter what heinous crimes they have committed. They care only about how they look to others, and whether they can get away with it.

'And, as you say, no one apart from our nefarious letter-writer seems to think Pandy's death was unlawful,' McCrodden went on. 'He was an extremely wealthy man— owner of the Combingham Hall Estate and former owner of several slate mines in Wales. That's how he made his fortune.'

'Mines?' I recalled my conversation with the Super, and the minor/miner misunderstanding. 'Did your son John used to work in a mine?'

'Yes. In the north, near Guisborough.'

'Not in Wales, then?'

'Never in Wales. You can abandon that idea.'

I did my best to look as if I had abandoned it.

'Pandy was ninety-four when he drowned in his bath,' said McCrodden. 'He had been a widower for sixty-five years. He and his wife had one child, a daughter, who married and had two daughters of her own before dying, along with her husband, in a house fire. Pandy took in his two orphaned grandchildren, Lenore and Annabel, who have both lived at Combingham Hall ever since. Annabel, the youngest, is not married. The older sister, Lenore, married a man by the name of Cecil Lavington. They had two children, Ivy and Timothy, in that order. Cecil died of an infection four years ago. That's all I've managed to find out, and none of it is interesting or suggestive of what steps to take next. I hope Poirot can do better.'

'There might be nothing to find out,' I said. 'They might be a quite ordinary family, in which no murder has been committed.'

'There is plenty to find out,' McCrodden corrected me. 'Who is the letter-writer, and why did he or she fix upon my son? Until we know these things, those of us who have been accused remain implicated.'

'You have been accused of nothing,' I said.

'You would not say that if you saw the note John enclosed with the letter!' He pointed at the floor, where the letter still lay by my feet. 'He accused me of putting Poirot up to it, so that John would have no choice but to take up the law in order to defend himself.'

'Why would he think you might do that?'

'John believes I hate him. It could not be further from the truth. I have been critical of the way he conducts his affairs in the past, but only because I want him to prosper. He seems to wish the opposite for himself. He has squandered every opportunity I've created for him. One of the reasons I know he cannot have killed Barnabas Pandy is that he does not have the animus to spare. All of his ill will is directed towards me—erroneously.'

I made a polite noise that I hoped was expressive of sympathy.

'The sooner I can speak to Hercule Poirot, the better,' said McCrodden. 'I hope he will be able to get to the bottom of this unsavoury business. I long ago gave up hope of changing my son's mind about me, but I should like to prove, if I can, that I had nothing do to with that letter.'

CHAPTER 7

An Old Enemy

While I was in the offices of Donaldson & McCrodden on Henrietta Street, Poirot was also in the offices of a firm of solicitors: Fuller, Fuller & Vout, only a short distance away on Drury Lane. Needless to say, I did not know this at the time.

Frustrated by his inability to find me, my Belgian friend had set about discovering all he could about Barnabas Pandy and almost the first thing he found out was that Pandy had been represented in all matters of a legal nature by Peter Vout, the firm's senior partner.

Poirot, unlike me, had made an appointment—or rather his valet, George, had made one for him. He arrived punctually and was shown into Vout's office by a girl far less obtrusive than Rowland McCrodden's Miss Mason. He tried to conceal his shock when he saw the room in which the solicitor worked.

'Welcome, welcome,' said Vout, rising from his chair to shake his visitor's hand. He had an engaging smile and snow-white hair that peaked and curled in random tufts. 'You must be Herc-*ule* Poir-*ot*—is that correct?'

'*C'est parfait*,' said Poirot approvingly. Rare indeed was the Englishman who could pronounce both the Christian name and the family name correctly. Was it appropriate, however, to feel admiration for any man who could work in conditions such as these? The room was an extraordinary sight. It was large, about twenty feet by fifteen, with a high ceiling. Pushed up against the wall on the right were Vout's large mahogany desk and green leather chair. In front of those stood two straight-backed armchairs in brown leather. In the right-hand third of the room there was also a book-case, a lamp and a fireplace. On the mantelpiece above the fire there was an invitation to a dinner of the Law Society.

The other two thirds of the available space were occupied by scruffy cardboard boxes, piled high, one atop another, to form an enormous and uneven edifice that was breath-taking in its grotesqueness. It would have been impossible to walk around or through the boxes. Effectively, their presence reduced the size of the room to a degree that any sane person would have found intolerable. Many of the boxes were open, with things spilling out of them: yellowing papers, broken picture frames, old cloths with dirt stains on them. Beyond the gargantuan box-structure was a window at which hung strips of pale yellow material that could not hope to cover the glass in front of which they dangled.

'*C'est le cauchemar*,' Poirot murmured.

'I see you've spotted the curtains.' Vout sounded

apologetic. 'One could make this room more appealing to the eye if one replaced them. They're terribly old. I'd have one of the office girls pull them down, but, as you can see, no one can reach them.'

'Because of the boxes?'

'Well, my mother died three years ago. There's much to be sorted out, and I've yet to make inroads, I'm afraid. Not all the boxes are Mama's possessions, mind you. A lot of it is my own . . . paraphernalia.' He sounded quite happy with the situation. 'Please, do be seated, M. Poirot. How may I be of assistance?'

Poirot lowered himself into one of the available armchairs. 'You do not mind working in here, with . . . the paraphernalia?' he persisted.

'I see you're fascinated by it, M. Poirot. I expect you're one of those chaps who likes everything to be ship-shape at all times, are you?'

'Most assuredly I am, monsieur. I am inordinately fond of the shape of the ship. It is necessary for me to be in a tidy environment if I am to think clearly and productively. It is not so for you?'

'I'm not going to let a few old boxes bother me.' Vout chuckled. 'I don't notice them from one day to the next. I'll tackle them at some point. Until then . . . why let them worry me?'

With a small twitch of the eyebrows, Poirot moved on to the subject he had come to discuss. Vout expressed regret at the death of his dear old friend Barnabas Pandy, and regaled Poirot with all the same facts that Rowland

McCrodden was (perhaps at that very moment) relating to me: Welsh slate mines; Combingham Hall Estate; two grand-daughters, Lenore and Annabel; two great-grandchildren, Ivy and Timothy. Vout also offered a detail about Barnabas Pandy that was absent from Rowland Rope's account: he mentioned the faithful and long-serving Kingsbury. 'More like a younger brother to Barnabas, was Kingsbury. He felt like a member of the family more than a servant— though he was always most conscientious when it came to performing his tasks. Naturally, Barnabas made arrange-ments for him to be looked after. A bequest . . .'

'Ah yes, the will,' said Poirot. 'I would like to hear about it.'

'Well, I don't see what harm it would do to tell you. Barnabas wouldn't have minded, and his testamentary affairs were very simple—just what one would expect, in fact. But . . . might I ask why you're interested?'

'It has been suggested to me—indirectly—that Monsieur Pandy was murdered.'

'Oh, I see.' Vout laughed and rolled his eyes. 'Murder, eh? No, not a bit of it. Barnabas drowned. Fell asleep while in the tub, sank under the water and, sadly . . .' He left the obvious conclusion unstated.

'That is the official story. However, the possibility has been raised that the death was made to look like an acci-dent, when in fact it was deliberate.'

Vout was shaking his head emphatically. 'Tommyrot! Goodness me, someone's been rumour-mongering for all he's worth, eh? Or she—it's usually the ladies who like to gossip. We chaps are much too sensible to waste our time stirring up trouble.'

'You are certain, then, that Monsieur Pandy's death was accidental?' asked Poirot.

'Couldn't be more so.'

'How are you able to state this with such conviction? Were you present in the bathroom when he died?'

Vout looked affronted. 'Of course I wasn't in the bathroom with him! Wasn't there at all! Seventh of December, wasn't it? My wife and I were at my nephew's wedding that day, as it happens. In Coventry.'

Poirot smiled politely. 'I simply wished to suggest that if you were not in the room when he died, and not at Combingham Hall, then you are not in a position to say definitively that the death of Monsieur Pandy was accidental. If someone had crept into the bathroom and pushed him under the water . . . How would you know this had happened, or had not happened, if you were at a wedding in Coventry?'

'It's only that I know the family,' Vout said eventually, with a concerned frown. 'I'm a dear friend to them all, as they are to me. I know who was at the Hall when the tragedy occurred: Lenore, Annabel, Ivy and Kingsbury, and I can assure you that none of them would have raised a finger against Barnabas. The idea is unthinkable! I have witnessed their grief first-hand, M. Poirot.'

Poirot mouthed to himself the words '*C'est ca*.' His suspicion had been correct. Vout was one of those people who believed in things like murder, and evil, and all forms of serious unpleasantness only when they did not affect him personally. Were he to read in a newspaper that a maniac had chopped five members of the same family into small pieces, he would not question it. Suggest to him, though, that a man he regarded as a friend might have been murdered, and you would never succeed in persuading him that it was possible.

'Please tell me about Monsieur Pandy's will,' said Poirot.

'As I say, Kingsbury was left a tidy sum: enough to be comfortable for the remainder of his days. The house and estate are left in trust for Ivy and Timothy, on the understanding that Lenore and Annabel may continue to live there for the rest of their lives. All the money and other assets, of which there are plenty, go to Lenore and Annabel. Each is now, in her own right, an extremely wealthy woman.'

'So an inheritance might provide a motive,' said Poirot.

Vout sighed impatiently. 'M. Poirot, please hear what I'm trying to tell you. There is simply no circumstance—'

'Yes, yes, I hear. Most people would assume that a man of ninety-four will die reasonably soon. But if someone needed money immediately . . . if to wait a year would have dire consequences for that person . . .'

'I tell you, you're barking up the wrong tree, man!' There was alarm in Vout's eyes and in his voice. 'They are a delightful family.'

'You are their good friend, monsieur,' Poirot reminded him gently.

'Quite! I am! Do you think I would continue a friendship with a family that contained a murderer? Barnabas was not murdered. I can prove it. He . . .' Vout stopped. A new pinkness suffused his cheeks.

'Anything you are able to tell me will be most helpful,' said Poirot.

Vout looked glum. Having said something he hadn't intended to say, he now lacked the gumption to find an ingenious way out of it.

'Well, I suppose it won't do any harm if I tell you.' He sighed. 'I can't help thinking Barnabas knew he was going to die. I saw him shortly before his death and . . . well, he seemed to know that his time was coming to an end.'

'What gave you this impression?'

'The last time I saw him, he struck me as a man from whose shoulders a great weight had been lifted. It was as if he was at peace. He smiled in a particular way, made certain oblique remarks about the need to set certain matters straight *now* before it was too late. I had the sense that he thought death was imminent, and it turned out to be so, sadly.'

'*Dommage,*' Poirot agreed. 'Still, it is better to meet the inevitable end with a peaceful spirit, is it not? Which matters did Monsieur Pandy wish to set straight?'

'Hmmph? Oh, there was a man who had been his . . . well, his *enemy* really, if the word doesn't sound fanciful. Vincent Lobb, the chap's name was. At our last meeting, Barnabas announced that he wished to send a letter to this fellow and suggest that the two of them might perhaps be reconciled.'

'A sudden urge to forgive an old enemy,' muttered Poirot.

'That is interesting. If someone wanted this making of peace not to take place . . . Was this letter to Monsieur Lobb ever sent?'

'It was,' said Vout. 'I told Barnabas I thought it was an excellent initiative, and he sent it off that very day. I don't know if he received a reply. It was really only a few days later that he . . . passed on. Very sad. Though he'd had a good innings at ninety-four! I suppose an answering letter might have arrived after his death, but I think Annabel or Lenore would have told me if it had.'

'What was the cause of the ill will between Messieurs Pandy and Lobb?' Poirot asked.

'I'm afraid I can't help you there. Barnabas never told me.'

'I should be grateful if you could tell me about the family,' said Poirot. 'Was it—is it—a happy household at Combingham Hall?'

'Oh, very happy. Very happy indeed. Lenore is a tower of strength. Both Annabel and Ivy admire her enormously. Annabel adores Lenore's children—and her beloved dog, of course. Hopscotch. He's a character! A big beast. Likes to leap up and lick you! Stubborn, mind you, but very affectionate. And as for young Timothy—that boy will go far. He is possessed of a shrewd mind and heaps of determination. I can see him being Prime Minister one day. Barnabas often said so. "That boy could be anything he set out to be," he often said. "Anything at all." Barnabas was devoted to them all, and they to him.'

'Truly you describe the perfect family,' said Poirot. 'Yet

no family is without its troubles. There must have been something that was less than perfect.'

'Well . . . I wouldn't say . . . I mean, obviously life is never without its infelicities, but for the most part . . . As I said before, M. Poirot: it is ladies who enjoy scurrilous gossip. Barnabas loved his family—and Kingsbury—and they loved him back. That is all I shall say. As there is no question of the death being anything but an accident, I see no reason to delve into a good man's private life and that of his family in search of unsavoury morsels.'

Seeing that Vout had resolved to disclose no more, Poirot thanked him for his help and left.

'But there is more to be disclosed,' he said to nobody in particular as he stood on the pavement of Drury Lane. 'Most certainly, there is more, and I shall find out what it is. Not one unsavoury morsel will escape from Hercule Poirot!'

CHAPTER 8

Poirot Issues Some Instructions

I found Poirot waiting for me in my office when I returned to Scotland Yard. He appeared to be lost in thought, muttering soundlessly to himself as I entered the room. He looked as dandified as ever, his remarkable moustaches appearing particularly well tended.

'Poirot! At last!'

Startled out of his reverie, he rose to his feet. '*Mon ami* Catchpool! Where have you been? There is a matter I wish to discuss with you that is causing me much consternation.'

'Let me guess,' I said. 'A letter, signed in your name although not written or sent by you, accusing Rowland McCrodden's son John of the murder of Barnabas Pandy.'

Poirot looked dumbfounded. '*Mon cher* . . . Somehow, you know. You will tell me how, I'm sure. Ah, but you say "letter", not "letters"! Does that mean you are unaware of the others?'

'Others?'

'*Oui, mon ami*. To Mrs Sylvia Rule, Miss Annabel Treadway and Mr Hugo Dockerill.'

Annabel? I knew that I had heard the name recently, but could not think where. Then I remembered: Rowland McCrodden had told me that one of Pandy's granddaughters was called Annabel.

'Quite correct,' said Poirot, when I asked. 'Miss Treadway is indeed the granddaughter of Monsieur Pandy.'

'Then who are the other two? What were their names again?'

'Sylvia Rule and Hugo Dockerill. They are two people— and Annabel Treadway is a third, and John McCrodden a fourth—who received letters signed in my name, accusing them of the murder of Barnabas Pandy. Most of these people have presented themselves at my home to berate me for having sent these letters that I did not send, and failed to pay attention when I explained that I did not send them! It has been enervating and discouraging, *mon ami*. And not one of them has been able to show me the letter they received.'

'I might be able to help on that front,' I told him.

His eyes widened. 'Do you have one of the letters? You do! You must, then, have the one sent to John McCrodden, since his was the name you mentioned. Ah! It is a pleasure to be in your office, Catchpool. There is no unsightly mountain of boxes!'

'Boxes? Why should there be?'

'There should not, my friend. But tell me, how can you have the letter that John McCrodden received? He told me he tore it into pieces and sent those pieces to his father.'

I explained about the Super's telegram and my meeting with Rowland Rope, trying to omit nothing that might be important. He nodded eagerly as I spoke.

When I had finished, he said, 'This is most fortuitous. Without realizing it, we have been highly efficient and—how do you say it?—in concert with one another! While you were speaking to Rowland McCrodden, I was speaking to the solicitor of Barnabas Pandy.' He then told me what he had found out and what he had failed to find out. 'There is something more, perhaps a great deal more, that Peter Vout did not wish to tell me about the family of Barnabas Pandy. And, since he is absolutely certain that Pandy was not murdered, he feels no obligation to divulge what he knows. Still, I have an idea—one that Rowland Rope might be able to assist with, if he is willing. I must speak with him at the earliest opportunity. But first, show me John McCrodden's letter.'

I handed it over. Poirot's eyes blazed with anger as he read it.

'It is inconceivable that Hercule Poirot should write and send such a thing as this, Catchpool. It is so poorly formulated and inelegantly written! I am insulted to think that anyone could believe it came from me.'

I tried to cheer him: 'None of the recipients knows you. If they did, they would have known, as I did the moment I saw it, that it was not your handiwork.'

'There is much to consider. I will make a list. We must get to work, Catchpool.'

'I'm afraid *I* must get to work, Poirot. By all means, speak to Rowland Rope—he is eager to speak to you—but I'm afraid you will have to count me out if you're planning to take any further action with regard to Barnabas Pandy.'

'How can I not act, *mon ami*? Why do you think the four letters were sent? Someone wishes to put in my head the idea that Barnabas Pandy was murdered. Is it not understandable that I am curious? Now, there is something I need you to do for me.'

'Poirot—'

'Yes, yes, you need to do your work. *Je comprends.* This I will allow you to do, once you have helped me. It is only a small task, and one that can be accomplished far more easily by you than by me. Find out where all four were on the day that Barnabas Pandy died: Sylvia Rule, Hugo Dockerill, Annabel Treadway and John McCrodden. The solicitor, Vout, told me that Mademoiselle Treadway was at home when her grandfather died, at Combingham Hall. Find out if she says the same thing. Now, it is of vital importance that you ask each of them in *precisely the same way*: the same questions, in the same order. Is that clear? I have realized that this is the way to distinguish most effectively one person's character from another's. Also, I am interested in this Eustace with whom Madame Rule is so obsessed. If you could—'

I waved at him to stop, like a railway signalman in the face of an out-of-control train hurtling towards him.

'Poirot, please! Who is Eustace? No—don't answer that. I have work to do. Barnabas Pandy's death has been officially recorded as an accident. I'm afraid that means I can't very well go around demanding that people furnish me with alibis.'

'Not straightforwardly, of course,' Poirot agreed. He stood up and started to smooth imaginary creases from his clothing. 'I am sure you will find an ingenious way around the problem. Good day, *mon ami*. Come and see me when you are able to give me the information I require. And—yes, yes!—*then* you will do your work assigned to you by Scotland Yard.'

CHAPTER 9

Four Alibis

Later that same evening, John McCrodden received a telephone call at the house where he lived. His landlady answered.

'It's John McCrodden you're after, is it? Not John Webber? McCrodden, yes? All right, I'll get him. Saw him a minute ago. He's probably upstairs in his room. You need to talk to him, do you? Then I'll get him. You wait there. I'll get him.'

The caller waited nearly five minutes, imagining a startlingly inefficacious woman who could well fail to find a person in the same house as herself.

Eventually a male voice came on the line: 'McCrodden here. Who is this?'

'I'm telephoning on behalf of Inspector Edward Catchpool,' said the caller. 'From Scotland Yard.'

There was a pause. Then John McCrodden said, 'Are you now?' He sounded as if he might be amused by the notion if he were not so weary.

'Yes. Yes, I am.'

'And who might you be? His wife?' he asked sarcastically.

The caller would not have minded telling McCrodden who she was, but she had been given explicit instructions not to do so. She had in front of her, on small cards, the precise words she was supposed to say and she intended to stick to them.

'I've got a few questions I'd like to ask you, questions to which Inspector Catchpool would like to know the answers. If you—'

'Then why doesn't he ask me himself? What is your name? Tell me at once, or this conversation is at an end.'

'If you provide me with satisfactory answers, then Inspector Catchpool hopes it won't be necessary for him to interview you at the police station. All I want to know is this: where were you on the day that Barnabas Pandy died?'

McCrodden laughed. 'Kindly tell my father that I'm not willing to put up with his campaign of harassment for one second longer. If he will not cease his devious persecution of me, then he is strongly advised to take precautions to ensure his own safety. Tell him I haven't the slightest clue when Barnabas Pandy died because I know no Barnabas Pandy. I don't know that he lived, died or joined the circus as a trapeze artist, and I don't know *when* he did those things, if he did them at all.'

The caller had been warned that John McCrodden might respond uncooperatively. She listened patiently as he continued to address her with icy disgust.

'Additionally, you may tell him I'm not as stupid as he thinks I am, and that I'm quite certain that if Scotland Yard employs an inspector by the name of "Edward Catchpool"— which I very much doubt—then that man knows nothing about this telephone call, and that you are in no way authorized to make it. Which is why you refuse to tell me your name.'

'Barnabas Pandy died on the seventh of December last year.'

'Did he? I'm delighted to hear it.'

'Where were you on that date, sir? Inspector Catchpool believes that Mr Pandy died at his home in the country, Combingham Hall—'

'Never heard of it.'

'—so if you can tell me your whereabouts on that date, and if anyone can vouch for you, then Inspector Catchpool might not need—'

'My whereabouts? Why, of course! Seconds before Barnabas Pandy breathed his last, I was standing over his prone body with a carving knife in my hand, ready to plunge it into his heart. Is that what my father would like me to say?'

There was a loud banging sound, and then the line went dead.

On the back of one of her question cards, the caller made a note of what she felt were the essential points: that John McCrodden believed his father to be behind the telephone call, that he had questioned the existence of Edward Catchpool and—most importantly, the caller thought—that he had not known, or had claimed not to know, the date of Barnabas Pandy's death.

'No alibi given,' she wrote. 'Said he was standing over Pandy with a knife just before Pandy died, but he said it like I was not supposed to believe it.'

After twice reading through what she had written, and after thinking for a few minutes, the caller picked up her pencil again and added, 'But maybe it *was* true, and the lie was the way he made his voice sound when he said it.'

'Is that Mrs Rule? Mrs Sylvia Rule?'

'Yes it is. To whom am I speaking?'

'Good evening, Mrs Rule. I'm telephoning on behalf of Inspector Edward Catchpool. From Scotland Yard.'

'Scotland Yard?' Sylvia Rule sounded instantly frightened. 'Has something happened? Is it Mildred? Is Mildred all right?'

'This isn't about anything to do with any Mildred, ma'am.'

'She was supposed to be home by now. I was starting to worry, and then . . . Scotland Yard? Oh, dear!'

'This is about something different. There's no reason to think anything's happened to Mildred.'

'Wait!' Sylvia Rule barked, causing the caller to jerk her head away from the telephone mouthpiece. 'I think that's her. Oh, thank the heavens! Let me . . .' A few grunts and panted breaths later, Mrs Rule said, 'Yes, it's Mildred. She's safely home. Do you have children, Inspector Catchpool?'

'I said I was telephoning on *behalf* of Inspector Catchpool.

I am not, myself, Inspector Catchpool.' Damned fool! Did Mrs Rule not know that women could not be police inspectors, no matter how much they might want to be or how talented they were? The caller resented being compelled to reflect upon this unwelcome fact and how unfair it was. She harboured a secret belief that she would make a better police inspector than anyone she knew.

'Oh, yes. Yes, quite,' said Sylvia Rule, who sounded as if she was not fully listening. 'Well, if you have children, then you'll know as well as I do that whatever age they are, one frets about them constantly. They might be anywhere, and how would one know? And with the most despicable degenerates! *Do* you have children?'

'No.'

'Well, I'm sure you will one day. I hope and pray you never suffer what I'm suffering now! My Mildred is engaged to be married to the most detestable man . . .'

The caller looked down at the notes she had been given. She guessed that, imminently, she was about to hear the name Eustace.

'. . . and now they've set a wedding date! Next June, or so they say. Eustace is more than capable of persuading Mildred to marry him in secret before that date. Oh, he knows I'm going to spend every waking moment from now until next June trying to make the wretched girl see sense— not that she will! Who ever listens to their mother? I think he's taken the opportunity to play a cruel trick on me.'

'Mrs Rule, I have a question—'

'He wants me to believe I have a full sixteen months to

talk Mildred out of marrying him, so that I won't set about it in a hurry. Oh, I know the way his disgusting mind works! It wouldn't surprise me if he and Mildred were to turn up already married in a month's time and say, "Surprise! We've tied the knot!" That's why I'm a bag of nerves whenever she leaves the house. Eustace could make her do anything. I don't know why the silly girl is so comprehensively unable to stand up for herself.'

The caller had some ideas about why this might be.

'Mrs Rule, I need to ask you a question. It's about the death of Barnabas Pandy. If you can give me a satisfactory answer then it might not be necessary for Inspector Catchpool to interview you at the police station.'

'Barnabas Pandy? Who is he? Oh, I remember! The letter Eustace induced that dreadful continental detective to send to me—what a reprehensible little toad he is! I used to hold Hercule Poirot in high esteem, but anyone who would allow himself to be bent to Eustace's will in that way . . . I refuse even to think about him!'

'If you can give me a satisfactory answer then it might not be necessary for Inspector Catchpool to interview you at the police station,' said the caller patiently. 'Where were you on the day that Barnabas Pandy died?'

A gasp came down the telephone line. 'Where was I? You are asking me where I was?'

'Yes.'

'And you say that Inspector—what name did you say?'

'Edward Catchpool.'

It sounded as if Sylvia Rule was making a note of the

name: 'And Inspector Edward Catchpool of Scotland Yard wishes to know this?'

'Yes.'

'Why? Doesn't he know that Eustace and that foreigner have cooked up this nonsense between them?'

'If you could just tell me where you were on the day in question?'

'What day? The day a man named Barnabas Pandy was murdered—a man I don't know, whose name was unknown to me until I received that odious letter? How should I know where I was when someone killed him? I have no idea when he died.'

The caller made a note of three things: first, Sylvia Rule seemed to accept that Pandy was murdered; second, this was understandable if she believed this telephone call to have hailed from Scotland Yard; third, she professed not to know when Pandy died, which might indicate that she had not killed him.

'Mr Pandy died on the seventh of December,' said the caller.

'Wait a moment and I shall go and look at last year's diary,' said Mrs Rule. 'Incidentally, whether or not Inspector . . .' There was a pause. The caller pictured Mrs Rule glancing down at a piece of paper. 'Whether or not Inspector Catchpool judges it necessary to interview me, I should very much like to speak to him. I wish to make it clear that I have murdered nobody and am not the kind of person who would do such a thing. Once I've explained to him about Eustace, I'm sure he will see this unsavoury business for what it is: an attempt to frame me for a crime of which I am innocent. He will find it as shocking as I do, I have no doubt—a woman of my reputation and distinction! I'm rather pleased that this has happened, for I expect it to be Eustace's downfall. Obstructing the proper investigation of a murder with slanderous accusations is a crime, is it not?'

'I would have thought so,' said the caller.

'Well, then! I shall check my diary. The seventh of December last year, you say?'

'Yes.'

The caller waited, listening to the sounds of Sylvia Rule's house. There was much stomping, doors opening and closing, footsteps on stairs. When Mrs Rule returned, she said triumphantly:

'I was at Turville College on the seventh of December, from ten in the morning until supper time. My son Freddie is a pupil there, and it was the day of the Christmas Fair. I didn't leave until well past eight o'clock. What is more, there were *hundreds* present—parents, teachers and pupils—and *all* of them will confirm what I have told you. Oh, how delightful!' Sylvia Rule sighed. 'Eustace's plan is doomed to fail. Wouldn't it be simply marvellous if he were to hang for his lies and calumnies against me—the very fate he had in mind for me?'

After John McCrodden and Sylvia Rule, Annabel Treadway was a positive pleasure to interrogate. She had no obvious grudges, no Eustace equivalent, and did not speak venomously and at length about any person in whom the caller had no interest. Furthermore, she had relevant information to impart.

'I was at home on the seventh of December,' she said. 'We all were—all of us who live at Combingham Hall. Kingsbury had just returned from a few days away. He drew the bath, as he always did, and he was the one who . . . who found Grandy under the water a while later. It was upsetting for all of us, but it must have been especially awful for Kingsbury. To be the person who *discovers* such a tragedy . . . By the time Lenore, Ivy and I reached the bathroom we knew something was wrong. I won't say we were prepared—how can one ever be, for something so terrible?—but we'd had warning. The way Kingsbury cried out when he saw . . . Oh, poor Kingsbury! I shall never forget the way his voice cracked as he called out to us.'

Annabel Treadway made an anguished noise. 'Kingsbury is neither a young man nor a strong one, and since Grandy's passing, he has grown so much older and weaker. Not in actual years, of course—but he looks ten years older. He had been with Grandy for most of his life.'

'Who is Kingsbury?' This question was not on the caller's list, but she felt it would be remiss of her not to ask.

'He's Grandy's manservant. Or *was*, I should say. Such a sweet, kind man. I've known him since I was a child. Really, he is more like a member of the family. We're all terribly worried about him. We're not sure how he'll manage now Grandy's gone.'

'He lives at Combingham Hall?'

'He has a cottage in the grounds. He used to spend most

of his time with us at the hall, but since Grandy died we haven't seen nearly as much of him. He does his work and then slips away, back to his cottage.'

'Apart from Kingsbury, does anyone else live in the grounds of Combingham Hall?'

'No. We have a cook and a kitchen maid, and also two housemaids, but they live in the town.'

'And who lives at Combingham Hall?'

'There were only the four of us. And my dog, Hopscotch. And then, since Grandy died, only my sister Lenore, my niece Ivy, Hopscotch and me. Oh, and Timothy for some of the exeats and school holidays, of course, though he often goes off with some friend or other to their house.'

The caller studied the notes in front of her. She had laid everything out neatly on the table so that she could see, at the same time and without shuffling papers, all potentially useful information and also all the questions that she needed to ask each of the four suspects, if 'suspects' was an accurate description of what they were. 'Timothy's your nephew, is he, Miss Treadway?' she asked.

'Yes. He's my sister Lenore's son. Ivy's younger brother.'

'Was Timothy at Combingham Hall when your grandfather died?'

'No. He was at his school's Christmas Fair.'

The caller nodded in satisfaction as she jotted this down. The notes said that Timothy Lavington was a pupil at Turville College. It seemed that Sylvia Rule had told the truth about the school's fair taking place on the seventh of December.

'Was there anyone else at Combingham Hall when Mr Pandy died apart from you, your sister Lenore, your niece Ivy, and Kingsbury?'

'No. Nobody,' said Annabel Treadway. 'Normally our cook would have been there too, and a maid, but we had given them the day off. Lenore, Ivy and I were supposed to be going to the Christmas Fair, you see, which would have meant luncheon and supper at Turville. Though in the end we didn't go.'

The caller tried not to sound too curious as she asked why the plan to attend the Christmas Fair had been abandoned.

'I'm afraid I don't remember,' Annabel said quickly. The caller did not believe her.

'So the manservant Kingsbury found Mr Pandy dead in his bathwater at twenty minutes after five, and he cried out for help? Where were you when you heard him call out?'

'This is how I know that Grandy cannot have been murdered.' She sounded glad to have been asked the question. 'I was in my niece Ivy's bedroom, with Ivy and Lenore and Hopscotch—while Grandy was still alive *and* when he must have died. Between those two times, none of us left the room, not for a second.'

'Between which two times, Miss Treadway?'

'I'm sorry, I haven't expressed myself very well. Shortly after Lenore and I went into Ivy's bedroom to talk to her, we heard Grandy's voice. We knew he was taking his bath—I had passed the bathroom on my way to Ivy's room and seen Kingsbury preparing it. The water was running. Then a little later, when Lenore and I had been in Ivy's room for ten minutes or so, we all heard Grandy shouting—so he was certainly alive then.'

'Shouting?' asked the caller. 'Do you mean shouting for help?'

'Oh, no, nothing of the sort! He sounded quite robust. He bellowed, "Can't a fellow bathe in peace? Is this cacophony necessary?" He definitely used the word "cacophony". He meant us, I'm afraid: Lenore, Ivy and me. We were probably all talking over each other the way we do when we're in high spirits. And often when we're making a commotion, Hoppy joins in with a yelp or a bark. For a dog, you'd be amazed—he has such an impressive range of noises that he makes, but I'm afraid they all annoyed Grandy, and never more so than at that moment. After he shouted at us, the three of us remained in Ivy's bedroom with the door firmly shut until we heard Kingsbury calling out in distress.'

'How much later was that?'

'It's hard to recall at a distance of so many weeks, but I should say perhaps thirty minutes later.'

'What were you talking about, in high spirits, with your sister and your niece for all that time?' asked the caller, who by now had chosen to forget that she was not an inspector with Scotland Yard.

'Oh, I couldn't tell you that, not so long afterwards,' said Annabel Treadway. Once again, the answer came a little too fast. 'I don't expect it was important.'

The caller thought it probably was. She wrote down the

words 'Bad liar' and underlined them twice for emphasis.

'The important thing is that this proves nobody could have murdered Grandy—don't you see? He fell asleep and drowned in his bath, as any man might who was as old and infirm as he was.'

'Kingsbury could have pushed him under the water,' the caller could not resist pointing out. 'He had the opportunity.'

'What?'

'Where was Kingsbury while you three ladies were talking in your niece's bedroom with the door closed?'

'I don't know, but . . . you can't honestly think . . . I mean, Kingsbury *found* Grandy. You're not suggesting . . .'

The caller waited.

'It is impossible to think that Kingsbury murdered my grandfather,' Annabel Treadway said, once she had composed herself. 'Completely impossible.'

'How can you know if you don't know where he was or what he was doing when Mr Pandy died?'

'Kingsbury is a dear, dear friend of our family. He could never be a murderer. Never!' It sounded as if Annabel Treadway had started to cry. 'I must go. I've neglected Hoppy today—poor little boy! Please tell Inspector Catchpool . . .' She stopped, then sighed loudly.

'What?' asked the caller.

'Nothing,' said Annabel Treadway. 'It's only that . . . I wish I could make him promise not to suspect Kingsbury. And I wish I hadn't answered any of your questions. But it's too late, isn't it? It's *always* too late!'

*

'Seventh of December, eh?' said Hugo Dockerill. 'I couldn't tell you where I was. Sorry! Probably pottering about at home.'

'So you weren't at Turville College's Christmas Fair?' asked the caller.

'Christmas Fair? Of course—wouldn't miss it!—but that was much later.'

'Really? What was the date of the fair?'

'Well, I can't remember the date—don't have a head for that sort of thing, I'm afraid. But I can tell you when Christmas is: twenty-fifth of December, same as every year!' Dockerill chuckled. 'I expect the fair was the twenty-third or something. What, my dearest?'

A woman's voice could be heard in the background: brisk and slightly weary.

'Aha . . . Ah! Wait a moment!' said Hugo Dockerill. 'My wife Jane has just reminded me that we would have broken up for the Christmas holidays long before the twenty-third. Yes, of course, she's quite right. You're quite right, Jane, dear. So . . . Ah! If you'd be good enough to hold on, Jane's going to check last year's calendar to see when exactly the fair was. What's that, my dearest? Yes, yes, of course, you're absolutely correct. She's quite correct. Of course the Christmas Fair was not the day before Christmas Eve— ridiculous notion!'

The caller heard a woman's voice say, 'Seventh of December.'

'I have it on good authority that our Christmas Fair last year was on December the seventh. Now, what was the date you wanted to ask me about again? I'm rather confused.'

'December the seventh. Were you at the fair that day, Mr Dockerill?'

'Indeed I was! Jolly affair, it was. Always is. We at Turville know how to . . .' He broke off suddenly, then said, 'Jane says you won't be interested in what I'm saying and that I should stick to answering your questions.'

'From what hour until what hour were you at the fair?'

'Start to finish, I expect. There was a supper afterwards, which usually finishes . . . Jane, when does . . . ? Thank you, my dearest. Around eight o'clock, Jane says. Look here, it might be simpler if you were to speak to Jane directly.'

'I would be glad to,' said the caller. Within the space of a minute, she had all the information she needed: according to Jane Dockerill, she and Hugo had been at the Christmas Fair on the seventh of December from when it started at eleven in the morning until when the supper finished at eight. Yes, Timothy Lavington had been present too, but not his mother, aunt or sister, who had been planning to attend but cancelled at the last minute. Freddie Rule had been there too, with his mother Sylvia, his sister Mildred and his sister's fiancé Eustace.

The caller said thank you and was about to say goodbye when Mrs Dockerill said, 'Wait a moment. You don't get rid of me that easily.'

'Was there something else, ma'am?'

'Yes, there is. Hugo has twice mislaid the letter he was

sent, accusing him of murder, which I realize is distinctly unhelpful. Well, I'm pleased to say that I've found it. I shall take it to Inspector Catchpool at Scotland Yard as soon as I am free to come to London. Now, I don't know if Barnabas Pandy was murdered or not—I'm inclined to think not, since to accuse four people of the same murder strikes me as more of a parlour game than a serious accusation, particularly when one fraudulently signs the name "Hercule Poirot" at the bottom of those letters—but just in case Mr Pandy *was* murdered, and in case this is a serious investigation and not some demented person's idea of a joke, there are two things I should tell you straight away.'

'Go on,' said the caller, her note-taking pencil at the ready.

'Sylvia Rule and her future son-in-law loathe one another. And poor Mildred, trapped in between them, is understandably perplexed and distraught about it all. Something must be done to avoid the direst consequences for the whole family. Poor Freddie is quite miserable enough already. I don't know how this relates to the death of Barnabas Pandy, but you asked about the Rule family, so I thought you should know, in case it's relevant.'

'Thank you.'

'The other thing I need to tell you is about the Lavingtons—Timothy's family, the family of Barnabas Pandy. It was I who answered the telephone to Annabel on the morning of the fair. Annabel is Timothy's aunt. She lied to me.'

'About what?'

'She told me that she and her sister and niece couldn't come to the fair because of a problem with the motorcar that was supposed to bring them. I don't believe that was the truth. She sounded upset and . . . shifty. Not at all her usual self. And later, Lenore Lavington, Timothy's mother, referred to having missed the fair on account of being very tired that day. None of it added up. Now, I don't know what all this means, or how my husband has managed to get himself drawn into it, but then I'm not a police inspector, so it's not my job to find out, is it? It's your job,' said Jane Dockerill.

'Yes, ma'am,' said the caller, who, at that moment, had quite forgotten that her job was something altogether different and nothing to do with investigating crimes that might or might not have been committed.

THE SECOND QUARTER

CHAPTER 10

Some Important Questions

'What the devil possessed you, Catchpool?' Superintendent Nathaniel Bewes roared in my ear.

'What do you mean, sir?'

He had been shouting for some time about my many deficiencies, but so far it had all been rather abstract.

'Last night! The telephone call you made—or, should I say, had some woman make for you!'

Ah, so that was it.

'You told me the letter to John McCrodden was not sent by Poirot, and I fell for it! Well, I'm not falling for any more clap-trap, so you needn't bother feeding me any. Do I make myself clear? I send you to see Rowly McCrodden to straighten things out, and what do you do instead? Collude with Poirot to pester Rowly's son still further. No, don't pretend this had nothing to do with you. I know that Poirot came here to see you—'

'That was because—'

'—and I know that the woman who telephoned John

McCrodden and demanded to hear his alibi for the day that this Pandy fellow died said she was doing so "on behalf of Inspector Edward Catchpool of Scotland Yard". Do you think I'm an imbecile? She was not acting on your behalf at all, was she? She was doing the bidding of Hercule Poirot! Like you, she is a mere cog in his machine. Well, I won't stand for it, do you hear me? Please explain to me why you and Poirot are determined to accuse an innocent man of a murder that wasn't a murder at all. Do you understand the correct meaning of the word "alibi", Catchpool?'

'Yes, s—'

'It does not mean where someone was at a particular moment. I am presently in my office talking to you, more's the pity, but that is my *whereabouts*, not my *alibi*. Do you know why? Because *no murder has been committed* while I stand here talking to you. I shouldn't have to explain this to you!'

He was bound to be wrong, I thought. Somewhere in the world, a murder was probably being committed, or had been committed, since he had started to bellow at me some twenty minutes earlier. More than one murder, very likely—and the Super was jolly lucky not to be among this potentially large and international group of victims. If I were someone who could ever be pushed over the edge into performing an act of violence, that moment would surely have come approximately ten minutes ago. Instead, and to my great regret, I seem to be a person who can balance quietly on the edge he is pushed towards for as long as anybody feels inclined to yell at him.

'Why does John McCrodden need to offer an alibi when *the death of Barnabas Pandy is not a criminal matter?* Why?' Bewes demanded.

'Sir, if you would allow me to answer . . .' I stopped, and there followed an awkward silence. I had expected the Super to interrupt me.

'If a telephone call was made to John McCrodden last night, it had nothing to do with me,' I said. 'Nothing at all. If someone used my name in order to find out where John McCrodden was on the day Barnabas Pandy died, then I can only think that . . . well, that person must have hoped to use the authority of Scotland Yard to make McCrodden talk.'

'Poirot must be behind it,' said the Super. 'Poirot and some other little helper of his.'

'Sir, the letter to John McCrodden was not the only one. Four were sent. Three other people also received a letter— signed in Poirot's name, though not from him—accusing them of the murder of Barnabas Pandy.'

'Don't be ridiculous, Catchpool!'

I told him the names of the other three recipients, and that one of them was Pandy's granddaughter, who had been in the house with him when he died. 'I spoke to Rowland McCrodden yesterday, as you asked me to, and he was keen to find out as much as he could about who sent the letters. He wants Poirot to investigate, so if Poirot *has* had some woman ask John McCrodden for an alibi, it might be . . . you know . . . helpful to Rowland McCrodden in the long run. If it sheds any light on anything, I mean.'

The Super groaned. 'Catchpool, from whom do you imagine I heard about the call to John McCrodden?'

I was feeling relieved that he'd lowered the volume of his voice, until he bellowed, 'From Rowly, of course!' next to my ear. 'He wants to know why I've permitted someone from Scotland Yard to demand an alibi from his son instead of doing what I promised I would, which was to put a stop to the whole infernal business! You can tell Poirot that it's very likely John McCrodden was in Spain in December when Pandy died. Spain! Can't kill someone in England if you're in Spain, can you?'

I took a deep breath and said, 'Rowland McCrodden wants to understand what's going on. He might have been angry to hear that his son was asked for an alibi, but I'm sure he still wants to pursue some form of enquiry until he gets an answer. There is only one way to put a stop to this: by working out who sent the four letters, and why. If there's a chance that Barnabas Pandy was murdered—'

'If I hear you make that suggestion again, Catchpool, I might just swing for you!'

'I know his death was recorded as an accident, sir, but if someone believes that it wasn't—'

'Then that someone is wrong!' In one of his more reasonable moods, and in a circumstance that did not cause distress to 'Rowly' Rope, the Super would have conceded that of course it was possible a mistake might have been made, that a crime had gone undetected. There was no point trying to persuade him of this today, however.

'You're right about one thing, Catchpool,' he said. 'Rowly

does want answers, and quickly. Therefore, until this matter is resolved, you are relieved of all official duties. You will assist Poirot in bringing this matter to a satisfactory conclusion.'

I was unsure how I felt about this. I used to worry about not knowing how I felt in certain situations, but I had more recently decided to treat them as a convenient opportunity to feel nothing at all. The Super had made his decision, and there could be no argument.

I discovered, when he next spoke, that it was not merely a decision that had been made but also concrete arrangements: 'You will find Poirot waiting for you in your office.' Bewes glanced at his watch. 'Yes, he will certainly be there by now. The two of you are expected at Rowly's offices in fifty minutes' time. That should be long enough for you to get there. Off you go! The sooner this strange affair is resolved, the happier I shall be.' He smiled unexpectedly, as if to tempt me with a glimpse of what his future happiness might look like.

Poirot was waiting for me in my office as advertised. '*Mon pauvre ami!*' he cried when he saw me. 'You have had the down-dressing, I think, from the superintendent?' His eyes twinkled.

'How did you guess?' I asked.

'He was ready to direct his fury at me, until I suggested to him that if he did so, I would leave without delay and offer no further assistance to his good friend Rowland Rope.'

'I see,' I said testily. 'Well, you needn't worry. He got it all out of his system in the end. I don't suppose he told you about Spain, did he?'

'Spain?'

'John McCrodden might have been too obstinate to volunteer an alibi, but his father told the Super that he was probably in Spain when Pandy died.'

'Probably? No sound alibi contains the word "probably".'

'I know that. I'm only telling you what the Super said.'

As we left the building, Poirot said, 'It is another question to add to the list: was John McCrodden in Spain on 7 December or not?'

I had assumed we would walk to the offices of Donaldson & McCrodden, but Poirot had arranged for a car to take us. As we set off, he produced a small piece of paper from his pocket. 'Here, you see, is the list,' he said. 'A pencil, please, Catchpool.'

I passed him one from my pocket, and he added the newest question at the bottom of the page.

The list was headed 'Important Questions' and was so much the sort of thing that Poirot would compose—so quintessentially him—that I found the last of my annoyance dissolving away.

The list read as follows:

Important Questions
1. Was Barnabas Pandy murdered?
2. If so, by whom, and why?
3. Who wrote the four letters?
4. Does the writer of the letters sincerely suspect all four? Or does he only suspect one of them? Or does he suspect none of them?

5. If the author of the letters suspects none of the four, what was the purpose of sending the letters?
6. Why were the letters signed in the name of Hercule Poirot?
7. What information is Peter Vout withholding?
8. Why were Barnabas Pandy and Vincent Lobb enemies?
9. Where is the typewriter on which the four letters were typed?
10. Did Barnabas Pandy know he was going to die?
11. Why does Annabel Treadway seem so sad? What secrets is she keeping?
12. Did Kingsbury, Barnabas Pandy's valet, kill him? If so, why?
13. Why did Annabel Treadway and Lenore and Ivy Lavington decide not to go to the Turville College Christmas Fair?
14. Was John McCrodden in Spain when Barnabas Pandy died?

'Why do you suspect Kingsbury?' I asked Poirot. 'And why is the typewriter important? One is much the same as another, surely?'

'Aha, the typewriter!' He smiled. Then, as if he had just answered my second question, he went back to the first. 'I ask about Kingsbury because of what Annabel Treadway said on the telephone last night, *mon ami*. If she was in Ivy Lavington's bedroom with Lenore and Ivy when Monsieur Pandy died, then only Kingsbury was in the house and unobserved at the relevant time. If the death was murder, he is the most likely murderer, *non?*'

'I suppose so. But then, isn't it peculiar that he received no letter? He's the only person who had the opportunity to commit the crime, and yet four people with no opportunity are accused of it.'

'Everything that has happened is peculiar in the extreme,' said Poirot. 'I begin to think that I was wrong to rush ahead and think about alibis . . .' He shook his head.

'Now's a fine time to tell me this, after the battering my eardrums have just taken.' I could still hear the Super's rage ringing in my head.

'Yes, that is unfortunate,' said Poirot. 'Ah, well. We must not regret what we have discovered. It will all prove useful, I have no doubt. But now? Now, it is time to think more deeply. For example, if Kingsbury is our killer, then for him not to have received a letter that four *innocent* people received is perhaps not peculiar at all.'

I asked him what he meant, but he made an enigmatic noise and would say no more.

At the offices of Donaldson & McCrodden, as we climbed the stairs, I prepared for my second encounter with Miss Mason. I had not warned Poirot about her. Instead, I dared to hope for a smoother passage on this occasion, given that Rowland McCrodden was expecting us.

I was soon disappointed. The pink-faced young woman almost threw herself into my arms. 'Oh, Inspector Catchpool! Thank goodness you're here! I don't know what to do!'

'What's the matter, Miss Mason? Has something happened?'

'It's Mr McCrodden. He won't open his door. I can't get in. He must have locked it from the inside, which he *never* does. And he's not answering his telephone, and when I knock and call his name, he doesn't answer. He *must* be in there. I saw him, with my own eyes, go into his room and close the door less than thirty minutes ago.'

Miss Mason turned to Poirot. 'And now you're here, and Mr McCrodden *knows* you've got an appointment, and he still won't open his door. I can't help thinking, what if he's had a fit of some sort?'

'Catchpool, can you break down Mr McCrodden's door?' said Poirot.

I reached out to touch it, preparing to assess how hard it might be to kick it down, when the door opened and there stood Rowland McCrodden. He looked perfectly well—not at all like a man who had suffered an unexpected seizure.

'Oh, thank heavens!' said Miss Mason.

'I must leave at once,' McCrodden said. 'I'm sorry, gentlemen.' Without another word, he walked past us and out of the office. We listened as his feet descended several flights of stairs. Then a door slammed loudly.

Miss Mason rushed after him, calling out, 'Mr McCrodden, this is most irregular. You can't go. These two gentlemen are here to see you.'

'He has already gone, mademoiselle.'

Miss Mason ignored Poirot and continued to howl into the now-empty stairwell: 'Mr McCrodden! *They have an appointment!*'

CHAPTER 11

Emerald Green

When I arrived at Scotland Yard the next morning, I was advised by the Super that Rowland McCrodden was keen to meet Poirot and me at our earliest convenience, though there was one condition: it could not be at the offices of Donaldson & McCrodden. We agreed, and an arrangement was made for the three of us to meet at Pleasant's at two o'clock.

The coffee house was, for once, a suitable temperature—warm but not too hot—and smelled pleasingly of cinnamon and lemons. Our friend Fee Spring rushed over to us. I had expected to be the main focus of her attention, as I usually am, but today she had eyes only for Poirot . . . and very intensely focused eyes, too. She pushed him into his chair, demanding, 'Well? Have you done what you promised you would?'

'*Oui*, mademoiselle. But we must postpone our discussion of the Church Window Cake until later. Catchpool and I are here for an important meeting.'

'With someone who isn't here yet,' said Fee. 'There's plenty of time.'

'The two of you are going to talk about Church Window Cake?' I said, confused.

They both ignored me. 'And if we begin and are then interrupted?' said Poirot. 'I prefer to do things in a more orderly fashion, one at a time.'

'Look at the teapots,' said Fee. 'Dusted 'em all, I did. Specially for you. Put all the spouts pointing the same way. Mind you, I can easily put them back how they were before . . .'

'Please refrain from doing so, I beg of you.' Poirot looked up at the shelves where the teapots stood. '*C'est magnifique!*' he declared. 'I could not have done better myself. Very well, mademoiselle, I will tell you. I visited Kemble's Coffee House as you asked me to. There I found the waitress Philippa and I ordered a slice of the Church Window Cake. I engaged her in conversation about it. She admitted to having made it herself.'

'See!' Fee hissed. 'Even if she'd denied it, I wouldn't believe a single word that came from her.'

'I asked her where the recipe came from. She told me that it came from a friend.'

'She's no friend of mine, and hasn't ever been! Working next to someone doesn't make them your friend.'

'What is this about?' I asked. Again, Poirot and Fee ignored me. Meanwhile, Rowland Rope was late.

'I asked her what was the name of the friend who gave her the recipe,' said Poirot. 'At once, she became furtive in her bearing and turned her attention to another customer.'

'That's all the proof I need,' said Fee. 'She knows she's stolen from me, right enough—but I'll deal with her! And now, I'll bring you a slice of *my* Church Window Cake with the compliments of the house.'

I glanced at my watch. Fee said, 'He'll be here in five minutes or so, your gent with the big forehead. I told him to return at fifteen minutes after two.' She smiled and made off towards the kitchen before either of us could admonish her.

'I sometimes wonder if she is a little unhinged,' I told Poirot. 'When ever did you find time to undertake this investigation into cake recipe theft?'

'I am lucky, *mon ami*. Whether I am doing my work or pursuing my own interests, I need nothing more than the opportunity to think. Sitting amid strangers and eating, slowly, a slice of cake . . . these circumstances are most conducive to the functioning of the little grey cells. Ah, Rowland McCrodden *est arrivé*.'

So he had.

'Monsieur McCrodden.' Poirot shook his hand. 'I am Hercule Poirot. You caught a glimpse of me yesterday, but I did not have the opportunity to introduce myself.'

McCrodden looked suitably embarrassed. 'That was unfortunate,' he said. 'I hope we will make good progress this afternoon, to compensate for the time lost.'

Fee brought coffee and a slice of Church Window Cake for Poirot, tea for me and water for Rowland McCrodden, who wasted no time in getting down to business.

'Whoever sent John that letter has escalated his campaign

of persecution,' he said. 'Last night a woman telephoned, pretending to be a representative of yours, Catchpool, and of Scotland Yard. She told John the date on which Barnabas Pandy died and asked him for an alibi.'

'That is not quite accurate,' I said. Poirot and I had agreed in advance that we would tell him the truth—most of it, at any rate. 'I believe she said that she was telephoning *on behalf of Inspector Catchpool* of Scotland Yard. Which she was—though not in connection with any Scotland Yard business. She certainly did not say that she herself was an employee of the Yard.'

'What the dickens . . . ?' McCrodden scowled at me across the table. 'Do you mean to say that *you* were responsible? That you put her up to it? Who was she?'

I made a point of not looking in Fee Spring's direction. Poirot, I assume, did the same. I could have made the four telephone calls myself, but I had wanted to add a layer of protection. Knowing there was a chance the Super might end up hauling me over the coals for it, I had decided that I would more plausibly be able to deny all knowledge if the voice on the other end of the telephone was reported to have been a woman's. Coward that I am, I calculated that if Fee took care of the matter for Poirot—as that was how I thought of it—then I could happily tell myself I was so uninvolved as to be guiltless. Fee had none of my qualms about the unorthodoxy of the plan; it was instantly apparent that I had made her day by asking her to do it.

'It is I who must take responsibility, monsieur,' Poirot told Rowland McCrodden. 'Do not alarm yourself. From this point forward, the three of us will work together to solve this mystery.'

'Work together?' McCrodden recoiled. 'Do you have any idea what you have done, Poirot? John came to my house after receiving that wretched telephone call, and told me that he was no longer my son and I no longer his father. He wishes to sever ties altogether.'

'He will change his mind as soon as the true identity of the letter-writer is known. Do not distress yourself, monsieur. Instead, place your trust in Hercule Poirot. May I ask . . . why did you insist on meeting today in a different place? What is in your offices that you do not wish me to see?'

McCrodden made a strange noise. 'It's too late for that,' he said.

'What do you mean?'

'Nothing.'

Poirot tried again: 'Why did you lock yourself in your room, then free yourself, only to disappear?'

We sat in silence while he considered the question.

'Monsieur? If you could please answer.'

'The reason has nothing to do with the matter at hand,' said McCrodden stiffly. 'Will that satisfy you?'

'*Pas du tout.* If you will not explain, I will have no choice but to guess. Could it be that you are afraid we will find a typewriter?'

'A typewriter?' McCrodden looked frustrated and a little bored. 'What do you mean?'

'E!' said Poirot enigmatically.

McCrodden turned to me. 'What does he mean, Catchpool?'

'I don't know, but you'll notice his eyes have turned a striking shade of emerald green. That usually means he has worked something out.'

'Emerald?' McCrodden growled, pushing his chair back from the table. 'You know, don't you? You both know. And you're taunting me. But how *could* you know? I have spoken to nobody.'

'What is it that you think we know, monsieur? About the typewriter?'

'I don't care a tuppenny damn for your typewriter! I'm talking about the reason I couldn't bear to stay in my offices a second longer yesterday and the reason I refused to meet you there today. I'm talking about Emerald, as well you know. That's why you said "emerald green", isn't it?'

Poirot and I exchanged a look of utmost confusion.

'Monsieur . . . what is this emerald?'

'Not what. *Who*. She's the reason I cannot go to my own place of work—which is most inconvenient. Miss Emerald Mason.'

'Miss Mason?' I said. 'The lady who works for you?'

'I suppose I shall have to tell you now—not that it's any of your business. Miss Mason's Christian name is Emerald. I thought you knew. When you said "emerald green". . .'

'*Non*, monsieur. Why does the presence of this woman drive you out of your building?'

'She has done nothing wrong,' said McCrodden despondently. 'She's diligent, well turned out—in every respect the model employee. The firm's affairs seem to matter to her as much as they do to Donaldson and me. I cannot fault her.'

'And yet?' Poirot prompted.

'I find her more insufferable by the day. Yesterday, I reached the point where I could bear it no longer. I had mentioned to her that I couldn't make up my mind whether to invite a particular client to attend the forthcoming Law Society dinner as my guest—there are reasons for and against, with which Miss Mason is familiar—and she reminded me *three times* in the hour that followed that I needed to decide as a matter of urgency. I know the date of the Law Society dinner as well as she does, and, what is more, she knows I do. It was clear that if she could have compelled me to make up my mind on the spot, she would have! The third time I told her I had not yet come to a decision, she said . . .' He gritted his teeth at the memory. 'She said, "Oh, dear. Well, perhaps you should have a little think." As if I were five years old. That was the last straw. I locked my office door and thereafter, when she addressed me from the other side of it, I ignored her.'

Poirot chuckled. 'And then, Catchpool and I . . . we arrive.'

'Yes. By then it was too late. The black mood that had me in its grip was . . . well, it was quite irrational.'

'If you find Miss Mason so enervating, why do you not tell her that you have no further need of her services?' said Poirot. 'Then you could once again go to work without dread in your heart.'

McCrodden seemed disgusted by the idea. 'I have no intention of turning her out on to the street. She is conscientious and has done nothing wrong. Besides, Stanley Donaldson, the firm's other partner, has no objection to her, as far as I know. I must try to overcome my aversion to her, and stop indulging in this . . . whatever it is.'

'Indulging,' said Poirot thoughtfully. 'That is an interesting way to describe it.'

'It *is* an indulgence,' said McCrodden. 'Avoiding the office, avoiding *her*, is satisfying in a way that it ought not to be—because I know how it will frustrate her.'

'This is fascinating indeed,' said Poirot.

'No, it isn't,' said McCrodden. 'It's childish of me and not what we're here to discuss. I want to know, Poirot, how you're proposing to find out who sent that letter to my son.'

'I have several ideas. The first involves your Law Society dinner. What is the date of it? I am wondering if it might be the same one to which Barnabas Pandy's solicitor, Peter Vout, has been invited.'

'It must be,' said McCrodden. 'There is only one on the horizon. Peter Vout was this Pandy fellow's solicitor, you say? Well, well.'

'Do you know him?' asked Poirot.

'A little, yes.'

'Excellent. Then you are ideally placed.'

'For what?' McCrodden asked suspiciously.

Poirot rubbed his hands together. 'As they say, *mon ami* . . . you are going to perform for us the under-the-cover investigation!'

CHAPTER 12

Many Ruined Alibis

'That's the most atrocious idea I've ever heard,' said Rowland McCrodden, once he knew the detail of Poirot's proposed plan. 'It's out of the question.'

'You might think so now, monsieur—but as the evening of the Law Society dinner draws nearer, you will come to see that it is a most advantageous opportunity, and that you are more than capable of playing your role to perfection.'

'I will not participate in a deception, however good the cause.'

'*Mon ami*, let us not argue. If you do not wish to do as I propose, then you will not do it. I cannot insist that you do.'

'And I shan't,' said McCrodden forcefully.

'We shall see. Now, will you agree to allow Catchpool here to inspect all the typewriters used by your firm?'

McCrodden's mouth tightened to a thin line. 'Why do you return to the subject of typewriters time after time?' he asked.

Poirot produced from a pocket the letter that had been sent to John McCrodden. He passed it across the table. 'Do you notice anything about any of the letters?' he said.

'No. I can't see anything worth remarking upon.'

'Study them closely.'

'No, I . . . Wait. The letter "e" is incomplete.'

'*Précisément.*'

'There's a gap in the straight line. A small hole of white.' McCrodden dropped the letter on the table. 'I see. If you find the typewriter, you find the sender of the letter. And since you've just asked permission to search my offices, I can only conclude that you suspect me of being that person.'

'Not at all, my friend. It is a mere formality. Everybody connected to this puzzle who is in possession of a typewriter we will investigate: the home of Sylvia Rule; that of Barnabas Pandy, of course; Turville College, where Timothy Lavington and Freddie Rule are pupils and Hugo Dockerill is a housemaster . . .'

'Who are all these people?' asked Rowland McCrodden. 'I've never heard of them.'

I took the opportunity to tell him that his son had not been the only person to get an accusatory letter, then watched as he struggled to digest the information. He said nothing for some time. Then: 'But why didn't you tell John, in that case, that he wasn't the only one? Instead, you allowed him to believe that he alone stood accused.'

'I did no such thing, monsieur. Assuredly, I informed your son that he was not the sole recipient of such a letter. My valet told to him the same thing—Georges testified on my behalf that I spoke the truth—but your son would not listen. He was steadfast in his belief that you must be responsible.'

'He's a blind, stubborn fool!' McCrodden banged his fist down on the table. 'Always has been, since the day he was born. What I don't understand is *why*. Why would anybody send letters to four different people, accusing them all of the same murder, and sign them in your name instead of his own?'

'It is puzzling,' Poirot concurred.

'Is that all you have to say? May I suggest that, instead of sitting around hoping the answer falls into our laps, we use our brains and try to solve the problem?'

Poirot smiled graciously. 'I did not wait, *mon ami*. I have, in fact, started without you to use the little grey cells of the mind. But, please, join me.'

'I can think of two reasons why someone might do it,' I said. 'Reason one: if he signs the letters in your name, Poirot, they are more likely to frighten the life out of those unlucky enough to receive them: the police listen when Hercule Poirot says somebody is guilty of murder. Therefore, if the letter-writer wants to give people a nasty shock, using your name is the way to do it. Even an innocent person would worry that to be accused of murder by you might prove fatal for them.'

'I agree,' said Poirot. 'What is the second reason?'

'The letter-writer wants you to look into the matter,' I said. 'He or she thinks Barnabas Pandy was murdered, but doesn't know for sure. Or *does* know it was murder, but doesn't know who did it. He or she comes up with a plan to make you curious enough to investigate. Going to the police won't work because the official record already states that Pandy's death was accidental.'

'Very good,' said Poirot. 'Both of those reasons I had thought of myself. But tell me, *why these four people*, Catchpool?'

'Not being the letter-writer myself, I'm afraid I can't answer that one.'

Poirot said to McCrodden, 'According to Monsieur Pandy's granddaughter, Annabel Treadway, there were five people at Combingham Hall on the seventh of December: she herself; Barnabas Pandy; his other granddaughter, Lenore Lavington; her daughter, Ivy; and Monsieur Pandy's manservant, Kingsbury. Let us assume for a moment that it was indeed a murder. The obvious people who ought to have received these letters of accusation are the four who were at Combingham Hall that day and are still alive: Annabel Treadway, Lenore Lavington, Ivy Lavington, and Kingsbury. Of those, only one got a letter. The other three letters were sent to two people who, if they are to be believed, were busy all of that day at the Turville College Christmas Fair—Sylvia Rule and Hugo Dockerill—and to John McCrodden, who, so far, does not appear to be in any way connected to the deceased man.'

'John is likely to have been in Spain when Pandy died,' said his father. 'I'm sure it was early December last year that I tried to track him down at the market where he works, and was told that he had gone to Spain and would remain there for several weeks.'

'You do not sound sure,' Poirot told him.

'Well . . .' McCrodden hestitated. 'It was December, undoubtedly. There were Christmas trinkets for sale on all the market stalls: shiny, useless pieces of rubbish. It might have been later in December, I suppose.' He shook his head in apparent disgust, as if he had caught himself red-handed in the act of lying to protect his son. 'You're right,' he admitted. 'I don't know where John was when Pandy died. I *never* know where he is. Poirot, believe me, I would not allow my judgement to be clouded by sentiment. Even though he is my only child, if John committed a murder, I would be the first to notify the police and I would support his execution as I support the death penalty for all murderers.'

'Is that so, monsieur?'

'It is. One must stick by one's principles or else the fabric of society crumbles. If a child of mine deserved it, I would hang him myself. But, as I told Catchpool, John would never kill another person. This I know for a fact. Therefore, his precise whereabouts on the day in question are irrelevant. He is innocent, and that's the end of the matter.'

'Those words, "the end of the matter". . . they are only ever used when the matter in question has only just begun,' said Poirot, much to Rowland McCrodden's consternation.

'Why would John go to Spain?' I asked.

A look of disapproval passed across Rowland McCrodden's face. 'He goes there regularly. His maternal grandmother lived there for a time and, when she died, she left her house to John. It's close to the sea and the weather is far superior to our climate. John is happier in Spain than in any part of England—he has always said so. And more recently, there has been a woman . . . Disreputable, of course. Not at all the sort of girl I'd have chosen for him.'

'People need to choose for themselves in these matters,' I said before I could stop myself, thinking about the 'ideal wife in waiting' whom my mother had recently found and attempted to inflict upon me. She was probably a delightful young woman, but I would forever blame her for those dismal few days in Great Yarmouth that I had felt obliged to offer Mother as compensation.

McCrodden emitted a hollow laugh. 'Matters of the heart, do you mean? Oh, John cares not a jot for the woman in Spain. He makes use of her, that's all. It's unsavoury and immoral, the way he carries on. I've told him what I think—I've told him his mother must be weeping in her grave—and do you know what he does? He laughs at me!'

'I wonder . . .' Poirot said quietly.

'What?' I asked.

'I wonder if, by pretending he is me, the letter-writer conceals a more important identity.'

'Do you mean the identity of the murderer?' asked McCrodden. 'The murderer of Barnabas Pandy?'

Something about the way he said it, in his woodwind-instrument voice, sent a shiver through me. It is hard to warm to a man who proudly announces that he would hang his own child.

'No, my friend,' said Poirot. 'That is not what I mean.

It is another possibility that occurs to me . . . a most interesting one.'

I knew he would say no more about it for the time being, so I asked McCrodden about his own whereabouts on the seventh of December. Without hesitation, he said, 'I was at my club, the Athenaeum, all day—with Stanley Donaldson. In the evening the two of us went to see *Dear Love* at the Palace Theatre. Please feel free to confirm that with Stanley.'

Seeing that I was surprised by how readily he had answered my question, he said, 'As soon as I discovered the date of Pandy's death, I asked . . .' He stopped, grimaced, then continued, 'I asked Miss Mason to bring me last year's appointments diary. I thought that if I recalled my own whereabouts, it might help me to know where John was. If it were a day on which I had attempted to communicate with him and been rebuffed, for instance . . .' The reedy voice shook. He tried to disguise it with a cough. 'In any case, I am in the fortunate position of having a far better alibi than some of the other players in this unpleasant little drama. School Christmas Fair!' he snorted contemptuously.

'You are unenthusiastic about Christmas, monsieur? About the shiny—what did you call them?—ah, yes, the trinkets. On the market stalls. And now also about the Christmas Fair of Turville College.'

'I have no objection to a Christmas Fair, though I would not attend one myself if I had a choice,' said McCrodden. 'But frankly, Poirot, the notion that someone's presence at the Christmas Fair of a large school is any sort of alibi at all is complete and utter bunkum.'

'Why do you say so, my friend?'

'It's a long time since I last attended such an event, but I recall them only too well from my youth. I remember trying to get through the day without speaking to anyone at all. It's something I still do at large gatherings, which I loathe. I shall certainly try to do it at the Law Society dinner. The secret is to pass by everybody with a friendly smile, while looking as if you're on your way to rejoin another little group that is waiting for you just over there. No one notices if you ever *do* join those towards whom you seem to be striding so urgently. Once you've passed them, they don't notice where you go or what you do.'

Poirot was frowning. His eyes darted up and down. 'You make a valuable point, monsieur. He is correct, is he not, Catchpool? I too have attended the large gatherings of this kind. It is the easiest thing in the word to disappear and reappear some while later, and no one will notice because everybody is busy talking to somebody else. *Je suis imbécile!* Monsieur McCrodden, do you know what you have done? You have brought ruination to the alibis of many people! And now we know less than we knew before we started!'

'Come now, Poirot,' I said. 'Do not exaggerate. Who are these many people with ruined alibis? Annabel Treadway still has hers: she was with Ivy and Lenore Lavington in Ivy's bedroom—though that will need checking. John McCrodden might have been in Spain—that too needs to be established. At most, this Christmas Fair problem you're so worried about leaves only two alibis looking shaky: Sylvia Rule's and Hugo Dockerill's.'

'You are wrong, *mon ami*. Also at the Christmas Fair at Turville College on the seventh of December were Jane Dockerill, the wife of Hugo, and Timothy Lavington, Barnabas Pandy's great-grandson. Oh—and young Freddie Rule, *n'est-ce pas?*'

'Why are they relevant?' Rowland McCrodden asked. 'No one has accused them of anything.'

'No one has accused the manservant Kingsbury either,' said Poirot. 'This does not make him irrelevant. No one has accused Vincent Lobb, Barnabas Pandy's old enemy. And we must not forget Sylvia Rule's hated Eustace. He, too, might be significant. I prefer to think of everybody as relevant—all of the people whose names arise in connection with this puzzling affair—until I can prove otherwise.'

'Are you suggesting that one of the people at the Christmas Fair that day might have left the grounds of Turville College, gone to Combingham Hall, and murdered Barnabas Pandy?' I said. 'They would need to have driven, or been driven, since it's a good hour's drive. And then what? They drowned Barnabas Pandy in his bathtub, then returned to the fair, where they walked around making sure lots of people observed their presence?'

'That could have happened,' said Poirot grimly. 'All too easily.'

'We mustn't forget that Barnabas Pandy's death is likely to have been an accident,' I said.

'But if it was murder . . .' Poirot said with a faraway

expression on his face. 'If it was murder, then the murderer has a powerful incentive to cast suspicion on someone other than himself, does he not?'

'Not if no one suspects him in the first place, because the death has been accepted to be an accident,' I said.

'Ah, but perhaps not everybody has accepted it,' said Poirot. 'The killer might discover that the truth is known by at least one person, and is about to be revealed. So—he casts the suspicion! Even more ingeniously, he casts suspicion on four innocent people simultaneously. That is more effective than simply to accuse one innocent person.'

'Why?' McCrodden and I asked at the same time.

'If you accuse only one person, the matter is concluded too quickly. The accused produces his alibi, or else no proof can be found to tie him to the crime, and that is that. Whereas if you accuse four people, and sign the name of Hercule Poirot to those accusations, what happens? Chaos! Confusion! Denials from many different quarters! That is the situation in which we now find ourselves and it is assuredly the most brilliant screen of smoke, is it not? We know nothing. We see nothing!'

'You're right,' said Rowland McCrodden. 'The way the letter-writer has conducted himself . . . it's rather ingenious. He has posed a question: which one of the four is guilty? He doubtless hopes that Poirot will investigate. A question that appears to have one of only four possible answers sets up a choice with an illusory limit. In truth, many more answers might be possible, and somebody entirely other might be guilty.' McCrodden leaned forward and said urgently, 'Poirot, do you believe, as I do, that the letter-writer is likely to be Barnabas Pandy's murderer?'

'I try to make no assumptions. As Catchpool says, we do not know, yet, if Monsieur Pandy was murdered. What I fear, *mes amis*, is that we may never know. I am at a loss as to how to pursue . . .' He left the sentence unfinished and, whispering something inaudible in French, pulled the plate on the table towards him. He picked up his cake fork. Holding it over the slice of Church Window Cake, he looked up at Rowland McCrodden and said purposefully, 'It is your son John that I will pursue.'

'What?' McCrodden scowled. 'Haven't I told you—'

'You misunderstand me. I do not mean that I think he is guilty. I mean that his position in the structure fascinates me.'

'What position? What structure?'

Poirot put down his cake fork and picked up a knife. 'See here the four squares in the cake,' he said. 'In the top half, a yellow and a pink square side by side, and in the bottom half the same. For the purposes of this exercise, these four little squares, these four quarters of the one slice, represent our four letter-recipients.

'At first I thought that there were two pairs of two.' Poirot cut the slice of cake in half, to illustrate his point. 'Annabel Treadway and Hugo Dockerill were one pair, both connected to Barnabas Pandy. Sylvia Rule and John McCrodden were the other pair. They both told me that they had never heard of Monsieur Pandy. But then . . .' Poirot cut one of the halves in half again, and pushed the newly detached pink square towards the half-slice that was still intact, leaving one solitary yellow square isolated at the bottom of the plate. 'Then I discover that Sylvia Rule's son, Freddie, is at school with Timothy Lavington, Barnabas Pandy's great-grandson. So now we have *three* people with a clear link to Monsieur Pandy and to each other: Annabel Treadway refused a marriage proposal from Hugo Dockerill. Hugo Dockerill is a housemaster at the school attended by Sylvia Rule's son, who is at school with Annabel Treadway's nephew. Only John McCrodden has, as far as we can see at the moment, nothing linking him to any of the others, or to Barnabas Pandy.'

'He *might* also have a connection to Pandy, though,' I said. 'One that just hasn't emerged yet.'

'But all of these other connections are very clear to see,' said Poirot. 'They are unmistakeable, straight away visible, impossible to miss.'

'You're right,' I conceded. 'John McCrodden does rather feel like the odd one out.'

Rowland McCrodden looked stricken, but said nothing.

Poirot pushed the lone yellow square of cake off the plate and on to the tablecloth. 'I wonder if this is what the writer of the letters wants me to think about,' he said. 'I wonder if he—or she—wants me to consider, above all, the guilt of Monsieur John McCrodden.'

CHAPTER 13

The Hooks

That evening, Poirot and I sat in front of a crackling log fire in the excessively decorated and alarmingly furnished drawing room of my landlady, Blanche Unsworth. We had sat like this many times, and no longer noticed the lurid shades of pink and purple, or the quite unnecessary fringes and trims appended to the ends and edges of every lampshade, armchair and curtain.

We each held a drink in our hand. Neither of us had spoken for some time. Poirot had been staring into the flickering flames for nearly an hour, occasionally nodding or shaking his head. I had just filled in the last clue of my crossword puzzle when he said quietly, 'Sylvia Rule burned the letter she received.'

I waited.

'John McCrodden tore his into pieces, which he sent to his father,' Poirot went on. 'Annabel Treadway first scribbled over the words of her letter, then tore it up and then burned it, and Hugo Dockerill lost his. His wife Jane subsequently found it.'

'Are any of these facts important?' I asked.

'I do not know what matters and what does not, my friend. I sit here and think more furiously than I have ever thought before, and *I find no answer to the most important puzzle of all.*'

'Whether Pandy was murdered, you mean?'

'No. There is a question still more important than that: *Why should we pursue this matter at all?* It is not the first time I have tried to discover if an accidental death might be a murder in disguise. *Pas du tout.* This I have done many times, but only ever when a person who appears to be of reliable character tells me that all might not be as it seems, or when I have the suspicion myself, based on my own observations. None of these conditions pertains to our present problem.'

'No,' I agreed, acutely aware that while I indulged the whims of Poirot, Rowland McCrodden and the Super, work would be mounting up on my desk at Scotland Yard.

'Instead, we have the suggestion that Monsieur Pandy's death was murder coming from a character we know to be untrustworthy—a person who writes letters and signs them with a name that is not his own. We know beyond the reasonable doubt that the sender of these letters is a fraud, a liar, a maker of the mischief! If I were to decide to take no further steps and turn my attention to other things, no one could fault my decision.'

'I certainly wouldn't,' I told him.

'And yet . . . the hooks, they have been successfully planted in the mind of Hercule Poirot. I would like to know why is Mademoiselle Annabel Treadway so sad? Who sent the letters, and why? Why four? And why to these four people? Does the person responsible truly believe that Barnabas Pandy was murdered, or is it some sort of trick or trap? What if he is the murderer as well as the letter-writer? Is it one culprit I must identify, or two?'

'Well, if the author of the letters *is* also the murderer, he or she must be one of the biggest fools that ever lived and breathed! "Dear Hercule Poirot, I should like to draw to your attention to the fact that I committed a murder in December of last year and I appear to have got away with it." No one would be so idiotic.'

'Perhaps. It is possible, Catchpool, that somebody who is not at all the idiot seeks to manipulate me—to what end I cannot and do not know.'

'Why not retaliate with a manipulation of your own? Do absolutely nothing. That might provoke the mischief-maker into sending more letters. He may write to you directly the next time.'

'If I had the patience . . . but it is not in my nature to do nothing. So . . .' Poirot clapped his hands together. 'You will start immediately to check all of the alibis and all of the typewriters.'

'In the world? Or only all the typewriters in London?'

'Very amusing, *mon ami*. No, not only in London. Also at Turville College, and Combingham Hall. I want you to test every typewriter you can find that might have been used by any of the people involved in this matter. Even Eustace!'

'But, Poirot—'

'Also, you must find Vincent Lobb. Ask him why he and Barnabas Pandy were enemies for so long. And, finally—for I do not want to burden you with too many tasks—please find a way to persuade Rowland McCrodden to do what we need him to do at the Law Society dinner.'

'Can't you tackle McCrodden?' I said. 'He's more likely to listen to you than to me.'

'What is your opinion of him?' Poirot asked.

'Frankly, I've been less favourably inclined towards him since hearing him say he would be pleased to hang his own son.'

'*If* his son were a murderer . . . and Rowland McCrodden is adamant that John is not. Therefore, when he says he would willingly hang him, it is not, in his mind, his son, but a fantasy version of John. This is why he is able to say it and believe he means it. Be assured, *mon ami*: if John McCrodden ever committed a murder, his father would do everything he could to save him from punishment. He would tie himself in the complicated knots and find a way to believe that John was innocent.'

'You are probably right,' I said. 'Do you think he might have sent the four letters? Think of it this way: he deliberately places his son in hot water so that he can rush to the rescue, thereby forcing John to acknowledge that he's a devoted father and not the hateful ogre John thinks he is. If at some point soon he is able to say to John, "I set Hercule Poirot to work on your behalf and he has exonerated you," and if John can see that is undeniably true, relations between them might improve greatly.'

'And he sends the letters to three other people as well, so that it does not look as if the whole exercise is about John?' said Poirot. 'It is possible. I have been thinking of Annabel Treadway as our most likely letter-writer, but it might be Rowland McCrodden.'

'Why Annabel Treadway?' I asked.

'Do you recall, I spoke of an identity that the sender of the letters might have sought to conceal? Rowland McCrodden asked me if I meant the identity of the murderer of Barnabas Pandy.'

'Yes, I remember.'

'What I meant, *mon ami*, is the identity of the *harbourer of suspicions*. I have been developing this theory with Annabel Treadway in mind.'

I sipped my drink, waiting for him to elaborate.

'It seems to me that if anyone murdered Monsieur Pandy, the most likely person is his manservant, Kingsbury,' Poirot went on. 'From what we have been told, he had the opportunity. The three women of the household were in a room together with the door closed, probably talking in an animated fashion; they would not have seen or heard anything.

'Let us say that Mademoiselle Annabel—who did not strike me as a brave or confident woman—suspects that Kingsbury killed her grandfather. She cannot prove it, so she places her faith in a gamble. She decides it is possible that Hercule Poirot might be able to prove her suspicions to be correct. Why, in that case, did she not come to me and ask more straightforwardly for help?'

'I can't think of any reason why she wouldn't do precisely that,' I told him.

'What if she was afraid of Kingsbury finding out that she had done so? She might have anticipated how difficult it would be to prove that a very old man was pushed underwater while in his bath. How could it ever be proven, if only Monsieur Pandy and Kingsbury were in the room at the time?'

'I see. So you're saying she'd have thought it likely that Kingsbury would get away with it?'

'Exactly. The law would be powerless to punish him, on account of the lack of evidence. Meanwhile, he—a murderer—would know that it was Annabel Treadway who had reported her suspicions to me. What is to stop him killing her next?'

I wasn't at all convinced by this theory, and I said so. 'If that was her fear, there was a far simpler plan of action available to her. She could have accused Kingsbury in an anonymous letter *to* you, rather than accusing herself and three other people in letters purporting to be *from* you. That would have been far more straightforward.'

'Indeed,' Poirot agreed. 'For her purposes, it would have been *too* straightforward. Kingsbury might have suspected her of writing such a letter, as she was at Combingham Hall when Monsieur Pandy died. She would have been one of three obvious suspects, and the other two would have been her sister and niece, to whom she seems devoted—she would not have wished to risk their lives either. No, no. My theory is better. The four letters having been sent to this strange collection of people, including Annabel Treadway herself, she now stands accused of her grandfather's murder. This, I think, would not lead Kingsbury to believe that she suspected him of the crime. Do you see, Catchpool?'

'Yes, but—'

'She signs the four letters as "Hercule Poirot", and, in doing so, she secures my involvement. Once I am involved, once I am successfully hooked like a fish and reeled in, then she sits back and hopes that her efforts were not in vain— that I will investigate and discover the guilt of Kingbury and a means of proving it.'

'All right, but then why accuse the three others? She could have sent *one* letter, to herself, signed in your name, accusing her and nobody else of her grandfather's murder.'

'She is a woman of extreme caution and trepidation,' said Poirot.

'Is she really?' I laughed. 'Then you've disproved your own colourful theory! No one of a cautious temperament would attempt a scheme like this.'

'Ah, but you must consider also her desperation.'

'I fear we have entered the realm of pure invention,' I told him.

'Maybe so. Then again, maybe not. I hope, one day soon, to know. The next step, in any case, is clear.'

'Not to me it isn't.'

'Yes, it is, Catchpool. I have given to you the clarity: Vincent Lobb, alibis and typewriters.'

I was relieved that persuading Rowland McCrodden to turn the Law Society dinner into a pantomime of Poirot's devising seemed to be off the list. 'And what will you be doing, while I search for faulty letter "e"s?'

'Is it not obvious?' asked Poirot. 'First thing tomorrow, I shall depart for Combingham Hall. We will see what answers I may find.'

'Be a sport and check the typewriters while you're there,' I said with a grin. 'Since you're going anyway.'

'Of course, *mon ami*. Poirot, he shall be the sport!'

CHAPTER 14

At Combingham Hall

There were many reasons, thought Poirot as he stood and stared at its façade the next day, why Combingham Hall ought to have looked appealing. The sky was bright with winter sun, and the temperature mild for February. In an apparent invitation for all visitors to enter, the front door stood half open. No one could have disputed that this was a fine and handsome building. It was surrounded by all that one might wish for: attractive lawned gardens and, further from the house, a lake, a tennis court, two cottages, an orchard and a substantial wooded area, all of which Poirot had seen from the windows of the motorcar that had brought him here from the nearest railway station.

Yet he lingered outside, reluctant to enter the Hall. One might be proud to own and live in such a building, but could one grow fond of it? The open door was more suggestive of carelessness than of active welcome. Instead of nestling in its natural environment as buildings ought to, it protruded in an ungainly fashion—loomed, almost—as if an ill-wisher had reached down from above and balanced it where it stood, with the aim of tricking people into thinking it belonged there. 'Or else I am a foolish old man who imagines these things,' Poirot said to himself.

A woman of perhaps forty or a few years more, wearing a yellow dress with a thin belt, appeared in the doorway. She stared at Poirot without smiling.

'Strangeness upon strangeness,' Poirot thought to himself. The woman had something in common with the building from which she had emerged. She was undoubtedly beautiful, with golden hair and every feature perfectly designed and precisely in proportion with the others, yet she looked . . .

'Uninviting,' Poirot murmured to himself.

He produced his best smile and walked briskly towards her. 'Good afternoon, madame,' he said before introducing himself.

She extended her hand for him to shake. 'It's a pleasure to meet you,' she said, though her face remained impassive. 'I'm Lenore Lavington. Please come in. We are ready for you.'

Poirot thought this a strange thing to say: as if he was an ordeal to be endured. He followed her into a large, bare entrance hall with a staircase of dark wood on the far left and a row of three archways straight ahead. Beyond these was a vaulted corridor and then a further three archways which led into a dining hall that contained a wooden table, long and narrow, with many chairs around it.

Poirot shivered. It was colder in the house than outside. The reason for this was obvious. Where were the walls?

Where were the doors separating one room from another? From where he stood, Poirot could not see none. It was quite wrong, he decided, to walk into a house and be able to see, in the distance, its dining table.

He felt greatly relieved when Lenore Lavington led him to a small, warmer sitting room with pale green wallpaper, a lit fire and a closeable door. Two other women awaited him there: Annabel Treadway, and a much younger, broad-shouldered woman with dark hair, intelligent eyes and an untidy filigree of scars trailing down one side of her face and, along her neck under her ear. This must be Ivy Lavington, thought Poirot. She could have covered some of the scarring by arranging her hair differently, but had evidently chosen not to.

A large dog with a lot of brown, fluffy hair—curly in places—was sitting on Annabel Treadway's feet, his head balanced in her lap. When Poirot appeared, he roused himself and trotted across the room to greet the new visitor. Poirot patted him, at which the dog lifted his front paw and patted him back.

'Ah! He greets me!'

'Hoppy's the friendliest boy in the world,' said Annabel Treadway. 'Hopscotch, meet M. Hercule Poirot!'

'This is my daughter, Ivy,' said Lenore Lavington. There was no suggestion in her tone that she intended this remark as a reproach to her sister.

'Yes, of course—this is Ivy,' said Annabel.

'Hello, M. Poirot. It is an honour to meet you,' said the younger woman. Her voice was warm and deep.

Hopscotch, still at Poirot's feet and staring up at him, raised his paw and patted the air between them, as if not quite daring to touch the great detective a second time.

'Oh, how sweet! He wants you to play with him,' said Annabel. 'In a moment he'll lie on his back and expect you to stroke his tummy.'

'I'm sure M. Poirot has more important things to think about,' said her sister.

'Yes, of course. I'm sorry.'

'No apology is necessary,' Poirot told her.

The dog was now lying on his back. Poirot stepped around him and, invited by Lenore Lavington to sit, lowered himself into a chair. This could not be Combingham Hall's main drawing room, he thought. It was far too small, though perhaps it was the only part of the house warm enough for human habitation.

He was offered refreshments, which he declined. Lenore Lavington sent Ivy to find Kingsbury and instruct him to prepare something to eat and drink 'in case M. Poirot changes his mind'. Once her daughter had left the room, she said, 'There is no need to wait until Ivy returns. Perhaps you could tell me why you are here?'

'You don't mind explaining, do you?' added Annabel quickly. 'You will do it so much better than I would.'

'Do you mean to say, mademoiselle, that you have not told Madame Lavington about the letter you received?'

'*C'est vraiment incroyable*,' Poirot said silently to himself. People: their strangeness had no limits. How could one sister tell another that the famous detective Hercule Poirot was to visit them at their home and not reveal the reason for the visit? And how could the other sister not demand to know, in advance of the detective's arrival?

'Annabel has told me nothing. I should very much like to know what this is about.'

As efficiently as he could, Poirot explained the situation. As she listened, Lenore Lavington paid close attention, nodding now and then. If his story surprised her, she showed no sign of it.

When he had finished, she said, 'I see,' and then, 'An unpleasant business—though not as unpleasant, I suppose, as if there was a chance the accusations were true.'

'You are going to tell me there is no such chance?'

'None whatever. Grandfather wasn't murdered, either by my sister or by anybody else. There was no one in the house when he died apart from Annabel, me, Ivy and Kingsbury—as you know, because *you* have just told me. Annabel is quite correct: she, Ivy and I were together in Ivy's bedroom between when Grandfather called out to us and when Kingsbury alerted us and we all ran to the bath-room to find Grandfather dead. None of us left the room in between.'

Poirot noted that she referred to Barnabas Pandy as 'Grandfather', not 'Grandy', as her sister called him. 'What about Kingsbury?' he asked.

'Kingsbury? Well, he wasn't in the room with us . . . but Kingsbury, kill Grandfather? It's unthinkable. I expect you'll wish to speak to him too before you leave?'

'*Oui*, madame.'

'Then you will soon see how absurd an idea it is. May I ask why you are pursuing this investigation, M. Poirot, when no police force and no court seems to have the slightest suspicion that Grandfather's death was anything but an accident? Has someone sent you? Or are you here simply to satisfy your own curiosity?'

'I am curious, I will admit. Always, I am curious. Also, the father of Monsieur John McCrodden, who received one of the four letters, asked for my help in clearing the name of his son.'

Lenore Lavington shook her head. 'This has gone too far already,' she said. 'Clear his name? It's laughable. He wasn't here in the house when Grandfather died. There: his name is cleared, and there is no need for you or the father of this Mr McClodden to waste any more of your time.'

'Though we are happy to answer your questions, of course,' said Annabel, stroking the dog under his chin. He had returned to his mistress and was once more draped across the lower part of her legs.

'May I ask? When I arrived, the front door stood open.'

'Yes. It's always open,' said Lenore.

'It's because of Hopscotch,' said Annabel. 'He likes to come and go quite freely between the house and garden, you see. We'd like it better—Lenore would like it better—if we could let him out, or in, and then close the door, but . . . well, he barks rather loudly, I'm afraid.'

'He requires the door to be left open, and Annabel insists that we indulge him.'

'Hoppy's extremely clever, M. Poirot,' said Annabel. 'He prefers the front door to be open so that whenever he wants to go out, he can, without having first to summon one of us.'

'If the door is habitually left open, is it not possible that somebody entered the house while your grandfather was in his bath on 7 December last year?' Poirot asked.

'No. It is not.'

'No,' Annabel echoed her sister. 'Ivy's bedroom is at the front of the house. One of the three of us would have seen someone coming up the driveway, whether they were in a vehicle or on a bicycle or on foot. It's impossible that none of us would have noticed.'

'What if a person approached the house from the back?' Poirot asked.

'Why would they?' asked Annabel. 'It's far easier from the front. Oh—I suppose if they didn't want to be seen . . .'

'*Précisément.*'

'The back door is also left open most of the time, though Hoppy prefers to go in and out at the front.'

Lenore said, 'The dog would have brought down the house with his barking if someone had been prowling around. He'd have smelled a stranger.'

'He did not bark when I came into the room,' Poirot pointed out.

'That's because you came in with Lenore,' said Annabel. 'He saw that you were a welcome guest.'

Lenore Lavington raised her eyebrows a little at that. 'Let us proceed,' she said. 'Do you have more questions, M. Poirot, or are you satisfied?'

'Alas, I am not yet satisfied,' Poirot told her. 'Is there a typewriter in the house?'

'A typewriter? Yes. Why do you ask?'

'May I use it before I leave?'

'If you wish.'

'Thank you, madame. Now, I should like to ask you about Vincent Lobb. He was an acquaintance of your grandfather's.'

'We know who he was,' said Lenore. 'He and Grandfather knew each other a long time ago. They were great friends, until something happened to turn them into enemies.'

'Before you ask, we don't know what happened,' said Annabel. 'Grandy never told us.'

'Perhaps you know that not long before he died, Monsieur Pandy wrote a letter to Monsieur Lobb in which he expressed a wish to end the *froideur* that existed between them?'

The sisters exchanged a look. Then Lenore said, 'No. We did not know. Who told you that?'

'Your grandfather's lawyer, Monsieur Peter Vout.'

'I see.'

'It makes me happy to think that Grandy did that.' Annabel sighed. 'And I'm not surprised to hear it. He was terribly kind and forgiving.'

'Annabel, you do say the most puzzling things,' said her sister.

'Do I, Lenore?'

'Yes, you do. Grandfather, forgiving? Whatever Vincent Lobb did, it was fifty years ago. Grandfather held a grudge for fifty years. I'm not saying he was wrong or cruel to do so—most people hold grudges, though not you, Annabel.'

'You do, Lenore.'

'Yes, I do,' her sister agreed. 'And *you* are the one with the forgiving nature. Not Grandfather.'

'No, I'm not!' Annabel seemed distressed by the suggestion. 'Who am I to forgive anybody? I'm . . .' She blinked away tears. Then she said, 'It's true, I forgave Grandy for ignoring Hoppy, and Skittle before him, and for preferring Lenore to me. I forgave him because he forgave me! He found me to be a dreadful disappointment, but he did his best not to show it. I knew how he felt about me, but I appreciated his daily efforts to hide it.'

'My sister is upset,' Lenore Lavington told Poirot. There was a small, neat smile on her face. 'She tends to exaggerate. I wonder where Ivy has got to? I do hope she's not eating the food intended for you, M. Poirot.'

'Why did your grandfather find you disappointing?' Poirot asked Annabel.

'I think it was because I had a superior older sister,' she said.

'Oh, really, Annabel!'

'No, Lenore, it's true. You *are* superior to me. I think so, and Grandy thought so too. Lenore was always his favourite, M. Poirot, and rightly so. She's so determined and efficient and strong, just like Grandy was. And she married and gave him great-grandchildren. Continued the family line. Whereas I seemed to want spend all my time with my dogs, and, worst of all, I'm a spinster with no children.'

'Annabel received many proposals of marriage,' Lenore told Poirot. 'She wasn't short of offers.'

'Grandy thought I hid away with animals because I couldn't hold my own with people. Maybe he was right. I *do* think animals are less bothersome than people, and they're certainly more loyal. They love one in spite of one's flaws. Oh—I'm not complaining about Grandy or anybody else. I should hate you to think that! He did his best, and I let him down so badly, I let—' She stopped with a sharp intake of breath. 'Here comes Ivy,' she said. It was a rather obvious attempt to change the subject.

'What do you mean, mademoiselle?' Poirot asked, wondering why she suddenly looked so frightened—as if the ghost of Barnabas Pandy himself had walked into the room.

The door opened and Ivy Lavington entered. She saw her aunt's face and looked alarmed. 'What has happened?' she asked.

'Nothing,' said Lenore Lavington. Considering that Ivy had not yet heard Poirot's explanation of why he was at Combingham Hall, this was an inadequate answer in every respect.

'How did you let your grandfather down?' Poirot asked Annabel Treadway again.

'I've told you already,' she said in a voice that sounded choked. 'He would have liked for me to marry and have children.'

There was something that she was determined not to say, thought Poirot. He decided not to pursue the matter now. There would be an opportunity to ask her later, he hoped. Perhaps when her sister and niece were not present, she would speak more freely.

He turned to Lenore Lavington. 'If it would not be too upsetting for you, madame, would you show me the bathroom in which your grandfather drowned?'

'That's rather morbid, isn't it?' said Ivy.

Her mother ignored her. 'Yes, of course,' she said to Poirot. 'If you think it's necessary.'

Annabel stood to follow them, but Lenore said, 'No.'

Annabel accepted the command without question, and sat down again.

'Why don't you tell Ivy what's happened?' Lenore suggested to her. 'Come with me, M. Poirot.'

CHAPTER 15

The Scene of the Possible Crime

The journey to the bathroom in which Barnabas Pandy had died was a relatively long one. Poirot had been inside many large country houses, but none with corridors as seemingly endless as those of Combingham Hall. When he saw that Lenore Lavington had no intention of conversing as they walked, he took the opportunity to go over in his mind the events that had taken place in the sitting room downstairs.

It had struck Poirot immediately, upon encountering Annabel Treadway a second time, that her air of unhappiness was less pronounced today. It was not that she seemed any happier, or happy at all—she did not, in spite of the presence of the dog whom she plainly loved. No, it was more that . . .

Poirot shook his head. He could not have said what it was, and that unnerved him. His thoughts moved on to Lenore Lavington. He decided that she was one of those rare people to whom one might speak for hours and still come away knowing nothing about their character. The only thing he felt he had learned about her was that she liked to make sure events unfolded in a certain way. There was an air about her of being always on duty. Poirot wondered if she was afraid of whatever it was that her sister had stopped herself from saying.

'Ah!' he exclaimed, as Lenore led him past another sequence of doors.

She stopped. 'Did you say something?' she asked him with a polite smile.

'*Non. Pardon*, madame.'

He had not intended to make a sound, but was relieved to have worked out what it was about Annabel Treadway that had struck him: although an atmosphere of melancholy still lingered around her, she had determinedly pushed her own emotions to one side in order to think only about her sister's.

'Yes, that is it,' thought Poirot to himself with satisfaction. Both of the sisters had been so acutely aware of the other, so attuned to every word, expression or gesture coming from the other . . . Why? he asked himself. It was as if Lenore had placed Annabel—and Annabel, in turn, had placed Lenore—under a form of secret surveillance. Each sister had of course known that the other was in the room, listening to whatever she said, but both had pretended to listen in an ordinary, casual way, when in fact each one had been obsessively focused on the other.

'They share a secret,' Poirot thought. 'The two sisters share a secret, and each is afraid that the other will give it away to Hercule Poirot, a stranger, who has come here to poke his nose into their private affairs!'

'M. Poirot?'

Distracted by his theorizing, he had failed to notice that Lenore Lavington had stopped walking. 'This is the bathroom in which the tragedy occurred. Please, do go in.'

'Thank you, madame.'

As they entered, the floorboards creaked, making a strained noise that sounded like someone in great pain trying not to attract attention, thought Poirot wistfully. The room was sparsely furnished: only a bathtub in the middle of the room, one chair, a shelf with a crumbling edge, and in one corner a low squat chest of drawers with elaborate carvings around the edges of each drawer. Poirot had previously heard such pieces described as 'tallboys', but that name wouldn't have suited this one, which was more of a 'shortboy'. The wood ought to have been shiny, but instead had the dull look of furniture that nobody had polished for years.

On the shelf stood one solitary item: a small bottle of purple glass. 'What is that?' Poirot asked.

'In the bottle? It's oil of olives,' said Lenore Lavington.

'In the bathroom, not the kitchen?'

'Grandfather . . .' She stopped. More quietly, she started again, 'Grandfather never bathed without oil of olives.'

'In his bathwater?'

'Yes. It was good for his skin, he said, and he liked the smell—goodness knows why.' She turned away and walked over to the window. 'I'm sorry, M. Poirot. It's surprising: I find it easy to discuss his death, but that little bottle . . .'

'*Je comprends*. It is harder to talk about the bottle because it was something he enjoyed while alive. That is the thought that makes you sad.'

'Yes, it is. I was fond of Grandfather.' She said it as though this was something that might require explanation, not a fact to be taken for granted.

'You are quite sure, madame, that you heard Monsieur Pandy speak—that you heard him, alive, and that it could only have been him? And from that moment until you saw that he had drowned in his bathwater, you were together with your sister and your daughter? Not one of you left the company of the other two, even for a few moments?'

'I am quite, quite sure,' said Lenore Lavington. 'Annabel, Ivy and I were chatting away and he called out to us that we were disturbing him. He liked the house to be quiet.'

'Mademoiselle Ivy's bedroom is near this room?'

'Yes, just across the corridor and a little to the right. We had closed the door, but it makes no difference in this house. He would have heard our conversation clearly.'

'Thank you, madame.'

'I would be grateful if you could tread carefully when you speak to Kingsbury,' she said. 'He has been rather withdrawn since Grandfather died. I hope you won't need to bother him for too long.'

'I shall make it as brief as possible,' Poirot promised.

'Nobody killed Grandfather, but if anybody had, that person could never have been Kingsbury. For one thing, his clothes would have been wet, and they weren't. Annabel, Ivy and I all heard him cry out when he found . . . when he saw what had happened and, seconds later, we were all in here together. Kingsbury's clothes were completely dry.'

'You did not try to pull your grandfather out of the water?'

'No. It was apparent that it was far too late to save him.'

'Then your sister's garments were also dry?'

Lenore seemed angered by the question. '*All* of our clothing was dry. Including Annabel's. She was wearing a blue dress with white and yellow flowers on it. Long sleeves. She stood right beside me, here. I would have noticed at once if she had water dripping from her sleeves! I am an observant person.'

'I do not doubt it,' said Poirot.

'Surely you do not take this accusation against my sister seriously, M. Poirot? The same letter was sent to four people. What if it had been sent to a hundred people? Would you consider each one a possible culprit, even if the police had no suspicions and the death had already been judged by a coroner's court to be an accident?'

Poirot started to answer, but Lenore Lavington had not yet finished. 'Besides, the idea of Annabel murdering anybody is quite ludicrous,' she said. 'My sister has the wrong constitution for any sort of unlawful action. If she broke even a minor law it would torment her for ever. She would never risk a murder. She wouldn't even risk getting a different breed of dog.'

Ivy Lavington walked into the room. 'Lots of people stick with one breed,' she said. 'Hopscotch is an Airedale and so was Skittle, the one before him,' she explained to Poirot.

'Have you been listening outside the door?' asked her mother.

'No,' said Ivy. 'Have you been saying things you don't want me to overhear?'

'My sister is like a second mother to Ivy and my son Timothy, M. Poirot. They both tend to leap to her defence, having first imagined I am attacking her when I'm not.'

'Oh, Mummy, stop feeling sorry for yourself!' said Ivy with good-humoured impatience. 'It's Aunt Annabel who has been accused of murder, not you. She absolutely couldn't have done it, M. Poirot.'

Poirot decided he liked Ivy Lavington. She had a youthful energy about her, and she struck him as the only normal member of the household—though of course he had yet to meet Kingsbury. 'Was Hopscotch with the three of you in your bedroom, Mademoiselle Ivy, while your Grandfather took his bath?'

'Of course he was,' Lenore Lavington answered the question on her daughter's behalf. 'Wherever Annabel goes, the dog follows. He can go off on his own, but she isn't allowed to. The day she travelled to London to see you, he howled for nearly an hour after she left. It was horribly inconvenient.'

'Madame, may I tell you the names of the other three people who received letters accusing them of Monsieur Pandy's murder?'

'Very well.'

'John McCrodden. Hugo Dockerill. Sylvia Rule. Do you know any of these names?'

'Hugo Dockerill is Timothy's housemaster at school. I have never heard the other two names apart from when you spoke of Mr McCrodden earlier.'

'Don't be silly, Mummy.' Ivy laughed. 'Of course you know who Sylvia Rule is.'

'That's not true.' Lenore Lavington looked confused. 'Do *you* know who she is?' she asked Ivy. 'Who is she?' It was as if her daughter knowing something she did not was a prospect she found intolerable.

'She's the mother of Freddie Rule. He's in Timmy's house at school. He started at Turville about six months ago. He was horribly bullied at his last school.'

Poirot watched with interest as the colour drained from Lenore Lavington's face. 'F-Freddie?' she stammered. 'Strange, lonely Freddie? His family name is *Rule*?'

'Yes. And his mother is Sylvia. You *must* have known that! Why do you look so queer?'

'Fred-die,' her mother said again, more slowly, her eyes glazed and remote. By merely uttering the name, she managed to imbue it with a peculiar sort of horror.

'Why do you object so strongly to poor Freddie, Mummy? What harm has he ever done to you?'

Ivy's robust question ruptured the tense atmosphere.

'None,' Lenore Lavington answered crisply. She seemed restored to her old self. 'I didn't know his family name, that's all. I'm surprised you do.'

'I spoke to him once when we went to visit Timmy at school. I noticed a boy on his own looking rather glum, so I went over to speak to him. We had a long and quite interesting chat. He introduced himself as Freddie Rule. At some point he must have mentioned his mother, Sylvia, because I know that's her name.'

'That awful hermit boy is no friend of Timothy's,' Lenore Lavington told Poirot. 'I've advised Timothy to avoid him, in fact. I think he's peculiar in the head—the sort of boy who might do anything.'

'Mummy!' Ivy laughed. 'Did you really? Have you lost your wits? Freddie's the most harmless boy in the world.'

Poirot said, 'On the day your grandfather died, the two of you and Mademoiselle Annabel were supposed to be attending the Christmas Fair at your son's school. That is correct, is it not?'

'Yes,' said Lenore.

'But you did not go to the fair, in the end.'

'No.'

'Why not?'

'I can't remember.'

Poirot turned to Ivy. 'Do you recall the reason, mademoiselle?'

'Perhaps Mummy wanted to avoid Freddie Rule, and that's why she changed her mind about going.'

'Don't be absurd, Ivy,' said Lenore.

'It's only that you looked so ghastly when I mentioned his name, Mummy. Why? I know you're not going to tell me, but I should very much like to know.'

So, too, would Hercule Poirot have liked to know.

CHAPTER 16

The Opportunity Man

Kingsbury's small cottage was a short walk from the main house. Immediately outside it was a compact kitchen garden with borders of lavender, rosemary and hyssop.

Poirot approached the front door, eager to meet 'The Opportunity Man', as he had begun to think of Kingsbury. If the ladies of Combingham Hall were telling the truth, then Kingsbury was the only person who could have murdered Barnabas Pandy. Could it be as simple as that? Poirot wondered. Might he extract a confession from the manservant and solve the mystery today?

He knocked on the door, and soon afterwards heard shuffling footsteps behind it. It opened. A skeletally thin man with creased, papery skin and eyes of a peculiar yellow-tinged green stood in the doorway. He looked at least seventy years old. Poirot suspected that he believed himself to be smartly dressed, though the bottoms of his trousers were covered in dust. What little hair he had hung in isolated strands of white, as if remnants of a wig he had once worn had adhered to his scalp.

Poirot introduced himself to the old man and explained his presence at Combingham Hall, starting with his visit from Annabel Treadway. Kingsbury squinted and bent his head forward, as if struggling to see and hear him. It was only when Poirot referred to his conversation with Lenore Lavington and mentioned that she had sent him to the cottage that the servant's manner changed. His eyes cleared and his back straightened. He invited Poirot inside.

Once uncomfortably seated on a hard chair in a room that clearly served as both sitting room and kitchen, Poirot asked Kingsbury if he thought it possible that Barnabas Pandy had been murdered.

The old man shook his head—a movement that rearranged the white strands on his scalp. 'Couldn't have been,' he said. 'The girls were all in Miss Ivy's room having a to-do, causing a commotion, and the only other person around was me.'

'And you, naturally, had no reason to want Monsieur Pandy dead?'

'Not *him*,' said Kingsbury, with a strong emphasis on the last word.

'There is, then, somebody else that you wish to kill?'

'Not to kill. But I'll not lie to you, Mr Porrott: I've thought to myself many times since Mr Pandy's been gone, it'd be a mercy if the Lord were to take me too.'

'He was a good friend as well as your employer, *n'est-ce pas?*'

'Best friend a man could have. He was a fine fellow. I don't do much of anything, now he's gone. Doesn't feel like there's a point to doing anything. I do my work, of course,' he added hurriedly. 'But I never go up to the Hall when I'm not needed, not now he's gone.'

Watching the fluttery, bird-like movements of Kingsbury's hands as he spoke, Poirot doubted he would have the strength to drown anybody. How had he helped an even older man into his bath? Perhaps Pandy, though older, had been physically stronger and able to get in and out of the tub without assistance.

Kingsbury leaned towards Poirot and said confidingly, 'Mr Porrott, I can promise you that Mr Pandy wasn't murdered. If that's the only reason you've come to Combingham Hall . . . well, you could have saved yourself the bother.'

'I hope that you are right. All the same, if you will permit me to ask you a few questions . . . ?'

'Ask if you want, but there's no more I can tell you than what I've just said. There's nothing more to tell.'

'Where were you while Monsieur Pandy took his bath and the ladies of the house were in Mademoiselle Ivy's bedroom causing the commotion?'

'I was here, unpacking my suitcase after having been away for a short spell. I drew Mr Pandy's bath for him, and put in the oil of olives like I always did, and then knowing he liked to soak in the tub for a good forty, forty-five minutes, I thought to myself, "I know what I'll do: I'll unpack that case." So that's what I did. Then I went back over to the Hall, thinking Mr Pandy would be wanting to get dried and dressed round about then. That's when I found him.' The old man's chin trembled at the memory. 'He was lying under the water. Dead. It was a terrible sight, Mr Porrott. His eyes and mouth were open. I'll not forget that in a hurry.'

'I am told that the front door to the Hall is usually left ajar,' said Poirot.

'Oh, yes. Dog won't stand for it being shut, not before nine o'clock at night, which is his bedtime, and Miss Annabel's. He doesn't mind it being shut then.'

'Could a stranger have entered the house and drowned Monsieur Pandy while the ladies were in Ivy Lavington's room and you were here unpacking your suitcase?'

Kingsbury shook his head.

'Why not?' asked Poirot.

'Dog,' said the old man. 'He'd have gone wild. I'd have heard him from over here. A stranger, creeping around the Hall? They wouldn't get out alive, not if Hopscotch had anything to do with it.'

'I have met Hopscotch,' Poirot told him. 'He seemed to me to be an affectionate creature.'

'Oh, yes, if you're a friend to the family, or an invited guest . . . but he's quick to take fright, and he'd know something was wrong if he got wind of an intruder prowling around.'

'I understand that you have been left a significant sum of money in the will of Monsieur Pandy?'

'I was left it, but I'll not be spending it—not so much as a farthing of it will I spend. It can go to one of that Dr Barnardo's homes for poor children. Mrs Lavington's said she'll arrange it all for me. What would I do with it? Money can't bring Mr Pandy back, and if he weren't gone, I'd not have had it as a worry. And now I won't again, as I'll be giving it all away.' Kingsbury spoke with apparent sincerity and conviction, but Poirot had encountered many talented liars in the past. It would be prudent, he decided, to check in due course that the sum intended for Dr Barnardo's had ended up there and not gone astray *en route*.

'*Alors*, you found a most distressing scene when you returned to the bathroom. When you cried out in shock and the three ladies soon afterwards appeared in the bath-room, were their clothes wet or dry?'

'Dry. Why would they be wet? It wasn't any of them that was in the tub, was it?'

'You are certain you would have noticed if, for example, somebody's sleeves or dress had been wet?'

The old man shook his head. 'A flock of geese could have wandered in and I'd not have noticed—not with Mr Pandy staring up at me from under the water.'

'Then . . .' Poirot sighed quietly. 'Never mind. There is a more important question I must ask you. The loud commo-tion that the three ladies were making while Mr Pandy bathed—'

'It was hard on the ears, I don't mind telling you,' said Kingsbury. 'Mrs Lavington and Miss Ivy were screaming at each other, and Miss Annabel was screaming at them to stop, and crying her heart out. And then Mrs Lavington shouted at her that she wasn't Miss Ivy's mother and she'd do well to remember that. It was a terrible to-do. Mr Pandy didn't like it and I can't say as I blame him. He shouted at them to be quiet.'

'You were still in the main house when you heard this?' asked Poirot.

'No, I was outside the cottage, just about to let myself in. The bathroom window was open—he always had it open. Liked his bathwater hot, he did, and the air in the room cold. Said the two balanced each other out. Oh, I heard him loud and clear.'

'After his plea for peace and quiet, were you able to hear if the argument ended?'

'I'm afraid not. Miss Ivy's bedroom is at the front of the house. But I don't think it had finished. No, I'm sure it hadn't. Or else it stopped and then started again, 'cause it was still going when I returned to the main house. Mr Pandy's death was what stopped it. They all saw him under the water and that was that.'

'If the dog was in a room full of people screaming at one another, and if he saw his mistress was upset, is it not possible that Hopscotch might, just this once, have failed to notice that a stranger had entered the house?' Poirot asked. 'The door to Ivy Lavington's bedroom was closed, according to Mrs Lavington. Might the dog not have failed to smell or hear the intruder, preoccupied as he must have been by his mistress's unhappy state?'

Kingsbury considered it. Finally he said, 'I'll admit, I'd not considered that until now. You're right, Mr Porrott. With Miss Ivy's door being closed, he *might* not have noticed if there was a stranger in the house. He would certainly have been worried by Miss Annabel's distress, and he wouldn't have left her side with her in that state. I'd still say there's a good chance he would hear a stranger on the prowl, but I'd not swear to it.'

They sat in silence, questions hanging in the air. Instead of feeling vindicated, Poirot felt defeated. The possibilities were once again endless. Barnabas Pandy might not have been murdered at all, or he might have been killed by Kingsbury, or by anybody who could have crept into the estate's grounds and illicitly entered Combingham Hall that day: Sylvia Rule, Hugo Dockerill, Jane Dockerill, Freddie Rule, John McCrodden . . . anybody.

What this puzzle lacked, thought Poirot despairingly, was parameters. There was an abundance of suspects for something that stood every chance of not being a crime. And if Rowland McCrodden had persuaded Stanley Donaldson to provide him with a false alibi for 7 December, or if Ivy and Lenore Lavington and Annabel Treadway were lying about all being together in Ivy's room, why, then the number of potential suspects grew even larger.

'Motive,' Poirot murmured. 'It is *motive* that will lead me to the answer, when too many people had the opportunity.'

'What's that you say?' Kingsbury roused himself from his reverie—and Poirot was ready to start again.

'What can you tell me about Vincent Lobb?' he asked.

'Mr Pandy wouldn't have nothing to do with him. Not for fifty years he wouldn't. Mr Lobb let him down badly.'

'How so?'

'I'm not able to tell you that, I'm afraid. Mr Pandy never told me. Didn't like to talk about the particulars, though he talked a lot about the treachery of it. "You'd never betray me, would you, Kingsbury?" he'd say, and I'd tell him I never would. I wouldn't have, and I never did,' the old man concluded proudly.

'What was the subject of the argument between Annabel Treadway and Ivy and Lenore Lavington?' Poirot asked.

'Oh, Miss Annabel wasn't part of the row. That was Mrs Lavington and Miss Ivy. Miss Annabel was trying to stop it.'

'What was the cause of the problem? Were you able to hear?'

'I'm not one to eavesdrop, if that's what you're suggesting. Anyone who wasn't deaf would have heard it. Still, I did my best not to listen. And I'm not sure Mrs Lavington would want me telling you what was said between her and her daughter.'

'But it was Mrs Lavington who told me that you were the person I must speak to! And you have told me a little already, have you not?'

'Not the particulars, I haven't,' said Kingsbury. 'Mrs Lavington could have told you herself if she'd wanted you to know.'

'My friend, I would be deeply grateful if you could help me in this matter. Now that we agree that the dog might not have heard a stranger enter the house, the possibility that Barnabas Pandy was murdered . . . well, let us say that it cannot be ruled out. If he was murdered, we must not let his murderer escape justice.'

'Now there I agree,' said Kingsbury grimly. 'Wring his neck with my bare hands, I would.'

'Please do not do that. Instead, help me by telling me about this argument you could not help hearing.'

'But if a stranger killed Mr Pandy, then a little family to-do can't be important to the solving of it,' said Kingsbury.

'You must trust me,' Poirot told him. 'I have solved many cases of murder.'

'I haven't,' Kingsbury interjected, his tone gloomy. 'I've never solved even one.'

'One never knows what is of vital importance, or where the connections lie, until the solution is apparent. The most inconsequential-seeming detail can be the one that matters most.'

'Well, if you think it might help, though I can't see how it could . . . It was something that Mrs Lavington had said to Miss Ivy that Miss Ivy had taken badly. And then she'd accused Mrs Lavington of intending it badly, if you follow me? She thought she'd said it purposefully to wound her, but Mrs Lavington swore she'd done no such thing and that Miss Ivy was making too much of it. Mind you, there was probably more to it than that.'

'Why do you say that?'

'Nothing had been right at the house since that dinner a few days earlier.'

'Which dinner?'

'You're going to be disappointed, Mr Porrott, because I

didn't overhear anything at all on that occasion, but that's when the trouble started. I'd left them all at the table and gone to do my last few jobs around the Hall. I was on my way to say goodnight to the family before leaving for the night, but I never got as far as the dining hall before Miss Ivy came running at me. Ran past like a mad thing she did, sobbing. Then Miss Annabel did the same, and then Mrs Lavington marched past very quickly with a face like . . . well, I don't know how to describe it, but it shocked me. There was a look in her eyes like I'd not seen before. I tried to speak to her but she didn't see or hear me, Mr Porrott. It was the strangest thing. I thought something frightful must have happened.'

'This was only a few days before Barnabas Pandy died, you say?'

'That's right. I don't remember how many, I'm sorry to say, but it might have been three or four days. Five at the most.'

'What did you do, when you suspected something dreadful had happened?'

'I hurried to the dining table, hoping to find Mr Pandy, hardly daring to wonder what state I might find him in. He was seated at the head of the table where he always sat, and . . .' Kingsbury stopped. 'Mr Porrott, don't think I didn't hear all that you said about how much the small details matter, but there's certain things I know Mr Pandy wouldn't have wanted anyone to hear about.'

'Would he have wanted his murderer to go unpunished?' said Poirot.

The old man shook his head. 'I hope I'm not doing wrong by telling you, or else Mr Pandy might give me a good hiding when we next meet in a better place.' He blinked a few times, then said, 'There's no need for you to pass on what I'm about to tell you to anybody else, mind.'

'If it has no bearing on any criminal matter, it will go no further. You have my promise.'

'Like I said: I found Mr Pandy sitting alone at the dining table, but that's not all he was doing.' Lowering his voice, Kingsbury said, 'He was *crying*, Mr Porrott. Crying! I'd not seen him do that before, not in all the years I'd known him. It was just the one tear, but I saw it clearly by the light of the candles on the table. Mr Pandy noticed me coming towards him and shook his head. He didn't want me any closer, not with him as he was, so I came back here, to the cottage. And—this is where you'll not be pleased with me, Mr Porrott—I never got to find out what had made him shed that tear and sent everyone else running from the table. I knew Mr Pandy wouldn't want to talk about it, so I never asked. It wasn't my place to ask.'

On his return to Combingham Hall, Poirot was met by Lenore Lavington, Annabel Treadway and Hopscotch the dog, who had an orange rubber ball in his mouth. 'I hope Kingsbury was helpful?' said Lenore.

'He confirmed much of what you had both already told me,' said Poirot matter-of-factly, not wishing to reveal how much he had learned in the servant's cottage. He now had more questions to ask of both sisters, but he would need to think of a clever way to do it—one that did not endanger the old man.

Did that mean, he asked himself, that he believed one of these two women standing before him to be a murderer? If one of them had killed Pandy then the other, as well as Ivy Lavington, must be lying about all being in Ivy's room together. Instinctively, Poirot had trusted Ivy. Did that mean that he distrusted Lenore Lavington and Annabel Treadway, or was he merely ambiguous about both of them? To avoid these difficult questions, he asked an easier one.

'If I might, before I leave, use your typewriter, madame?'

Lenore Lavington nodded, from which Poirot gathered that she was about to acquiesce. Then she said, 'M. Poirot, while you were with Kingsbury, Annabel and I discussed this ludicrous and rather sordid situation in which we find ourselves—and in which you are also involved—and we both feel it necessary to put a stop to it. No one has been murdered, and no one believes anybody has been murdered. The story is pure invention, and we don't even know who invented it, or what exactly their story is, though we may surmise that they were motivated by malice.'

'All of this is true, madame, but the letter I wish to type before I leave is a different thing altogether. It is . . . a personal matter.'

'Is it? Or do you want to check if our typewriter here is the same one used to type the four letters?'

Poirot gave a little bow and smiled his most charming smile. 'You are shrewd indeed, madame. I apologize a

166

thousand times for my little trick. However, if you would be so generous as to—'

'I would be generous if I could convince myself it was the right thing to do.'.

'Lenore's right, M. Poirot,' said Annabel. There was a pleading tone to her voice. 'I should never have come to you. I should have gone straight to the police, who could have assured me that they suspect me of having committed no crime, because, as is quite clear now, there was no crime committed.'

Her sister said, 'We understand that it must be immensely frustrating for you, M. Poirot, to have your name used in the way that it was by a devious person intent on stirring up trouble for *you* as much as for anybody else . . . but the thing to do, when something like this happens, is to ignore it and get on with one's life. Don't you agree?'

'I cannot ignore it, madame, until I understand why these letters were sent.'

'Then the letter-writer has won,' said Lenore Lavington. 'Against you, he has won. Well, I'm certainly not going to let him defeat me. Which is why, with regret, I'm afraid I must now ask you to leave.'

'But madame . . .'

'I'm sorry, M. Poirot. I have made my decision.'

Nothing Poirot said could persuade her to change her mind, and his attempts to do so seemed to cause almost physical pain to Annabel Treadway. Thirty minutes later, he left Combingham Hall without having caught so much as a glimpse of its typewriter.

CHAPTER 17

Poirot's Trick

Whenever possible, Rowland McCrodden replied in the negative to the social invitations he received. Once in a while, however, he felt duty-bound to attend events that he knew he would not enjoy, and the Law Society dinner was one such occasion. The din alone was nearly enough to make him turn on his heel and leave: all those open mouths filling the air around him with pointless chirping. Everybody seemed to be talking and no one listening, as was always the way at such gatherings. McCrodden found them draining in the extreme.

The dinner was at the Bloxham Hotel, an elegant establishment, famous for its afternoon teas. McCrodden had decided not to do what he normally did, which was to move from one part of the excessively full room to another, trying to avoid being engaged in dialogue. Tonight, he had resolved to submit rather than resist. He would stand still and allow himself to be endlessly accosted. At least that would involve less effort on his part.

'Well, well, well, if it isn't old Rowly Rope!' said a booming voice.

McCrodden turned and found himself face-to-face with a man whose name he was supposed to know but stood no chance of remembering. He had certainly never asked this man to call him Rowly—or Rowland, for that matter.

'Haven't you got a drink, old chap? You don't want to be slow off the mark when it comes to the drink—not in this company! It'll be all gone before you know it!'

From the loose-mouthed way the man spoke, McCrodden had the sense that vast quantities of liquor had already gone down his throat and were at that moment sloshing around inside his barrel-shaped form.

'Tell me, old boy, how's the lovely Mrs Rope? Haven't seen her at one of these shindigs for a long time. Seem to remember she was something of a stunner!'

McCrodden, whose wife had died many years ago, bristled. 'You are mistaking me for someone else.' At that moment, he caught sight of Peter Vout approximately eight chandeliers away, on the opposite side of the large ballroom. 'Would you please excuse me?' he said to the barrel, who was shaking his head as if preparing to mount another challenge. McCrodden walked purposefully away from him. He would not, after all, stand still—not if that meant spending his evening with the most objectionable man in the room.

He had told Poirot that he would not deceive Peter Vout, but now, with Vout within easy reach, he found himself wondering: was Poirot right? Would Vout fall for such an obvious trick? McCrodden knew that he himself could not be similarly fooled . . . or perhaps he only thought that because he knew his own aim. It is natural to imagine that one's intention is obvious when one knows it oneself. Peter Vout was unaware that Rowland McCrodden and Hercule Poirot were acquainted. Furthermore, the redness of Vout's face and the two empty champagne glasses in his hand suggested he might be less vigilant than usual.

McCrodden had stopped a short distance from where Vout was standing. He could not deny that he was tempted. He was an intellectually curious man, and wanted to see if he could win. The only thing that concerned him was the idea that to do so would be to capitulate to Poirot's will. And then Fate seemed to decide the matter, as Peter Vout caught sight of McCrodden lurking nearby.

'Rowland McCrodden!' Vout strode towards him. 'What are you doing without a drink? Waiter!' he called out. 'Champagne for this gentleman, please! And for me, if you'd be so kind.'

'None for me, thank you,' McCrodden told the young waiter. 'I'll take some water instead.'

'Water? Well, that's rather dull!'

'Champagne should be reserved for celebrations,' said McCrodden. 'I'm hardly in a celebratory mood this evening.' He said this pointedly, to suggest that there was a story to be told—one that he was only too ready to tell. So far, nothing he had said had been an outright lie. The next part would be difficult, however.

'Oh, dear! Well, that's bad luck!' Vout commiserated. 'I'm sorry to hear that. Yes, indeed. Waiter, bring two glasses of champagne anyway, if you'd be so good. You never know, I might succeed in lifting my friend's spirits, and if I don't, well . . . the extra glass won't go begging. Haha!' He slapped the waiter on the back, and the young man scurried away.

'Now, then, McCrodden, you'd better tell me how you fetched up in this disconsolate state. Whatever the problem, I'm sure it's not as bad as you think it is. Things generally aren't, you know.'

Rowland McCrodden made an effort to imagine what fortuitous and alien life experiences, so vastly divergent from his own, might induce a person to utter those words and believe them to be true.

'It is not so much a problem as an irritant,' he said. 'There's nothing to be done about it—or rather, I've already done the thing that needed doing; I've told the impertinent fellow to buzz off, except I'm afraid I didn't put it quite so politely. Still, some things leave a decidedly unpleasant taste in the mouth—one that cannot be washed away with champagne!'

Rowland McCrodden had done no acting since his school days. He had a memory of loathing it and being terrible at it. This was only going to work if he drew upon his true feelings—indignation and revulsion—to bolster the false words he was about to utter. He thought about his son being accused of murder by a coward who had not dared to sign his own name, and also about John's conviction that he was hated by his father, when the opposite was true.

He said to Vout: 'A detective chap came to see me today. He bombarded me with questions about private matters involving one of my most valuable clients—a man whose affairs I have handled for years. He's an old friend, really, as much as anything else. And this intrusive, grubby little man wasn't even an officer of the law! He was some sort of sleuth-for-hire, with no good reason to offer as to why I should supply him with answers to a series of really *most* intrusive questions. I sent him on his way, as I say, but . . . one wonders how such people sleep at night, undisturbed by pangs of conscience.'

Vout looked interested.

McCrodden went on, 'My client recently, and through no fault of his own, found himself in a sensitive situation that he wouldn't wish anybody to find out about. There was a young lady involved—a charming girl—and an estate to be disposed of, and a family with particular . . . sensitivities. In fact, it's a perplexing business all round and one that I should very much like to discuss with somebody impartial and unconnected to my client, but I was hardly about to chew over the details with *that* unsavoury individual!'

Rowland McCrodden pretended to be struck by a sudden thought. 'I wonder if I might consult you about it, Vout? Not tonight, of course, but perhaps if you have a spare hour next week? I don't see any harm in telling you all about it if I don't tell you the name of the chap in question.'

An expression of delight appeared on Vout's face. 'Of course! I would be only too happy to help.'

'Thank you. That's generous of you. And I'm sorry to burden you with my woes.'

'I'm very glad you did, old fellow. It's quite remarkable— but then, coincidences do happen, don't they? I recently had a similar experience to the one you've just described.'

'You did?'

'Yes. A detective—a rather well-known one, whose name in the interests of discretion I had better not mention—came to see me and asked if a longstanding client and old friend of mine might have been *murdered*. He had not, of course. He drow—Ahem!' Vout cleared his throat to cover his mistake. 'His death was a tragic accident. There was nothing deliberate or criminal about it, and nobody—no police officer and no court in the land—thought there was, apart from this detective. I told him there was no question of it being a murder, absolutely no question. This is a respectable family we're talking about. The idea is laughable! But my visitor continued to badger me. He wished to know if there was anything else I could tell him. I told him one more thing, in the spirit of helpfulness.'

'That was very decent of you and more than he deserved,' said Rowland McCrodden.

'Hmmph? Well, I didn't see that it would do any harm. The old man—my late friend and client—seemed to have an inkling that he was not long for this world. Having always tended towards a rather fiery and combative attitude, he was suddenly overcome by a desire to make peace with a chap who had been his enemy for many years. I didn't see that it would do any harm to tell the detective that much, and so I did. Was it enough for him? No! He asked the same question again: could I give him more information, about the family, their relationships? I *could* have told him considerably more, but why on earth should I share a story that I don't entirely understand myself and that has no bearing on anything now that my client's dead? It would cause great unhappiness to certain members of his family if they were to learn the truth, and how do I know that this chap won't spread it around?'

'You absolutely do not,' said Rowland McCrodden. 'You did the right thing in saying nothing. And, of course, you mustn't feel obliged to tell me any more than you have. I wouldn't want you think that because I wish to consult you about *my* client's affairs, I expect you to reciprocate in any way. After all, *your* client is deceased, and it sounds as if there is no immediate problem to be resolved, so perhaps there is no need for you to understand whatever it is that remains unclear.'

Vout frowned. 'I should like to understand, all the same. And I never have. But you're right: there is nothing to be resolved, because the story is one of something that *didn't* happen, not something that did. If I had been inclined to confide in this detective fellow, which I was not, I'd have had to tell him of events that had failed to transpire—and what would be the point of that?'

The waiter reappeared with two glasses of champagne and one of water. McCrodden took the latter, and Vout whipped the other two off the tray in a proprietorial manner. He did not raise again the question of whether McCrodden might, after all, want some champagne.

'You've aroused my curiosity,' said McCrodden, as Vout glugged down the contents of the two glasses in quick succession. 'Unlike this ill-mannered detective, I would never ask anybody to be indiscreet . . .'

'I can't see that it would do any harm to tell you, if I keep the names out of it,' said Vout. 'Would you like to hear the story?'

Rowland McCrodden indicated that he would, without displaying anything as vulgar as enthusiasm. Was it possible that this evening might have to be remembered as the only Law Society dinner he had ever enjoyed?

'The family is not one you're likely to encounter,' said Peter Vout. 'They don't live in London. And in any case, you're not an unknown quantity in the way the detective chap was. I have no doubt I can rely on you not to spread any of this about.'

'Of course.'

'Well, then: the event that did not occur was the changing of a will.'

'I see.'

'My client was an elderly gentleman who had always planned for his two granddaughters to inherit precisely equal amounts of his considerable fortune. He had no living children, you see, and was very much a father figure to his granddaughters, who had lost their parents at a young age.'

'Tragic,' Rowland McCrodden said dutifully.

'About a week before he died, my client invited me to his home to discuss what he described as "a sensitive matter". For the first time in our long acquaintance, he was particularly—one might say—cagey. He lowered his voice and kept glancing at the drawing room door, saying, "Did you hear someone?" or "Was that footsteps on the staircase?"'

'He did not want anybody to overhear the conversation?'

'No, he didn't. Which was odd, because usually he was rather blunt about his opinions and what he wanted to happen. But in this case, he wished to make a new will that would have adversely affected one of his granddaughters.'

'Only one?' McCrodden asked.

'Yes,' said Vout. 'The other would have ended up a spec-tacularly wealthy woman if the new will had been made, but, as I say, that didn't happen. Barn—Ahem! My client died in a tragic accident before the new will could be drawn up and signed. And, although she is quite unaware of it, the younger of his two granddaughters would not be the rich woman she is now if her grandfather had lived a little longer, for he planned to cut her off completely, without so much as a penny!'

'Goodness me.' Rowland McCrodden forgot that he was supposed to be acting a part. His surprise was genuine. He could only hope that Vout would not sense his excitement.

The younger of his two granddaughters . . . That was Annabel Treadway. Could she be a cold-blooded killer?

McCrodden wondered. Never having met her, he had no trouble believing that she could. He had known many people who were. And in spite of Barnabas Pandy's best efforts, Miss Treadway might have learned of his intentions and decided to take drastic action to safeguard her inheritance.

'I tried to make my client see sense, but he was a stubborn old cove,' said Peter Vout. 'Wouldn't listen. Did his usual trick of arguing vigorously with me until I abandoned all attempts to persuade him. It always worked! I've never known a man so sure of his own mind and desires as Barn—Ahem! And so full of energy to defend his position, however wrong-headed it was.'

'Am I to understand that you disagreed with his decision, then? You felt he was treating the younger granddaughter unfairly?'

'I did.'

'In your opinion, she had done nothing to deserve it?'

'I don't know what she had done, because my friend did not tell me. He was peculiarly oblique in his narration—told me as little as possible. Which made no sense, since I would have needed to know the details in due course in order to arrange the new will. Perhaps he was afraid of being overheard, or perhaps he was merely considering making this change and had not yet finally decided upon it.'

'Was your client in the habit of inflicting heinous punishments upon those who did not deserve them?' asked McCrodden.

'Not as a rule, no. Though, as I say, he had one

longstanding enemy—and on the same day, the day he spoke to me about the need to draw up a new will, he announced that he also wished to broker a reconciliation with this chap. I urged him to reflect upon his eagerness to make peace with this fellow, and asked if he might not employ the same approach in relation to his granddaughter. I'm afraid he laughed at me. And then he said something I have remembered ever since.'

'What was that?' Rowland McCrodden asked.

'He said, "There is a difference, Peter, between an unforgivable *act* and a person of unforgivable *character*. What matters is not what people have done but who they are. A chap might put not a foot wrong his entire life, and do nothing outward to which the world would vociferously object, yet he might be rotten to the core."'

'What was the cause of the longstanding enmity between your client and this other man?'

'I don't know, I'm afraid. Ah, well—I don't suppose it matters, now that he is no longer with us, poor fellow. And, thankfully, his death put a stop to the plan to make a new will, with the result that both granddaughters are equally well provided for. It's a relief to think that neither of them ever suspected anything was afoot.'

'You are fond of both women?' McCrodden asked.

Vout lowered his voice and said, 'I am. The truth is, I have always felt rather sorry for poor Annab—Ahem!—for the younger granddaughter. The older one was my client's favourite, and he made no attempt to hide it. She—the eldest—made a good marriage, had two children. The younger granddaughter is . . . different. My friend found her hard to fathom and was regularly irritated by her refusal to explain herself.'

'Was there something in particular that he wished her to explain?' asked McCrodden.

'Oh, she refused numerous offers of marriage, from a range of deserving and delightful suitors,' said Vout. 'My client believed it was fear that stopped her from accepting any of them, and any sort of timidity provoked him to anger. I heard him call Annabel a coward in her presence, more than once. Each time he did, she would start weeping. The worst thing was, she would always *agree*. It was most unpleasant. I never understood how he could berate her in the way he did, even in the face of her sobbing and pleading guilty to every character flaw that he accused her of possessing.'

McCrodden waited for Vout to realize that he had spoken her name aloud, but he showed no sign of having noticed his mistake. How many glasses of champagne had he taken? He must have worked his way through a bottle by now.

'There was also the dog, which was a point of bitter contention,' he went on. 'Dogs, I should say. First Skittle and then Hopscotch.'

No anonymity was to be granted to the canines of the family, then.

'The younger granddaughter loved one and loves the other as if they were fully human members of the family,' said Vout. 'My client mocked her mercilessly, I'm afraid. Called her disgusting for allowing them to sleep on her bed, but to her they were like children. *Her* children. Once the old boy locked Skittle out of the house for a whole night. It wasn't especially cold, but the dog was used to cuddling up with his owner at night, and she thought he'd be bereft to be banished. She was nearly screaming with panic, and my client only laughed at her. In fairness, Skittle didn't seem particularly perturbed to be excluded. And, in my client's defence, it *was* the day that Skittle had . . .' Vout came to an awkward halt without finishing his sentence.

'What were you about to say?' asked McCrodden.

Vout sighed. 'It's funny, but I feel as if telling you *that* story would be to speak ill of the dead. A dead *dog*, admittedly, but . . . Poor Skittle was a lovely animal, really, and he had the best of intentions. Still, the old man was not best pleased.'

McCrodden waited to be enlightened.

Vout took a further glass of champagne from a passing tray—only one this time. He said, 'My client's great-grandaughter, Ivy, nearly drowned when she was a little girl. Oh, dear! Whoops! I've just told you her name. Ah, well, never mind. You wouldn't be able to identify her by her Christian name alone. In any case . . . her name is Ivy. She's the daughter of my client's older grand-daughter.'

Ivy, Skittle, Hopscotch, a careless and undetected 'Annabel', and an old man with a name that began with 'Barn—'; Rowland McCrodden thought these snippets might well be sufficient for identification, assuming he had cared enough to pursue the matter—and had he not already known which family Vout was talking about.

'I think Ivy was three or four years old when it happened,' said Vout. 'She was out with her aunt and the dog, walking by a river, and she fell into the water. Her aunt had to leap in after her and haul her out, risking her own life in the process. There was a strong current. They both very nearly died.'

'Her aunt—do you mean the younger granddaughter?' asked McCrodden. He was thinking that this story showed Annabel Treadway as being far from a coward.

'Yes. She was walking a little ahead and had no reason to suppose little Ivy was in any danger. And nor would she have been, except that, being a mischievous child, she decided to roll down the slope of the bank. I don't know why, but young children can never resist rolling down green slopes, can they? I was the same as a boy.'

'Unless I have missed part of the story, you have not yet spoken ill of the late Skittle,' said Rowland McCrodden.

'Nor shall I,' said Vout. 'It wasn't his fault. He was a dog, and that's all there is to it. One can't hold a dog responsible . . . yet I'm afraid my client did. You see, the aunt—the younger granddaughter—wasn't the only one who tried to save young Ivy's life. Skittle did, too. But the poor creature's efforts at rescue were more of a hindrance than a help—and he scratched Ivy's face rather badly while trying to save her. *Very* badly, I'm afraid. From what I hear, he panicked and rather lashed out. Ivy was left badly scarred. Her face . . . It was most unfortunate. It *is* unfortunate. I know her mother worries that no man will want her as a wife, for instance, though I'm sure that's not true. But one can see that it might be a worry.'

'And your client blamed Skittle for Ivy's scarred face?'

Vout considered the question. 'I think he was rational enough to know that the dog meant well. It was more that, well, that he blamed Skittle for *existing*. And he blamed Annabel—whoops! Still, I trust you to be discreet, old chap—he blamed Annabel *even though she saved Ivy's life*, because if it weren't for her, there would have been no Skittle there in the first place. No one else in the family cares for dogs at all. Interestingly, though, when I last visited my client at his home, I witnessed something I had never seen before . . .'

McCrodden waited.

'I saw him give Hopscotch—the current dog—a pat on the head. I thought I must be imagining things. All I had ever seen before was him shooing the dogs away and making cruel remarks about them. Used to say they were nothing but overgrown rats. It brought tears to Annabel's eyes whenever he said it, which was a source of great amusement to him. "Grow up and stop being a baby," he would say to her. I think he hoped he could toughen her up. He loved her as much as he loved her older sister, I'm sure of it—he just didn't approve of her in the same way. And then, of course . . . well, he must have decided he didn't love her at all,' said Vout sadly.

'Because of his plan to change his will?'

'Yes. The way he spoke about her when we discussed it

. . . it was clear to me that there was no love left. Something had killed it.'

'Yet, on that same day, you saw him pat her dog on the head in an affectionate manner?'

'I did—and most peculiar it was too. He didn't merely pat Hopscotch: he stroked him under his chin and I'm sure he called him a good boy. It was most unlike him, as I say. Now, where's that young chap with the drinks?'

CHAPTER 18

Mrs Dockerill's Discovery

'You fascinate me, monsieur,' said Poirot to Rowland McCrodden. 'Time after time you insist that you will *not* do for your friend Poirot this small favour—'

'There was nothing small about it,' McCrodden protested.

'—that you will not use the method I suggested to try to extract from Peter Vout the information he is hiding. Then, having refused, you do the very thing I wanted you to do, and you play your part to perfection! No acclaimed actor could have done better!'

The three of us were at Whitehaven Mansions. I had suggested to McCrodden that Poirot and I might meet him at his firm's offices, but he wouldn't hear of it. I strongly suspected that he was once again avoiding Miss Mason.

'I'm rather ashamed that I did it,' said McCrodden. 'I do not like to behave deceitfully.'

'You did so in the best of causes, *mon ami.*'

'Yes, well . . . This new information about Pandy's will changes everything, doesn't it?'

'I should say so,' I agreed.

'You are both wrong,' Poirot told us. 'It is true that each new fact is potentially useful, but this one, as with so many others we have unearthed, does not seem to take us anywhere.'

'You are surely not serious?' said McCrodden. 'Annabel Treadway had a most persuasive reason to want to do away with her grandfather. It couldn't be clearer: he was about to alter his will and leave her penniless.'

'But Lenore and Ivy Lavington have assured me that Mademoiselle Annabel cannot have killed him.'

'Then they're lying.'

I tended to agree with McCrodden. 'However fond they were of Pandy, they might nevertheless lie to protect Annabel,' I said.

'I agree,' said Poirot. 'That they would lie to save Mademoiselle Annabel's life and that she might be capable of committing murder in order to secure her material security, given the fearfulness of her nature—both are quite possible. There is, however, a problem: she was ignorant of her grandfather's wish to alter his will. It cannot be her motive if she was unaware of it.'

'Vout might be mistaken about that,' I said.

'A "might" gets us nowhere, Catchpool. Yes, she *might* have overheard the conversation about the planned new will after all, and yes, her sister and niece *might* be lying in order to save her—but one cannot rest any certain conclusions upon two "mights" of this kind.'

He was right. When you are desperately casting about

for a solution, and suddenly you learn that a vast fortune was at risk of being lost because of a proposed change to a will, it is far too tempting to decide that that must have been the motive.'

'I should like to know what Annabel Treadway did so soon before Pandy died,' said Rowland McCrodden. 'It must have been something truly appalling and shocking to him if it induced him to make peace with an enemy he had made tens of years earlier.'

'We do not know that the two are connected,' said Poirot.

'They have to be,' said McCrodden. 'When your antipathy towards one person becomes all-consuming, you find that . . . well, you might decide to dispense with all other feuds and grudges. Nobody wishes to think of himself as having a tendency towards bitterness and hatred.'

'I find this interesting,' said Poirot. 'Please, continue, my friend.'

'Well, if an unkind impulse towards one person begins to grow inside us at a rapid rate and perhaps get rather out of control, it is only natural that we should feel the need to balance that out with a sort of . . . ostentatious benevolence. If I were to guess, I should say that, when Pandy decided to cut off Miss Treadway, he balanced this out with a few clear acts of kindliness: seeking to reconcile with his old enemy Vincent Lobb, playing with the dog he usually ignored . . .'

'To make himself appear a good and charitable man in his own eyes?' said Poirot. '*Oui, je comprend.* Then . . . we might also guess that, when he made that decision,

Monsieur Pandy's bitterness towards Mademoiselle Annabel was very great indeed.'

McCrodden nodded. 'It would need to have been, yes, for my theory to be correct.'

'It is your experience with Miss Emerald Mason that has led you to this conclusion?' Poirot asked him.

'Yes. When I was first struck by the extent to which I irrationally loathed her, I felt a need to . . . well, to relinquish a few of my less important grudges.'

'Did you have many?' I asked.

'A few. Doesn't everybody?'

'I don't,' I said. 'I can't think of a single one. Do you have any grudges, Poirot?'

He was prevented from answering by a knock at the door. The valet, George, entered the room. 'There is a lady here to see you, sir. I told her you were busy, but she said it was urgent.'

'Then, if it is urgent, we must see her. Did she tell you her name?'

'She did, sir. Most thoroughly. She identified herself as Jane Dockerill, and also as Mrs Hugo Dockerill, the wife of the housemaster of Timothy Lavington and Frederick Rule at Turville College.'

'Please show her in, Georges.'

Jane Dockerill was a tiny slip of a thing, with curly dark brown hair, glasses with severe black frames, and a large brown bag that she carried into the room with both hands. It was wider than she was. She moved and spoke quickly.

When Poirot stood and introduced himself, she shook his hand at the same time as saying, 'And who are these other two gentleman?'

'Rowland McCrodden, solicitor, and Inspector Edward Catchpool of Scotland Yard.'

'I see,' said Jane Dockerill. 'I take it you've been discussing this business in which we are all involved?'

We all nodded. It did not occur to us to hold anything back. Jane Dockerill was the most naturally commanding person I could remember being in a room with. Even the Super might have done her bidding without question.

'Good,' she said. Then, without pausing for breath, 'I came here to deliver two items: one you already know about; the other you do not. The first is Hugo's letter, the one in which he is accused of murder. I thought you would probably need it.'

'Indeed, madame. Most helpful.' Poirot had never sounded more like an obedient schoolboy.

Jane Dockerill pulled the letter out of her bag and handed it to him. He read it, then passed it to me. Apart from the recipient's name and address and the words 'Dear Mr Dockerill' at the top, it was identical to the letter received by John McCrodden, right down to the missing ink from the horizontal bar of each letter 'e'. I passed the letter on to Rowland McCrodden.

'And now for the item that you were not expecting,' said Jane Dockerill. 'Neither, I should like to say, was I expecting it. I was shocked to discover it where I did, and I sincerely hope it does not mean what I think it means.'

She produced from her bag an object that I did not immediately recognize. It was blue—or, rather, there was something blue inside it: blue with tiny flashes of white and yellow. Whatever it was, it was wrapped in cellophane to make an odd-looking parcel.

'What is inside this package, madame?' Poirot asked.

'A dress. It was wrapped when wet. I found it taped to the underside of Timothy Lavington's bed. I like to keep all the dormitories spotlessly clean, which means—if you're going to do a thorough job, which I like to—looking under the beds regularly to check there is no rubbish piled up there, or forbidden items stashed away out of sight.'

'Very commendable, madame.'

Jane Dockerill moved briskly on. 'Before yesterday, the last time I looked under the beds in Timothy's dormitory was four weeks ago. I know precisely when it was because it was my first inspection since the holidays. Four weeks ago, this package was not there. Then, yesterday, there it was—taped, as I say, to the bottom of the frame of the bed: Timothy Lavington's bed. I unwrapped it in Timothy's presence, to see if he knew what it was. He recognized the dress as belonging to his aunt, but was baffled by its presence in his dorm.' Pointedly, Jane Dockerill added, 'A stiff, badly-dried dress, still damp in places. Belonging to his aunt, Annabel Treadway.'

'This causes you to suspect something?' Poirot asked her. 'May I ask what?'

'Is it not obvious? I suspect—though I pray it's not true—that Annabel Treadway murdered Barnabas Pandy by drowning him in his bath, for that was how he died. Her dress got wet in the process, and, afraid it would incriminate her, she hid it at Turville, under Timothy's bed.'

'As far as we know, Mr Pandy's death was an accident,' I felt obliged to say. 'From an official point of view—'

'Oh, that means nothing,' said Jane Dockerill. 'I now believe Mr Pandy was murdered, whatever anybody else thinks.'

'Upon what do you base this belief?' asked Poirot.

'Common sense and probability,' she told him. 'Most accidental deaths are not followed by multiple accusations of murder and strange packages taped to bed frames. This one has been—therefore it seems likely to me that it was indeed a murder.'

Poirot gave a small nod. It was not suggestive of whole-hearted agreement.

'Aren't you going to open the package?' said Mrs Dockerill.

'*Oui, bien sûr*. Catchpool, if you would be so kind.'

It was easy enough to pull off the tape and unwrap the cellophane. We all looked at the pale blue fabric as it was freed from its wrapping. The spots of yellow and white turned out to be tiny flowers. Parts of the material, deprived of air for weeks, had become slimy.

'Notice the smell,' said Jane Dockerill.

'It is the oil of olives,' said Poirot. 'I smell it distinctly. This is the dress that Annabel Treadway wore the day that Barnabas Pandy died. Lenore Lavington described it to me: blue, with flowers of white and yellow. Only in one respect is the fabric of this dress different from the one Madame Lavington described.'

'For goodness' sake, don't keep us in suspense,' said Jane Dockerill. 'How is it different?'

'This dress was clearly wrapped while it was still wet,' I said.

'*Précisément*, Catchpool. Lenore Lavington told me that the dress of his sister was not wet when they stood together in the bathroom on 7 December. She offered this as proof that her sister could not have drowned their grandfather. The dress of Annabel Treadway, according to Lenore Lavington—her blue dress, with yellow and white flowers— *was completely dry.*'

CHAPTER 19

Four More Letters

'This is quite a development, isn't it?' said Jane Dockerill.

'It is,' Poirot agreed.

'I have known Timothy's mother for many years. She would certainly lie to protect a member of her family—no question about it. Hugo and I can't say a word to Timothy without her swooping down upon us in a mist of quiet fury to make a range of exaggerated threats: she'll see to it that Hugo is fired, she'll remove Timothy and, with him, the kind donations upon which the school so relies.'

Jane Dockerill uncrossed her legs, then crossed them the other way. 'Schools are terribly unfair places, you know. There are some boys—the ones whose parents have a suitable respect for authority—who are ordered to tuck in their shirts, straighten their ties, pull up their socks, and we do our well-intentioned ordering around safe in the knowledge that no member of those boys' families will turn up in due course to make our lives a misery. Other boys—and I'm afraid both Timothy Lavington and Freddie Rule fall into this category—can walk around with their blazers torn and their ties all askew, and we all contrive not to notice. Heaven forbid that we should provoke an avoidable encounter with a parent of Lenore Lavington's stripe!'

'Madame, who could have taped the parcel containing the dress to the underneath of Timothy Lavington's bed?' Poirot asked her.

'Almost anybody. Timothy himself—though I know he didn't do it. He was as surprised to see it as I was. His mother, sister or aunt could have done it during one of their visits. I or my husband could have done it. I didn't, of course, and neither did Hugo.' She laughed. 'The very idea! Hugo would never in a thousand years have been able to find adhesive tape, even if he were to have the bright idea to stick a dress to the frame of a bed.'

'Is there anybody else?' asked Poirot.

'Oh, yes, said Jane Dockerill. 'As I said: almost everybody. Any of the boys in our house, any boy from one of the other houses who crept in when Timothy's dorm room was empty. Any teacher. Any parent.'

I heard myself sigh. Poirot murmured, 'No parameters.'

'We can narrow it down a bit, you'll be glad to hear,' Jane Dockerill said with a wry smile. 'A person not known at Turville wouldn't have stood a chance of sneaking in without being stopped and thoroughly interrogated. Like all communities, we suspect outsiders of being bent on our destruction and expel them from the premises whenever we stumble upon them.' She looked irritated by our lack of reaction. 'That was a joke.'

Obediently, but too late to please her, Poirot, McCrodden and I all laughed.

'So it could have been any person from within the school community, including the parent of a pupil?' Poirot said.

'It could, I'm afraid.'

'Have you ever, in this school community or associated with it, encountered a man by the name of John McCrodden?'

At the mention of his son's name, Rowland McCrodden twitched slightly.

'No,' said Jane Dockerill. Her denial appeared genuine.

'The family of Timothy Lavington . . . have they visited him at school since Barnabas Pandy died, and since the day you checked under the bed four weeks ago when there was no package stuck there?'

'Yes. Lenore, Annabel and Timothy's sister Ivy were at Turville about two weeks ago. Any one of them could have taped the parcel containing the wet dress to the bed frame during that visit.'

'When did Madame Sylvia Rule last come to the school?' Poirot asked.

'Last week,' said Mrs Dockerill. 'With Mildred and her fiancé, Eustace.'

'You put Freddie in the "boys who don't get ordered around" category,' I said. 'Does that mean that Sylvia Rule is as fearsome a prospect as Lenore Lavington?'

'Sylvia's unbearable,' said Jane Dockerill. 'I should explain that, having lived and worked at Turville for so long, I find approximately two thirds of the parents unbearable, in so many different ways. They are generally far more difficult than the boys. Freddie Rule, Sylvia's son, is a sweetheart. His good nature must come from his father.'

'He is a loner, is he not?' said Poirot.

'He's not a popular boy,' said Jane Dockerill with a sigh. 'He's sensitive, complicated, quiet—not a person of high social status. And he feels things very deeply. He couldn't be more different from Timothy Lavington. Timothy has no use for boys like Freddie. His friends are all like him: loud, confident show-offs. The highest rung of Turville's social ladder. It broke my heart to see Freddie on his own all the time. I decided that if those stupid boys didn't want to be his friend, then I would. And I am.' She smiled. 'Freddie has become my little helper around the house. I don't know what I'd do without him. Everybody at Turville knows now: if they bully Freddie, they will have me to deal with.'

'He has been bullied?' I asked. 'Not by Timothy Lavingon, I don't suppose?'

'No, never by Timothy, but by plenty of others.' Jane Dockerill looked angry, suddenly. 'It's terribly unfair. Freddie is seen by many as tainted. It's his mother. There are rumours about her, you see—that she, um, makes her living in a way that is both immoral and unlawful. I don't expect there's a shred of truth in these lurid stories.'

'I see. Madame Dockerill, may I ask you about the Christmas Fair on 7 December? Freddie Rule was there, yes? With his mother and sister, and Eustace?'

'Yes, they were all there.'

'And Timothy Lavington, and you and your husband?'

'Of course. I was dashing about all day like a mad creature.'

'Of the people I have listed, can you be certain that any of them were at the fair for the entire day, from when it started until it closed?'

'I've just told you: they were all there,' said Jane Dockerill.

'You were watching them, with your own eyes, for every second of the day?'

She looked surprised. 'No. How could I? I was desperately busy.'

'Then, pardon me, madame, but how do you know that they were there all day?'

'Well, they were certainly all at the supper in the evening. And I saw them now and then throughout the day. Where else would they have—?' She stopped abruptly. 'Oh. I see what you mean. You're wondering if one of them might have slipped out to go and kill Barnabas Pandy, then slipped back in?'

'Is it possible?' asked Poirot.

'I suppose, in the sense that you mean . . . yes, it is possible. Any of them could have absented himself or herself for the required time. They would have needed a means of getting to Combingham Hall, of course.'

After successfully dodging her questions about what next steps he planned to take, Poirot thanked Jane Dockerill, and she left.

'She has an unhealthy attachment to the Rule boy,' said Rowland McCrodden, once she had gone.

'I don't think that's true,' I told him. 'She feels protective towards a lonely boy is how I should describe it.'

'I'd be surprised if there were not as many rumours about Mrs Dockerill and young Freddie Rule as there are about Sylvia Rule being a lady of the night,' said McCrodden.

'Catchpool, when you visit Turville College, try to hear as many of these rumours as you can,' Poirot said.

'The boys are hardly likely to say anything unseemly in the presence of a Scotland Yard inspector,' I said. 'Or am I to disguise myself as a bun in the tuck-shop?'

'You will find a way, Catchpool.'

Poirot ran his fingers along the slimy fabric of the blue dress, then produced a handkerchief to wipe his hand. 'The dress of Mademoiselle Treadway,' he murmured. 'What does it mean? Does it mean that the three ladies of Combingham Hall have lied to me, and Kingsbury also? That they all know Annabel Treadway murdered Monsieur Pandy, and seek to conceal the truth? Or . . . ?' He turned to me.

'Or,' I took my cue, 'is somebody trying to frame Annabel Treadway?'

'*Exactement!* If the aim were to protect Mademoiselle Annabel, the most sensible plan would have been to wash and dry the dress immediately.'

'What if traces of olive oil would still be detectable even after washing?' I said. 'Perhaps the dress had to disappear so that no one would ever ask the question: "Why would there be olive oil on this dress?"'

Poirot said, 'Mes amis, we have met Jane Dockerill only once. Annabel Treadway has met her many more times, on her visits to Timothy at school. Would she not assume that Madame Dockerill would check every dormitory in her boarding house most thoroughly? Having met her once, that is what I would assume. There must be hundreds of beds at Turville. Why not choose one that belongs to a stranger?'

'You think, then, that the hiding of the dress under Timothy's bed is more likely to be an attempt to frame Miss Treadway than evidence of her guilt?' asked McCrodden.

'I do not yet know enough . . .' Poirot began thoughtfully. 'Notice that the dress is equally damp all over. Mademoiselle Annabel's clothing, if she drowned her grandfather, would not have been. The arms would have been extremely wet, but the bottom of the dress? The back of it? *Non*. These would have been much drier, perhaps not wet at all. And yet, if at the time of wrapping in the cellophane the arms were drenched, while other parts of the dress were dry, the water could have soaked through to wet the dress in its entirety.'

'We may invent as many theories as we like, Poirot, but we know nothing,' said McCrodden wearily. 'There are too many possibilities. Reluctant as I am to admit defeat—'

'You think we ought to give up?' said Poirot. 'No, no, my friend. You are quite wrong. There are indeed many possibilities—but we much closer, now, to the truth!'

'Are we?' I said. 'How? Why?'

'Catchpool, do you not see what is now clear?'

I did not. Neither did Rowland McCrodden.

Poirot laughed at us both, in our ignorance. 'Thanks to this dress, I am confident that I will soon have all the answers. I do not have them yet, but I will. I intend to set myself a challenge and put a deadline in place. Let us see if Hercule Poirot can beat the clocks!'

'What do you mean?' I asked him.

He laughed again. 'It astonishes me that neither of you sees what I see. A pity, but never mind. Soon, I will explain. *Alors, maintenant*, it is time for me compose four letters, to be sent to Sylvia Rule, Annabel Treadway, John McCrodden and Hugo Dockerill. And this time, they will be from the real Hercule Poirot!'

THE THIRD QUARTER

CHAPTER 20

The Letters Arrive

Eustace Campbell-Brown was reclining in the drawing room of his fiancée Mildred's London townhouse when Mildred's mother bustled into the room holding a letter and a torn envelope with the very tips of her fingers, as if to touch them any more thoroughly might contaminate her. Sylvia Rule gasped in horror at the sight of her future son-in-law, though she had seen him many times before, and sitting in this exact position: with a cigarette in one hand and a book in the other.

'Good morning,' said Eustace. He did not think he could get into trouble for saying something so simple.

'Where is Mildred?'

'Upstairs, getting dressed. I'm taking her out for the day.' He smiled.

Sylvia Rule stared at him for a long time. Then she said, 'How much do you want?'

'I beg your pardon?'

'To leave Mildred alone and disappear for ever. There must be an amount of money that would tempt you.'

Eustace placed his cigarette in the ashtray on the table beside him and put down his book. So, he thought to himself, it had come to this, despite his best efforts to win the esteem of his soon-to-be mother-in-law.

It was time, at last, to stop trying—to stop being polite and charming and to say what he felt like saying for once.

'Finally, an enticement of money,' he said. 'I've been wondering how long it would take you. Just think, you could have made me an offer this time last year and I'd have been out of your life long ago.'

'Then . . . there is a sum . . . ?'

'No, Sylvia, there is not. I was teasing you. The fact is, I love Mildred and she loves me. The sooner you get used to that, the happier you will be.'

'Oh, you are a vile, disgusting man!'

'I don't think I am,' said Eustace quite reasonably. 'Neither does Mildred. Have you ever considered, Sylvia, that you might be the ghastly one? You are, after all, a murderer. Mildred might not know the truth about you, but I do. Don't worry—I have no wish to distress her by telling her what I know. But I don't suppose there's any chance you might lay off me for a while, is there? In return for my keeping your secret, I mean.'

'You're a liar!' Sylvia Rule's face had turned white. She lowered herself into an armchair.

'No, I'm not,' said Eustace. 'If it were not true, you would be saying, "What do you mean?" and "What on earth are you on about?" You know perfectly well what I'm talking about.'

At that moment Mildred Rule appeared in the drawing room wearing the blank expression she always wore in the company of her mother and her fiancé. She did not ask why Sylvia looked so ashen-faced, nor why Eustace was glowing with a new, peculiar energy, one she had not seen in him before. She knew that something important had probably happened in her absence, and hoped to avoid finding out what it was. Mildred had recently decided that it was better for her to know nothing about what passed between Sylvia and Eustace, and not to enquire about her mother's loathing for the man she loved more than anything.

She noticed the letter and torn envelope that her mother was holding. 'What's that?' she asked. If her mother was upset about something other than Eustace, then Mildred was interested to know what it was.

'It's another letter from Hercule Poirot,' said Sylvia Rule.

'Accusing you of murder again, is he?' Eustace sneered.

Sylvia passed the letter to Mildred. 'Read it aloud,' she said. 'It mentions you. And *him*.'

'"Dear Madame Rule,"' read Mildred. '"It is of vital importance that you attend a meeting at Combingham Hall, home of the deceased Barnabas Pandy, on 24 February, at 2 o'clock. I will be present and so will Inspector Edward Catchpool of Scotland Yard. Others will be present as well. The mystery of the death of Barnabas Pandy, in which we are all interested parties, will be resolved, and a murderer apprehended. Please extend this same invitation to your daughter Mildred and to her fiancé Eustace. It is important that they attend also. Yours sincerely, Hercule Poirot."'

'I don't suppose we have any way of knowing if the letter's from the real Hercule Poirot this time?' said Eustace.

'What shall we do?' asked Mildred. 'Shall we go? Or shall we ignore it?' She hoped that her mother and Eustace would, for once, agree upon a course of action. If they disagreed, Mildred knew her mind would freeze and be unable to make sense of anything.

'I have no intention of attending,' said Sylvia Rule.

'We have to go,' said Eustace. 'All of us. Don't you want to know who this murderer is, Sylvia? *I* do.'

John McCrodden touched the arm of the woman in his bed. He couldn't remember her name; it might have been Annie, or Aggie. She was lying on her front, facing away from him. 'Wake up. Wake up, will you?'

'I'm awake.' She rolled over with a yawn. 'Lucky for you. I don't take kindly to being woken when it's my day off work. Though, since it's you . . .' She grinned and reached out to touch John's face.

He pushed her hand away. 'I'm not in the mood. Sorry. Look, I've got things to do, so you'd better be on your way.' A peculiar letter had arrived for him and he wanted to read it again, more carefully. He couldn't concentrate with her still here.

The woman sat up, covering herself with the bed-sheet. 'Well, you're charming, aren't you? Is this how you treat all the girls?'

'As a matter of fact, it is. I never intend them any harm, but they always take it badly. No doubt you will too.'

'I suppose you'll promise to take me out again, as soon as you can, and then I'll never hear from you again,' said the woman resentfully, tears forming in the corners of her eyes.

'No. I'm promising nothing. And I don't want to take you anywhere. I enjoyed last night, but that's all it was: one night. You won't see me again, unless by chance. You may scream at me as you leave, if it makes you feel better.'

Once he'd said that, she was out of his room in seconds. She would doubtless think him callous, but she would be wrong. The cruel thing would have been to allow her to build up her hopes. When he was much younger, John had met a woman and known within moments that here was a person he could love for ever. He had not felt that way about anybody else, before or since. Nor had he spoken of the feeling to a single soul, for it had been too powerful to describe and, in any case, no one would have believed it possible who had not personally fallen into a similar chasm of longing. Humans, as a rule, were doggedly determined not to believe in the experiences of anyone but themselves.

John dressed and took the strange letter over to the chair by the window. He read it once more, shaking his head. Instead of deciding that the four accusations sent in his name were no more than a prank, and resolving to think no more about them, Hercule Poirot had evidently assigned to himself responsibility for solving this murder.

Had anyone paid him to undertake the task? John doubted it. Like Annie or Aggie or whatever her name was,

Poirot had chosen to make life more difficult and complicated than it needed to be. He had now sent letters of invitation to a 'meeting' about Barnabas Pandy's death to John and no doubt many other people. Making matters worse, his letter to John contained the unwelcome line: 'Others will be present as well, including your father, Rowland McCrodden.'

John was no fool. He had known for some time that he had unfairly maligned both his father and Hercule Poirot. He now believed that neither man was responsible for the letter in which he had been accused of murdering Barnabas Pandy. Apologies were owed; there was no getting away from that, but there was nothing John hated more than admitting he had been wrong—especially to two men whose work sometimes led to nooses being placed around people's necks.

'I'll go to Poirot's meeting,' he thought. 'That will have to do, by way of apology. And maybe I'll find out who sent me that letter.'

John wrote a short note to Poirot saying that he would be at Combingham Hall on 24 February as instructed. He put it in an envelope, which he was about to seal when he remembered Catalina.

Ah, Catalina, his Spanish lady-friend. Now there was a sensible, resourceful woman. Damned attractive, too. She let John come and go as he pleased, without ever applying pressure or crying all over him. She enjoyed his company but managed perfectly well without him, as he did without her. John had not met many people, men or women, whom he felt were his equals, but Catalina most certainly was: a brilliant woman and, now, a brilliant alibi. Good old Catalina!

John walked over to his bed and reached under it for the bundle of her letters that he kept there. Most of them were about King Alfonso XIII and the precariousness of General Miguel Primo de Rivera's hold on power. Catalina was a committed Republican. John smiled. He did not care for politics. What people claimed to stand for meant very little, he had always found, and told you nothing about their true character. It was like judging a person by their choice of socks or handkerchief.

He selected Catalina's letter dated 21 December 1929 and inserted it in the envelope he would send to Poirot. Pulling out the letter he'd just written, he added, beneath his signature, the words: 'Alibi for 7 December enclosed'.

'Oh, dear,' cried Annabel Treadway. 'Hoppy, what shall I do? A meeting, here? He doesn't say how many people he's invited. Lenore will be furious. We shall have to think about the catering, and I haven't got a head for it at all—not even to talk to Kingsbury or Cook about it. But . . . oh, goodness. I'm going to have to tell Lenore, and . . . look, he says that a murderer will be apprehended. Oh, dear!'

Hopscotch lifted his head from Annabel's lap and gave her a questioning look. They were in the morning room at Combingham Hall, having recently returned from a ball game in the meadow. Hopscotch eyed Annabel hopefully, trying to work out if her latest exclamation might mean that she would soon be ready to run back outside and play a little more.

'I'm frightened,' said Annabel. 'I'm so frightened. Of everything, except you, darling Hoppy.'

The dog rolled over, wanting his tummy to be scratched.

'What if Lenore forbids Poirot from holding his meeting here?' As she spoke these words, Annabel was struck by a sudden, powerful realization. 'Oh!' she gasped. 'Even if she forbids it, the truth will come out. There is no way to stop it, not now that Hercule Poirot is involved. Oh, Hoppy, if it weren't for you . . .'

She left the sentence unfinished, not wishing to alarm the dog by saying what she would do if she were not so reluctant to leave him alone in the world. Lenore didn't care about him. Ivy claimed to, but she didn't love him the way Annabel did, as if he were a fully-fledged member of the family—which he absolutely was. Skittle had been too. 'One day,' thought Annabel, 'the world will be a more enlightened place and we will treat dogs as well as we treat people. Oh, but—I am a dreadful hypocrite!' She started to cry.

Hopscotch rolled over and placed his paw in her hand in a consolatory manner, but she continued to weep.

'Look at this, Jane.' Hugo Dockerill tried to pass his wife the letter he'd just opened. 'That trickster is pretending to be Poirot again. I suppose I ought to tell him. Poirot, I mean.'

Jane balanced a large pile of laundry on the arm of the nearest sofa, and snatched the paper out of her husband's hand. She read aloud: "Dear Monsieur Dockerill, It is of vital importance that you and your wife Jane attend a meeting at Combingham Hall . . ." She mouthed the rest of the words silently. Looking up at Hugo, she said, 'Why do you think this isn't from the real Poirot?'

He frowned. 'Do you think it might be?'

'Yes. Look at the signature. It's quite different from the one on the other letter. *Quite* different. Having met Poirot, I should say that this could well be his handwriting: very neat, with a few fancy touches here and there.'

'Golly,' said Hugo. 'I wonder why he wants us to go to Combingham Hall?'

'Have you read the letter?'

'Yes. Twice.'

'It explains why he wants us to go.'

'Do you think he's got to the bottom of it all, then? Who else do you suppose he's invited?'

'I would imagine the other three people who were accused in the first lot of letters will be there,' said Jane.

'Yes, that would make sense. What do you think, dearest one? Shall we go?'

'What do you think, Hugo? Do you want to go?'

'Well, I . . . I mean . . . I rather thought you might take a view on that, my dear. I mean . . . Well, it's hard to know. Am I . . . Are we busy on that day?'

Jane laughed affectionately and linked her arm through his. 'I'm teasing you. We're busy every day, or at least I am, but of course we must go. I want to know what the great Hercule Poirot has worked out, and who this murderer is. I wish we didn't have to wait nearly a week. I want to know *now* what he intends to tell us all.'

CHAPTER 21

The Day of the Typewriters

The Day of the Typewriters, as I will always think of it, turned out to be more interesting than I had expected it to. For one thing, it proved Poirot right: it really is a good test of character to put several people in the exact same situation and examine the difference in their reactions. I had been making a list as I went along, and dreading the moment when I would have to show it to Poirot and hear all about how vastly superior his list would have been. Mine read as follows:

Offices of Donaldson & McCrodden Solicitors
Stanley Donaldson allowed me to test his typewriter. Its letter 'e' was not faulty. (Donaldson also confirmed that Rowland Rope was with him for the whole of Saturday 7 December, first at the Athenaeum Club and then at the Palace Theatre.) None of the typewriters that I found in the firm's offices was the one we are looking for. I tested all of them, and then Miss Emerald

Mason insisted on testing them again just to make sure.

Home of Sylvia and Mildred Rule
There was one typewriter in the house. Mrs Rule tried to forbid me from entering and told me I had no business invading her privacy and hounding her when she had done nothing wrong, but then her daughter Mildred persuaded her to cooperate. I tested the typewriter and the letter 'e' was perfectly normal.

Eustace Campbell-Brown
Finally we know his last name! Mildred told me where I would find him. I visited him at home. He seemed pleased to find me on his doorstep and was happy for me to test his typewriter. It was not the one we are looking for. As I was leaving, Mr Campbell-Brown said, 'If I wanted to send letters accusing people of murder, signed in the name of Hercule Poirot, the very first thing I should do is check that the machine I was typing them on had no irregularities that might identify me.' I did not know quite what to make of this.

John McCrodden
John McCrodden told me, in a rude and surly manner, that he does not own a typewriter. His landlady does, but she assured me that McCrodden had never used it.

Peter Vout
Mr Vout was gracious enough to allow me to check all the typewriters in his firm's offices, and I found them all to be in good working order.

All Typewriters Not Based in London
Combingham Hall typewriters—Poirot tried to check, but was prevented from doing so.

Turville College's typewriters—still need to be checked. (I shall go tomorrow.)

Vincent Lobb—does he own a typewriter? If so, it needs to be checked. Still no luck tracking down Lobb.

CHAPTER 22

The Solitary Yellow Square of Cake

'Good morning, Monsieur McCrodden. You are surprised to see me here, *non?*'

John McCrodden looked up to find Hercule Poirot peering down at him where he sat cross-legged on the floor beside his market stall, a cloth bag full of coins in his lap. There were no customers around; the market had only just opened. 'What do you want?' McCrodden asked. 'Didn't you get the letter I sent to you?'

'From a woman by the name of Catalina? Yes, it arrived.'

'Then you also received my note in which I undertook to present myself at Combingham Hall on the date you want me there—so why are you here now?'

'I wished to see you before our meeting at Combingham Hall, at which others will be present. I should like to speak to you alone.'

'I have customers to deal with.'

'You do not have them now,' said Poirot with a polite smile. 'Tell me, who is this Mademoiselle Catalina?'

McCrodden grimaced. 'What does it matter to you? She's nobody you know. If you're suggesting she isn't real and I've fabricated an alibi for myself, why don't you go to Spain and talk to her yourself? Her address is on all of her letters, including the one I sent you.'

Poirot produced the letter from his pocket. 'It is most convenient for you, this letter,' he said. 'It is dated 21 December last year, and it refers to "fourteen days ago today" when you and Mademoiselle Catalina were together in . . .'—Poirot glanced down at the paper in his hand—'. . . Ribadesella. If you were in Ribadesella on 7 December, you cannot also have been at Combingham Hall, drowning Barnabas Pandy.'

'I'm glad we agree about that,' said McCrodden. 'Since we do—since we both know that I couldn't have murdered Pandy—would you care to explain your continued interest in me? Why must I attend a meeting at Combingham Hall on 24 February? And why, when I agree to do so, do you come and pester me at my place of work? It might not be the sort of work that impresses the likes of you and my father, but it's work all the same. It's how I earn my living, and you're getting in my way.'

'But still you have no customers,' Poirot pointed out. 'I interrupt nothing.'

McCrodden sighed. 'It's slow at the moment, but it'll pick up,' he said. 'And if it doesn't, I'll do something else to earn a crust. What my father has never understood about me is that I don't much care what I do. It's only work, and life's more interesting if you try a few different things. I've tried telling him that's how I see it. You'd think he wouldn't care if I move from one employment to another, wouldn't you, when he's disapproved of every single job I've ever had? He hated me being a miner—didn't want his son getting his hands dirty digging into the cliff like a commoner—but then he didn't like it when I worked at the clean end either. Didn't like me making and selling the trinkets, didn't like me working on a farm, and doesn't like me working here at the market. Yet he complains when I move around because he only approves of people who stick at things.'

'Monsieur, I am not here to talk about your father.'

'Answer me one thing, Poirot.' John McCrodden leapt to his feet. 'Do you approve of this legal form of murder that we have in our country? Because as far as I'm concerned, you're no better than a murderer yourself if you're in favour of killing those who have committed crimes—even the most serious crimes.'

Poirot looked around. The market had started to fill with people and noise. Still nobody approached John McCrodden's stall.

'If I answer your question, will you answer one of mine?' he asked.

'I will.'

'*Bien.* I believe that the loss of life, for whatever reason, is a tragedy. However, when the most heinous of crimes has been committed, is it not fitting that the perpetrator should suffer the most severe of punishments? Does justice not demand it?'

McCrodden shook his head. 'You're just like my father.

You profess to care about justice, while not having the faintest idea of what it means.'

'Now it is my turn to ask the question,' said Poirot. 'Think carefully, please, before answering. You have told me that you were not acquainted with Barnabas Pandy.'

'I never so much as heard his name until your . . . until that letter arrived.'

'Listen to these names and tell me if any of them are familiar to you: Lenore Lavington, Ivy Lavington, Timothy Lavington.'

McCrodden shook his head. 'Never heard of any Lavingtons,' he said.

'Sylvia Rule, Freddie Rule, Mildred Rule.'

'I have heard the name Sylvia Rule, but only from you,' said McCrodden. 'Or, rather, from the man who works for you. Don't you recall? You had him come into the room and tell me that Mrs Rule had also received a letter in your name, accusing her of murder.'

'*Oui*, monsieur, I remember.'

'Then why ask me, if you know I know the name? Some sort of test?'

'What about Mildred Rule and Freddie Rule?' asked Poirot.

'I agreed to answer one question,' McCrodden reminded him. 'You've used up your allowance, mate.'

'Monsieur McCrodden, I do not understand you. You seem to disapprove of the taking of life when it is done by the law. Do you not also disapprove of the lives taken by unlawful murderers?'

'Of course I do.'

'Then believe me when I tell you that I am trying to catch such a person: a meticulous and careful murderer, driven not by passion but by calculation. Why should you not want to help me?'

'You sound as if you've worked out who killed this Pandy fellow. Have you?'

Poirot had not. All he knew was that there was a murderer to be caught: a dangerous and wicked person who must be stopped. He had never before announced, in advance, a date on which he would reveal facts of such importance *that he did not yet know*. Why, then, had he chosen to do so in the case of Barnabas Pandy? Poirot was not sure he knew the answer. He wondered if it might be a strange sort of prayer, disguised as an exciting and alarming challenge.

Avoiding John McCrodden's question, he said, 'I am still waiting for an answer from you.'

McCrodden cursed under his breath, then said, 'No, I've never heard of Mildred Rule or Freddie Rule.'

'What about Annabel Treadway, or Hugo and Jane Dockerill? Or Eustace Campbell-Brown?'

'No. None of these names mean anything to me. Should they?'

'Not necessarily, no. Do you know Turville College?'

'I've heard of it, naturally.'

'But you have no personal connection with the place.'

'No. My father sent me first to Eton and then to Rugby. I was expelled from both.'

'Thank you, Monsieur McCrodden. It seems that you are truly the solitary yellow square of cake, all alone at the edge of the plate. But *why*? That is the question: why?'

'Cake?' snarled John McCrodden. 'Nothing that's happened recently makes sense to me. That's why I shan't bother to ask you what I have in common with a piece of cake! I'm sure I wouldn't understand, even if you told me.'

CHAPTER 23

Meaning Harm

As I set off to Turville College two days later, in the hope of talking to Timothy Lavington and examining all available typewriters, I could not help but feel hard done by. Poirot was also travelling, and I wished I could have swapped places with him. He was on his way to Llanidloes in Wales to talk to a woman by the name of Deborah Dakin. Vincent Lobb, we had learned the day before from one of Poirot's mysterious 'helpers', had died some thirteen years earlier. Mrs Dakin, the widow of Lobb's eldest son, was the only surviving member of the family.

I should have liked to go with Poirot to speak to her. Instead, with time running away from us and Poirot's quite unnecessarily self-imposed deadline of 24 February looming, I had been assigned the Turville trip.

I did not relish the prospect of venturing inside a boys' boarding school. I attended such a school myself and, despite the education I received, I would not wish the overall experience on anybody.

I felt slightly more comfortable once I was inside Coode House, the boarding house run by Hugo and Jane Dockerill. It was large and wide with a flat façade and a symmetrical distribution of windows, like an enormous doll's house. Inside, it was warm, clean and generally tidy, though as I waited to be shown to Hugo Dockerill's study I spotted one pile of books and one of papers that had been abandoned on the floor close to the front door. Notes had been placed on top of the piles: 'Hugo, please move these' and 'Hugo, please find a proper place for these'. Both were signed 'J'.

A short, bespectacled boy appeared, the third who had helped me so far. This one, like the previous two, was wearing the full Turville uniform: maroon blazer, dark grey trousers, maroon and yellow striped tie. 'I'm to take you to Mr Dockerill's study,' he said.

I thanked him and followed him past the foot of the staircase into a wide corridor. We had turned several corners before he stopped and knocked at a door.

'Come in!' called a man's voice from within.

My pupil guide entered, mumbled something about a visitor, then ran away as if he feared there might be repercussions for his having introduced me to the room. The man, with almost no hair and a wide smile on his face, came towards me, hand extended.

'Inspector Catchpool!' he said warmly. 'I'm Hugo Dockerill, and this is my wife Jane, whom I understand you have met? Welcome to Coode House! We like to think it's the best of all the boarding houses, but of course we are biased.'

'It *is* the best,' said Jane Dockerill matter-of-factly. 'Hello again, Inspector Catchpool.' She sat in a leather armchair in the corner of the room. Books lined every wall from top to bottom, and there were many piles of them on the floor. Presumably this was where those wrongly positioned piles near Coode House's front door would eventually be moved to.

On Jane Dockerill's left, on a straight-backed sofa, sat a boy with dark hair that fell over his large brown eyes. He was a strange-looking character: he was tall, and the eyes, hair and bone structure suggested he ought to be handsome, but the lower part of his face had a clumsily-assembled look about it. He wore an embattled expression and had the bearing of someone who expected to be harangued or punished.

'Good morning, Mrs Dockerill,' I said. 'A pleasure to meet you, Mr Dockerill. Thank you for fitting me into your busy day.'

'Oh, we're delighted to have you. Delighted!' proclaimed the housemaster.

'And this is Timothy Lavington, the late Barnabas Pandy's great-grandson,' said his wife.

'Is it true that you believe Grandy was murdered?' Timothy asked without looking at me.

'Timothy . . .' There was a warning tone in Jane Dockerill's voice. She evidently feared the question might be the prelude to some impertinence on Timothy's part.

'It's perfectly all right,' I told her. 'Timothy, I want you to feel free to ask me whatever questions spring to mind. This must be horrible for you.'

'I would describe it as frustrating rather than horrible,' said the boy. 'If it was murder and not an accident, is it too late to catch whoever did it?'

'No.'

'Good,' said Timothy.

'Though I think it most unlikely that Mr Pandy was murdered. You must try not to worry.'

'I'm not worried. And, unlike you, I *don't* think it's unlikely,' he said.

'Timothy,' warned Jane Dockerill again, obviously knowing that impertinence was now inevitable

He gestured towards her without looking at her and said to me, 'As you can see, I'm prevented from speaking freely by Mrs Dockerill's desire for me to say only the sorts of things that grown-ups think boys my age *should* say.'

'Why don't you think it unlikely that your great-grandfather was murdered?' I asked him.

'Several reasons. Mother, Aunt Annabel and Ivy were supposed to come to the Christmas Fair here on the day Grandy died. They cancelled at the last moment, and couldn't explain why—not to my satisfaction. Something must have happened at home, something they all decided not to tell me. Whatever it was, that something might have led to one of them killing Grandy. Even the weakest woman could easily have pushed him under the water and held him there. Physically, he was weaker than a daddy-long-legs.'

'Go on,' I said.

'Well, then someone stuck a dress belonging to my Aunt

Annabel to the bottom of my bed here—a *soggy* dress. And Grandy died while in the bath. That's extremely suspicious—don't you think so, Inspector?'

'It's certainly something that requires an explanation,' I said.

'I'll say! And what about the letters that were sent, accusing four people of killing Grandy? One of them was sent to Aunt Annabel.'

'We perhaps should not have told Timothy as much as we did,' said Jane Dockerill ruefully.

'Ivy would have told me, if you hadn't,' Timothy said. 'Oh—Ivy won't have killed Grandy, Inspector. You can cross her off your list. And Kingsbury—it definitely won't have been him.'

'Are you suggesting that your mother or your aunt might have done it?' I asked.

'One of them must have, I suppose. They've both got heaps of money now he's dead.'

'Timothy!' said Jane Dockerill.

'Mrs Dockerill, I'm sure the inspector wants me to tell the truth—don't you, Inspector? I can quite see Mother killing anyone who crossed her. She does so like to be in charge of everything. Aunt Annabel is quite the opposite, but she's a strange lady, so who knows what she might do?'

'Strange in what respect?' I asked.

'It's difficult to describe. It's as if . . . even when she's at her happiest, one sort of feels she might be pretending. Rather like . . .' Timothy nodded to himself, as if pleased with the idea that had just struck him. 'Have you ever known anyone whose skin is ice-cold, even when they're sitting in front of a roaring fire in a swelteringly hot room? If you substitute feelings for body temperature, you've got Aunt Annabel.'

'That doesn't make an awful lot of sense, Timothy,' said Jane Dockerill.

'I think I understand,' I told her.

'It's been difficult for Timothy since his father died a few years ago, Inspector.'

'Mrs Dockerill is right,' said Timothy. 'I was sad to lose my father. That does not, however, invalidate my thoughts and observations on other matters.'

'Were you also sad to lose your great-grandfather?' I asked him.

'In a theoretical sort of way, yes.'

'What do you mean?'

'The end of any life is sad, isn't it?' said Timothy. 'I definitely *thought* it was sad that Grandy was dead, but he was old, and we weren't close. He didn't speak to me much. It was amusing, actually: sometimes, at home, he saw me coming and pretended to remember something that required him to turn and walk in the opposite direction.'

'Why would he avoid you?' I asked, feeling that I knew the answer.

'He thought I was hard work. I *am* rather hard work. He was too—which meant that he preferred to speak to Mother, Aunt Annabel, Ivy and Kingsbury. They all pandered to him.'

'It did not upset you, that he displayed a preference for your sister?'

'Hardly. Mother prefers me, so it all evens out. I'm her precious little boy who can do no wrong. We have preferences, in our family. Grandy never liked Aunt Annabel anywhere near as much as he liked Mother—while I think *I* like Aunt Annabel more. She's a far nicer woman.'

'Come now, Lavington,' said Hugo Dockerill vaguely.

'One cannot choose how one feels and about whom, Mr Dockerill. Can one, Inspector?'

I had no intention of taking sides.

'Don't look so shocked, Mrs Dockerill,' said Timothy. 'You like Freddie Rule more than all the other Coode House boys, and I'm sure you can't help that any more than I can help the way I feel.'

'That's not true, Timothy,' said Jane Dockerill. 'I would treat any boy who was lonely exactly as I treat Freddie. And you need to learn the difference between truthfulness and giving voice to every idea that passes through your mind. One is helpful; the other is not. I think you have said enough this morning. Please can you return to your lessons now?'

Once Timothy had been dismissed, I asked about typewriters. Hugo Dockerill said, 'By all means, old chap—you may inspect mine to your heart's content. Oh . . . I wonder where it is. Jane, dearest, do you happen to know?'

'I'm afraid not, Hugo. I haven't seen it for weeks. Last time I saw it, it was in this room, but it's not here now.'

I tried to look as if this piece of information was of no great interest or relevance. 'Do you remember moving the machine, Mr Dockerill?' I asked.

'No. No, I'm afraid I don't. I don't think I *did* move it. Yet it's not here. How funny.'

'Why do you need to see our typewriter?' asked his wife.

I explained to her about the faulty 'e's in the four letters, and told her that if possible I should like to examine all of Turville College's typewriters.

'I suspected as much,' she said. 'Inspector, you said your visit here today was *not* official police business.'

'That's true.'

'Then there is no Scotland Yard investigation into the sending of those four letters?'

'No. For the time being, Poirot and I are simply poking around, with your kind permission, to see if we can make sense of this perplexing business.'

'I understand, Inspector—but there's a difference between a short conversation of the kind we've just had, and allowing you to test all our typewriters. I'm not sure how the boys' parents would feel about that, or the headmaster. I think he might say that, really, you ought to supply a warrant if that is what you wish to do.'

Hugo Dockerill's missing typewriter was becoming more intriguing by the second.

'May I ask a blunt question, Mrs Dockerill? Are you hoping to protect somebody?'

She looked at me carefully before speaking. 'Whom do you think I would wish to protect? I can assure you, I have not stashed Hugo's typewriter away in a secret place. Why would I have? I could not have anticipated that you would ask to see it.'

'Nevertheless, now that I have, you might not like the idea of me finding it and perhaps identifying it as the machine on which the four letters were typed.'

'Jane, dearest, you don't imagine *I* sent those letters?' Hugo Dockerill sounded alarmed.

'*You?* Don't be ridiculous, Hugo. I am simply suggesting that Inspector Catchpool ought to speak to the headmaster. Turville is his kingdom. If he finds out that a detective was allowed to prowl around without his permission, inspecting school property, we will never hear the end of it!'

To the credit of Jane Dockerill, she did her best to convince the headmaster that cooperating with me would be the sensible and correct thing to do. He seemed amenable to her arguments until he heard of the involvement of Hercule Poirot, at which point his demeanour changed and he became as impassable as a road buried under heavy snow. He made it abundantly clear that, although there were many typewriters at Turville College, I was to be shown none of them.

As I crossed the main quadrangle on my way out, I was thinking of one of these unseen machines more than any of the others: Hugo Dockerill's. Who might have made it go missing? I wondered.

'Inspector Catchpool!'

I turned to see Timothy Lavington, satchel over one shoulder, hurrying towards me.

'Do you have any more questions you'd like to ask me?' he panted.

'I do, as a matter of fact. I'd like to ask you about the Christmas Fair.'

'You mean the day Grandy died?'

'Yes, but I'm interested in the fair.'

Timothy winced. 'Why? It's a stupid waste of time, every year. I wish they'd abolish it.'

'Were you there all day?'

'Yes. Why?'

'Did you see Freddie Rule there, and his mother? And Mr and Mrs Dockerill?'

'Yes. Why are you asking? Oh, I see! You're wondering if one of them might have murdered Grandy. No, they were all here.'

'Can you be certain they were here all day? Would you have noticed if one of them left, then returned an hour or two later?'

Timothy considered the question, then said, 'No, I don't suppose so. Mrs Rule, in particular, might have done that.'

'Why do you say that?' I asked.

'She drove herself here on the day of the fair. I saw her arrive, because Freddie rushed over to greet her. And she is hardly a paragon of virtue—though Mrs Dockerill would say "Timothy!" if she had heard me tell you that.'

'You are referring, I take it, to the rumours about Sylvia Rule?'

Timothy's eyes widened in surprise. 'Do you know about her? I didn't think you would. Who told you?'

'It is possible to pick up a lot of information wandering around a large school,' I said, pleased with my carefully-chosen words.

'Then . . . you know that she kills babies? Oh! You *didn't* know.'

I must have looked as surprised as I felt. Jane Dockerill, when she had brought the dress to Whitehaven Mansions, had said something about Mrs Rule earning money in a manner that was both illegal and immoral. Poirot, Rowland McCrodden and I had all assumed she was referring to a different sort of unlawful immorality.

'It's perfectly true, you know,' said Timothy.

'When you say that Sylvia Rule kills babies . . . ?'

'Women go to her when they're expecting babies they don't want. Only the ones who can afford to pay through the nose, of course. Mrs Rule doesn't care about them—or the babies, obviously. Only about getting richer. That's why I think she might have killed Grandy. Don't you think murder could become a habit? I mean, once a person has taken one life, why not carry on? Grandy would have been an ideal victim. The very old, like the very young, can't fight back.'

Timothy's theory struck me as fanciful. What motive might Sylvia Rule have had for murdering Barnabas Pandy?

'Could Mrs Rule have stuck the dress to the bottom of your bed?' I asked.

'Easily. Though I don't know how she'd have got hold of it. It belongs to my Aunt Annabel.'

I was about to ask Timothy if he knew the whereabouts

of his housemaster's typewriter when he said, 'I want to show you something. It concerns my father. You must promise to tell nobody, if I tell you. Especially not Mother. She doesn't deserve to know. She was always so cold to Father—never showed any affection towards him that I ever saw.

'I'm not sure I can promise to keep secrets, Timothy. If, for instance, there were to be anything criminal about—'

'Oh, it's nothing like that. It's the opposite, actually.' He opened his satchel, pulled out an envelope and passed it to me. It was addressed to him—not at Combingham Hall, but here, at Turville. 'Open it,' he said.

I pulled out the letter, unfolded it and began to read:

Dear Timmy,

I am sorry to have taken so long to write and inform you that, contrary to what you have been told, I am not dead. I am alive and well, and engaged in important work on behalf of His Majesty's Government. Our country is under threat, and must be protected. It has fallen to me to be one of its protectors. My work has placed me and others in a certain amount of danger, and so it was decided that I had to disappear. I am afraid that I cannot tell you any more than I have without endangering you too, which is the very last thing I would ever wish to do. I should not be writing to you at all, and you must promise never to tell anyone that I have. This is very important, Timmy. I do not know if I shall ever be able to return to my old life, but I will certainly write to you whenever I can. This must be our little secret. As soon as I can, I will send an address at which you can write to me. Then we can have a proper corre- spondence. I am immensely proud of you, Timmy, and think of you every single day.

Your loving father,
Cecil Lavington

The letter was dated 21 June 1929: nearly eight months ago.

'Goodness me,' I said, suddenly aware of my heart pounding in my chest.

'I don't think Father would mind my showing you the letter,' said Timothy. 'It's Mother and Ivy and Aunt Annabel who can't be allowed to know. He surely couldn't object to my telling a policeman. And I've been bursting to tell somebody. It was so infuriating to have to sit quietly while Mrs Dockerill explained to you that I must be so sad about my dead father. She has no idea he's as alive as you and I. They must have buried an empty coffin. Ha! Your face is a picture. I knew the letter would shock you.'

'Indeed it has,' I said quietly, staring at the words 'Coode House, Turville College' typed on the envelope. Five letter 'e's; five tiny pieces of proof. And many more in the letter itself.

The horizontal bar of each 'e' had a tiny hole in it where the white paper showed through. Many months before our Hercule Poirot impersonator had decided to accuse four people of murdering Barnabas Pandy, he or she had sent this letter to Timothy Lavington.

The question, as ever, was: why? And how did all the pieces fit together?

CHAPTER 24

Ancient Enmities

In the heart of Wales, Hercule Poirot sat at a heavily scarred kitchen table opposite Deborah Dakin, a stout woman with iron-grey hair, who had talked a lot in the short time Poirot had known her about the need to put her feet up and the impossibility of ever doing so. She had delayed the start of their conversation for nearly twenty minutes while she bustled around her kitchen, assembling a plate of cakes that a detective of Poirot's eminence might deem worthy of his gastronomic attention. Finally, she had sat down and was now rubbing her ankles, grimacing and murmuring to herself about her feet as Poirot read the letter she had placed on the table, alongside the cakes.

Finding Mrs Dakin had been no easy task. Her little cottage had turned out to be not in the town of Llanidloes, as the address had led Poirot to believe, but in a sort of forest nearby, two miles up a steep, narrow track and many miles from what could reasonably be termed 'civilization'. No other houses were visible from any of the cottage's windows, only dense trees. If he had not had the reassurance that a driver was waiting for him as close to the house as it was possible for a motorcar to park, and in a reliable vehicle that would soon take him back to a railway station, Poirot would have been feeling decidedly anxious.

He read the letter a second time. It had been sent by Barnabas Pandy to Vincent Lobb at an address in Dollgellau in Wales, late the previous year. The date on it was 5 December, just two days before Pandy had died.

Pandy had written:

Dear Vincent,

You will be surprised to receive this letter from me, I am sure. For my part, I am surprised to be writing it. I have no way of knowing if, after all these years, you will be as glad to receive it as you would once have been, or if you long ago resolved to cast me from your mind and never think of me again. I asked myself if I might do more harm than good by sending a communication of this sort after so many years, when we are both old men with not much time left to us. In the end, I felt compelled to make an attempt to repair the damage that was done so many years ago.

I wish you to know that I forgive you. I understand the choice you made, and that you would have chosen differently had you not believed yourself to be in mortal danger. I should not have blamed you so unremittingly for your weakness, particularly when you endeavoured to atone for your error by telling me the truth in due course, which is something you need not have done. It was brave of you to do it.

I wish now that I had made a greater effort to see the matter from your perspective. I wish I had, much sooner than now, admitted to myself that, in your position, I too might have been afraid and thought only of saving my own life and the lives of my family, and not about justice and the morality of the situation—and so I write to beg you to be more forgiving towards me than I have been towards you. I am sorry, Vincent, truly. I regret my unyielding condemnation of you. My lack of compassion towards you was a worse sin, I now realize, than anything that you did.

Please forgive me,

Barnabas

Poirot looked up from the letter. 'You received this only three weeks ago?' he asked Deborah Dakin.

She nodded. 'With Vincent being dead, it lay around unopened for a while, until someone decided to enquire as to whether he had family anywhere—and, before you ask me, I don't know who that someone was. All I know is, one day I came home and found it sitting on my doormat. It might easily have been lost for ever and read by no one. It's lucky it got here, if it's important—and I'll admit, Mr Prarrow, that that's the *only* lucky side to it. Otherwise, if it hadn't turned out to be important, and helpful to you . . . well, I'd prefer not to have read it.'

'What do you mean, madame?'

'Only that I nearly wept tears of joy when you told me who you were, and asked if I knew anything about a letter Mr Pandy had sent to Vincent. "The Lord truly does work in mysterious ways," I thought to myself. There was I wishing I'd never clapped eyes on the wretched thing—wishing Mr Pandy had never bothered to write it—when a famous detective tells me it might help with an important investigation! I don't mind the upset it's caused me if it helps you, Mr Prarrow. I can't pretend I'll be sorry if it turns out someone *has* murdered Mr Pandy—because I won't. Not at all. Not for *his* sake. All the same, murder's wrong and I'll willingly do my duty if there's a murderer to be caught.'

'It sounds, madame, as if I ought to ask you where you were on the day Monsieur Pandy died. You speak as if you might have hated him enough to kill him.'

'Enough?' Deborah Dakin looked puzzled. 'Oh, I hated him enough all right, Mr Prarrow. But it's not a question of "enough" or "not enough". I'd never allow myself to kill a person. It's against the law, and so I wouldn't do it. That's what the law's for, isn't it? To tell us what we can and can't do? But please don't think I didn't kill Mr Pandy on account of not hating him *enough*.'

'Why did you hate him?'

'Because of what he did to Vincent. I dare say you'll have heard *that* story already, from Mr Pandy's side.'

Poirot told her he had not.

'Oh.' She looked surprised. 'Well, it goes back to the mine. Slate mine, it was, near Llanberis. Mr Pandy had a few of them—it's how he made his money. This was . . . oh, it must have been fifty years ago. I wasn't even born.'

She was younger than fifty, then. Poirot had thought she was older.

'Mr Pandy was the owner of the mine, and Vincent worked for him as a supervisor. The two of them became good friends—the *best* of friends. What you'd call lifelong friends, except it didn't last, and that was Mr Pandy's doing.'

'He did something to destroy the friendship?' said Poirot.

'Some slate was stolen, and a young man named William Evans was blamed for it. He also worked in the mine, and Mr Pandy thought he was a good lad, by all accounts. Well, Mr Evans got sent to prison, where he took his own life—and he didn't waste any time about it either. He left behind a note saying he wouldn't allow anyone to punish him for a crime he hadn't committed. Well, that made no sense, did it? When he put that rope around his neck, he punished himself worse than the prison was punishing him. And that wasn't yet the worst of it: his grief-stricken wife followed his example and did away with herself *and* their young child.'

'*Bouleversant*,' murmured Poirot, shaking his head.

'It was a terrible tragedy: three lives lost, and all for nothing. It turned out, you see, that he was *right*. About being innocent. William Evans wasn't the guilty one. But I'm getting ahead of myself. I'll admit, Mr Prarrow, I've had no practice at talking to famous detectives in my own kitchen.'

'Please, tell me the story however you wish, madame.'

'You're very kind, Mr Prarrow. Well . . . Mr Pandy was upset by the deaths of the Evanses. Very upset indeed. He wasn't one to count his profits and not care about his workers, I'll say that for him. Fair's fair, much as I hate the man. Hated, I suppose I ought to say, since he's dead.'

'Hatred can survive long after the one who inspired it is gone,' said Poirot.

'You don't have to tell me that, Mr Prarrow! I'm the expert!'

'Was the true culprit ever identified—the one who stole the slate?'

'Oh, yes. With the Evanses dead, Vincent wasn't himself at all, and Mr Pandy noticed some strange behaviour. He wanted to know why Vincent should be so wretched about it when he and William Evans had not been particular friends. Fearing Mr Pandy had guessed the truth, Vincent told him that he'd known all along that William Evans hadn't been the one to steal the slate. The guilty party was a horrible dirty beast of a man—Vincent never told us his name. Didn't want to put it in our heads, he said. Vincent told Mr Pandy that lots of the mine men had known. It wasn't only him. They all kept quiet, though, after the thief threatened to cut their throats and their wives' and children's throats if they spoke up about what they knew.'

'An evil man,' said Poirot quietly.

'Oh, without a doubt, Mr Prarrow. Without a doubt. But that didn't make Vincent evil for not saying anything, did it? He was frightened—frightened that he and his wife and their son, my late husband, would be murdered in their beds if he told Mr Pandy what he knew. Do you see? Could you or I or any of us say we wouldn't be too afraid to speak up? And besides, Vincent *did* speak up eventually. Thanks to him, that beast got what he deserved in the end.'

'But Monsieur Pandy could not forgive him? He blamed him for the death of the Evans family?'

'That he did, Mr Prarrow. And Vincent blamed himself. And I don't deny it made sense for Mr Pandy to be angry with him at first. Anyone would have been, and there was the shock of it as much as anything else. Oh, Vincent understood the way Mr Pandy felt, all right. He never could forgive himself, and neither did Mr Pandy. He treated Vincent as if he'd murdered William Evans and his family with his own bare hands. Even after twenty, thirty years, when Vincent tried again and again to say how deeply he regretted it . . . Even then Mr Pandy wouldn't see him or read his letters. Sent them all back unopened, he did. In the end, Vincent stopped trying.'

'I am sorry, madame.'

'You should be,' Deborah Dakin said. 'Well, not you, Mr Prarrow, I don't mean *you* . . . but Mr Pandy should have been sorry—very sorry—for the way he treated poor Vincent. It destroyed him. As he grew older and life got harder, and no kind word arrived from Mr Pandy, Vincent came to see his old and once so dear friend's judgement upon him as . . . well, as a kind of doom.'

'Tragedy upon tragedy,' said Poirot.

'That makes it sound as if it's no one's fault, when it was,' said Deborah Dakin. 'It was Mr Pandy's fault. Vincent died believing himself to be damned. In the last years of his life, he barely spoke a word.'

'Then . . . pardon me, madame, but why do you describe this letter as "wretched"? Were you not pleased to read it? To know that, after so many years, Monsieur Pandy relented and forgave your father-in-law?

'No, I'm not! This letter makes the whole thing so much *worse*—surely you can see that? Either Vincent committed an unforgivable sin or else he didn't. We always thought that, to Mr Pandy, that's what it was: unforgivable. Then, suddenly, after fifty years, he decides it's no such thing? He made Vincent suffer all that time, only to decide when it was too late, and when it suited *him*, that he got it wrong?'

Poirot said, 'An interesting opinion, madame—though perhaps not entirely rational.'

Deborah Dakin looked affronted. 'What do you mean it's not rational? Of course it is! Doing the right thing much too late is worse than never doing it at all.'

The same logic could be applied to Vincent Lobb's actions, thought Poirot. Evidently this had not occurred to his daughter-in-law, and Poirot decided not to extend his visit any longer than necessary by pointing it out to her.

CHAPTER 25

Poirot Returns to Combingham Hall

Poirot had been expecting a driver to collect him from the railway station. He was surprised to alight from his train and find Lenore Lavington standing on the platform under a navy blue umbrella. She offered no conventional greetings or pleasantries, and instead said, 'I hope I won't regret allowing you to visit us again, M. Poirot.'

'I hope so too, madame.'

They walked to her motorcar in silence, followed by the porter who carried Poirot's cases.

As she started up the engine a few minutes later, Lenore Lavington said, 'Your telegram need not have been as cryptic as it was. Am I to understand that you have found evidence that Grandfather was murdered, and that you plan to expose a murderer during your stay with us? Do you already know . . . ?' She left the question unfinished.

'I will admit, madame, that the picture is not yet complete. In three days' time, however, I hope to be able to tell you and others the whole story.'

Three days. The words loomed large in Poirot's mind. 24 February had seemed a safe distance away when he had sent his letters of invitation. Since then, several interesting new pieces of information had come his way. Any one of them might prove to be the key that unlocked the mystery, but when, he wondered, would the unlocking happen? For the sake of Poirot's peace of mind, he hoped it would be soon.

'At our gathering, you will learn the truth about your grandfather's death,' he said, fervently hoping he would not be proved wrong. 'One of the assembled company will know the truth already, of course.'

'Do you mean Grandfather's murderer?' asked Lenore. 'But that person won't be among the assembled company, as you put it. The only people at the Hall will be you, me, Annabel, Ivy and Kingsbury. None of us murdered Grandfather.'

'You are wrong, I am afraid, madame. Many more people are to join us. They will arrive tomorrow. Inspector Edward Catchpool of Scotland Yard, Hugo and Jane Dockerill, Freddie Rule and his mother Sylvia. Also, there will be Freddie's sister Mildred, and her fiancé Eustace Campbell-Brown, and John McCrodden and his father Rowland McCrodden. And—please be careful!'

The motorcar swerved violently, narrowly missing another vehicle travelling in the opposite direction, then stopped by the side of the road. Lenore Lavington switched off the engine.

'And also your son Timothy,' Poirot said in a faltering

voice, producing a handkerchief from his pocket to wipe his brow.

'Do you mean to tell me you have invited an assortment of complete strangers to my home, without my permission?'

'It is irregular, I know. In my defence, I will say only that it is necessary—unless you wish a murderer to escape justice.'

'Of course I don't, but . . . that does not mean that you can fill my house with strangers and people I dislike without consulting me.'

'Whom do you dislike? Freddie Rule?'

'No. I didn't mean Freddie.'

'Yet you dislike him, do you not?'

'Not at all.' She sounded bored.

'You said when we last met that you had advised your son Timothy to stay away from him.'

'Only because he's so peculiar. I was thinking of the Dockerills, if you must know.'

'What is your objection to Hugo and Jane Dockerill?'

'They are unfair to my son. They punish him for the most minor of misdemeanours, while other boys, the ones who present an angelic façade, get away with . . .' Lenore Lavington stopped.

'Murder?' Poirot suggested.

'I shall have to have lots of bedrooms made up. How long do you plan for all these people to stay? And why so many?'

Because any one of them might have murdered Barnabas Pandy—and I do not yet know which one.

Poirot withheld his true answer and said instead, 'I would prefer to wait until the final pieces of the puzzle fall into place before I say any more.'

Lenore Lavington sighed. Then she started up the engine, and they were once more on their way, along narrow country roads lined with beech trees and silver birches. 'I find it quite impossible to believe that one of these people you have invited could have entered the house on the day Grandfather died without any of us noticing,' she said. 'Still . . . if you're certain, and as an inspector from Scotland Yard is taking the trouble to come to the Hall, you will have my family's full cooperation.'

'*Merci mille fois*, madame.'

'As soon as we arrive at the house, you may look at the typewriter, if you still wish to do so.'

'That would be useful.'

'We have a new one, since you were last here—the old machine was past its best.'

Poirot looked alarmed. 'Do you still have the old typewriter?'

'Yes. I've asked Kingsbury to put both machines out for you to look at. The new one was still in the shop when those horrible letters were typed, but if I don't present it for inspection, you might think I am hiding something.'

'It is sensible to be always thorough and check everything,' Poirot told her. 'Which is why I should like to ask you some questions about the day Monsieur Pandy died.'

'Are you going to ask about the discussion Ivy and I

were having while Grandfather took his bath? Go ahead. I've told you: I am willing to cooperate if it will help bring an end to all this unpleasantness and uncertainty.'

'Kingsbury described it as an argument, not a discussion,' said Poirot.

'It was a horrible row, made worse by Annabel's endless wailing at us to stop,' said Lenore. 'She cannot tolerate any sort of conflict. Nobody likes it, of course, but most of us accept that not every exchange can be a pleasant one. I'm sure Ivy and I would have resolved our dispute far sooner if Annabel had not constantly interrupted with her demands that we be kind to one another. That only inspired me to be rather unkind to *her*, as I recall. Her sympathies were with Ivy, as always, yet she took care to ingratiate herself with me too.'

'Madame, I am grateful for your frankness, but it would be more useful to me if you could tell me first the cause of the *contretemps* between you and your daughter.'

'Yes, I am being frank, aren't I?' Lenore Lavington sounded surprised. 'Franker than I've been in a long time. It's rather intoxicating.'

Yet she also sounded worried by it, Poirot thought.

'The harsh words that passed between Ivy and me in her bedroom that day were not the start of the trouble. A few days earlier, there was a family dinner that ended in disaster, and several months prior to that there was an equally ill-fated trip to the beach. That's really when it all began. And it was my fault, all of it. If I had exercised a little more self-control, none of it would have happened.'

'Tell me the story from the beginning,' said Poirot.

'I will, on one condition,' said Lenore Lavington. 'That you promise not to speak of it to Ivy. I have her permission to tell you about it, but I fear it would be dreadfully embarrassing for her if you were to raise the subject in her presence.'

By way of response, Poirot made a noise that was carefully calibrated to sound like assent. The next words he heard surprised him.

'I made an unfortunate remark about Ivy's legs, while we were at the beach together.'

'Her legs, madame?'

'Yes. I will forever regret it—but, once made, a remark cannot be cancelled out of existence, however often one apologizes. It lives on in the memory of the one wounded by it.'

'The remark was an insulting one?' Poirot asked.

'It certainly wasn't intended to be. You will have noticed, I'm sure, that Ivy's face is badly scarred. Of course you have. No one could fail to notice. As her mother, I naturally worry that the disfigurement will make it difficult if not impossible for her to attract a husband. I should like her to have one—and children. My own marriage was not a success, but Ivy would make a better choice than I did, I have no doubt. She is more realistic than I was at her age. If only she would understand that marriage is about being chosen as much as it is about choosing.'

Lenore made an impatient noise. 'It is impossible to tell

this story without saying things that you might judge to be unforgivable, M. Poirot. I'm afraid I cannot help how I feel. Ivy is lucky that most of her face is unaffected by the scarring. She could easily conceal it if she arranged her hair in the right way—which she perversely refuses to do. She could if she chose to, of course, and I have never believed that her scars would deter any man from ever taking an interest in her. Ivy has a lively and engaging way about her.'

'Most engaging,' Poirot agreed.

'I *do* think, however, that she ought not to add to the problem by eating until she's the size of a small house. What man would want a wife with scars on her face *and* a hugely fat body? If I sound angry, M. Poirot, it is only because I have never said this to Ivy, though it's often in my mind. Nothing has ever mattered more to me than my children's happiness. For *their* sake, I was a dutiful and loving wife to their father, my late husband, until the day he died. For *their* sake, I allow Annabel to fuss over them and interfere in their lives as if she's as much their mother as I am. I know how much they love her, and I have always put their needs and feelings before my own. In order not to hurt Ivy's feelings, I have sat at the dinner table night after night and watched her pile extra helpings on to her plate, and I've said *nothing*—not a word—though I can hardly bear to watch. She was a large, stocky child and will always be a well-built girl, of course. She takes after Cecil, her father. Still, I cannot help watching the way she eats and wondering what on earth she thinks she's doing.

She seems not to worry at all about her figure. I can't understand it.'

Lenore Lavington exhaled loudly. 'There. I've said it. Those are my true feelings. Do you think I'm a cruel, unloving mother, M. Poirot?'

'Not unloving, madame, but . . . if you will permit me to make an observation?'

'By all means.'

'Mademoiselle Ivy is a perfectly attractive young lady of a quite normal shape and size. You are, in my opinion, worrying unnecessarily. It is true that she does not have the exceptionally fine-boned frame that you and your sister both have, but many women do not. Look around at the world! It is not only those with the waist I could encircle between my forefinger and thumb who fall in love and make successful marriages.'

Lenore Lavington shook her head vigorously as Poirot spoke. The moment he'd finished, she said, 'If Ivy continues to heap potatoes on to her plate at her present rate, she will soon have no waist to speak of. That was what started the trouble at the disastrous dinner: she helped herself to one potato, then another, then another, until I simply couldn't stop myself.'

'From what?' asked Poirot.

'All I said was, "Ivy, two potatoes are enough, surely?" I thought I had chosen my words carefully, but she flew into the wildest rage, and all her resentments came pouring out, including the full story of what had happened on the beach. Grandfather and Annabel were terribly shocked and upset, and *I* was upset because I was made to seem like the villain of the piece, which I suppose I was—and that only made it even worse!'

'Tell me the story of the beach,' said Poirot.

'It was last summer,' said Lenore. 'A blisteringly hot day. Annabel had influenza, and couldn't even get up to play with Hopscotch in the garden. He was howling and whining at the foot of her bed, and it was causing her great distress. She asked us to take him out for the day, away from Combingham Hall. I wasn't thrilled by the prospect—I am not a dog lover, I'm afraid—but Ivy said that Annabel would recover more quickly if she wasn't worried about Hopscotch, so I agreed.

'We went to the beach. Ivy nearly drowned as a young girl—did you know that? That's how she acquired those horrible scars. She rolled down a river bank into the water. Annabel's dog before Hopscotch—Skittle, his name was—he tried to stop her from rolling into the water, but only ended up scratching her face to ribbons. It wasn't his fault, of course.'

'Mademoiselle Annabel saved your daughter's life, did she not?' said Poirot.

'Yes. If it weren't for my sister, Ivy would have drowned. They both nearly drowned. The current was easily strong enough to carry them both away, but, somehow, Annabel managed to drag Ivy out of the water and save her, and save herself too. They were very lucky. I can hardly bear to think about what might have happened. Annabel has had a strong aversion to water ever since.'

'To water,' Poirot murmured. 'This is most fascinating.'

'Ivy was also scared of water for a long time, but at the age of fourteen, she set herself the task of conquering her fear, and soon became a regular and enthusiastic swimmer. She now drives to the beach for a dip as often as she can—the same beach to which she and I took Hopscotch the day Annabel was sick.'

'Commendable.'

'Yes. Though all that swimming has given her legs and arms a rather muscular quality. And there is no need to tell me that many women with the limbs of male athletes have happy marriages, M. Poirot. I don't doubt it. I simply want my daughter to look as attractive as she can, that's all.'

Poirot said nothing.

'I am not a regular swimmer myself,' said Lenore. 'I had not seen my daughter in a bathing costume for many years, until the day we took Hopscotch to the beach. Ivy swam for half an hour, then came to sit with me. Hopscotch was playing in the waves, and Ivy and I were sitting near the trees. She was eating some sort of picnic. Then the dog came running over to us, having noticed that there were goodies available, and the strangest thing happened: Ivy turned pale and began to shake. She was staring at Hopscotch, her mouth wide open, trembling as if she might faint.

'I asked her what was wrong, but she couldn't speak. A memory had come back to her, you see—a memory of the day she nearly drowned. She was able to tell me this only later, on the way home. Having remembered hardly any of the details for so many years, she had suddenly remembered her head being under the water, and being unable to breathe or free herself from whatever was trapping her there. Suddenly, she remembered all of it vividly. She remembered there had been *trees* on the river bank, like the ones she and I were sitting near on the beach, and she remembered seeing Skittle's legs . . . How well do you know dogs, M. Poirot?'

'I have made the acquaintance of several over the years, madame. Why do you ask?'

'Have you ever known a dog like Hopscotch? One with a thick, wiry coat?'

Had he? Poirot did not think that he had. He said so.

'Hopscotch is an Airedale Terrier,' said Lenore. 'You will have noticed, I'm sure, that the hair on his four legs is fluffy and voluminous—almost as if he's wearing furry trousers.'

'*Oui*. That is a good description.'

'Skittle, the dog that tried to save Ivy, was an Airedale, just like Hopscotch. When dry, the legs of Airedale Terriers look much wider than they are—the hair fluffs out instead of lying flat. When Hopscotch ran over to Ivy that day, in the hope of sharing her picnic, his legs were wet from playing in the sea, and so they looked much thinner—like two brown sticks. It took Ivy back, in the most vivid way, to the day she nearly drowned.

'She remembered seeing Skittle's wet legs, you see, and thinking, only for a second or two, that they were brown tree trunks. Because they were so thin, she said she imagined they must be far away, and thought this meant that she was trapped far out from the bank of the river with no hope of rescue. I think she was probably delirious with fear.

'Moments later, Annabel reached her and suddenly there was hope! Ivy noticed that there was a thick tree trunk beside the thin ones—that was when she knew that the thin ones were not tree trunks at all. She realized they were moving back and forth, and that they were attached to the dog. Everything started to make sense again.'

Lenore Lavington's breathing had a jagged sound to it. 'You can imagine how distressing it was for me to hear all this, M. Poirot. It brought it all back: the shock of discovering that I had so nearly lost my daughter. If Ivy and I had not taken Hopscotch to the beach that day, if he hadn't got his legs wet in the sea, those memories might never have surfaced. I wish they hadn't, and I wish *I* hadn't said what I said afterwards, but one cannot undo the past, can one?'

'Are we coming now to the unfortunate remark about the legs?' Poirot asked. He had been wondering if she would ever get to it.

'We were driving back. After what Ivy had told me, I was not myself—not at all. I tried to concentrate on getting us home without crashing into anything. I desperately wanted her to stop talking so that I could gather my wits . . . and the words just came out! I didn't *choose* to say what I said.'

'What words came out, madame?'

'I said that Skittle wasn't the one whose legs resembled tree trunks. And I said that Ivy ought to think about doing a little less swimming, because her legs would look more and more like tree trunks the more muscular she became. I regretted it as soon as the words were out of my mouth. Still, there was one benefit: Ivy was immediately furious with me. The horrible old memories of her near-drowning were no longer in her mind. All she could think about was how much she loathed her heartless mother. I didn't say what I said to hurt her—I don't *really* think her legs look like *actual* tree trunks—I only wanted her to think about something else instead of the memories that were upsetting her. I wanted her to turn her attention to her future, not the past. I must have spent hours apologizing to her, and I thought we'd put it behind us, I really did—but then *months* later at dinner . . . well, I've already told you about that.'

'Mademoiselle Ivy told your sister and your grandfather the story of what happened at the beach, and what you had said to her?'

'Yes.'

'What was their reaction?'

'Annabel was distraught, naturally,' said Lenore with a weary impatience. 'For every tear shed by anybody else, Annabel must always produce a flood of her own.'

'And Monsieur Pandy?'

'He said nothing, but he looked terribly unhappy. I don't think it was my careless remarks so much as the thought of how frightened Ivy must have been, thinking she was about to die. She perhaps should have kept her newly discovered memories to herself. It's Annabel's influence. Ivy never used to have these outbursts of emotion. Even after a dinner had been ruined, it wasn't enough for her! On the day Grandfather died, I was walking along the landing and I heard loud sobbing. It is possible to cry quietly, you know, M. Poirot.'

'Indeed, madame.'

'I'm afraid I decided I could not tolerate such self-pity any longer. My daughter used to be a robust, sensible girl. I told her so, and she screamed at me: "How am I supposed to feel when my own mother has compared my legs to tree trunks?" Then of course Annabel dashed up the stairs to meddle where she wasn't needed, in the guise of peace-keeping, and soon afterwards Grandfather shouted from his bath that we were all making a horrible din and could we please desist? If Annabel had kept out of it and let me speak to my daughter privately, there would have been far less of a commotion, because Ivy and I had to raise our voices to make ourselves heard above her ceaseless wailing. Grandfather was no fool—he knew it as well as I did. It was Annabel he was shouting at. By then, he had already decided . . .'

Poirot turned to see why Lenore Lavington had stopped speaking. Unsightly blotches had appeared on her face. She stared straight ahead, at the road.

'Please go on,' said Poirot.

'If I do, you must promise to repeat it to nobody. No one knows apart from me, now that Grandfather is dead.'

'You are going to tell me, I think, that Monsieur Pandy had decided to make a new will?'

The car jerked dramatically. '*Sacre tonnerre!*' cried Poirot. 'You are surprised to discover that Hercule Poirot knows so much, I understand, but it is no reason to kill us both.'

'How can you know about the will? Unless . . . You must have spoken to Peter about it, Peter Vout. That's funny. Grandfather said I was only one he had told. Perhaps he meant the only one of the family. Annabel must never know, M. Poirot. You must promise me. It would destroy her. I have been saying things about her that are not entirely complimentary, I know, but nevertheless . . .'

'Nevertheless, she is your sister. And she saved the life of your daughter.'

'Quite,' said Lenore. 'After Grandfather died, it was the one thing I was thankful for: that he did not have the chance to alter his will, and so Annabel would never have to find out. I would have made sure she was well looked after, naturally, but that's hardly the point. To be cut off so brutally . . . I think she might have fallen apart.'

'Did you try to persuade Monsieur Pandy to change his mind, when he told you what he intended to do?'

'No. It would only have strengthened his resolve. To try to persuade someone out of a feeling . . .' She broke off with a firm shake of the head. 'It's the very essence of futility. It never works, whether directed at oneself or at others. Grandfather rarely, though occasionally, saw that he had been wrong about something, but never when told by somebody else.'

'I see,' said Poirot.

What was it, he asked himself, that did not fit? He knew

he had heard something that jutted out awkwardly. He knew, furthermore, that he had heard it since getting into the car with Lenore Lavington. *What was it?*

'You might be thinking that my sister had the perfect motive to commit murder,' Lenore said. 'She did—but she didn't *know* she did. Therefore, she didn't.'

'Mademoiselle Annabel has also been given the most unshakeable alibi by you and your daughter,' Poirot reminded her.

'You say that as if it's a lie. It's *not* a lie. Ivy and I were with Annabel every single second, M. Poirot. And when we all stood in the bathroom together, summoned by Kingsbury, every inch of Annabel's dress was dry. It is quite impossible that she killed Grandfather.'

'Tell me, madame: has Mademoiselle Ivy forgiven you?' Poirot asked. 'Or does she still keep alive the grievance?'

'I don't know. I have no intention of raising the subject again, but I hope that she has. The other day, for the first time, she wore a bracelet I gave her. I think that might have been a sort of peace offering. I gave it to her when Grandfather died, you see. She definitely had not forgiven me then! She told me she would rather die than wear it, and threw it across the room at me. It was a beautiful, hand-carved mourning bracelet made of jet—one I cherished. I suppose I thought that giving it to Ivy would be proof of my love for her. She knew it was precious to me—a treasured gift from a seaside holiday with my late husband Cecil—but she chose to interpret it in the worst possible way.'

'In what way did she interpret it?' The gates to the Combingham Hall Estate were now visible in the distance.

'She accused me of only ever giving her gifts that were things I already owned, not presents I had bought especially for her. She went to her bedroom and started pulling drawers out of chests, looking for a hand-held fan I had once given her—more evidence against me! The fan was also a treasured possession of mine. It had a picture on it of a beautiful lady, dancing, and of course her waist was *tiny*. Trust Ivy to remember that when I had given her the fan I'd said, "The dancing lady looks like you, darling"—because she *did,* with her black hair and pale skin. Ivy had loved the fan when I first gave it to her, and taken the comparison as the compliment I intended it to be. Suddenly, however, in the light of the unfortunate events I have already described, she decided I had been duplicitous, and had wanted her to notice the difference between the fan-lady's dainty waist and her own larger one.'

'Human relationships are extremely complicated,' said Poirot.

'People make them more complicated than they need to be,' said Lenore disapprovingly. 'Though, as I say: Ivy recently wore the mourning bracelet I gave her. She made sure that I saw her wearing it, too. It must have been her way of letting me know that she has forgiven me. What else could it mean?'

CHAPTER 26

The Typewriter Experiment

When Lenore Lavington and Poirot arrived at Combingham Hall, they found Kingsbury standing guard beside a small table in the entrance hall. On the table sat two typewriters, side by side.

'I've set up the two machines for Mr Porrott, like you asked, Mrs Lavington,' he said.

'Thank you, Kingsbury. That will be all for now.'

The manservant shuffled away. Nobody made a move to close the front door.

Poirot managed to suppress his urge to ask why, in a house the size of Combingham Hall, with so many rooms presumably empty and without function, did such things as dining and the testing of typewriters need to take place in the entrance hall? It made no sense! If Poirot had owned the building, he would have put a grand piano here where the small table had been placed. That was the only thing that might look as if it belonged in this particular spot.

'Is there a problem, M. Poirot?' Lenore Lavington asked.

'Not at all, madame.' He turned his attention to the two machines in front of him. One was new and shiny; the other had a crack in its side and a deep scratch on its front. Kingsbury had set out, next to the two typewriters, the paper and carbon paper that Poirot would need later to conduct his experiment.

Once he had made himself at home in the bedroom that had been assigned to him, and taken some refreshment, Poirot sat down at the little table and tried first one typewriter, then the other. Both had identical letter 'e's with no ink missing at all. There was no need to search for other differences, though search he did. If one did not look, one gave oneself no opportunity to spot any detail that could not have been anticipated, but was nonetheless highly significant.

In his mother tongue of French, Poirot gave thanks to a higher power when he saw that such a detail was present in this instance. He was busy comparing the two pieces of paper on which he had typed precisely the same words when first he heard and then saw Hopscotch. The dog came running down the stairs and across the hall. He leapt up to greet Poirot. Annabel Treadway ran down the stairs after him. 'Hoppy, *down*. Down, boy! M. Poirot doesn't want to have his face licked, I'm sure.'

Indeed Poirot did not. He patted the dog instead, hoping Hopscotch would accept this as a reasonable compromise.

'Look how pleased he is to see you, M. Poirot! Isn't he a lovely, affectionate boy?' Annabel managed to sound sad about it: as if no one but she could appreciate the dog's good nature.

Eventually Hopscotch remembered that he had been on his way outside, and trotted off into the garden.

Annabel, spotting the two sheets of paper in Poirot's hands, said, 'I see you've begun your typewriter investigation. Oh, don't let me interrupt you. Lenore gave me strict orders to leave you alone and let you do your detective work.'

'I have concluded the experiment, mademoiselle. Would you like to see the results? Tell me, what differences do you notice?' He passed her the two sheets of paper.

She stared at them for a while before looking up at Poirot. 'I don't see anything at all,' she said. 'Nothing worthy of note, I mean. The letter "e" is fully present and correct on both pages.'

'It is. But there is more to look at than the many letters "e".'

'The same words are typed on both sheets of paper—"I, Hercule Poirot, have arrived at Combingham Hall, and I will not leave until I have solved the mystery of the death of Barnabas Pandy." The two versions are identical in every respect, aren't they? What am I failing to notice?'

'If I were to tell you the answer, Mademoiselle, I would deprive you of the chance to work it out for yourself.'

'I don't want to work anything out. I want you to tell us if we're in danger from a murderer roaming about the place, and protect us if we are, and then . . . then all I want is to forget!'

'What do you wish to forget?'

'All of it. Grandy's murder, and the reason for it, whatever that turns out to be, and the sickening letter I can't get out of my mind, even though I burned it.'

'And a wet blue dress with white and yellow flowers on it?' Poirot asked.

She looked at him, wide-eyed and apparently uncomprehending. 'What do you mean?' she said. '*I* have a blue dress with white and yellow flowers on it. But it isn't wet.'

'Where is it?'

'In my wardrobe.'

'Are you certain it is there?'

'Where else would it be? It's the dress I wore the day Grandy died. I haven't felt like wearing it since.'

She had not, then, looked for the dress and found that it was missing. *Assuming she is telling the truth*, Poirot said to himself.

'Mademoiselle, were you aware that, before he died, your grandfather decided to make a change to his will? He did not, in the end, do so. His death prevented it. But it was his intention to alter his testamentary provisions quite considerably.'

'No, I didn't know that. Though Peter Vout, his solicitor, came to the house and the two of them secluded themselves in the drawing room to talk in private, so perhaps that was . . .'

Annabel gasped suddenly, and reeled backwards. Poirot moved quickly to catch her, in case she fell.

He helped her to a chair. 'What is the matter, mademoiselle?'

'It was me, wasn't it?' she said in a whisper. 'He wished to cut me off. That was why he summoned Peter Vout. Even though I saved Ivy's life—once he knew, he couldn't forgive me! Which means I must deserve never to be forgiven,' Annabel said fiercely. 'If Grandy was going to alter his will to punish me, that means I deserve nothing. Only to suffer. He was always fair. I never imagined he could love me the way he loved Lenore, but *he was always fair.*'

'Mademoiselle, please explain to Poirot. For what could your grandfather not forgive you?'

'No! Oh, he will get what he wanted—I won't stand in the way of his wishes—but I will never tell you or anybody. *Never!*' Sobbing, she ran up the stairs.

Poirot stared after her, bemused. Then he looked at the house's open front door, and thought about how easy it would be for him to go back to London and to Whitehaven Mansions, and never return. Officially, no crime had been committed, so he could hardly be blamed for failing to solve a murder.

But of course he would not leave. He was Hercule Poirot! 'Three days,' he said to himself. 'Only three days.'

CHAPTER 27

The Bracelet and the Fan

The next morning, Poirot was on his way to take breakfast when Ivy Lavington ambushed him in the hall. Hopscotch was at her side. He did not try to lick Poirot this time. He seemed, in fact, rather subdued.

'Where is Aunt Annabel?' Ivy demanded. 'What have you done with her?'

'Is she not at home, here in the house?' he asked.

'No. She's taken one of the cars and gone off somewhere without Hoppy—which she never does. Absolutely never. Not without saying a word to me or Mummy. Did you say something to upset her?'

'*Oui, c'est possible*,' said Poirot with a heavy heart. 'Sometimes, if lives are to be saved, one must ask unwelcome questions.'

'Whose lives must be saved?' asked Ivy. 'Are you suggesting that whoever killed Grandy intends to kill again?'

'Without doubt, a murder has been planned.'

'So is it one life, or more than one? You said "lives".'

'Mademoiselle! *Sacre tonnerre!*'

'What is it? You look as if you've seen a ghost.'

Poirot opened his mouth, but could make no words come out. He was thinking too fast to speak at all.

'Are you quite well, M. Poirot?' Ivy looked concerned. 'Did I say something that frightened you?'

'Mademoiselle, you said something that has helped me greatly! Please now say nothing for a short while. I need to follow the logic of the theory that is growing in my mind, to see if I am right. I *must* be right!'

Ivy stood, arms folded, and watched him as he put the various pieces together. Hopscotch, still by her side, also stared at him quizzically.

'Thank you,' Poirot said eventually.

'Well?' said Ivy. 'Are you right?'

'I believe so, yes.'

'Jolly good! I'm looking forward to hearing your theory. I haven't been able to think up any of my own.'

'Do not try,' Poirot advised. 'Your speculations would be based upon an entirely false premise, and so you would fail.'

'What do you mean, a false premise?'

'All in good time, mademoiselle. All in good time.'

Ivy made a face at him that suggested a mixture of annoyance and admiration. 'I expect Mummy told you all about the fight we had the day Grandy died?' She grinned. 'You'll know all about my tree-trunk legs. And Mummy will have told you not to say a word to me, for fear of upsetting me all over again.'

'Mademoiselle, if I might be permitted to say so, you are most pleasing to look at, and there is nothing at all wrong with your size or shape.'

'Well, I've got my scars,' said Ivy, pointing to her face. 'But apart from that, I agree. I am a normal, healthy person, and that suits me fine. Mummy thinks I ought to aspire to be no wider than a pipe-cleaner, but food is a madness of hers. She doesn't eat properly. Never has. Did you notice last night, at dinner?'

'I am afraid I did not,' said Poirot, who had been too busy eating his own delicious meal.

'She puts the odd sliver of something in her mouth every now and then, and swallows it grudgingly, like someone taking a prescribed medicine, but she spends most of each meal prodding things with her fork as if she suspects them of plotting against her. She imagines that the reason I was so angry with her was because I couldn't bear to hear the truth about my horrible legs. What nonsense! I'm perfectly happy with my legs. What upset me was finding out that Mummy looks at me and sees only, or mainly, a bundle of physical flaws. And her dishonesty—that also enrages me.'

'Your mother is not honest?' said Poirot.

'Oh, she can't bear the truth. She is almost allergic to it. She would do or say *anything* to keep me and Timmy happy—I think she feels it's her duty as a mother—but every so often a scrap of truthfulness slips out, and when it does, she bends over backwards afterwards to deny what is plain to see. I shall *never* believe her when she says she thinks I'm beautiful. I know it's a lie. She'd be far better off admitting that she would love it if I starved myself skinny. Instead, she lies and lies about how much she loves me the way I am, and tells herself she's keeping me happy by doing so.' Ivy spoke thoughtfully and analytically, with no trace of resentment in her voice. She was, Poirot reflected, a happier and more stable woman than either her mother or her aunt.

'The thing is, if you try to deny the truth, it creeps out in other ways. I don't suppose Mummy told you about the time she gave me a fan as a present?' Ivy laughed. 'There was a picture of a dark-haired woman on it, and Mummy said, "Doesn't she look like you, Ivy? Her hair is the same colour, and her dress." All of which was true—but the woman on the fan had the tiniest waist I had ever seen! And *I* happened to be on my way out to a dance wearing a rather attention-seeking black and red dress which, looking back, probably didn't suit me, and would have looked better on someone with a more slender figure, but I didn't care. I liked the dress, so I wore it. Mummy couldn't bear it, though, because it accentuated my waist—so she presented me with a rebuke in the guise of a gift. I imagine she hoped I would take one look at the woman on the fan, notice the contrast, and immediately decide to change into something that disguised my waist and made me look smaller.'

'Your mother told me that she gave to you also a bracelet,' said Poirot.

Ivy nodded. 'That was after Grandy died. I took one look at it and thought that I wouldn't be able to squeeze my hand through it if I tried for a hundred years. It was Mummy's, and must have fitted her perfectly, but it wasn't designed for someone of my build. As it turned out, the bracelet *did* fit me, but only just. I wore it recently, but I don't think I will again. I wanted Mummy to see it on my wrist at least once. I know she still worries that she's damaged me irreparably by allowing me to discover that she would like me to be slimmer, and I wanted to show her that I've forgiven her. She can't help being the way she is. And, in my anger, I was terribly unfair to her. The bracelet and the fan were both things she loved and would never have parted with—if she hadn't given them to me, I mean— but I accused her of giving me second-hand gifts and being unwilling to spend her money on me.'

Ivy gave a rueful smile. 'I am no more perfect than Mummy is, M. Poirot. I think it's important to understand that one's nearest and dearest are *not* perfect. If one cannot accept that . . . well, that way lies madness.'

No person, Poirot agreed, could ever be perfect. On the other hand, a puzzle and its solution, once all the loose and messy ends were neatly wrapped up . . .

'Did you know, mademoiselle, that your grandfather intended to change his will, and that he died before he could do so?'

'No.' Ivy's eyes took on a sharper look. 'How did he plan to change it?'

'Both his solicitor and your mother tell me that he intended to cut off Mademoiselle Annabel—to leave to her nothing at all.'

'Why on earth should he want to do that?' said Ivy. 'Aunt Annabel is a kind, selfless, entirely good person. There are not many people like her. I am not always kind. Are you, M. Poirot?'

'I try to be, mademoiselle. It is important to try.'

'But . . . it makes no sense,' Ivy muttered. 'It can't be true. Grandfather always favoured Mummy, but he would never have demonstrated his preference so starkly. He knew as well I do that Aunt Annabel would never hurt anybody. I always believed he felt rather guilty for finding her maddening, because he knew she had done nothing to deserve it.'

'I must ask you one more question, mademoiselle,' said Poirot. 'It is a strange one, and I apologize if it causes you distress.'

'Is it about tree trunks?' Ivy said.

'No. It concerns your late father.'

'Poor Daddy.'

'Why do you say that?'

'I don't know. I don't think Mummy loved him very much. Oh, she played the role of a good wife to perfection, but her heart was not engaged. She *might* have been able to love him more if she had only been honest from the start. Instead, their relationship followed her usual pattern: she tried to do and say whatever she thought would keep him happy, and, as a result, neither of them was able to be happy.'

'Did she deceive him about something in particular?' Poirot asked.

'No, it was worse than that,' said Ivy. 'She deceived him in their ordinary, everyday life. Mummy is terribly clever, you know. Well organized, astute, capable. She tends to assume that things will go her way. Having that attitude has often made the obstacles in her path disappear. Or rather, I should say, it has since Daddy died. Daddy would fret awfully about the tiniest things, and was forever saying they shouldn't try to do this or that because they wouldn't succeed—leaving Combingham Hall, for instance, and making a home of their own. Mummy wanted to, but Daddy didn't, and so Mummy pretended to agree with him. Knowing that she could have made it work brilliantly if she'd only had the chance must have eaten away at her. She should have told him to stop being so silly instead of pandering to his timid approach to life. I imagine it must have been rather a relief to her when he died.'

'Did she express relief?'

'Goodness me, no. She'd have died too rather than admit it. She really is terribly clever. She has thoroughly enjoyed being in charge of herself and making all her own decisions since Daddy died—but without once saying, "What a relief to be free!" as many women in her position might have. To say anything like that would be too direct for Mummy.'

Ivy smiled. 'Listen to me chattering away. What did you want to ask me about Daddy? I never gave you the chance.'

'Since your father's death, have you received any letters purporting to be from him?'

'Letters from my dead father? No. Not a one. Why do you ask?'

Poirot shook his head. 'It does not matter. Thank you for taking the time to talk to me, mademoiselle. Our conversation has been most illuminating.'

'I should say it matters quite a lot,' Ivy called after him as he set off for the dining hall, where his breakfast awaited him. 'First letters from you that aren't from you, and now letters from my dead father that can't be from him . . . I hope you're going to explain all of this, M. Poirot. I want to understand every single baffling aspect of this whole peculiar business.'

'So do I,' said Poirot to himself as he sat down to eat. 'So, very much, do I.'

CHAPTER 28

An Unconvincing Confession

I was sitting in my office at Scotland Yard, grappling with a particularly difficult crossword clue, when the Super knocked on my door. 'Sorry to interrupt, Catchpool,' he said with a smile. 'There's a Miss Annabel Treadway here to see you.'

Since learning that Rowland Rope was finally convinced that neither Poirot nor Scotland Yard had accused his son of murder, the Super had been the soul of reasonable discourse and moderation.

'I'll see Miss Treadway immediately,' I said.

The Super showed her into the small room, then made himself scarce. I took one look at the woman standing before me and wondered why she struck me so powerfully at that moment as being the embodiment of a tragic fate. It was as if the room had turned darker with her arrival. But why? She wasn't crying; she wasn't dressed in mourning garments. It was a puzzle.

'Good afternoon, Miss Treadway.'

'You're Inspector Edward Catchpool?'

'That's right. I was expecting to see you tomorrow afternoon at Combingham Hall. I was not expecting you to come to me in London.'

'I have a confession to make,' she said.

'I see.' I sat down and invited her to do the same, but she remained standing.

'I killed my grandfather. I acted alone.'

'Is that so?'

'Yes.' She raised her chin and looked almost proud. 'Three other people also received letters accusing them of his murder, but they are all innocent. I killed him.'

'You murdered Barnabas Pandy—is that what you're telling me?'

'Yes.'

'How?'

She frowned. 'I'm not sure what you are asking.'

'It's quite simple. You say you killed Mr Pandy. I'm asking how.'

'But I thought you knew. He drowned in the bathtub.'

'Don't you mean *you* drowned him?'

'I . . . Yes. I drowned him.'

'That's a different story from the one you told Hercule Poirot,' I said.

Annabel Treadway lowered her eyes. 'I'm sorry.'

'For what? Killing your grandfather? Lying to Poirot? Lying to me? All three?'

'Please don't make this any harder for me than it needs to be, Inspector.'

'You've just confessed to a murder, Miss Treadway. What were you hoping for: a mug of cocoa and a pat on the back? Your sister and niece have both told Poirot that you couldn't possibly have killed Mr Pandy—that you were with them from when the three of you heard him complain about the noise you were making until Kingsbury found him dead around thirty minutes later.'

'They must be mistaken. We were all together in Ivy's bedroom, but I left the room for a few minutes. Lenore and Ivy must have forgotten. It's hard to remember events clearly at a distance of many weeks.'

'I see. Do you remember what you were wearing when you killed your grandfather?'

'What I was wearing?'

'Yes. Your sister Lenore described a particular dress.'

'I . . . I was wearing my blue dress with the yellow and white flowers.' That, at least, tallied with her sister's account.

'Tell me, where is that dress now?' I asked.

'At home. Why does everybody keep asking me about my dress? Why does it matter? I haven't worn it since the day Grandy died.'

'Did it get wet, when you forced your grandfather's head under the bathwater?' I asked her.

She looked as if she might faint. 'Yes.'

'Your sister Lenore told Poirot that your dress was completely dry.'

'She . . . she must not have noticed.'

'And what if I were to tell you that Jane Dockerill found

this blue dress of yours—that it had been wrapped in cellophane while it was sopping wet, and taped to the underside of Timothy Lavington's bed at school?'

There was no mistaking the shock on Annabel Treadway's face.

'You're making this up, to confuse me,' she said. 'You're doing it deliberately!'

'Putting you off your well-rehearsed story, am I, with some inconvenient facts?'

'You're twisting my words! Won't you please just accept my confession?'

'Not yet. Are you sure you didn't tape the dress to the frame of your nephew's bed? You weren't worried that someone would notice that it was wet and smelled of olive oil? You didn't have the bright idea to hide it somewhere far from the house?'

She said shakily, 'All right, then: yes, I did.'

'Yet, when I asked to confirm that you'd hidden the dress under Timothy's bed, you said it was at home. Why would you lie about that when you've already confessed to murder? I don't think you would.'

'There is only one thing that matters, Inspector: I killed my grandfather. I will swear to it in court. You may arrest me immediately, and do whatever you do with criminals— but would you promise me something, in exchange for my full confession? I don't want Hoppy to be stuck at Combingham Hall once I'm gone. He wouldn't be properly attended to. Promise me you'll find someone who will love and care for him properly.'

'*You* will continue to do both,' I told her cheerfully. 'It's quite clear to me that you haven't killed anybody.'

'I did. Put a Bible in my hands and I will swear on it.'

'A Bible, eh? Would you swear on the life of your dog, Hopscotch?'

Annabel Treadway's mouth set in a hard line. Tears came to her eyes. She said nothing.

'All right, Miss Treadway, tell me: *why* did you drown your grandfather?'

'That I can answer easily.' There was tangible relief, both in her voice and in her eyes. I sensed that she might be about to speak the truth, or at least some of it. 'Grandy found out something about me. He was going to cut me out of his will because of it.'

'What did he find out?'

'I shall *never* tell you that,' said Annabel Treadway. 'And you cannot compel me to.'

'You're right. I can't.'

'Are you going to arrest me for murder?'

'Me? No. I shall consult with M. Poirot, and perhaps contact the relevant police constabulary after doing so.'

'But . . . what should I do now? I wasn't expecting to have to go home again.'

'Well, I'm afraid you will have to—unless you've got somewhere else to go. Go home, walk your dog, and wait and see if anyone turns up to arrest you for murder. I think it's pretty unlikely that anyone will, but you never know. You might be lucky!'

CHAPTER 29

An Unexpected Eel

As I turned the corner into my own street later that same evening, I saw that the door of the house where I lived was standing open and that my landlady, Mrs Blanche Unsworth, had planted herself in the doorway and looked ready to burst out of it at the first sight of me. 'Oh, no,' I muttered to myself.

She hopped from one foot to the other and waved her arms about as if someone had asked her to impersonate a tree being blown by a storm. Did she imagine that I might not yet have spotted her?

I produced my best smile, and called out, 'Hello, Mrs Unsworth! A fine evening, isn't it?'

'Am I glad you're back!' she said. As soon as I was within her reach, she pulled me into the house. 'A gentleman paid a call while you were out. I didn't like the look of him. Strange piece of goods, he was. I've known all sorts, but he was like no one I've ever met.'

'Ah,' I said. The best thing about Mrs Unsworth is that

you never need to ask her a question. Within minutes of encountering her, she will have provided you with a complete list of every thought in her head and every incident she has witnessed or been involved in since the last time you saw her.

'Stood there like a china figurine, he did. As if someone had made him from pottery! His face barely moved as he spoke. He was ever so polite—almost too polite, as if he was putting it on.'

'Ah,' I said again.

'I had a funny feeling from the moment I set eyes on him. "Don't be silly, Blanche. What are you fretting about?" I said to myself. "Gentleman's nicely turned out, nice and polite, a bit reserved, maybe, but that's nothing to be concerned about. If only every gentleman caller should be so well mannered." Then he gave me a parcel to give to you, and he said it was for Inspector Edward Catchpool, and it's addressed to you, so I've left it well alone. It's all wrapped up, and I'm sure it's nothing *too* nasty, but you just never know, do you? It looks a bit lumpy to me.'

'Where is the parcel?' I asked.

'I must say, I didn't like the look of it any more than I liked the look of him,' said Mrs Unsworth. 'I'm not sure you should open it. I wouldn't, if I were you.'

'You don't need to worry about me, Mrs Unsworth.'

'Oh, but I do! I do worry.'

'Where is the parcel?'

'Well, it's in the dining room, but . . . Wait!' She stood in front of me to prevent me from proceeding along the hall. 'I can't let you open it without warning you. What happened next put the wind up me good and proper. You need to hear the whole story.'

Did I? I tried my best to look patient.

'I asked the gentleman's name and he ignored me. Acted as if I'd never asked! That's what I mean: he tried to seem ever so polite, but would a true gentleman ignore a reasonable question like that from a lady? I'm telling you, he was a piece of goods. He had a cunning glint in his eye.'

'I'm sure he did.'

'A funny smile, too. Not the sort of smile you see every day. And then he opened his mouth and said—and I'll never forget it, as long as I live! One of the most peculiar things as ever happened to me! He said, "*Tell Inspector Catchpool that the eel feels down at heel.*"'

'What?'

Blanche Unsworth obediently repeated the words.

'The eel feels down at heel?' I said.

'Those very words! Well, I thought to myself: no point being the gracious hostess if he's going to toy with me in such an unpleasant manner. "Please tell me your name," I said, and he'll have known I hadn't taken kindly to his nonsense, but he didn't care. Just said it again, didn't he? "The eel feels down at heel."'

'I must see the parcel,' I said. This time, mercifully, my landlady stood aside and allowed me to pass.

I stopped abruptly when I saw the wrapped package on the dining room table. I knew straight away what it was.

'The eel feels down at heel! Ha!'

'Why are you laughing? Do you know what it means?' Mrs Unsworth asked.

'I think I do, yes.'

She stood back, covered her mouth with her hands and gasped as I pulled off the wrapping. Once the object was revealed she said with reverence, 'It's . . . it's a typewriter.'

'I need some paper,' I told her. 'I'll explain in due course, once I've tested this thing to find out if I'm right.'

'Paper? Well, I'm sure I . . . It's no trouble, of course, but—'

'Then please bring some, without delay.'

Soon afterwards, with Mrs Unsworth standing behind me, I inserted a sheet of writing paper into the machine. I typed, 'The eel feels down at heel'. It sounded as if it might be the first line of a funny music hall song. The next line, I thought, might be, 'He kneels beside a wheel'. I typed that too.

'Who is this eel?' asked Mrs Unsworth. 'And why, I should like to know, is he kneeling beside a wheel?'

I pulled the paper out of the typewriter and surveyed the results of my creativity. 'Yes!' I said.

'If you don't tell me what this is all about, I shan't get a wink of sleep tonight,' Mrs Unsworth threatened.

'For some time, Poirot and I have been looking for a particular typewriter. This, it turns out, is the one. It has a faulty letter "e". Look closely.' I passed her the piece of paper.

'But . . . what does that have to do with an eel?' she asked.

'Whoever delivered the typewriter obviously wanted me to test it by typing a phrase that contains lots of "e"s. That's all that matters—not the eel and not the wheel, either. They're not real. What matters is: who was the strange man who came here, and whose is this machine?'

I had been imagining how pleased Poirot would be when I told him about this new development, but in fact—as I would have realized straight away if I weren't such a cloth-headed fool—it moved us no further forward.

'I expect the man you met was merely a messenger, not the true sender,' I told Blanche Unsworth. 'It's not his name we need, it's the name of whoever put him up to it.'

I excused myself, went up to my room and lay down on the bed, feeling as down at heel as our friend the eel. Somebody was taunting me—someone who had gone to great lengths to draw my attention to my own ignorance: 'Here is the typewriter you're after. Now all you have to do is work out where it came from—which you can't, can you? And you never will, because I'm cleverer than you.' I could almost hear the words being spoken in a sneering tone of voice.

'You might be cleverer than I am,' I said, though the person I was addressing had no chance of hearing me, 'but I wouldn't assume you're cleverer than Hercule Poirot.'

CHAPTER 30

The Mystery of Three Quarters

The next day, battling against the foul weather, I travelled to Combingham Hall with Rowland McCrodden. It was not an enjoyable journey. I spent much of it pondering why it should be the case that conversations between Poirot, McCrodden and me flowed easily, while McCrodden and I, minus Poirot, couldn't seem to talk in a way that was not stilted and—on his part, at least—ill-tempered.

Combingham Hall had a bland, institutional frontage. Though it was evidently an old building, it had an oddly temporary look about it, as if it had been positioned, rather than rooted, in its surrounding landscape. I found it strange to think that, the following day, everybody involved in the peculiar puzzle surrounding the death of Barnabas Pandy would congregate here, on Poirot's orders.

Rowland McCrodden and I found the front door of the Hall ajar, in spite of the driving rain. Unsurprisingly, the front part of the tiled floor was wet, and there was some mud mixed in with the water. I immediately thought about

Poirot's poor shoes and the suffering they might already have endured. There were a few muddy paw prints dotted about—the handiwork of Hopscotch the dog, I assumed. (Or 'paws-iwork', I smiled to myself.)

There was no one to greet us. McCrodden turned to me with a dissatisfied expression and seemed about to make a complaint when we both heard a shuffling sound. An elderly man had appeared from the vaulted corridor ahead and was making slow progress towards us.

'I see you've found your way in, gentlemen,' he said. 'My name is Kingsbury. Let me take your hats and coats, and then I'll show you to your rooms. Nice rooms, you've both got. Pleasing aspect. Oh—and then Mr Porrott has requested that you both join him in Mr Pandy's study.' As he shuffled closer, I noticed that he was shivering. Still, he made no move to close the front door before inviting us to follow him upstairs.

The bedroom assigned to me was enormous, austere, uncomfortable and cold. The bed had a lumpy mattress and a lumpy pillow: a disheartening combination. The view had the potential to be delightful as soon as the rain stopped lashing at the windows.

Kingsbury had told us how to find the room he still called 'Mr Pandy's study', and once I was ready to go downstairs I knocked on McCrodden's door, which was next to mine. When I asked him if his bedroom was to his liking, he replied coldly, 'It contains a bed and a washbasin, which is all I require.' The clear implication was that only a cosseted degenerate would hope for more.

We found Poirot installed in a high-backed leather armchair in the study, with a striped blanket in orange, brown and black draped around his shoulders. He was drinking a tisane. I smelled it as soon as we entered the room and could see the steam rising from it.

'Catchpool!' he said in a tone of anguish. 'I do not understand what is the matter with you English. It is as cold in this room as it is outside!'

'I agree. This house is like a glacier with walls and a roof,' I said.

'Will you two stop fussing?' Rowland McCrodden barked. 'What's that, Poirot?' He pointed to a piece of paper that lay face-down on what Kingsbury would doubtless have called 'Mr Pandy's desk'.

'Aha!' said Poirot. 'All in good time, *mon ami*, all in good time.'

'And what's in the brown paper bag?'

'I will answer your questions *bientôt*. But first . . . I am so very sorry, my friend, but it is my duty to inform you of the most terrible news. Please, will you sit down?'

'Terrible . . .' The flesh on McCrodden's face seemed to drop. 'Is it John?'

'*Non, non*. John is perfectly well.'

'Well, what is it, then? Spit it out!'

'It is *la pauvre* Mademoiselle Mason. Emerald Mason.'

'What about her? You haven't invited her here, have you? Poirot, I will swing for you if you've—'

'Please, *mon ami*.' Poirot put his finger to his lips. 'I beg of you, silence.'

'Just tell me, for pity's sake,' McCrodden snapped. 'What has Miss Mason done now?'

'There has been the most unfortunate motorcar accident. Miss Mason was in a vehicle when a . . . a horse moved unexpectedly in front of it.'

'A horse?' I said.

'Yes, Catchpool, a horse. Please do not interrupt. Nobody else was hurt, but poor Mademoiselle Mason . . . Oh! *C'est vraiment dommage!*'

'Are you saying that Emerald Mason is dead?' asked McCrodden.

'No, my friend. It would perhaps be better for her if she were. A young lady, with her whole life ahead of her . . .'

'Poirot, I demand that you tell me at once—' began McCrodden. His face had turned as red as a beetroot.

'Of course, of course. She is to lose both legs.'

'*What?*' McCrodden exclaimed.

'Good Lord!' I said. 'That's horrible.'

'A surgeon is, at this moment, removing the two limbs. There was no way to save either one. Too much damage had been sustained.'

McCrodden produced a handkerchief and started to mop his brow. He said nothing. Then he shook his head several times. 'That . . . that is . . . How unspeakably . . . I can't believe it. *Both* legs?'

'Yes, both legs.'

'We must . . . The firm must ensure she has everything she needs. And flowers. A basket of fruit. And money, damn it! As much as she needs, and the best medical expertise available. There must be specialists who train people after accidents like this, so that they can . . .' McCrodden's mouth twisted. The redness had drained from his face. Now his skin looked almost transparent. 'Will she be able to come back to work? If she can't, it will kill her. Truly, it will. She loves her work.'

'Monsieur McCrodden, I am so sorry,' said Poirot. 'You do not care for the young woman, I know, but this must nevertheless be a terrible shock for you.'

Rowland McCrodden moved slowly to the nearest chair, lowered himself into it, and covered his face with his hands. At the very same moment, Poirot turned to me and winked.

I made a questioning face at him. He winked again. A powerful sensation of disbelief gripped me. Could this really be happening?

I made another, more severe, questioning face. Was Poirot trying to signal to me that he had told McCrodden a lie? Was Emerald Mason perfectly fine, with two functioning legs still attached to the rest of her body, and no one angling to chop them off? In which case, what on earth was Poirot up to?

I wondered if I ought to speak up. What would happen if I were to say to Rowland McCrodden, 'Poirot just winked at me twice; I think he's pulling your leg'? That would hardly be the ideal phrase to use, in the circumstances.

'*Mon ami*, would you prefer to retire to your room?' Poirot asked him. 'Catchpool and I, we can hold up the fort if you do not feel well enough to continue.'

'Continue with what? I'm sorry, I . . . This appalling news has distracted me.'

'That I can see,' said Poirot.

'Catchpool, I'm sorry,' said McCrodden, almost inaudibly.

'For what?' I asked him.

'I have been atrocious company today. You've been a saint to put up with me. I've treated you unconscionably and you did nothing to deserve it. Please accept my most sincere apologies.'

'Of course,' I said. 'It's forgotten.'

'Gentlemen, we have much to discuss,' said Poirot. 'Monsieur McCrodden, you asked me about this sheet of paper. You may look at it now if you wish. So may you, Catchpool, if our friend is too distressed.'

'He looks distressed to me,' I said pointedly. 'Doesn't he to you?'

Poirot smiled. That was when I knew for certain that Emerald Mason's legs were in no danger of being chopped off. I was cross with myself. There was nothing to stop me telling McCrodden he had been tricked, so why wasn't I speaking up? Instead, I said nothing, trusting in the grand plan of Poirot, as if he were a deity.

I walked over to the desk, picked up the piece of paper and turned it over. On it were typed six words: 'The eel feels down at heel.'

'What the blazes . . . ?' I muttered.

Poirot began to laugh.

'*You* sent me the typewriter?' I said.

'Ah! *Oui, c'etait* Poirot! I had Georges deliver it, and gave him instructions about what to say. He played his part most satisfactorily. To Mrs Unsworth, he gave the message about the eel.'

'Enough games, Poirot. Why didn't you simply tell me you'd found the typewriter?'

'A thousand apologies, *mon cher*. Poirot, he has every now and then the mischievous impulse.'

'Where did you find it?'

'Where did I found the down-at-heel eel? Here at Combingham Hall. Do not breathe a word, please, Catchpool. Nobody here knows that a typewriter is missing.'

'Then . . . the four letters signed in your name were typed by somebody here?'

'The letters were typed here, yes.'

'By whom?'

'That is indeed the question! I have a suspicion—but that is all it is, and I cannot prove I am right. The certain knowledge . . .' He sighed. 'After much hard work, it still eludes me.'

'Haven't you promised to reveal all at two o'clock tomorrow?' I reminded him.

'Yes. Time is starting to run out for Poirot.' He smiled, as if the idea pleased him. 'Will he make the enormous fool of himself? No, he cannot! He must think of his reputation! He must preserve his good name—the most excellent name of Hercule Poirot. *Alors*, there is, then, only one thing to do! This mystery must be solved before two o'clock tomorrow afternoon. I am very close, my friends . . . very close. I feel it here.' He pointed to his head. 'The little grey cells are hard at work. The running out of time . . . it is invigorating, Catchpool. It inspires me! Do not worry. All will be well.'

'I'm not worried,' I told him. 'I haven't promised any answers to anybody. I was only reminding you that *you* ought to be worried.'

'Very amusing, Catchpool.'

'What's in the brown paper bag?' I asked.

'Ah, yes, the bag,' said Poirot. 'We will unwrap it now. But first, I must confess something. Monsieur McCrodden, I see that you are still unable to speak, so please listen to what I am about to say. The story I told you about Miss Mason, that she is to lose both her legs—it was not true.'

McCrodden's mouth fell open. 'Not . . . not *true*?'

'Not in the least. To the best of my knowledge, that young woman has suffered no unfortunate accident, and both of her legs are still in the condition of the mint.'

'But you . . . you said . . . *Why*, Poirot?'

I found it peculiar that McCrodden was not angry. He seemed, rather, to be in a funny sort of trance. His eyes looked glazed.

'That, *mon ami*, along with much else, I will explain at our gathering tomorrow. I am sorry to have caused you distress with my little story. In my defence, I can only say that it was absolutely necessary. You do not know it yet, but you have helped me greatly.'

McCrodden nodded vaguely.

Poirot walked over to the desk. I heard a rustling noise as he took something out of the brown paper bag. Then he stood back so that we could see what it was.

'Isn't that . . . ?' I started to say. McCrodden laughed.

It was a small plate of blue and white patterned china, with a slice of Church Window Cake on it.

'Yes, indeed—it is Mademoiselle Fee's cake. One slice. That is all I need!' said Poirot.

'To keep the wolf from the door until dinner?' said McCrodden, before letting out another delirious laugh. He had evidently undergone some kind of transformation, and Poirot was responsible, yet it was hard to know if the effect was accidental or deliberately engineered.

'It is not for the stomach but for the little grey cells,' Poirot said. 'Here, my friends, in this small slice of cake, *we have the solution to the mystery of who killed Barnabas Pandy!*'

'Goodness me, what a horrible house,' said Eustace Campbell-Brown, as he, Sylvia Rule and Mildred alighted from the car that had brought them to Combingham Hall. He stared up at the building's façade. 'A person surely couldn't *live* here? Look at it! And to think, they could sell it for a fortune and buy any number of swanky, well-appointed flats in London, Paris, New York . . .'

'I don't think it's as bad as all that,' said Mildred.

'Neither do I,' said Sylvia Rule. 'You're right, Mildred—it's a very handsome building indeed. Eustace doesn't know what he's talking about. He's only displaying his ignorance.'

Mildred looked at her mother, then at her fiancé. Then, without a word, she set off towards the house. Sylvia and

Eustace watched her walk in through the open front door.

'May I suggest a truce?' said Eustace. 'At least until we return to London.'

Sylvia turned away. 'I am allowed to think that the house is attractive if that is what I happen to think,' she said.

'Doesn't it bother you that you have, once again, driven Mildred away? Don't you mind being as unbearable as you are?' Eustace held up his hands. 'That one was my fault. I will desist from making hostile remarks if you will too. How about it? We need to think not about ourselves but about Mildred. You and I might be enjoying our little war, but I don't think she can stand much more of it.'

'You called me a murderer,' Sylvia reminded him.

'I should not have said that. I apologize.'

'Do you truly believe it? Answer me honestly.'

'I have said I'm sorry.'

'But not meant it! You have no understanding of the suffering of others—of women like me. You're a demon.'

'Now that you've got that off your chest, how about that truce?' said Eustace.

'Very well. For as long as we are at Combingham Hall, I shall try my best.'

'Thank you. I will too.'

Together, they entered the house. They found Mildred standing alone in the entrance hall. She flinched at the sight of them, then looked up at the ceiling and quietly started to sing one of her favourite songs, 'The Boy I Love Is Up in the Gallery', her arms stretched out on either side. She looked as if she wanted to fly away.

Eustace thought: 'I've got to get her away from Sylvia's influence or we'll both be driven quite mad.'

Mildred's voice shook as she sang:

'Now, If I were a Duchess who had a lot of money,
I'd give it to the boy that's going to marry me.
But I haven't got a penny, so we'll live on love and kisses,
And be just as happy as the birds on the tree.
The boy I love is up in the gallery . . .'

'Does anyone hear singing?' asked Rowland McCrodden. 'I'm sure someone's singing.'

'Poirot, how can a slice of cake be the solution to an unsolved murder?' I asked.

'Because it is a whole slice: undivided, intact. Not separated into quarters. It is the solution to what I have thought of, for some time, as the Mystery of the Three Quarters! Unless . . .'

Poirot hurried over to the cake and, producing a small knife from his pocket, cut off the yellow square in the top left-hand corner. He pushed it to the edge of the plate, separating it from the rest of the slice. 'Unless *this* is the case,' he said. 'But I do not believe it is. No, I do not believe that at all.' He pushed the yellow square back to its original position, so that it was touching the other squares.

'You are suggesting that one square is not separate, but connected to the three other squares,' I said. 'Which means that . . . all four people who received letters accusing them of murder know one another?'

'*Non, mon ami*. Not at all.'

'John does not know any of the others,' said Rowland McCrodden. 'That's what he told me, and I believe him.'

'Then what does Poirot mean by the whole, undivided slice of cake being the solution?'

We both looked at him. He smiled enigmatically. Then McCrodden said, 'Wait! I think I know what he means . . .'

'But I don't *know* where it could be,' said Hugo Dockerill in a panicked voice. 'I mean, it *might* be anywhere! All I know is that it's not here, and we're already hopelessly late. Oh, dear.'

'Hugo,' said his wife gently. 'Calm down. Nobody at Combingham Hall cares if we arrive at noon or at midnight. As long as we're there in time for tomorrow's meeting, that's all that matters.'

'Thank you for trying to make me feel better, dearest Jane. I know you're crosser about our lateness than you're letting me see.'

'I'm not cross, Hugo.' She put her hand in his. 'I wish I understood, that's all: what it must feel like to be you, the way you think and . . . carry on. I can't imagine it. I can't imagine needing to make three trips to post a letter because, on the first two trips, you forget to take the letter with you. I would never do that, and so it's hard for me to understand how it's possible.'

'Well, it got posted in the end. It's not the letter that's the problem, it's my blasted hat! Where *is* the damned thing?'

'Why don't you take a different hat?'

'I wanted to take this one. I mean, *that* one, the one that isn't here any more!'

'You said you had it in your hand very recently.'

'I'm sure I did, yes.'

'Well, then. Where did you go when you left the room a moment ago?'

'Only to the parlour.'

'Then might the hat be in the parlour?'

Hugo frowned again. Then an expression of utmost delight appeared on his face. 'It might! I shall go and have a look.'

He returned a few seconds later, hat in hand. 'Your method worked. Dearest Jane, you are marvellous. Right! Shall we go?'

Jane Dockerill sighed. 'We should—but isn't there something else we need to take with us, apart from your hat and all the things already waiting by the door?'

'No, I've got everything else. It's all in the overnight case. What else do we need?'

'Timothy Lavington and Freddie Rule?' She shook her head and smiled. 'Shall I go and find them?'

'Yes, please, darling. You'll do a better job of that than I would, I'm quite sure.'

'So am I. Hugo?'

'Yes, dearest?'

'Hold that hat in your hand the whole time I'm gone, won't you? I don't want you losing it again.'

'Absolutely. I shan't let it out of my sight.'

*

'If I'm right, Poirot, then what you mean is this,' said Rowland McCrodden. 'It's not that all four people who received letters accusing them of murder know one another. Neither is it that they all knew Barnabas Pandy. It is that they were all acquainted with the writer of the letters.'

'Yes—you are correct,' said Poirot.

McCrodden looked astonished. 'Am I?' he said. 'I wasn't expecting to be. It was only a guess.'

'It was a good one,' Poirot told him. 'At least . . . I am nearly certain that you are correct. There is still one important question I must ask, and that will require a trip to London.'

'London? But everybody's coming here,' I exclaimed. '*You've* brought them!'

'And here they must remain, until I return. Do not alarm yourself, *mon cher* Catchpool. I will be back in good time for our two o'clock appointment tomorrow.'

'But where are you going?'

'It must be . . . is it Peter Vout?' asked Rowland McCrodden.

'Another ingenious guess!' Poirot clapped his hands together.

'Hardly,' said McCrodden. 'Vout is just about the only person who might know anything who isn't here at Combingham Hall.'

'He will certainly know the answer to the question I shall ask him tomorrow morning,' said Poirot. 'He cannot fail to know it! After which, hopefully the complete picture will be clear—and just in time, too.'

*

John McCrodden arrived at Combingham Hall to find the front door standing wide open. He walked in. The floor of the entrance hall was wet and muddy. There were some unattended suitcases by the bottom of a staircase three times as large as any he had seen before.

'Hello?' he called out. 'Hello! Is there anybody here?'

No person appeared, and nobody answered his question. There was nothing John would have liked more than for it to turn out that he was, indeed, alone in this enormous building that was as cold as a grave—where he could build and light a fire in one of the rooms and spend a peaceful evening on his own—but he knew this was merely a fantasy. No doubt an assortment of affected society people would appear at any moment, and he knew he would loathe them all.

He was halfway across the hall in search of a kitchen where he could rummage for food and make himself a cup of hot, strong tea when a door to the right of him opened and at last someone appeared.

'I'm John Mc . . .' he started to say, turning. But he ran out of breath saying his own name.

No. It couldn't be. It was impossible to think clearly while his heart pounded so violently.

It couldn't be. Yet it was.

'Hello, John.'

'It's . . . it's *you*,' was all he could manage to say.

THE FOURTH QUARTER

CHAPTER 31

A Note for Mr Porrott

Freddie Rule had learned a lot since arriving at Combingham Hall yesterday. Much more than he had ever learned at school, in fact. The teachers did their best to stuff useful facts into him, and he was decent at remembering them, but hearing about something that had happened in the past, or about what some long-dead chap had worked out, wasn't the same as making the discovery yourself. When that happened—and not in a stuffy, almost-silent schoolroom, but in the course of one's everyday life—whatever it was that one had learned left a much deeper impression. Freddie was certain he would never forget the two lessons that his time at Timothy Lavington's house (as he thought of it) had so far taught him: the first was that a person only really needed one friend.

Miraculously, Timothy had decided that he liked Freddie. They'd had fun running around the garden together playing hide-and-seek, pinching food from the kitchen when Cook wasn't looking, and mocking old Dimwit Dockerill and some of the other people in the house: the Old Fossil of a butler who looked as if he might crumble to dust if he moved another inch, the Belgian that both Timothy and Freddie called 'the Egg with a Moustache', and the man who looked like a bust in a museum, with curly grey hair and the highest forehead in the world.

'People are really rather grotesque, aren't they, Freddie?' Timothy had said this morning. 'Especially when lots of them are gathered together in one place, like now—that's when I really notice it—or at school. I don't think much of our species, on the whole. *You're* all right, Freddie. And obviously I'm all right too. And I love my Aunt Annabel and Ivy and my father . . .' Here Timothy had stopped and frowned, as if thinking about his father bothered him.

'What about your mother, and all your friends at Turville?'

'I try to think well of Mummy,' Timothy had sighed. 'As for my friends at Turville, I loathe them all. They're the most insufferable dullards.'

'But then . . . ?'

'Why do I keep them as friends? Why do I spend all my time with them? Survival: that's the only reason. School is a savage place, Freddie, wouldn't you agree?'

'I . . . I'm not sure,' Freddie had stammered, looking down at his lap. 'My last school was more savage. I got my collarbone broken there, and my wrist.'

'You haven't been around long enough to notice Turville's subtle savagery. No limbs are broken—only spirits. When I started there, I immediately identified that group of boys—the group of which I'm now the leader—as the one most likely to ensure my survival. I chose correctly, I think. The fact is, I knew I wasn't strong enough to tough it out alone. That's why I admire you, Freddie.'

Freddie had been too astonished to speak and so had made no response.

'You don't feel the need to make the nauseating compromises I make in order to be popular. You spend most of your time with Dimwit Dockerill's wife, who's a good egg, all things considered. Taken you under her wing, hasn't she?'

'She is kind to me, yes.'

Freddie had found it hard to concentrate, so surprised was he by what Timothy was saying. He had barely managed to answer the question. He would have made endless nauseating compromises in order to be as popular as Timothy, but the opportunity to do so had never presented itself.

'I could be your friend at school,' he said. 'If you don't like your other friends, I mean. We don't have to speak to each other, but secretly we could know that we were friends. Only if . . .' Freddie had lost his nerve at that point, and started to mumble: 'It was just an idea. I'll understand if you don't want to.'

'Or we could be friends in the normal way, quite openly, and anyone who doesn't like it can go to the devil!' Timothy had said defiantly.

'No, you don't want to do that. You can't be seen to like me. You'd soon be as unpopular as I am.'

'I don't think that's true,' Timothy had said thoughtfully.

'I did such a good job of making myself popular when I joined the school, I'm fairly sure I can now take that popularity with me wherever I go, whatever groups I do or don't belong to. We shall see. Naturally, we'll need to make a few vital alterations to . . . well, to *you*, Freddie. Your demeanour, the way you conduct yourself at school.'

'Of course,' Freddie had hastily agreed. 'Whatever you think best.'

'Your clothes are a little too . . . I mean, there's school uniform and then there's school uniform, Freddie.'

'I see. Yes, of course.'

'Still, we needn't worry about the details now. It's funny, you know: I've always envied you. The rumours about your mother . . . I hope you don't mind my mentioning them?'

'I don't mind,' Freddie had said, though he did, very much.

'It's just that everybody thinks your mother's a baby-killer and a monster, and they all say so, while they all think *my* mother is the soul of respectability. Which she is. But that means nobody ever calls her a horror, which means I can't join in and say, "Yes, I think you might be right. I think she drove my father away with her cold-heartedness." I should like to say that, loudly and to a large crowd. I should like it very much. But *my* mother's deficiencies get no official recognition. And if I tried to explain, no one would understand or feel sorry for me.'

'The rumours about my mother are completely untrue,' said Freddie quickly and quietly. He could not have forgiven himself if he hadn't said it at all.

'As are the lack of rumours about mine,' said Timothy.

'How can a *lack* of rumours be untrue?'

'You are too literal-minded, Freddie.' Timothy smiled. 'Come on, let's see if we can find any tasty scraps in the kitchen. I'm starved!'

And so—although he feared his new-found state of delirious happiness might last only as long as he and Timothy were at Combingham Hall together, with no other boys of their age present—Freddie's life had changed beyond all recognition in the space of mere minutes. He had a friend! Mrs Dockerill, kind though she was, couldn't be his friend. She could only ever be a grown-up who pitied him and took care of him—but that didn't matter, because now Freddie had Timothy.

This was what had taught him that nobody needed more than one friend. He had only one, and it turned out to be the perfect number. He felt absolutely no need for more.

The second lesson Freddie had learned at Combingham Hall was that definitions of size, like 'big' and 'small', were relative. Until he had come here, Freddie had always thought of his own home in London as large. He knew he would not be able to think of it in this way ever again, not now that he'd seen Timothy's house, which was a mansion of the sort that a royal or aristocratic person might own, and had more extensive grounds even than Turville College. The Hall was so big, it was almost like being outside in the open air, except inside. One could run past as many doors as one would normally only see side by side on a long street, and still find new corners to turn, new staircases to climb.

Freddie had now been running for some time, looking for Timothy in their latest game of hide-and-seek. He had checked dozens of empty bedrooms and every nook and cranny he could find, and was now at the stage of simply dashing around calling out, 'Timothy! Timothy!'

He raced around another corner and nearly banged into the Old Fossil. 'Mind yourself, laddie!' the old man said. What was his name? Kingswood? Kingsmead? 'You nearly knocked me to the ground!'

'Sorry, sir,' said Freddie. Kingsbury: that was it!

'I should think so too. Now, have you by any chance seen Mr Porrott?'

'Who?'

'The French gentleman.'

The Fossil was talking about the Egg with a Moustache, Freddie realized. 'He's Belgian, isn't he? Not French.'

'No, he's French. I've heard him say French-sounding things since he got here.'

'Yes, but—'

'Have you seen him, laddie?'

At that moment, Timothy Lavington ran up behind the Fossil, shouting, 'Freddie! Found you!'

The old man staggered back. He steadied himself against the wall and put his hand on his chest. 'You boys'll put me in an early grave,' he said. Freddie nearly laughed at his use of the word 'early'. He must have been at least eighty years old.

'Why'd you have to tear around like wild things, and leap out at each other like monkeys from trees?'

'Sorry, Kingsbury,' Timothy said cheerfully. 'It won't happen again, I promise.'

'Oh, but it will, Master Timothy. I know it will.'

'You're probably right, old boy.'

'I thought I was supposed to be finding you?' Freddie said.

'And I need to find Mr Porrott, the Frenchman,' said Kingsbury. 'I've looked everywhere.'

'He's Belgian! His name's pronounced *Poirot* and he's in the drawing room,' said Timothy. 'That's where we all ought to be. It's ten minutes after two. I completely forgot that we were all supposed to be there at two o'clock. Poirot sent me to round everyone up, so here I am. Consider yourselves rounded!'

Like Timothy, Freddie had forgotten about the drawing room meeting at two o'clock. So, it seemed, had the Fossil, who nodded and said, 'It's quite true that I *haven't* looked for Mr Porrott in the drawing room since the clocks struck two. I looked for him in there nearly an hour ago, but not since. In fact, I despaired of ever finding him, so I ended up writing it all down in a note. If only I'd remembered . . . Yes, he *did* say two o'clock! Shall I get the note and take it to him, I wonder?'

'I should go straight to the drawing room if I were you,' Timothy advised. 'He's waiting for us all to turn up. Also, aren't you excited to hear what he has to say? I am! We're about to find out who murdered Grandy.'

'Do you think he *was* murdered?' Freddie asked. 'Mother says he died a perfectly innocent death and someone's trying to stir up trouble.'

'Well, let's hope not,' said Timothy. 'I miss him, of course, but . . . well, if people have to die, and it seems they do, it's far better if they're murdered. It's so much more interesting.'

'Hush, Master Timothy!' Kingsbury scolded. 'That's a wicked thing to say.'

'No, it's not,' said Timothy. 'Honestly, Freddie, every time I say anything that's true, somebody gripes about it. I sometimes feel as if the whole world is conspiring to turn me into a liar.'

CHAPTER 32

Where is Kingsbury?

Finally, all the chairs in Combingham Hall's drawing room were occupied apart from two. Since the number of chairs set out (by me, at some cost to my back) corresponded exactly to the number of people who ought to have been present for Poirot's meeting, there was no doubt that the emptiness of one of those two chairs constituted a problem. The other chair belonged to Poirot himself, because, unable to keep still on account of his mounting impatience, he was pacing up and down, looking every few seconds at the door, then at the empty chair opposite his own, then at the grandfather clock beside the window that looked on to the gardens. 'Soon it will be three o'clock!' he cried out in frustration, startling everybody. 'Why do people in this house not comprehend the importance of being punctual? I have been all the way to London and back, yet still I arrived here in good time.'

'M. Poirot, we need not wait for Kingsbury,' said Lenore Lavington. 'There is no question of his having murdered anybody or sent those foul letters. Could we not proceed without him? Perhaps you would like to tell us all why we are gathered here?'

Those gathered, aside from Poirot and me, were: Rowland McCrodden, John McCrodden, Sylvia Rule, Mildred Rule, Eustace Campbell-Brown, Lenore Lavington, Ivy Lavington, Annabel Treadway, Hugo Dockerill, Jane Dockerill, Timothy Lavington and Freddie Rule. Hopscotch the dog was also with us; he was lying on the carpet and had draped himself over Annabel's feet.

'*Non*,' said Poirot in a tone of grim determination. 'We wait. I called this meeting and it will not begin until I say so! It is essential for everyone to be here.'

'I'm so sorry, M. Poirot,' said Ivy Lavington. 'It was terribly rude of us all to keep you waiting. I am not normally late for anything. Neither is Kingsbury. This is most unlike him.'

'You, mademoiselle, were the first to arrive . . . twenty minutes after two o'clock. May I ask what delayed you?'

'I . . . I was thinking,' said Ivy. 'I must have lost myself in my thoughts more fully than I had realized.'

'I see. And the rest of you?' Poirot's eyes moved slowly from one person to another. 'What caused you all to be elsewhere at two o'clock, when you were supposed to be here?'

'Timothy and I were playing hide-and-seek. We forgot the time,' said Freddie.

'I was helping Hugo to find a pair of shoes that he eventually remembered he had left at home,' said Jane Dockerill.

'I could have sworn I packed them, darling. Beats me how I could have made a silly mistake like that.'

'I was looking after Mildred,' said Sylvia Rule. 'She had a most peculiar turn. For a long time she would not stop singing.'

'Singing, madame?' said Poirot.

'Mother, please,' murmured Mildred.

'Yes, singing,' said Sylvia Rule. 'When Eustace and I finally managed to make her stop, she was in a most irregular state and needed to lie down.'

'I was with Mildred,' Eustace told Poirot. 'I am eager to hear what you have to tell us, M. Poirot, and I would have been here as the clocks struck two, but Mildred seemed unable to speak or move for a while, and I'm afraid that was all I could think about. It put this little meeting right out of my head. I might have forgotten about it altogether if Timothy hadn't whizzed past and reminded me.'

'Well done for remembering, Timmy.' Ivy smiled at her brother.

'I didn't remember,' he said. 'I was hunting for Freddie. I thought I'd try the drawing room, even though I'd tried it already. I didn't find Freddie, but—'

'He found me,' said Poirot. 'It was past two o'clock and *nobody was here*. Only Catchpool and me. I sent Timothy to hunt not only for Freddie but for all of you.'

'I was looking for John,' said Rowland McCrodden. 'I left my bedroom with the intention of coming straight here, in fact, but as I made my way along the landing, I decided I would like to speak to my son privately first, before we joined the bigger group.'

'Why?' asked John.

'I don't know.' Rowland McCrodden lowered his eyes.

'Was there something particular that you wanted to say to me?'

'No.'

'You must have had a reason,' John insisted.

'You were perhaps hoping that you and Monsieur John could come to the meeting together, Monsieur McCrodden?' said Poirot.

'Yes. I was.'

'Why?' John asked again.

'Because you're my son!' bellowed Rowland McCrodden.

Once the shock of his outburst had subsided, John said to Poirot, 'If you're about to ask me why I was late, I decided at the last minute that perhaps I wouldn't indulge you—perhaps I would simply return home without hearing your explanation.'

'You came all the way here from London only to return home, monsieur?' Poirot raised an eyebrow.

'I did not return home, as you can see. I considered doing so, then decided against it.'

'What about you, Mademoiselle Treadway? And you, Madame Lavington? Why were you late?'

'I was out with Hoppy,' said Annabel Treadway. 'We were playing with his ball. He was having so much fun that I didn't want to disappoint him by coming inside. I . . . well, I suppose when you said two o'clock, I assumed you meant "or thereabouts". I was only a little bit late, wasn't I?'

'You were twenty-five minutes late, mademoiselle.'

'I was outside looking for Annabel,' said Lenore Lavington. 'I knew there was a danger she'd forget all about the time—she's far too soft on Hopscotch, and I knew he would want to play ball for *hours*. He always does.'

'And so, in order to prevent your sister from being late, you made yourself late.'

'As a matter of fact, I glanced in through that window when I heard the church clock strike the hour . . .'—Lenore pointed—'. . . and I saw all the empty chairs, and only you and Inspector Catchpool in here, and I thought, "Oh, well, plainly the meeting won't be starting on time." Which it didn't. I missed nothing. Now, may we please hear whatever it is that you have to say this afternoon, M. Poirot? Kingsbury is probably fast asleep in his bed. He often has a sleep in the middle of the afternoon. He is old and tires easily. Annabel and I will make sure he is informed of any developments.'

'He isn't in his cottage, or asleep,' said Timothy. 'Freddie and I talked to him upstairs, didn't we, Freddie? I told him Poirot was looking for him, and he said he'd forgotten all about this meeting, but when I reminded him, he set off for the drawing room.'

'He did,' Freddie Rule confirmed. 'He seemed upset about having forgotten and being late, and hurried off towards the stairs. I'm sure he was on his way here. He also said—'

'Stop, Freddie. Hush,' said Timothy suddenly. He stood up. 'M. Poirot, might I talk to you alone for a few moments?'

'*Oui, bien sûr,*' said Poirot.

The two of them left the drawing room together, closing the door behind them.

With Poirot gone, everyone looked at me as if they expected me to take over the proceedings. I hadn't the faintest notion of what to say, so I made a cheery remark about the fire, and how necessary it was on a cold day like today. 'I hope there's enough fuel at Combingham Hall to keep it going!' I said.

No one responded.

Thankfully, a few moments later, Poirot and Timothy Lavington returned. Poirot's eyes had a hard look about them. 'Catchpool,' he said. 'As quickly as you can, please, *check every room in the house*. The rest of us will wait here.'

'What am I looking for?' I asked, already on my feet.

'In my bedroom . . . Do you know where that is?'

I nodded.

'In my bedroom, you will look for a note that has been left for me by Kingsbury.'

I heard a gasp then: an uneven, staggered gasp. It sounded as if it came from a woman—yes, I thought, definitely a woman—but there was no way of knowing which one. Perhaps if I had been looking around the room at that moment . . . but my attention had been focused solely on Poirot.

'In my room, also, and in every room of this house, you will look for Kingsbury himself,' Poirot said. 'Quick, my friend. There is no time to lose!'

Annabel Treadway stood up. 'You're frightening me,' she

told Poirot. 'You sound as if you think Kingsbury is in danger.'

'I do, mademoiselle. He is in the most grave danger. Please hurry, Catchpool!'

'Then we must *all* look for him,' said Annabel.

'No!' Poirot stamped his foot on the floor. 'I forbid it. Only Catchpool. *Nobody else is to leave this room.*'

I don't know how many bedrooms there are at Combingham Hall, and my memory of my panicked dash around the place that afternoon is probably unreliable, but I would not be at all surprised if someone were to tell me that there were thirty bedrooms, or even forty. I raced from room to room, from floor to floor, feeling as if I was running around a sinister, deserted city instead of a family home. I distinctly remember an entire floor of bedrooms that were unused and almost derelict, with bare mattresses in some and, in others, bed frames without mattresses.

I discovered that I did not, in fact, know where Poirot's bedroom was. It felt like hours before I reached it, but I knew it was his as soon as I walked in and saw, laid out with geometric neatness beside a book and a cigarette case, the net he uses to protect his moustaches while he sleeps.

There was an envelope on the floor, between the bed and the door. It was sealed. In spidery handwriting, someone—presumably Kingsbury—had written 'Mr Herkl Porrott'. I put the envelope in my trouser pocket and continued with my search. 'Kingsbury!' I yelled as I ran along corridor after corridor, pushing open endless doors as I went. 'Are you here? Kingsbury!' I received no answer. All I could hear was my own words as they echoed back to me.

Eventually, after what felt like hours, I pushed open a door and found that I recognized the room behind it. It was the bathroom in which Barnabas Pandy had drowned. Poirot had insisted on showing it to me yesterday.

I was relieved to see an empty bathtub: no water and no dead body. I was busy telling myself that it was absurd to imagine I might find Kingsbury drowned in the same tub in which Pandy had died, when I noticed something on the floor. It was close to my feet, near the door. It was a towel: white with red patches and streaks.

I knew straight away that the red was blood.

I bent down to examine the towel more closely and I saw, between the feet of the bathtub, a dark shape lying on the floor behind it. The bath itself had initially blocked my view of it. I knew at once what it must be, though I prayed I would turn out to be wrong as I walked over to take a closer look.

It was Kingsbury. He lay curled on his side. His eyes were open. Around and beneath his head was a pool of red, forming an almost perfect circle. It resembled, in that moment and to my eyes at least, a sort of halo or crown— neither of which suited poor Kingsbury. One look at his face was enough to tell me he was dead.

CHAPTER 33

The Marks on the Towel

The next day, our meeting was reconvened in the drawing room of Combingham Hall. Two o'clock was again the agreed hour and, unlike on the previous day, everybody arrived promptly. Poirot confided to me later that he felt insulted by their punctuality. In his eyes, it was proof that they were all more than capable of arriving at the correct time when it mattered to them.

This meeting had been called not only by Poirot but also by a local police officer by the name of Inspector Hubert Thrubwell. 'We are treating Mr Kingsbury's death as murder for a very simple reason,' he told us all. 'There was a towel on the floor in the bathroom where he lay dead. Inspector Catchpool found the towel, and it was nowhere near the body of Mr Kingsbury. Isn't that right, Inspector Catchpool?'

'It is,' I said. 'The towel was next to the door, on the opposite side of the room. I almost trod on it as I walked in.'

Thrubwell thanked me and continued. 'When that towel

was examined by our police doctor, two distinct types of blood were found.'

'You do not mean different *types* of blood, *mon ami*,' said Poirot. 'All of the blood, if it belonged to Kingsbury, must have been of the same type. You are talking about the marks made by the blood on the towel, *n'est-ce pas?*'

'Yes, I am,' said Thrubwell. 'I am indeed!' He looked pleased to have been corrected. 'The police doctor found that Mr Kingsbury's death was the result of a serious head wound. He had either been pushed or fallen back, and hit his head hard on the sharp corner of the only cupboard in the room. Without the evidence of the towel that Inspector Catchpool found, it would have been impossible to know whether he was pushed or if he fell. Thanks to the towel, I think we can safely say that he was probably pushed—and even if he wasn't, he was certainly left to bleed to death by someone who wanted him gone. And that, in my book, is what I call murder!' Thrubwell looked at Poirot, who nodded his approval.

'I don't understand,' said Lenore Lavington. 'How does a towel prove anything?'

'Because of the two types of marks made by Mr Kingsbury's blood,' said Thrubwell. 'On one side of the towel was a large, thick, dark patch of blood, where Mr Kingsbury must have held it against his wound to try to stop the flow and save his own life. Now, if that's what he was trying to do, then why did the towel end up on the other side of the room, beyond the bathtub? I can't see that Mr Kingsbury would have had the strength to throw it all that way. It's a large room, and he was in a severely weakened state, and not the strongest of men even before he sustained his head wound. And then we come to the other blood marks. As well as the dense, dark patch of blood there were also five streaks on a quite different part of the towel. These were lighter in colour than the larger patch, and one of the five was shorter and lower down than the others.'

'Streaks?' said Ivy Lavington. She looked pale and serious. Annabel Treadway, in the chair beside Ivy's, was crying silently. Hopscotch stood next to her with one paw in her lap, occasionally whining and licking the side of her face. Most of the others present looked stunned.

'Yes, streaks,' said Inspector Thrubwell. 'It didn't take long for Mr Poirot here to figure out that they were finger marks. The shorter, lower one was made by the thumb.'

'The thumb of the person who left Mr Kingsbury to bleed to death?' asked Jane Dockerill.

'No, ma'am,' said Thrubwell. 'That person would have taken care not to touch any of the blood. The bloody finger streaks were made by the murder victim: Mr Kingsbury.'

'Here is what we believe must have happened,' said Hercule Poirot. 'The killer either pushed Kingsbury so that he fell and struck his head, or else the fall was an accident. Let us say it was an accident and give to our killer the benefit of the doubt in this one respect. Having fallen, it soon becomes apparent that Kingsbury is bleeding profusely. He is also old and weak, and has recently suffered the tragic loss of his dear friend Monsieur Pandy.

'The killer sees that Kingsbury is too weak to call for help and will probably die if nothing is done to save him. This is what the murderer wants. There is only one problem: as he fell, Kingsbury reached out for a towel that must have been draped over the side of the bathtub—a towel which he now holds in his hand and presses against his wound. This, thinks the killer, might staunch the flow of blood and save the old man's life. It becomes necessary, therefore, to snatch the towel away from Kingsbury, who suddenly finds he is no longer holding it. He tries to stop the bleeding with his hand. Now he has blood on his fingers. The killer is standing over him, perhaps taunting him with the towel, and Kingsbury reaches up to try to take hold of it again. He has no hope of retrieving it from the clutches of his strong and healthy tormenter, but he is allowed, briefly, to touch the towel before it is snatched away again, and dropped near the door as the killer leaves the bathroom—*and, in doing so, leaves Kingsbury to die.*'

'You're assuming rather a lot, aren't you?' said John McCrodden. 'What if Kingsbury got blood on his fingers *before* he ever reached for the towel? What if he *did* somehow manage to throw it across the room? Being close to death can give a person extraordinary strength.'

'He could not have thrown the towel and made it land where Inspector Catchpool found it,' Inspector Thrubwell replied. 'It would have been near impossible even for a strong man without a head wound.'

'Perhaps it would have, and perhaps it would not,' said Poirot. 'I will admit that, without all the other evidence, it might be difficult to say for certain. What you must not forget, Monsieur McCrodden, is that *I know there is a murderer among us today.* I have proof—proof that was given to me by Kingsbury himself.'

'Golly!' said Hugo Dockerill.

'I know who the killer is, and I know why that person wanted Kingsbury dead,' Poirot went on. 'That is why I am able to say to Inspector Thrubwell here that, happily, I have saved him some work. I had already solved the murder of Kingsbury before he arrived here at Combingham Hall.'

'And very grateful I am too, sir,' said Inspector Thrubwell.

'What proof was given to you by Kingsbury?' asked Rowland McCrodden. 'How can he have given you proof in the matter of his own murder while he was still alive? Or are you referring to the murder of Barnabas Pandy?'

'That is a good question,' said Poirot. 'As you know, before he died, Kingsbury was looking for me. There was something important that he wished to tell me. Unable to find me, he left a note in my bedroom. The note, when I read it, brought to mind certain facts I already knew. This meant that when I was informed of the death of Kingsbury, and told about the towel, and when I put all of these things together . . . I found that I knew who had so cruelly left Kingsbury to die. I knew it—I *know* it—beyond a doubt. That person is a cold-blooded murderer by nature, whether they pushed Kingsbury or not. What else are you, if you leave a man to die whom you might have saved?'

'Presumably the same person also murdered Barnabas

Pandy,' said Jane Dockerill. 'I hope you are not going to tell me that I'm sitting in a room with two murderers, M. Poirot? That I should find difficult to believe.'

'No, madame. There is only one.' Poirot pulled a piece of paper out of his pocket. 'This is not the note that I received from Kingsbury, but it is an exact copy of it. In it, though his use of English is flawed, Kingsbury nevertheless manages to make clear his meaning. You may all examine the copy of his letter in a moment. You will see that Kingsbury tells me that he has just overheard a conversation between Ivy Lavington and another person whose identity he does not know. Kingsbury heard this person crying, but not speaking. He believed it might have been a man or a woman. It was hard to tell, so anguished and uncontrolled was the crying.

'The conversation that Kingsbury overheard, one-sided as it was, took place in Mademoiselle Ivy's bedroom, with the door pushed closed, though not securely shut. He heard Mademoiselle Ivy say . . .'

Poirot stopped. He passed the piece of paper to me. 'Catchpool, would you please read the passage I have encircled? I find it too difficult not to make the necessary corrections. I am too much the perfectionist.'

I took the copied note from Poirot and began to read the indicated section.

'She were saying words to the effect of how carrying on like you're unfamiliar with the law isnt no defence. Theres wot your allowed to do, and theres those things your not allowed to, and pretending like you cant tell the one from the other is not going to wash with anyone. No one will believe you and being as your the only one of all of us as knows this John Modden . . .'

I stopped reading at that point and asked Poirot if Kingsbury had meant John McCrodden.

'*Oui, bien sûr.* Look around you, Catchpool. *Is* there a John Modden in the room?'

I read on:

'Being as your the only one of us all who knows this John Modden you should tell Mister Porrott the truth all of it like you told it to me. He will understand and after all no harm is done if you tell the truth now and if you dont he will.'

'Thank you, Catchpool. *Mesdames et messieurs*, you will understand, I hope, that most of what you have just heard was Kingsbury quoting what he heard Ivy Lavington say. He was not the most accurate of writers. No, he was not meticulous about the details. But in essence, on the important substance of what he overheard, he is accurate. We learn, then, that Kingsbury heard Ivy Lavington talking to somebody—we do not know whom—and warning them. *Words to the effect that ignorance of the law is no defence.* And that no one will believe in this ignorance of the law, for the person to whom Ivy Lavington was speaking is *the only one acquainted with John McCrodden.* And if that person does not tell me, Hercule Poirot, the full truth, perhaps, warned Mademoiselle Ivy, John McCrodden would do so.

'All of this seems to suggest, does it not, that Ivy Lavington was talking to the murderer of Barnabas Pandy? Or at least to the writer of the four letters signed in my name?'

'What it suggests to me is that Ivy must have been speaking to Rowland McCrodden,' said Jane Dockerill. 'If only one person here is acquainted with his son, then surely it must be him?'

'Yes, that's a reasonable assumption,' said Eustace Campbell-Brown.

'It's not true,' said Ivy Lavington. 'I will not tell you to whom I was speaking, but I can promise you that it wasn't Rowland McCrodden. Obviously he knows his own son. I meant that the person I was addressing was the only one of us who is not supposed to know John McCrodden, and yet does. I had no idea Kingbury was listening at the door, so I didn't take the trouble to be clear. Incidentally, Kingsbury's note is not accurate. He got much of it wrong. What he wrote . . . those were not my words. That was not what I said.'

Poirot beamed at her. '*Eh bien!* mademoiselle, I am delighted to hear you say that. Yes, Kingsbury got some of the words wrong. Nevertheless, he enabled Hercule Poirot to get everything right!

'In his note to me, Kingsbury also wrote that, as he listened outside Mademoiselle Lavington's door, a floorboard creaked loudly. His movement caused it to do so. He hurried away, and he heard, behind him, a door bang against the wall after being flung open—at least, this was how it sounded to Kingsbury. He believed he might have been seen. I too believe this. Kingsbury was killed—or left to die, if you prefer—for what he overheard. Minutes after he spoke to Timothy Lavington and Freddie Rule upstairs, somebody either forced him or followed him into the bathroom in which he was to die.

'Of course, his murderer did not know that, before he or she ended the old man's life, Kingsbury had left this helpful note for Poirot! Ladies and gentlemen, I can reveal that the murderer of Kingsbury is . . . the person with whom Mademoiselle Ivy was conducting this secret conversation.'

'And who was that?' John McCrodden asked bluntly.

'Ivy, what does he mean?' Timothy Lavington asked his sister. 'He seems to be saying that you were involved in a conspiracy to kill Grandy, and that your fellow conspirator then killed Kingsbury.'

'*Pas du tout*,' Poirot told Timothy. 'You will soon understand why this is not true. Mademoiselle Ivy, please tell us all: with whom were you conversing in your bedroom a short while before two o'clock yesterday afternoon?'

'I shall not tell you, and I don't mind if I'm punished for it,' said Ivy Lavington. 'M. Poirot, if you know who killed Kingsbury—or left him to die—then you know that it was not I. And if you know everything, as you claim to, then you do not need me to tell you anything.'

Annabel Treadway said, through her tears, 'It was *I* who murdered Grandy. I have already told Inspector Catchpool. Why will nobody believe me?'

'Because it isn't true,' I said.

Poirot continued: 'By forty minutes after two o'clock, we were all here in this room. Everybody, apart from Kingsbury. Catchpool and I were here at two, but no one else was. After I sent Timothy Lavington and Freddie Rule to rouse people and bring them here, at about five minutes after two, this was the order of arrival. First came Ivy Lavington at twenty minutes past two. She was very soon followed by Jane and Hugo Dockerill. Next, at twenty-five minutes after two, came Annabel Treadway, Freddie Rule and Timothy Lavington, then John McCrodden and then his father, Rowland McCrodden. The last to arrive were Mildred Rule, Eustace Campbell-Brown, Sylvia Rule and Lenore Lavington. I am afraid to say that any one of the people that I have just named could have been the one who pulled the towel out of Kingsbury's hand and left him to die. We can eliminate from suspicion only four people in this room: Inspector Thrubwell, Catchpool, me . . . and the fourth person, of course, is John McCrodden.'

'I don't see that we have eliminated Mr McCrodden,' said Sylvia Rule. 'It sounds to me as if he would have had ample time to injure Kingsbury and leave him in the bathroom to die before coming to the drawing room.'

'Ah, but think, madame,' said Poirot. 'If Kingsbury's killer is the person to whom Ivy Lavington said, "You are the only one of us who knows John McCrodden . . ."?'

'Oh, I see,' said Jane Dockerill. 'Yes, you're right. The person who said that cannot, then, be Mr McCrodden.'

'How encouraging,' said John McCrodden. 'I am no longer suspected of murder.'

'Yes, you are,' said his father. 'You are not suspected of murdering Kingsbury, but there is still Barnabas Pandy to consider.'

'Actually, *mon ami*, there is not,' said Poirot.

Everyone stared at him in astonishment.

'Barnabas Pandy died an accidental death,' he said. 'He drowned in his bathwater, as everyone first, and correctly, believed. There has been only one murder: that of poor Kingsbury, Monsieur Pandy's faithful servant. In addition to that, there has been an attempted second murder that will now, I am pleased to say, be unsuccessful. Or perhaps I should call Kingsbury's death the *second* murder and the attempted murder the *first*, since the attempt started long before Kingsbury died.'

'An attempted murder?' said Lenore Lavington. 'Of whom?'

'Of your sister,' Poirot told her. 'You see, madame, the writer of the four letters signed falsely in my name did everything he or she could to ensure—even though, as I have already said, he was not murdered—that *Annabel Treadway would hang for the murder of Barnabas Pandy.*'

CHAPTER 34

Rebecca Grace

'May I ask you a question, M. Poirot?' said Annabel Treadway.

'*Oui*, mademoiselle. What is it?'

'The killer of Kingsbury, the writer of the four letters, and the person who wanted me to hang for the murder of Grandy—are these three different people?'

'No. Only one person is responsible.'

'Then . . . I have unwittingly helped that person,' said Annabel. She had stopped crying. 'I have colluded in the attempted murder of myself by going to Scotland Yard and confessing to drowning Grandy in his bath.'

'Let me ask you now: did you murder your grandfather, Barnabas Pandy?'

'No. No, I did not.'

'*Bien*. Now you tell the truth. *Excellent!* It is time for the truth, finally, to be told. Mademoiselle Ivy, you believe very strongly in the power of the truth, do you not?'

'I do,' said Ivy. 'Did you really confess to a murder you

did not commit, Aunt Annabel? A murder that was not even a murder? That was foolish of you.'

Poirot said to Ivy, 'The murderer of Kingsbury told you the truth, yesterday, about his or her attempt to frame Annabel Treadway, your aunt, for the murder of your great-grandfather. You refuse to reveal that person's name. You protect a remorseless killer. Why? It is because of the power of the truth they told you!'

'Why do you assume that the person in question lacks remorse?' said Ivy.

'A contrite person would confess here and now,' said Poirot, looking around the room. Nobody spoke up, until Eustace Campbell-Brown said, 'Isn't it peculiar how, in circumstances such as these, one feels madly tempted to confess? I'm innocent, but I can't bear the silence. I feel an urge to cry out that it was *I* who killed Kingsbury. It wasn't, naturally.'

'Then be quiet, please,' Poirot told him.

'What if, instead of being remorseless, the person in question is simply more frightened than he or she has ever been?' Ivy Lavington asked Poirot

'It is gratifying to me that you seek to defend the killer of Kingsbury, mademoiselle. It confirms to me that I am right in every respect. The truth told to you by this person, while Kingsbury listened outside the door . . . it touched your heart, did it not? In spite of the inexcusable acts that you know were perpetrated by this guilty one, you cannot bring yourself to harden your heart against them.'

Ivy Lavington looked away. 'As I said before: you know

everything, M. Poirot. You do not need me to confirm what you know.'

Poirot turned to Sylvia Rule. 'Madame, with the exception of your daughter and future son-in-law, have you ever before seen the face of anybody in this room?'

'Of course I have,' she snorted. 'I have seen *your* face, M. Poirot.'

'I should have added "and apart from Hercule Poirot"! Is there anybody else in this room that you recognize?'

Sylvia Rule looked down at her hands, which were folded in her lap. After a few seconds, she said, 'Yes. I have met Mrs Lavington before—Lenore Lavington—though I did not know her true name when we met. It was thirteen years ago. She told me her name was Rebecca something. Rebecca Gray, or . . . no, Grace. Rebecca Grace.'

'Why do you think Madame Lavington felt it necessary to lie about her name? Please, do not try to hide the truth. Poirot, he knows everything.'

'Mrs Lavington was in the family way, and did not want to be,' said Sylvia Rule. 'When I was younger, I . . . helped women who found themselves in situations of that kind. I was good at what I did. I offered a service that was safe and discreet. Most of the ladies who came to me used other names, not their real ones.'

'Madame?' Poirot turned to Lenore Lavington.

'It's true,' she said. 'Cecil and I were unhappy together, and I thought it would only make things worse if we were to have another baby. In the end, however, I couldn't bring myself to go through with the procedure. At our first meeting, Mrs Rule told me that she too was expecting a baby. She wanted hers, but she said she could well imagine the distress of having to bear an unwanted child. When I heard those words—"an unwanted child"—I made my excuses and left. I never went back. My child, I realized, was not unwanted after all. I certainly could not bring myself to do away with it.'

Lenore Lavington threw a vicious look in Sylvia Rule's direction. She said, 'Mrs Rule tried to force the procedure upon me, once she saw I had changed my mind—so desperate was she not to lose a customer.'

Timothy Lavington rose unsteadily to his feet. There were tears in his eyes. 'The baby you didn't want was me, wasn't it, Mother?' he said.

'She didn't go through with it, Timmy,' said Ivy.

'I knew I would love you and want you as soon as I met you, Timmy,' Lenore told him. 'And I did. I truly did.'

'Did you tell Father that you were thinking of disposing of me in this barbaric fashion?' Timothy asked, his voice full of disgust.

'No. I told nobody.'

'Indeed,' said Poirot. 'You told nobody. This is very important.'

He gestured to me. This was my cue. I left the room, and returned a few moments later, carrying a small table, which I placed in the middle of the room so that everyone could see it. It was covered with a white sheet. Poirot had refused to tell me what was beneath the sheet, but I was pretty certain I knew what he was up to. So, from the look on his face, did Rowland McCrodden. Sure enough, Poirot lifted the sheet to reveal another slice of Church Window Cake, on a small china plate. Next to the plate was a knife. How many slices of that confounded cake, I wondered, had he brought with him to Combingham Hall? Fee Spring must have been delighted to have sold so many.

'Is this your way of telling us that solving the mystery has been a piece of cake, Poirot?' said Hugo Dockerill. 'A *piece of cake*, eh? That's a good one, isn't it?' He guffawed. His wife told him to be quiet and he fell silent, looking suitably chastened.

'I will now demonstrate to you, ladies and gentlemen, that when we solve the Mystery of Three Quarters, we are well on our way to solving the entire puzzle!'

'What is the Mystery of Three Quarters, Mr Poirot?' Inspector Thrubwell asked.

'I will explain, Inspector. You see here, as do we all, that there are four quarters to this slice of cake. On the top row, if I may call it that, we have the little yellow square and then the pink, and on the bottom row there is the pink and then the yellow. But we also have, because we have not yet used the knife, the whole slice, undivided.'

Dramatically, Poirot cut the slice into two halves, which he pushed to opposite edges of the plate. 'At first I thought that the four people who received letters from someone pretending to be me, accusing them of the murder of Barnabas Pandy, were two pairs of two: Annabel Treadway and Hugo Dockerill, who were connected to Monsieur Pandy, and Sylvia Rule and John McCrodden, who did not at first appear to be. Both told me they had never heard of Barnabas Pandy. Then I discovered from Hugo Dockerill that Madame Rule's son, Freddie, is a pupil at Turville College, the same school attended by Timothy Lavington. So! Then it appears to Poirot to be like this!' He took the knife and cut one half-slice of cake in half again.

He made a new arrangement of the yellow and pink squares on the plate: three of them close together and one alone and separate. 'This, *mes amis*, is what I referred to as the Mystery of the Three Quarters! Why is Monsieur John McCrodden the exception? Why was he—a stranger to Barnabas Pandy, a man who has never heard his name and has no obvious link to him—why was *he* chosen, when the other three choices were all people with visible connections to Monsieur Pandy or his family? Why should our composer of fraudulent letters choose these three and then this one?

'I asked myself if the writer of the letters wanted me to notice John McCrodden *in particular*. Then something occurred that puzzled me. I happened to be present when Mademoiselle Ivy mentioned the name of Freddie Rule to her mother. I noticed that Lenore Lavington looked aghast. Horrified. Almost frozen by shock. Why, I wondered, would she react so dramatically to the mention of a boy at her son's school?'

Poirot probably wanted to answer the question himself, but I could not help piping up with the one that struck me at that moment: 'Because she had not known, until you referred to Freddie Rule being at Turville College, that he was. She had no idea that the son of Sylvia Rule was at the same school as her son.'

'*Précisément!* She knew about a boy whom she described as "strange, lonely Freddie", but she did not know his family name. He had only been a pupil at Turville for a few months. Lenore Lavington was unaware that the Madame Rule she had met thirteen years earlier was the mother of strange, lonely Freddie until her daughter told her it was so. Then, in order to put me off the scent, she pretended at once to have a strong objection to Freddie, and to have warned Timothy not to associate with him. She did not wish me to suspect that it was Freddie's mother, and not Freddie himself, who had caused her to feel such horror. Later, she seemed to forget altogether that she had told me she disliked Freddie. When I next mentioned him, she displayed no animosity at all and seemed to have no interest in criticizing him. She has not objected to her son spending time with him here at Combingham Hall.

'I should say, ladies and gentlemen, that it was only once I was certain that the writer of the four letters was Lenore Lavington that this piece of the puzzle fell into place.'

'Wait,' said John McCrodden. 'If you believe that the same person killed Kingsbury, and tried to have Miss Treadway here hanged for murder . . . Are you accusing Mrs Lavington of those things too?'

'For the time being, I am saying that Madame Lavington wrote the letters accusing four people—including you, monsieur—of murder, and signed them in the name of Hercule Poirot. Madame Lavington, you were shaken by the mention of Freddie Rule because you had been so sure that the link between you and Sylvia Rule could never be known or guessed by anyone. You consulted her thirteen years ago in order to procure an illegal medical procedure. Of course, it would be in both of your interests to mention this to nobody. Then, in a most casual and coincidental manner, your daughter informs you that Mrs Rule's son, Freddie, is at school with your own son. Suddenly, a link between Sylvia Rule and Barnabas Pandy is plain for all to see.

'This, for you, was a disaster. You wanted the two-halves arrangement of the slice of cake, did you not? You wanted the recipients of your letters to be two people connected to your grandfather, and two who were completely uncon-nected. That way, no one would stand out. It would have been almost impossible to work out what was the aim of the letter-writer in those circumstances. However, thanks to the accident of Freddie Rule being a pupil at Turville, you realized to your dismay that you had unintentionally directed my attention towards John McCrodden as the special one, the *different* one. I knew then that there were only two possibilities: he was either the odd one out, or there was no odd one out—only the whole, undivided slice of cake.'

Poirot pushed the cake back together so that all four squares were once again touching. 'When I talk about the undivided slice of cake, I am referring to the possibility that the letter-writer might have had a personal connection to *all four people who received the letters*, including John McCrodden.

'You chose to sign your letters in my name, Madame Lavington. Why? You know that I am the best solver of crimes, *n'est-ce pas*? There is none better! And you wanted my attention. You wanted Hercule Poirot, after involving himself in the matter, to go to the police with a stiffened, pungent dress wrapped in cellophane and the opinion that your sister Annabel must have murdered your grandfather. Who else would sound so authoritative when saying all the things you thought you could manipulate me to say? Madame, I have never been at the same time and by the same person so flattered and so underestimated! You were foolish to believe that you could distract Hercule Poirot from the truth with a dress soaked in water and oil of olives.'

Inspector Thrubwell said, 'Mr Poirot, I'm a little confused. Are you suggesting that Mrs Lavington did *not* want you to think that Mr John McCrodden was the odd one out?'

'*Oui*, monsieur. She did not want me to wonder how he fitted into the picture. She did not wish me to ask myself: if Sylvia Rule turns out to be connected to Barnabas Pandy's family, might not the same be true of John McCrodden? Because, my friends, *Lenore Lavington is the only one in this room who personally has a link to all four people who received the letters.* She made a grave error when she constructed her plan. If she wished to accuse two complete strangers, she easily could have selected them at random from the telephone directory. Instead, she chose two people with whom she has a past connection—in both cases one that she believes is secret enough to be safe. She thinks that Poirot, he will soon discover that Sylvia Rule and John

McCrodden could not have murdered Barnabas Pandy because they were strangers to him and his family, and *nowhere near Combingham Hall on the day that he died.* They had neither motive nor opportunity. Madame Lavington imagines, therefore, that the names Rule and McCrodden will soon be eliminated from consideration.

'Ah, but this too goes wrong for her! It soon became clear to me that both Madame Rule and Monsieur McCrodden *could* have come here on the day that Barnabas Pandy died. As could Hugo Dockerill. They could have slipped in while the rest of the household was busy arguing or, in Kingsbury's case, unpacking a suitcase. They could have entered via the always-open front door, killed Monsieur Pandy, and then left in a hurry, without being seen by anybody. None of the three had strong alibis: a Christmas Fair from which it would have been easy to disappear for an hour or two without anyone noticing; a letter from a Spanish woman who might have been willing to say what-ever she had been told to say.'

Poirot stared at John McCrodden. He seemed to be waiting for him to speak.

Eventually McCrodden said in a low voice, 'I did not know her real name until I arrived at this house. She intro-duced herself to me as Rebecca Grace, as she did to Mrs Rule. Lenore.' He looked across the room at her. 'It's an unusual name. I am glad to know your name, Lenore.'

'Monsieur McCrodden, for the benefit of us all, will you please clarify the nature of your relationship to Lenore Lavington?' said Poirot. 'You were lovers, were you not?

'Yes. We were lovers for a short time. Too short. I knew she was married. How I cursed fate, for allowing me to meet her when it was too late and she already belonged to someone else.' His voice shook. 'I loved her with all my heart,' he said. 'I still do.'

CHAPTER 35

Family Loyalty

'I'm not ashamed of it,' said John McCrodden. 'I cannot be made to feel shame, as I am sure my father will be happy to tell you. Rebecca—Lenore—is the only woman I have ever loved, though we had only three days together. I have spent every hour of every day since then wishing it could have been longer—'

'John, please don't,' said Lenore. 'What good will it do now?'

'—but she insisted on returning to her husband, who, by the sound of it, was an uninspiring individual. She did her duty.'

'How dare you say that about my father?' protested Timothy Lavington. To his mother, he said coldly, 'Did *you* tell him Father was uninspiring? What other lies did you tell about him?'

Ivy touched her mother's arm and said, 'Tell him, Mummy. You have to.'

'Your father is dead, Timmy,' said Lenore. 'The letter that you received . . . I wrote it. I sent it.'

'What letter?' asked Jane Dockerill.

'Lenore Lavington sent a fifth letter,' said Poirot. 'One that most of you do not know about. She typed it on the same machine that she used for the other four: with the faulty letter "e". This letter was not an accusation of murder, however, and in it, Madame Lavington did not pretend to be Hercule Poirot. Instead, she pretended to be her late husband, Cecil Lavington. The point of the letter was to tell his son, Timothy, that he was not dead, though everybody believed that he was. Instead, he was busy with a secret government mission.'

'How could you lie about something like that, Mother?' said Timothy. 'I believed he was alive!'

Lenore Lavington looked away. Ivy touched her arm, at the same time giving Timothy a look that ordered him to stop.

Poirot continued: 'When Timothy Lavington showed to Catchpool here this letter that was supposedly from his father, Catchpool noticed at once the "e"s with the tiny white hole in the ink. He knew that the same person had sent the four letters in the name of Hercule Poirot, and that they had been typed on the same machine. You will all understand, I am sure, why we were determined to find it.

'When I first came to Combingham Hall, I asked Madame Lavington if I might test the typewriter here. She refused to allow it. Since there was no evidence to suggest that a crime had been committed, she was under no obligation to allow me to see anything in the house. Then, when I arrived at Combingham Hall the second time, I found that she had changed her mind and wished to cooperate.'

'We all wanted to help you, M. Poirot, but you tricked us,' said Annabel Treadway. 'You led us to believe that you could prove Grandy had been murdered. Now, however, you tell us his death was an accident, exactly as we had always believed.'

'Mademoiselle, I have been careful at every stage not to say a word that was not true. I told you only that I was certain there was a guilty person, a murderer, to be caught, and that, until that happened, there remained a great danger. I referred, mademoiselle, to the danger *to you*. Your sister wished to see you hang for the murder of your grandfather. When she admitted this to Mademoiselle Ivy—the conversation overheard by Kingsbury—she had not yet successfully killed anybody. Perhaps would not have continued with her plot to frame you? I do not know. But I do know this: a very short time later, thinking herself to be at risk of discovery and exposure, *she left Kingsbury to die*. Madame Lavington, I did not lie or even twist the truth when I described you as a murderer. It is a question of *character*. You became a murderer the moment you set out to arrange your sister's death.'

Lenore Lavington looked back at Poirot expressionlessly. She said nothing.

'Why did Lenore want her sister to hang?' asked John McCrodden.

'What about the other three letters?' said Annabel Treadway. 'Whatever Lenore's intentions with regard to me, why should she sent the same letter to Mr Dockerill, Mrs Rule and Mr McCrodden?'

'Mademoiselle, monsieur—please. I have not yet finished explaining. Since one cannot finish unless one starts somewhere, please allow me to start with the typewriter. Lenore Lavington used all of her cunning to try to deceive Poirot, but it did not work. Oh, yes, she was very clever. The typewriter I was forbidden to inspect when I first came here . . . it was the one I was looking for, with the imperfect letter "e".

'Between my first visit to Combingham Hall and my second, Lenore Lavington decided it would be wise for her to appear to want to help me in any way she can. I was told, upon arrival, that I could now inspect the typewriter, but that there had been purchased recently a new machine. The old one, said Lenore Lavington, was past its best. In order to appear helpful, Madame Lavington tells me she has kept the old one, *since that must be the one I will want to examine*. Naturally, the new typewriter, still unsold in the shop when the four letters were typed, cannot be the one I seek. Madame Lavington tells me she has asked Kingsbury to present me with both machines, new and old, so that I may test both. Ah, she was clever—but not clever enough.

'One of the typewriters looks new. The other looks new apart from a few scratches and cracks—which are easily made. *Alors*, Poirot, he performs the test, and he notices something most puzzling. The letter "e" is working exactly as it should on both machines, so both can be eliminated from suspicion. But it is not only the "e" that, in each case, is flawless. *It is everything.* I noticed no difference of quality. Apart from the scratches to one, *both* might have come brand new from the shop that very morning. I thought to myself: what if Lenore Lavington has lied to me and has, instead of new and old, given me two new machines to inspect? Why would she do that?'

'She would do it if she didn't want you to check the *real* old typewriter,' said Timothy Lavington. 'And she didn't— because it would have incriminated her.'

'Timmy, don't,' said Ivy. 'You needn't be the one to say it.'

'Family loyalty is the last thing in my mind at the moment,' her brother told her. 'I'm right, aren't I, M. Poirot?'

'Yes, Timothy, you are correct. Your mother was careless. She thought that telling me the old typewriter had not been working properly would be enough. She was not afraid that I would use both machines and notice that both seemed equally new, because of the many scratches she had inflicted upon one machine.

'I was nearly fooled! I asked myself: "Is it possible that the older machine is simply in excellent condition, and works well on occasions, though not on others?" I was asking myself this question when Annabel Treadway appeared and said to me, "I see you've begun your type-writer investigation. Lenore gave me strict orders to leave you alone and let you do your detective work."

'Why would Mademoiselle Annabel see *two* typewriters and *two* pieces of paper, both with words typed upon them, and conclude that I had only *begun* my typewriter experiment, rather than completed it? I could think of only one reason: she knew there were in fact *three* typewriters in the house—the two new ones, and the old machine that Lenore Lavington had hidden away.'

'Which is why Mrs Lavington told Miss Treadway to leave you alone,' said Eustace Campbell-Brown. 'If Miss Treadway knew that two typewriters had recently been purchased, she might have given the game away.'

'*Exactement*. And, remember, Lenore Lavington could not ask her sister to lie. If she did, Mademoiselle Annabel would suspect at once who had written and sent the four letters.'

'And . . .' Annabel Treadway began hesitantly '. . . when you asked me to look carefully at the two pieces of paper, and I could see no difference between them . . .'

'You were quite correct! I told you, did I not, that I had noticed something significant? *It was the absence of difference*. Often, the important thing to be noticed is a thing that is not there. I waited until I knew Madame Lavington was downstairs and not in her bedroom, and I searched that room. As I hoped I would, I found the old typewriter. It was in a bag under her bed. A quick test revealed that it was the one with the faulty "e".'

Timothy was staring furiously at his mother. 'You were going to kill me before I was even born,' he said. 'You were unfaithful to Father. You killed Kingsbury, and you would have allowed Aunt Annabel to hang if M. Poirot here hadn't stopped you. You're a monster.'

'That's enough!' John McCrodden told him.

To Poirot, McCrodden said, 'Whatever you suspect Lenore of having done, you surely cannot think it's acceptable for a boy to address his mother in such a manner, in front of strangers?'

'I do not suspect, monsieur. I *know*. Tell me—for you are not a stranger to Lenore Lavington—what did you do to anger her?'

McCrodden looked surprised. 'Anger her? How . . . how did . . .'

'How did I know? It is simple,' said Poirot. He often said this about things that were simple to nobody but him. 'Lenore Lavington wanted Annabel Treadway to hang—but she needed to conceal her true aim. She did this by sending the same letter of accusation to three other people. You, Monsieur McCrodden, were one of the three. Knowing that it would be a most unpleasant sort of letter to receive, Madame Lavington chose three people who, in her opinion, deserved to suffer a little. Not to hang for murder—that fate, she reserved only for her sister Annabel—but to worry, perhaps, that they might soon be charged with a crime they had not committed. So, I ask again: what did you do to anger Rebecca Grace, whose real name is Lenore Lavington?'

John McCrodden looked at Lenore as he spoke. 'We met at the seaside resort of Whitby. Rebec—Lenore was holidaying there with her husband. She . . . I'm afraid there is no nice way to put it. After we met, she abandoned him to spend three days with me. I don't know what she told him. I can't remember, all these years later. I seem to recall she made an excuse about having to rush off somewhere. Do you remember what it was, Lenore?'

She gave no answer. For some time, she had expressed no emotion, and done nothing but sit and stare straight ahead.

'At the end of the three days, I couldn't bear to let her go,' John McCrodden went on. 'I begged her to leave her husband and live with me. She said she couldn't do that, but that she would come to Whitby and see me whenever she could. She wanted our love affair to continue, but it was a prospect I found intolerable. The idea that she planned to stay with a man she neither loved nor desired . . . It would have been wrong. And I wasn't prepared to share her.'

'Whereas cavorting with a married woman is not wrong,' muttered Sylvia Rule.

'Be quiet,' John McCrodden told her. 'You know nothing of right and wrong, and you care even less.'

'So you forced upon Madame Lavington the stark choice?' said Poirot to McCrodden.

'Yes, I did. Him or me. She chose him, and she blamed me. To her mind, I had ended a love affair that might have continued—that she very much wanted to continue.'

'And she could not forgive you,' said Poirot. 'Just as she could not forgive Sylvia Rule for trying to force her to get rid of the baby she had decided she wanted to keep. Nor could she forgive Hugo for occasionally punishing Timothy for bad behaviour, as he had to every so often. That's why Monsieur Dockerill was chosen to receive one of the four letters.'

'How did you know that Lenore and I had had a love affair?' John McCrodden asked. 'I never said a word, not to a single soul. Neither did she, I am quite certain. It's impossible that you could know.'

'Ah, monsieur, this knowledge was not difficult to acquire. You and Madame Lavington told me yourselves, with a little help from Mademoiselle Ivy.'

'That cannot be true,' Ivy said. 'I myself only found out yesterday afternoon, when Mr McCrodden walked into the house and Mummy saw him again, and then she got so upset that I was able to force her to tell me everything. Before that happened, the name John McCrodden meant nothing to me, and you and I have barely spoken since then, M. Poirot.'

'*C'est vrai.* All the same, mademoiselle, you helped me to learn the secret without knowing it yourself. I put together things you had said with things I had heard from both your mother and Monsieur McCrodden, and—'

'What things?' John McCrodden asked. 'I'm still not sure whether to believe a single word that comes out of your mouth, Poirot.'

'You told me, if you recall, that your father disapproved of your choice of work. You referred to having worked as a miner somewhere in the north of England, on the coast, or near the coast. Your father did not approve this sort of labour, in which you got the dirty hands—but, you said, *he also did not approve when you worked at the clean end, making and selling the trinkets.* It was a strange expression, this "at the clean end". I did not know what it meant at the time. It struck me as not especially important, so I did not dwell upon it.

'I also did not at first realize what you might have meant by the word "trinkets". I had heard that word used recently—by your father, in fact. He used it to mean the decorations for Christmas, I think. But the word "trinkets" has another meaning too. It can mean jewellery. As for "the clean end", I decided that you must have been referring to the clean end *of mining*, for that was the subject we had been discussing. What you were trying to tell me, Monsieur McCrodden, was that you went from working in a mine—the dirty end—to the cleaner work of making jewellery from the substance that, previously, you had mined. That substance was the Whitby jet, was it not?

'Lenore Lavington told me that she had once owned a mourning bracelet made from jet, one that she later gave to her daughter, Mademoiselle Ivy. She described the bracelet to me as a treasured possession—a gift she herself was given during a seaside holiday with her late husband Cecil. From Ivy Lavington, I learned that the marriage of Cecil and Lenore Lavington was not a happy one—not, at least, on her part. Why, then, I asked myself, would she so treasure a gift bought for her by a husband she had not loved? She would not! The bracelet of Whitby jet had been given to her instead by a man she loved passionately: John McCrodden, the lover she took while on holiday.

'There was also, I learned, a second gift that Lenore

Lavington had given to her daughter: a fan—another item she described as a treasured possession. On the fan was a picture of a dancer with hair the same colour as that of Mademoiselle Ivy—a dancer wearing *a red and black dress*. Dark hair and a dress of red and black? This sounded very much to me like a *Spanish dancer*. I have seen such illustrations on ladies' fans that have been brought back as souvenirs from the continent. I knew, thanks to Rowland McCrodden, that his son John owned a house in Spain—that he loved the country and visited it often. Could John McCrodden have given that fan to Lenore Lavington, I wondered, during the three days they had spent together? I decided it was not merely possible but probable. Why else would an ordinary fan have become a treasured possession? Lenore Lavington had not forgiven John McCrodden, as we know—yet still, she treasured those gifts he had given her. Such is the complicated character of love!'

'It's a complicated business,' agreed Inspector Hubert Thrubwell. 'Not one of us could deny that, Mr Poirot.'

'The jet bracelet, the Spanish dancer fan,' Poirot went on. 'These things might have been mere coincidences, of course. Neither was proof that John McCrodden and Lenore Lavington knew one another. Then I thought: Lenore Lavington can be linked to Sylvia Rule, via Freddie; to Annabel, her sister; to Hugo Dockerill, housemaster of her son. Why not also to John McCrodden? Instead of being the odd one out, I decided it was likely that it was a case of one whole, undivided slice of cake . . .'—Poirot pointed dramatically at the plate on the table—'. . . and no odd ones out. *Lenore Lavington knew them all.*'

'Do you have anything to say about any of this, Mrs Lavington?' Inspector Thrubwell asked her.

She did not move an inch. Still, she said nothing.

John McCrodden said fiercely, 'I won't allow the woman I love to hang for murder, whatever she has done! I don't care if you're still angry with me after all these years, Lenore. I love you as much as I did then. Say something, for God's sake!'

'Poirot, I'm still not at all clear about the need for four letters,' said Rowland McCrodden. 'If Mrs Lavington hoped to see Miss Treadway punished for her grandfather's murder, why didn't she send only one letter, to her sister?'

'Because, my friend, she wished to conceal the fact that she was the accuser—the one with the suspicions! Lenore Lavington could not guarantee that her plan would work and that Mademoiselle Annabel would be sent to the gallows. If the plan did not work, she wanted to be free to try something different, perhaps—another form of revenge. This she would be better placed to do if Mademoiselle Annabel did not know she was an enemy to be feared. If one is feared, then at once precautions are taken. Lenore Lavington did not wish such precautions to be in operation. She wanted her sister *unguarded*.

'If she had been the only one accused of murder, Annabel Treadway would have asked herself, "Who might have done such a thing to me, and why?" If, on the other hand, she hears from Hercule Poirot that *four* people have been accused of the murder of Barnabas Pandy, then it seems to her that the accuser might be some person of whom she has never heard, perhaps. It seems to Mademoiselle Annabel that the accuser would surely *not* be her sister, who knows she could not have killed their grandfather because the two of them were together in a different room when he died. *Eh bien*, Lenore Lavington is protected from suspicion of being the one who suspects, the one who accuses; her quarry remains trusting of her and therefore vulnerable, which is how Lenore Lavington wanted her.'

'Wait a moment,' said John McCrodden. 'Lenore and Annabel were in a room together when their grandfather died? Did Lenore tell you that?' He sounded excited. I could not work out why.

'*Oui, monsieur*,' said Poirot. 'All three women told me this, and it is true.'

'Then Lenore provided Annabel with an alibi,' said McCrodden 'Why would she do that, if you say she wanted her to hang?'

Poirot looked at Rowland McCrodden. 'I'm sure you can enlighten your son on this point, *mon ami*.'

'The guilty tend to try to look as if they're not doing the very thing they *are* doing—the thing they're guilty of,' said Rowland McCrodden. 'If Mrs Lavington hoped to get her sister convicted of murder, what better way to look as if she's doing the opposite than by vigorously defending Miss Treadway and providing her with an alibi?'

'Is nobody going to ask the most important question?' said Jane Dockerill impatiently.

'I will,' said Timothy Lavington. 'Why on earth should Mother wish to revenge herself upon Aunt Annabel, M. Poirot? What harm had Aunt Annabel ever done to Mother?'

CHAPTER 36

The True Culprit

Poirot turned to Annabel Treadway. 'Mademoiselle,' he said. 'You know only too well the answer to your nephew's question.'

'I do,' said Annabel Treadway. 'It is something I can never forget.'

'Indeed. It is a secret you have kept for many years, and it has cast a shadow over your whole life, a shadow of terrible guilt and regret.'

'No. Not regret,' she said. 'It was not something I decided to do. It was something that just *happened*. Oh, I know I was the one who made it happen, but how can I regret it when I can't remember making the decision?'

'Then perhaps you feel additional guilt, not knowing whether, if you found yourself in a similar situation today, you would behave differently,' said Poirot.

'Can somebody please explain?' said Jane Dockerill.

'Yes, do get it over with, M. Poirot,' said Ivy Lavington. 'For many of us, this is not a pleasant experience. I accept that it is necessary, but please digress as little as possible.'

'Very well, mademoiselle. I shall tell everybody the secret that your mother told you yesterday, before Kingsbury came to listen outside the door.

'Shortly before Barnabas Pandy died, ladies and gentlemen, there was a dinner in this house. At the table were seated Monsieur Pandy, Lenore and Ivy Lavington and Annabel Treadway. Madame Lavington chastised Mademoiselle Ivy for eating too much. During an excursion to the beach several months earlier, she had told her that her legs resembled tree-trunks, and this story was told at the dinner table by an angry Ivy Lavington, who had now been twice insulted by her mother. The meal ended in misery: all three ladies left the table in distress, and Barnabas Pandy was also unhappy. The late Kingsbury told me that he came upon Monsieur Pandy sitting alone at the dinner table, crying.

'Now I must go back to when Ivy Lavington was a little girl, and Annabel Treadway took her for a walk by a river,' Poirot went on. 'Skittle, the dog, went with them. Mademoiselle Ivy decided it would be entertaining to roll down the river bank. Skittle, immediately alert to the danger, scrambled down the bank to rescue her but failed to stop her rolling into the water. Instead, he scratched her face and caused the scarring that remains to this day. Mademoiselle Ivy was soon afterwards trapped under the water, where she nearly drowned. Annabel Treadway had to climb into these lethal waters and rescue her. The current was very strong. Mademoiselle Annabel risked her own life to save her niece.

'*Alors*, now we must leap forward in time, *mes amis*, to the trip to the beach that I have already mentioned. Lenore and Ivy Lavington had taken the dog, Hopscotch, to the beach because Annabel Treadway was confined to her bed with the influenza. Mademoiselle Ivy loves swimming in the sea. She did not allow her near-fatal accident to make her afraid of water.'

'Hopscotch?' said Eustace Campbell-Brown. 'I thought the dog was called Skittle.'

'They are two different dogs, monsieur. Skittle is no longer with us. Hopscotch, a dog of the same breed, has replaced him.'

'*Replaced* him?' Tears sprang to Annabel Treadway's eyes. 'No one could replace Skittle, just as no one will be able to replace Hopscotch when he . . . when he . . . Oh!' She buried her face in her hands.

'Apologies, mademoiselle. I spoke without thinking.'

'Very good, so they're two different dogs,' said Rowland McCrodden. 'But, really, now is no time for us to be thinking about *any* dogs.'

'You are wrong,' Poirot told him. 'Dogs—or, to be precise, the late Skittle—is the very creature about whom we must think.'

'Why, for pity's sake?'

'I am about to explain. On the day of the trip to the beach, Lenore and Ivy Lavington were sitting near some trees. Hopscotch came running towards them, after first splashing in the waves. The sight of the dog's wet legs, which looked much thinner than they do when dry, reminded Mademoiselle Ivy of the day she nearly drowned. Memories flooded back to her, memories she had been unaware of until that moment. She told her mother that, as she had struggled under the water in her state of panic, she had mistaken the dog's wet legs for tree trunks on the river bank—even though they could not have been, because they were far too thin, and moving, not still. Then Annabel Treadway came to her rescue and Mademoiselle Ivy saw the *real* tree trunks: thick and stationary. She realized that the other things she had seen were the legs of Skittle and not tree trunks at all.

'This memory came back to her most powerfully that day on the beach many years later, thanks to the wet legs of Hopscotch. She told the story to her mother, and, as she listened, Lenore Lavington realized something. It was something of which Mademoiselle Ivy herself was unaware . . . and she remained unaware of it until her mother confessed everything to her yesterday in the conversation overheard by Kingsbury.'

'*What* did Mrs Lavington realize?' asked Rowland McCrodden, by now unable to conceal his desperation to understand. I myself was feeling a similar desperation.

'Is it not obvious?' said Poirot. 'Skittle's legs would only have been on that river-bank—to be observed by Mademoiselle Ivy—if, before saving her niece, Annabel Treadway had first pulled Skittle out of the water. There is no other logical conclusion to be drawn. *She must have saved her dog first, and only afterwards saved Mademoiselle Ivy.*'

As soon as Poirot had said it, I saw precisely what he meant. 'If Skittle tried to stop Ivy Lavington from rolling into the water and failed, he wouldn't simply give up and go and wait on the bank,' I said. 'No loyal dog would do that. He would leap into the water. He wouldn't ever stop trying to save whichever family member was in danger.'

'Exactly, *mon ami*,' said Poirot. He sounded rather proud of me, which I appreciated, though we both knew I would never have worked it out on my own. 'And once his mistress, Mademoiselle Annabel, jumped into the water also, Skittle would only have become more intent upon his rescue mission. He would not have left the water by choice, not with two people he loved still in peril. His own life would have been in danger, therefore, from the strong and fast-moving current. All three of them might have died.'

'And if Skittle's legs were thin and wet when Ivy Lavington saw them on the river bank, then they must at some point have been in the water,' said Rowland McCrodden. 'You're right, Poirot. No dog would decide to save only himself and scramble back up the bank in that situation. Someone must have dragged him out of the water and . . . tethered him to something.'

'*Oui*. Annabel Treadway tethered him securely, to prevent him from leaping back into the river and placing himself in danger once more. Only then did she return to the water to save Mademoiselle Ivy. You did not realize the significance of your memory, mademoiselle, when you described it to your mother—but she knew. She knew instantly. She pictured the wet legs of Skittle on the river bank as he struggled against whatever restraint his mistress had imposed upon him. She understood exactly what it meant. But here is the dilemma. . .

'Did Lenore Lavington ask herself if her sister might have dealt with the dog first only because he was flailing so wildly in the water that her attempt to rescue her niece was impeded? If that had been the case, would not Mademoiselle Annabel have told the truth? She would have—so it must have been otherwise. Annabel Treadway must have valued the life of her dog more than that of her niece, and chosen to save Skittle first—thereby taking the most enormous risk with Mademoiselle Ivy's life. She could so easily have drowned in the time that it took for Skittle to be carried to safety.'

By now, Annabel Treadway was weeping. She made no attempt to deny any of what Poirot had said.

Poirot spoke softly to her. 'You, mademoiselle, the first time we met, told me that nobody minds when very old people die, whereas if a child dies it is seen as a tragedy. That was your guilt speaking. It pained you that the life you had risked was that of a little child with such potential and so many years ahead of her. You knew society would judge you all the more harshly for that. It is a strange coincidence . . . When I spoke to the daughter-in-law of Vincent Lobb, your grandfather's lifelong enemy with whom he sought, finally, to be reconciled, she told me that it is a most terrible thing *to do the right thing too late*. That is what you did, mademoiselle: you saved the life of your little niece, but you did it too late.'

'And I have suffered ever since,' sobbed Annabel.

'You told me in our very first conversation that you had "saved lives". You then quickly corrected yourself, or so it seemed, and suddenly it was only one life that you had saved: the life of Mademoiselle Ivy. I thought you were embarrassed to have exaggerated—that you wanted to be strictly, scrupulously accurate, and not to claim any more credit than was your due. Only much later did it occur to me that there was another possibility, equally plausible: *that you had saved more than one life, but wanted to conceal the fact.* Your initial pronouncement—*lives*, plural—was the truth.

'It was during a conversation with Mademoiselle Ivy that this struck me. Knowing that somebody had plotted to bring about the death of Annabel Treadway, I had spoken of the need to save lives. Ivy Lavington asked me if it was one life or more that needed to be saved, and I admitted that it was only one that was in danger. Of course, I did not know then that Kingsbury would be killed. I noticed that my conversation with Mademoiselle Ivy reminded me of something, and wondered what it could be. It took me only seconds, after that, to solve the mystery: it was my first encounter with Annabel Treadway of which I had been reminded, and our exchange about saving lives, or perhaps it was only one life. Suddenly, in the light of what I had deduced about the day Mademoiselle Ivy nearly drowned, Mademoiselle Annabel's remarks about saving lives made perfect sense to me.'

I could not help shaking my head, amazed at how Poirot's

brain worked. Other people looked similarly impressed. We all sat transfixed as he continued with his account.

'The first time we met, after she had received a letter that she believed was from me, accusing her of the murder of Monsieur Pandy, Annabel Treadway said something else that struck me as unusual. She said, "You cannot know . . ." then stopped herself before she said any more. She felt, you see, as if morally she deserved to receive a letter accusing her of murder, even though she had murdered nobody and Mademoiselle Ivy had not, in fact, died that day in the river. What she meant to say was that I, Hercule Poirot, *could not know* that she was guilty; it was impossible.

'She will never stop thinking of herself as guilty, ladies and gentlemen. She has tried so hard to atone. Monsieur Dockerill, you told me that she declined your offer of marriage. She said that she would not be well suited to looking after the boys of Turville College. This, too, now makes sense: she did not believe she should be entrusted with the welfare of children, and so she did not allow herself to marry and have any of her own. At the same time, she doted upon her sister's two children and poured into them all the love that she could, to compensate for her secret failure all those years ago.'

'There must have been a considerable amount of fear, as well as guilt,' said Rowland McCrodden. 'At any moment, Miss Lavington might have remembered what happened that day at the river.'

'Indeed she might have,' Poirot agreed. 'And of that,

Annabel Treadway was terrified. Then, after many years, her worst fears were realized. During the disastrous dinner, Mademoiselle Ivy told the story about the tree trunks remark, and Annabel Treadway saw in her sister's face that she knew the truth—that she had known it since the day on the beach. Monsieur Pandy also quickly understood the meaning of Mademoiselle Ivy's newly unearthed memory— and Annabel Treadway saw that too.'

Poirot turned to Ivy Lavington. 'You, mademoiselle, were the only one seated at the dinner table that night who thought that it was only legs and potatoes and your mother's opinions about your size and shape that, together, were causing such trouble. The other three people at the table were thinking about something quite different.'

'Yes, and I had no idea,' said Ivy. 'None whatsoever. Aunt Annabel, you should have told me the truth as soon as I was old enough to understand. I would have forgiven you. I *do* forgive you. Please do not feel guilty any longer—I should not be able to bear it. It's such a waste of time, and you have made yourself suffer quite enough already. I know you are sorry, and I know you love me. That is all that matters.'

'Your aunt's guilt will not, I'm afraid, be so easily banished,' Poirot told her. 'Without it, I fear she would be quite lost. She would not know herself at all. For most people, that is a prospect too frightening to contemplate.'

'You might forgive me, Ivy, but Lenore never will,' said Annabel. 'And Grandy . . . he couldn't forgive me either. He was going to cut me out of his will—leave me with nothing.'

'That was the final straw for you, was it not, mademoiselle? It was what made you decide to go to Scotland Yard and confess to the murder of Monsieur Pandy, though you knew you were innocent.'

Annabel nodded. 'I thought, "If Grandy has decided to treat me in this way, if all my kindness and devotion in the intervening years counts for nothing . . . why, then I might as well hang for murder. Perhaps it is no more than I deserve." But Ivy, darling, I would like you to know this: that day by the river, I was like a mad thing. I only realized that I had made a *choice* after I had secured Skittle to a post by his leash. It was like waking from a dream. A nightmare! And you were still thrashing around in the water, and I saved you *then*, of course, but . . . I couldn't remember, and can't remember, *deciding* not to save you first. I truly can't.'

'How old was Skittle then?' Lenore Lavington asked.

I heard a few people gasp. It was so long since she had said anything.

'He was five, wasn't he? At most he could only have lived for another seven or eight years, and I believe he died when he was ten, in fact. You risked my daughter's life, your own niece's life, to save a dog who only went on to live for another five years.'

'I'm so sorry,' Annabel said quietly. 'But . . . you mustn't pretend that you don't understand about *love*, Lenore, and what it can make a person do. After all, we have all heard about your Mr McCrodden, with whom you spent only three days. Yet you loved him passionately, did you not?

And I can see—though no one else can, because no one knows you as I do—that you *still* love him. I loved Skittle, however short his life was doomed to be.

'Love!' Annabel turned to Poirot. 'Love is the true culprit, M. Poirot. Why did my sister try to frame me for murder? Because of her determination to avenge a wrong done to her daughter many years ago—because of how much she *loves* Ivy. So many sins and crimes are committed in the name of love.'

'That may be so,' said Rowland McCrodden, 'but can we postpone our discussion of emotional matters and stick to the facts for a little longer? In his note to you, Poirot, Kingsbury wrote that he had overheard Miss Lavington saying to her interlocutor—and we now know that person was her mother, Mrs Lavington—that ignorance of the law is no defence. What, if I may ask, is the relevance of that? At what point, and in relation to what, might Mrs Lavington have pleaded ignorance of the law? I'm sorry if the question is a pedantic one.'

'Ah, my friend.' Poirot smiled at him. 'It is Hercule Poirot who must be the greater pedant. What Kingsbury wrote in his note to me was that he had heard Mademoiselle Ivy saying *words to the effect that* ignorance of the law is not an acceptable defence. That means, does it not, that the point might have been made with different words? *Words that conveyed the same meaning.* Remember, Kingsbury also wrote "John Modden" instead of "John McCrodden". He was not a person who concerned himself with precision of language or nomenclature.'

'Quite, quite,' said Rowland McCrodden, 'but however Miss Lavington might have phrased it, she must have known that her mother would have been as aware as anybody in the land that to falsely accuse someone of murder and attempt to plant evidence incriminating them is unlawful. It's hardly the sort of thing about which one might plausibly say, "Sorry, M'lud, I had no notion that such behaviour was not permitted and viewed by everybody as entirely above board."'

'Wasn't that the very point Miss Lavington was overheard making to her mother?' said Jane Dockerill. 'That ignorance of the law would *not* be accepted by any court of law as a valid defence?'

'I can see why you might think so, Madame Dockerill— just as I can see the wisdom of the point made by Monsieur McCrodden. Both sides of this particular argument are, however, irrelevant, since Lenore and Ivy Lavington did not discuss *at all* the defence of not knowing the law and whether or not it might work in this instance. Not even for a moment did they discuss it!'

'What do you mean by saying that they didn't discuss it, Mr Poirot?' asked Inspector Thrubwell. 'Mr Kingsbury wrote in his note to you that he heard—'

'Yes, yes. Let me explain what Kingsbury heard. It is startlingly simple: he heard Mademoiselle Ivy warning her mother that she would soon be found out, for she was the only person connected to all four letter-recipients. I imagine she said something of this kind: "It will soon be discovered that you and John McCrodden know one another, and

Sylvia Rule's son Freddie is at school with Timothy, *so it will be pointless to say that you don't know the Rules. That will get you nowhere.* No one would believe you."' Poirot stopped and shrugged. 'Or, as Kingsbury wrote in his most helpful note, "words to that effect".'

'The Rules,' I repeated in a whisper. 'Ivy wasn't talking about the law, she was talking about the Rule family.'

'I see,' said Rowland McCrodden. 'Thank you for clearing that up, Poirot.'

'You are most welcome, my friend. And now there remains only one more thing that must be cleared up. Madame Lavington, there is something that I must tell you. It will, I think, be of great interest to you. You have patiently sat and listened as I explained to everybody else things that you knew only too well already. But now I have a surprise for you . . .'

CHAPTER 37

The Will

'Let's hear it then, Poirot,' said John McCrodden. 'What is this final revelation?' He spoke tauntingly, as if everything Poirot had told us so far might have been a lie.

'Barnabas Pandy had no intention of cutting off Mademoiselle Annabel. None at all! The granddaughter he planned to disinherit was Lenore Lavington.'

'That can't be true,' said Annabel. 'He adored Lenore.'

'I performed a little experiment,' said Poirot. 'Not with the typewriters this time. I used, instead, human beings. There is a woman working in the offices of Rowland McCrodden—a woman he has detested for some time, with, one might say, little cause.'

'She's not the easiest of people to deal with,' I felt obliged to say.

'Her name is Emerald Mason,' said Poirot. 'To test my theory about Barnabas Pandy's attitude to Annabel Treadway and how it might have affected his behaviour towards his old enemy Vincent Lobb, I played a little trick on Monsieur McCrodden. I told him that Emerald Mason had been in a terrible motorcar accident and was to lose both her legs. This was not true, and I soon revealed that I had created this little deception. Before I did so, however, Monsieur McCrodden apologized to Catchpool for having been uncongenial when they travelled here together from London. Having been not at all amiable for the duration of the journey, Rowland McCrodden transformed himself, immediately upon hearing about poor Mademoiselle Emerald's lost legs, into a humble and contrite man who could see exactly how trying he had been until that moment.

'Why did this change take place? Because Rowland McCrodden felt terribly guilty. He realized that he had been unduly harsh towards this relatively harmless woman, and now a terrible fate had befallen her. He felt, almost, responsible—as if her tragic fate had been his fault. This led him, directly, to think of other people whom he might have treated harshly. Catchpool came immediately to mind, and so Rowland McCrodden apologized to him—something that would not have happened had I not invented the story about the legs of Mademoiselle Emerald Mason.'

'Legs again!' said Hugo Dockerill. 'Golly!'

'You are probably right, monsieur,' Poirot smiled at him. 'The subconscious influence must have been at work. In any case, when I heard Rowland McCrodden apologize to Catchpool, I knew for a certainty the reason for Barnabas Pandy's sudden lightness of spirit, noticed by his lawyer Peter Vout. I knew that it must have been caused by his understanding, finally, the pain of the timid, sad granddaughter whom for so long he had judged and found wanting. Suddenly, he comprehends how she has suffered for so many years. He regrets, profoundly, his severe judgement of her. And he finds that he no longer feels antipathy towards Vincent Lobb. He can forgive not only Annabel Treadway's weakness but also Lobb's. What he cannot tolerate, he finds, is the harsh judgement he sees in the eyes and hears in the voice of his other granddaughter, Lenore Lavington. This reminds him of his own punitive way of looking at the world until so late in his life. *Eh bien*, he resolves to ensure that Lenore Lavington does not benefit after his death—and he resolves to compensate Annabel Treadway for his years of preferential treatment towards her sister that must have greatly increased Mademoiselle Annabel's suffering.'

'What are you talking about?' said Lenore Lavington. 'It's nonsense.'

'I am explaining, madame, that you were the one your grandfather would have cut out of his will, had he survived.'

'But . . . that cannot be true,' said Annabel Treadway. She looked utterly lost.

'I was in London this morning,' said Poirot. 'I asked Monsieur Peter Vout: did Monsieur Pandy state explicitly that it was Mademoiselle Annabel whom he planned to deprive of her inheritance? I was given the answer I expected: no, he had not specified which granddaughter he had in mind for this unfortunate fate. In fact, I was told by Monsieur Vout that Monsieur Pandy had been uncharacteristically oblique when speaking of his new will. His solicitor had merely assumed, as did Lenore Lavington when he told her of his intentions without naming any names, that Mademoiselle Annabel would be the one cut off without a penny, because she had always been the least favoured granddaughter.'

'Why would Mr Pandy behave in this deliberately misleading fashion?' asked Jane Dockerill. 'Surely one would only do that if one wished to deliver a surprise punishment from beyond the grave—one that was designed to come as a great shock.'

'*Précisément*, madame. Of course, Lenore Lavington was in no doubt that she would be the one to end up twice as wealthy as she would otherwise have been as a result of this new will. How could it not be so? Had Monsieur Pandy not learned, a day or two earlier, that Annabel Treadway had left his great-granddaughter to drown in a river while saving a dog? He had! And it was she, Lenore Lavington, who had been summoned, in secret, to be told of her grandfather's plan to make this change to his will. I expect he said—to use Kingsbury's phrase again—*words to the effect of* "Everybody will get what they deserve after I die. Those who deserve nothing will get nothing."'

'You are mistaken,' Lenore Lavington said. 'Even if he was able to forgive Annabel and Vincent Lobb, Grandfather had no reason suddenly to decide to cut me off.'

'I believe he did,' said Poirot. 'At the dinner table on the evening of the unpleasantness, I believe he noticed a cruel, unforgiving glint in your eye, when you saw that he had realized the truth about Mademoiselle Ivy's accident and your sister's actions on that day. He saw you watching him closely, hoping that this new knowledge would kill any feelings of affection or loyalty that he had towards your sister once and for all. He saw in your eyes pure, unforgiving hatred. It shocked him. He found it unbearable. Shall I tell you why? Because it reminded him of himself! Suddenly, he saw how cruelly unforgiving he had been to his once good friend, Vincent Lobb. He realized, perhaps, that the very worst sin of all is the inability to forgive the sins of others. That, Madame Lavington, is why he decided you deserved nothing.'

'This is quite shameless invention on your part, Poirot,' said John McCrodden. 'Truly, I don't see how you can claim to know any of this.'

'I make deductions based upon what facts I do know, monsieur.'

Poirot turned back to Lenore Lavington. He said, 'After the disaster of the dinner, your grandfather decided to make for you a test. He wanted to test whether you—knowing that guilt had consumed the life and soul of Mademoiselle Annabel, and knowing how much she loved Mademoiselle Ivy and how sorry she must be—would beg him to reconsider and to forgive. That is why he told you about his plan to make a new will. It is the only reason he did so. If you had said, "Please, do not punish Annabel, who has already suffered enough," he would have been content to let his existing will remain in place. But you did no such thing. Instead, you showed him that you were delighted by the prospect of your sister being doomed to live in poverty. You demonstrated that you had no compassion.'

'M. Poirot, if I understand you correctly, you are saying that Mother did in fact have a substantial motive for murdering Grandy,' said Timothy Lavington. 'Except that, one, he wasn't murdered, and two, Mother *didn't know* she had a motive to kill him. She believed Aunt Annabel would be the one to lose out under the terms of the new will, not her.'

'That is precisely correct,' Poirot said. 'Barnabas Pandy was not murdered, but it was his accidental drowning that caused the murder of poor Kingsbury and the attempted murder of Mademoiselle Annabel. I do not believe that Lenore Lavington would have tried to bring about the death of her sister if Monsieur Pandy had not died. He would have changed his will, and Lenore Lavington would have assumed the change was in her favour and to the detriment of her sister. That might have been enough for her—Mademoiselle Annabel's punishment of being entirely cut off from the family fortune—at least until Monsieur Pandy eventually died and she learned the truth about the changed will.

'Instead, her grandfather died *before* making the promised alterations to his testamentary affairs. This was too much for Madame Lavington to bear. Mademoiselle Annabel would not, after all, get her punishment of poverty! *That*, ladies and gentlemen, was when Lenore Lavington decided to see if she might be able to arrange for her sister to hang for a murder she did not commit. This last part, of course, is mere supposition. I cannot prove it.'

'That and the rest of what you've told us today,' said

John McCrodden coldly. 'Where is your proof that Mr Pandy would have disinherited Lenore, whom you yourself say he always favoured? Your silly experiment proves nothing.'

'Do you think so, monsieur? I disagree. I think everybody in this room who is not in love with Lenore Lavington can see the logic in what I have said. Let me tell you one more thing that might convince you: Kingsbury told me that on the night of the dinner disaster, he saw Monsieur Pandy sitting at the table and crying, once his granddaughters and great-granddaughter had left him alone. One single, solitary tear, Kingsbury said. Does this suggest that Barnabas Pandy was angry with Mademoiselle Annabel? *Non, mes amis.* One might cry from anger, but there would be a flood of passionate tears, would there not? He was not angry with Mademoiselle Annabel. He felt compassion for her. He was sad—sad and full of regret. With no knowledge of the terrible guilt she struggled with every day, he had treated her with impatience. Suddenly, this incomprehensible grand-daughter of his *made sense to him*: the invisible layer of tragedy that seemed always to surround her; her refusal to marry and bear children.

'It is not difficult to see how such thoughts—such a startling change of perspective—might lead him to reflect upon the other person whom he had treated with undue harshness: his enemy, Vincent Lobb. The analogy, when I considered it, was extremely strong, and convinced me I was right. Vincent Lobb, like Annabel Treadway, was guilty of cowardice. Too afraid of the possible consequences of choosing the right course of action, he chose the wrong one. He then felt guilty for the rest of his life—once again, like Annabel Treadway. Lobb did something terribly wrong, as did Mademoiselle Annabel, and both suffered greatly. Both were unable, thereafter, to enjoy their lives and live them to the full. In that moment, as he sat at the dinner table, Barnabas Pandy decided that he must forgive them both. It was a wise decision that he made.'

'It's all very well to spout about forgiveness, Poirot, when you are not personally the one with something to forgive,' said John McCrodden. 'You don't have children, do you? Neither do I, but I do possess an imagination. Do you believe you could ever forgive a person who left your four-year-old child to drown in a river, while saving a *dog* instead? I know I could not!'

'I know, monsieur, that I would never stick a wet dress to the bottom of a bed frame in the hope that it would be found by Hercule Poirot and result in the person I could not forgive being sent to the gallows for a murder she did not commit. That much I know.

'You made a fatal miscalculation, madame,' Poirot said to Lenore Lavington. 'The discovery of the dress provided me with a vital clue. It told me that that either your sister had murdered Monsieur Pandy, or else someone needed me to believe that she had. That was the moment when I knew there was a murderer to be caught: either one who had killed already, or one who intended to cause the death of Annabel Treadway, or perhaps both. Without the wet dress, I might not have pursued my investigation so assiduously, and the world might never have known of your guilt, madame.'

Annabel Treadway stood up. Hopscotch made a noise as he too rose from his seated position and stood by her side. It was as if he knew she had something important to say. 'My sister cannot be guilty of murder, M. Poirot. She was with me when Kingsbury was killed. Weren't you, Lenore? You were with me the whole time, between two o'clock and when we both arrived in the drawing room together. So you see, she cannot have done it.'

'I can see that you wish to follow your grandfather's example and be compassionate, mademoiselle. You intend to forgive your sister, *n'est-ce pas*, for her attempt to end your life? You cannot fool Hercule Poirot. If you and Madame Lavington had been together between two o'clock and when you arrived in the drawing room, you would have said so much sooner.'

'No, that's not true,' said Annabel. 'Lenore, tell him. We were together—don't you remember?'

Lenore Lavington ignored her sister. She looked at Poirot and said, 'I am a mother who loves her children. That is all.'

'Lenore.' John McCrodden knelt beside her and took her hand in both of his. 'You must be strong. I love you, darling. He cannot prove a damned thing, and I believe he knows it.'

A tear escaped from the corner of Lenore's eye and started, slowly, to creep down the side of her face. One single solitary tear: exactly like the one Barnabas Pandy had shed, described by Kingsbury to Poirot.

'I love you, John,' she said. 'I have never stopped loving you.'

'It turns out that you are capable of forgiveness after all, madame,' said Poirot. 'That is good. Whatever else has happened or will happen, that is always good.'

CHAPTER 38

Rowland Without a Rope

'The visitor you have been expecting has arrived, sir,' said George to Poirot late one Tuesday afternoon. Nearly two weeks had passed since Poirot and I had left Combingham Hall and returned to London.

'Monsieur Rowland McCrodden?'

'Yes, sir. Shall I show him in?'

'Yes, please, Georges.'

Rowland McCrodden entered the room moments later, looking defiant, then seemed to slump a little when he caught sight of Poirot and heard his heartfelt welcome.

'You need not be abashed,' Poirot said. 'I know what you have come to tell me. I expected it. It is quite natural that it should happen.'

'Then you've heard?' said McCrodden.

'I have heard nothing. I have been told nothing. Yet, still, I know.'

'That's impossible.'

'You have come to tell me that you will be assisting in the

defence of Lenore Lavington—is that not so? She is to plead not guilty to the charges of murder and attempted murder.'

'Someone *has* told you. You must have spoken to John.'

'My friend, I have spoken to no one. *You* have spoken to John at great length, though, have you not, since our time at Combingham Hall? The two of you have put aside all the unpleasantness that has passed between you, like the water under a bridge, *non*?'

'Well, yes. But I fail to see how you could have—'

'Tell me, is it possible that John will now follow you into the law, as you always hoped he would?'

'Why, yes, he . . . he expressed his intention to do so only yesterday,' said Rowland McCrodden suspiciously. 'Why won't you be straight with me, Poirot? It is simply not credible to think that anyone could guess correctly in so much detail. Even you.'

'It is not a guess. It is knowledge of human nature,' Poirot explained. 'Monsieur John, he wishes he himself could defend the woman he loves—though he is grateful for your efforts on his, and her, behalf. He shows his appreciation by deciding that, after all, it would not be such a bad thing if he were to practise the law. Especially now that his father has changed his mind about what ought to happen to those who have committed murder.'

'You talk about my own opinions and how they have changed as if you know more about it than I do,' said McCrodden.

'Not more—only the same amount,' said Poirot. 'I know what must be true, always. And in this case, it was all so easy to foresee. Your son loves Lenore Lavington, and you, *mon ami*, you love your son as any good father does. And so, although you believe that Poirot is right and that Madame Lavington is guilty, you will help to defend her. You know that if she were to hang for murder, your son's heart would break. His hopes of any future happiness would be crushed. You would do anything to prevent that, would you not? Having once lost him—seemingly irretrievably, and for so long—you will not now risk losing him again, neither on account of a disagreement about the law and its morality, nor to his own grief. And so, you help Lenore Lavington, and you change your mind about certain issues of law and justice. I imagine you now believe that no murderer should hang for his or her crime? Are we now to call you "Rowland Without a Rope"?'

'This is not what I came here to discuss, Poirot.'

'Or are you still an advocate for the death penalty in all cases apart from this one?'

'That would make me a hypocrite,' said McCrodden with a sigh. 'Isn't there another possibility? Might I not believe that Lenore Lavington is innocent?'

'No. You do not believe that.'

The two men sat for a few moments in silence. Then McCrodden said, 'I came here because I wanted to tell you in person that I shall be helping Lenore. I also want to thank you. When I first found out that John had received that horrible letter—'

'You refer to the letter sent to him *by Lenore Lavington*—the woman you intend to help?'

'I am trying to thank you, Poirot. I am grateful to you for exonerating my son.'

'He is not a murderer.'

'As you might be aware, Miss Treadway is sticking to her version of events,' said McCrodden.

'You mean she continues to insist that she was with her sister when Kingsbury died? That, too, I expected. It is her guilt at work—at work in the service of injustice. Madame Lavington is lucky indeed to have Mademoiselle Annabel to help her, and you, and your son. Less lucky are those she might kill in the future, if you all prevail. I'm sure you are aware, my friend, that once a person has allowed themselves to take one life, it is easy for them to kill again and again. This is why I pray that you will not prevail. The jury, I hope, will believe me—not because of my reputation but *because I will be telling the truth*.'

'All of the evidence against Lenore is circumstantial,' said McCrodden. 'You have nothing concrete, Poirot. No indisputable facts.'

'*Mon ami*, let us not argue the merits of our respective cases here and now. This is not a murder trial. Soon enough we will be in a courtroom, and we will see whom the jury believes.'

McCrodden nodded curtly. 'I bear you no ill will, Poirot,' he said on his way to the door. 'Quite the opposite.'

'*Merci*. And I . . .' Poirot found it hard to decide what to say. Finally he said, 'I am pleased to hear that relations between you and your son have improved. Family is very important. For your sake, I am glad that you do not find the price of reconciliation to be too high. Please do Poirot one little favour: ask yourself every day if this is the course you wish to pursue, and if it is the *right* course.'

'Kingsbury had no living relatives,' said McCrodden. 'And Annabel Treadway is not on her way to the gallows for a crime she didn't commit.'

'And so no harm is done if Lenore Lavington walks free? I disagree. When justice is deliberately distorted and denied, harm is done. You, your son, Lenore Lavington . . . and, yes, Annabel Treadway for her lies . . . if you are all lucky, you might not pay the price for your actions in this life. Beyond that, it is not up to Hercule Poirot to speculate.'

'Goodbye, Poirot. Thank you for everything you did for John.'

With these words, Rowland McCrodden turned and left.

CHAPTER 39

A New Typewriter

I am typing this final section of my account of 'The Mystery of Three Quarters' six months subsequent to the events of the preceding chapter, and on a brand new typewriter. All the letter 'e's in this last chapter are, therefore, perfect. Our friend the eel need no longer feel down at heel.

It's strange—I developed a strong aversion to the sight of those faulty 'e's as I wrote this story, but now that they are gone, I rather miss them.

The new typewriter was a gift from Poirot. A few weeks after the trial of Lenore Lavington was concluded, having noticed that I had sent him no new pages to read, he arrived at Scotland Yard with the most elegantly wrapped box I have ever seen. He said, 'You have abandoned your writing?'

I made a non-committal noise.

'Every story needs an ending, *mon ami*. Even if we do not like the resolution, it is still necessary to finish what we have started. The loose threads, they must be gathered in.'

He put the parcel down on my desk. 'This gift, I hope, will encourage you to complete your account.'

'Why does it matter?' I asked. 'There's a strong chance no one will ever read my scribblings.'

'I, Hercule Poirot, will read them.'

Once he had left my office, I unwrapped the package and stared at the shiny new machine. I was touched that he had cared enough to buy it for me, and, as always, in awe of his cleverness. Of course I would have to finish writing the story after a gesture like that. So, here I am, finishing it. Which means it is my duty to report that the trial of Lenore Lavington did not go the way I hoped it would. She was convicted of the murder of Kingsbury, and the attempted murder of Annabel Treadway, but, thanks to Rowland McCrodden's advocacy on her behalf, she was spared the gallows. I happen to know, though I should prefer not to know it, that Mrs Lavington receives regular visits in prison from a devoted John McCrodden—while poor, loyal Kingsbury lies dead.

'Do you believe justice has been done?' I asked Poirot, when we learned that Mrs Lavington would not pay with her life for the crimes she had committed.

'A jury found her guilty, *mon ami*,' he said. 'She will spend the rest of her days in prison.'

'You know as well as I do, she'd have hanged if it weren't for Rowland McCrodden's efforts, made for all the wrong reasons. Every judge in the land knows him to be the most passionate advocate of the death penalty, and suddenly he is on the side of compassion for a distraught woman who simply made a terrible mistake in a moment of weakness? That powerful speech delivered by Lenore Lavington's barrister was McCrodden's creation, and the judge knew it. The same Rowland Rope who has sent dozens of less fortunate fellows off to the gallows, without a thought for whom they might love or who might love them, purely because none of them happened to be his son! It's not right, Poirot. That isn't justice.'

He smiled at me. 'Do not torment yourself, my friend. I concern myself only with bringing to light the facts of the case, and securing the guilty verdict for the criminal, not with the punishment that follows. I leave such considerations to a higher authority. The truth has been recognized, in a court of law—that is what matters.'

We sat in silence for a few moments. Then he said, 'You perhaps do not know that there is somebody who has announced his intention to behave as if Lenore Lavington *were* dead—who has vowed never to write to her, and to burn any letters she might send to him.'

'Who?'

'Her son, Timothy. This, I think, will be an additional punishment. To be cast aside by one's own child, whatever one has done—it is a terrible thing.'

I did not know if Poirot meant, with this observation, to imply that I ought not to judge Rowland McCrodden too harshly. I decided that, if that was his intention, it would be unwise to prolong our discussion of the matter, so I said nothing.

And now, having come to the end of this account, I see that Poirot was absolutely correct: to record that a story ended unsatisfactorily is still, somehow, considerably more satisfying than to offer no resolution at all.

This, then, is the end of 'The Mystery of Three Quarters'.

Edward (with a flawless 'E'!) Catchpool

ALSO BY SOPHIE HANNAH

The Monogram Murders

'It is hate that makes people kill . . . not love.'

Hercule Poirot's quiet supper in a London coffee house is interrupted when a young woman confides to him that she is about to be murdered. She is terrified, but begs Poirot not to find and punish her killer. Once she is dead, she insists, justice will have been done.

Later that night, Poirot learns that three guests at the fashionable Bloxham Hotel have been murdered, and a cufflink has been placed in each one's mouth. Could there be a connection with the frightened woman? While Poirot struggles to connect the bizarre pieces of the puzzle, the murderer prepares a hotel bedroom for a fourth victim . . .

'Grips from the very start. Hannah gets it right in every particular.'
THE TIMES

'Immensely satisfying—an ingenious ending'
INDEPENDENT

'A highly readable locked-room mystery with a delectable twist.'
MAIL ON SUNDAY

'Superbly orchestrated . . . as exhilaratingly complicated as anything by Christie.'
SUNDAY TIMES

ALSO BY SOPHIE HANNAH

Closed Casket

'What I intend to say to you will come as a shock . . .'

Lady Athelinda Playford has planned a house party at her mansion, but it is no ordinary gathering. She announces that she has decided to change her will, cutting off her children and leaving her fortune to someone who has only weeks to live . . .

Among Lady Playford's guests are Belgian detective Hercule Poirot and Inspector Edward Catchpool of Scotland Yard, who have no idea why they have been invited . . . until Poirot starts to wonder if Lady Playford expects a murderer to strike. When the crime is committed, and the victim is not who Poirot thought it would be, will he be able to solve the mystery?

'Sparkling second outing for Hannah's reimagined Poirot'
SUNDAY TIMES

'Offers a clever twist which the Queen of Crime would have applauded'
DAILY EXPRESS

'Another satisfying addition to the Agatha Christie canon'
IRISH TIMES

'A novel fizzing with ideas and spikey dialogue'
SUNDAY EXPRESS

THE AGATHA CHRISTIE COLLECTION

Mysteries
The Man in the Brown
 Suit
The Secret of Chimneys
The Seven Dials Mystery
The Mysterious Mr Quin
The Sittaford Mystery
The Hound of Death
The Listerdale Mystery
Why Didn't They Ask
 Evans?
Parker Pyne Investigates
Murder Is Easy
And Then There Were
 None
Towards Zero
Death Comes as the End
Sparkling Cyanide
Crooked House
They Came to Baghdad
Destination Unknown
Spider's Web*
The Unexpected Guest*
Ordeal by Innocence
The Pale Horse
Endless Night
Passenger To Frankfurt
Problem at Pollensa Bay
While the Light Lasts

Poirot
The Mysterious Affair at
 Styles
The Murder on the
 Links
Poirot Investigates
The Murder of Roger
 Ackroyd
The Big Four
The Mystery of the Blue
 Train
Black Coffee*
Peril at End House
Lord Edgware Dies

Murder on the Orient
 Express
Three Act Tragedy
Death in the Clouds
The ABC Murders
Murder in Mesopotamia
Cards on the Table
Murder in the Mews
Dumb Witness
Death on the Nile
Appointment With Death
Hercule Poirot's
 Christmas
Sad Cypress
One, Two, Buckle My
 Shoe
Evil Under the Sun
Five Little Pigs
The Hollow
The Labours of
 Hercules
Taken at the Flood
Mrs McGinty's Dead
After the Funeral
Hickory Dickory Dock
Dead Man's Folly
Cat Among the Pigeons
The Adventure of the
 Christmas Pudding
The Clocks
Third Girl
Hallowe'en Party
Elephants Can
 Remember
Poirot's Early Cases
Curtain: Poirot's Last
 Case

Marple
The Murder at the
 Vicarage
The Thirteen Problems
The Body in the Library
The Moving Finger

A Murder Is Announced
They Do It With Mirrors
A Pocket Full of Rye
4.50 from Paddington
The Mirror Crack'd from
 Side to Side
A Caribbean Mystery
At Bertram's Hotel
Nemesis
Sleeping Murder
Miss Marple's Final Cases

Tommy & Tuppence
The Secret Adversary
Partners in Crime
N or M?
By the Pricking of My
 Thumbs
Postern of Fate

**Published as Mary
 Westmacott**
Giant's Bread
Unfinished Portrait
Absent in the Spring
The Rose and the Yew
 Tree
A Daughter's a Daughter
The Burden

Memoirs
An Autobiography
Come, Tell Me How You
 Live
The Grand Tour

Plays and Stories
Akhnaton
The Mousetrap and
 Other Plays
The Floating Admiral†
Star Over Bethlehem
Hercule Poirot and the
 Greenshore Folly

* novelized by Charles Osborne
† contributor

About the Authors

SOPHIE HANNAH is an internationally bestselling writer of crime fiction, published in more than 35 languages. Her novel *The Carrier* won Crime Thriller of the Year at the 2013 Specsavers National Book Awards. She lives with her husband, children and dog in Cambridge, where she is a Fellow of Lucy Cavendish College, and as a poet has been shortlisted for the TS Eliot Prize. Sophie has written two previous Hercule Poirot novels, *The Monogram Murders* and *Closed Casket,* both of which were top five *Sunday Times* bestsellers.

AGATHA CHRISTIE is known throughout the world as the Queen of Crime. Her books have sold over a billion copies in English with another billion in foreign languages. She is the most widely published author of all time, outsold only by the Bible and Shakespeare. She is the author of 80 crime novels and short story collections, more than 20 plays, and six novels written under the name Mary Westmacott.